StormTree

I0705906

The World of Alyssia

StormTree

E.D.E. Bell

Atthis Arts

Detroit, Michigan

Storm Tree

Copyright © 2024 by E.D.E. Bell

Cover illustration by Matthew Spencer
Book Design by E.D.E. Bell
Layout by G.C. Bell

All rights reserved.

Published by Atthis Arts, LLC
Detroit, Michigan
atthisarts.com

ISBN 978-1-961654-21-1

LCCN 2024942520

First Edition: Published October 2024

To 2 from 6.

It is my regret.

Contents

Somewhere in the Land of True Princesses.

You will know you found a mother.

Jubilee Cho 1998-2024

Preface

This book fought its way to publication from the thunder of my heart. My necessary urgency to position Atthis Arts amidst the increasing successes of my friends left this book positioned to wait, and wait again, and hope to someday be important, but it refused, and I indulged. So this volume grew up in the wild, and wouldn't even had an edit if it weren't for Greg. Every time it seemed this book would have to step back, the story and I danced defiantly in the pathways. And so, without further explanation of a situation that kept complicating on itself, any abundance of sentences gone wild should not be attributed to Stewart and Minerva* who were so, so kind to peek behind the proofreading curtain, understanding that much was already entangled and Emily was skipping around the pathways singing.

I am at a crossroads of preparation and power right now, but then, so is Xelle.

I love this book. I really love it. I've reached an attachment to my own storytelling that is comforting and also newly vulnerable. I feel hope and faith, and sometimes moments of promise.

A question I've been asking myself in more detail is: What is Alyssia as a work, rather than a world? I've used music analogies before with my writing, but I suppose that's how I view the temporal arts. I am an empath but also an *empathic writer* (rather than visual or linguistic, etc.), which perhaps relates to why sound is a stronger sense to me · than sight. Thus I have decided that if Diamondsong was a concerto, then Alyssia, or at least the story of Xelle within it, is an opera.

And thus, in an art form strongly tied to tradition (as with the fantasy epic), I know it can be jarring to some readers when I incorporate current and colloquial expression. Yet I am not writing in a historical setting, nor one modeled after one, and as I cannot truly answer whether the threading of slipstream into my fantasy is jarring because it does not match the world, or because it does not match the reader's expectations of form, I have decided to be mindfully instinctive.

See, look how fancy I can sound when I want to. With the sauce.

There is one thing I have struggled more with than anything in this series, and it is the balance between my desire to embrace a more serialized storytelling style, my strongly-felt approach to recalibrating our perception of 'stakes', and how those interact with my writing skills and limitations.

An opera needs acts, and an audience needs intermissions.

So, I will be looking to bring some closure to this first act at the end of the fifth book. A breath. And I'd like to do it not as a firm ending and beginning, but a satisfying point for a new or revisited entry. I look forward to approach this with all the enthusiasm and determination—and joy—that I feel.

I love my friends, and want to express, in the context of this book, my deepest gratitude: To Gwynn, Vance, and Vera, for their emotional support and infinite coolness. To Mura for her looking out, Xave for his hugs, and Tad for her companionship. To Matt Spencer for this electrifying and grounding cover that I really, really, love. To George C. Bell for his beautiful work, his continued understanding of what this series means to me, and our Jedi partnership. We have done and will continue to do amazing things together. Thank you for trusting my saber. To Tad Williams for his personal encouragement and understanding. To Ava Kelly, Seth Lindberg, Camille Gooderham Campbell, and Dimitris Tzellis for true friendship, the kind that stays, and to Brandon O'Brien who is family. To so many people whose love floods into my mind: Jenn, Jen, Jenn, Jen, Zig, Shadowed (Joe), Josh (#BouncyHorses),

Drew (Fancy), Cat, Val, Mom B, Shelley, Valya, Bogi, Marsalis, Richard, Laura, Tanouska, Joyce, Core, AJ, all the Atthis Arts team and family, and my chatfriends ♥. Meghan Cusack for her thoughtful alpha feedback and following me through all these bumps and curves now over the full last decade. To Stewart C Baker and Minerva Cerridwen for friendship, proofreading*, and their genuine love for this work! To Gregory A. Wilson, who offered thoughtful, caring, candid, and encouraging critiques. Our creative and personal friendship brings peace to my heart and fire to my soul, and you will *always* have my sunshine. Most of all, I want to thank *you*, whoever and whenever you are, for valuing my words enough to read them. I hope you enjoy.

Cheers —
E.D.E. Bell
Summer 2024

Until Now

This summary is meant as an optional refresher for those who haven't picked up the last books in a bit, or for those starting here who enjoy a bit of a brief. It can be skipped; feel free to dive in.

Xeleanor Du'Tam, she or e, has decided to grant herself the title of Mage, despite not being recognized as such by the Seven Towers of Alyssia because she has not pledged to one.

The boldness of this would have been unthinkable to Xelle just a year before, but having spent that year as an Apprentice (in status only) to an obnoxious Mage at Ever Tower, her view has shifted.

Status was not important to Xelle, but she was increasingly frustrated by the limitations her lack of title imposed on her. The dragons had relocated to the cold, harsh high mountains at her urging, and she wanted to help them return. There remains a group of pers, whom she calls 'the Hurts', both sowing discord at Arc Tower and also pursuing the dragons, and she wants to understand why.

At first, her main ally and source of information was the powerful Mage this group had previously compromised, Arc Spire Mage Kern, who now acts as a double-agent against their interests. Then, based on a tip from the mysterious Breath Mage Thyra, who claims to covertly work for the Labor Council of the city Wehj, Xelle learned that an exorbitantly rich couple, Irla and Mark Lunest, were suspected to be at the core of the Hurts. Kern began to form a plan to confirm this information, though not told its source.

Kern's artist cura (son), Tenne, who the Hurts had used to initially manipulate Mage Kern by falsely awarding him the prestigious E'lle Prize, has concluded his year's residence at the E'lle Gallery in Mytil, and is now living with the artist who would have won the prize, Owin, also as lovers. Tenne is very in love.

Xelle, feeling alone and constrained, began pouring her summer into constructing an enclosed space built into the branches of a tree in the forests behind To'Ever, and then enchanting it so the space would remain hidden and also increasingly loyal to Xelle over time (through its design; she does not believe enchantments are sentient). She calls this space her daygarden.

In this safe place to talk, Xelle began to open up to her friends. Study Kwillen Du'Satta, using eir connections as grandcura of one of the Seven Mages of Satta, was able to bring Xelle some startling (and still difficult to believe) information: That the Lunests' goal, stated as to return magic to working for the populace, is really greed—a plan to sell homes in the mountains with views of dragons and the ability to travel to Alyssia's sacred moons. Then Rayn, an Ever Study Xelle had met once on a shared moveroom, returned from six months at To'Grand, and Xelle decided to tell her what she knew.

Additionally, Xelle remembered Crown Mage Jehanne's council that Arc Spire Mage We'le could be trusted. Xelle visited her, during which time We'le said that the Amberborn, an affiliation used to tarnish Xelle's credibility, was likely not even real, but a distraction from the Hurts themselves (We'le is amused by Xelle's name). We'le does tell Xelle that she is a member of the Sevensense, a group she did not describe and stated firmly would not be mentioned by Xelle. She also told Xelle that the Arc Tower had not just a Front Desk for check-in, but an invitation-only Back Desk. The entrance, hidden by magic in Vi'Arc, allows Xelle to access To'Arc without being seen, except by the clerk, who at the time of Xelle's visit was Sec Lai Dvi'Arc.

Xelle, who had been trying to grow forbidden inkbloom in her hidden nightgarden at To'Arc, finally learned what the phyta craved was an emotional connection. With the inkbloom now flourishing, the thriving vines and blossoms allow Xelle to either travel (reminding her of her own travel cast, Xelle also calls this slinging) to a location and then return, still holding the cast—or to consume a pod provided by one of the blossoms. Each pod allows one transport, to anywhere the caster is able to connect.

Xelle also has three primary Frond Magic runes, one in her daygarden, one in her nightgarden, and a new one just outside of her nightgarden. The first time she used one, she had forgotten to make a second to leave the room. Her friend Helia, an Arc Mage, helped her leave the Tower without being seen (at that time she was not allowed to be there), but first, the two, who had previously casually dated, enjoyed an intimate day together in Helia's room.

With the help of the inkbloom's magic, Xelle was finally able to travel to visit Thunder and the other dragons. There, she confirmed they were unhappy on the frigid, difficult land. She also learned that they used to live not just in the mountains, but the lower lands of Alyssia, and whatever treaty there was between hu and dragon, the hu had repeatedly violated it—including Xelle when she asked them to leave. (Even though it was a request, and done for her concerns of their safety, this was still true.) She is quickly concluding that, whatever anyone does or doesn't know, no Mage is going to tell her anything about the dragons or the treaty.

The day before the last of the year, Xelle turned thirty years old. This struck her in difficult ways. She felt lost. Confused. She misses Arc Tower. And she still holds a place in her heart for her departed labmate, Ay'tea, whom she hasn't seen now since the day of her original petition at To'Arc. She has resolved to let him go. Her heart, unfortunately, has not agreed. She used some of the day to enchant a new cloak, that will adjust to her needs for warmth, concealment, or comfort. As pleased as she was at her accomplishment, somehow it only strengthened her feelings of emptiness.

After a day of thinking no one outside of her homevillage had remembered her birthday, she received a greeting from Helia, along with a request to meet for the new year's celebration the next day. They met at the tavern outside of the city, the Enchanted Forest, where Xelle also secretly has a room, for which she pays the bartender, Klein. Xelle and Helia had a lovely evening, and after a nearly magical kiss, Helia returned to To'Arc.

Soon after, Kern followed through on his ploy to present Xelle to the Lunests, telling them that via her sigil, she can always locate the dragons. He did this as a lure to prove the Lunests were, in fact, leading the Hurts (refusing Xelle's name, he calls them the conglomerate), and perhaps find out even more. Once there, Xelle realized the only way she could leave without exposing that Kern hoped she would leave (her theory) was to turn the magic, slicing through the slightest thickness of time, to cause Kern a momentary need to defend himself. The impacts of those events have not yet fully settled with her. Nor has she spoken to Mage Kern since.

Knowing she would now be pursued regardless, Xelle decided to operate in the open. She spent a day in Vi'Arc, learning that there was a whole subscription service dedicated to documenting news about her. While she did check this out (it was disgusting), she stayed with her original goal: to ask about Ascension. While populace sentiment seemed to be returning to Spire Mage Pelir ascending to the Crown Mage once Jehanne retired, support was growing for Kern as well. She worried that Kern would need to work even more to position himself as Crown Mage, in order to maintain his appearance of sincerity and leverage with the Lunests.

This quickly became moot.

Xelle fell asleep in her nightgarden, suddenly receiving a feeling of comfort from the obsidian sword Crown Mage Jehanne had given Xelle. The next morning, just before Xelle intended to return to Ever Tower, the bells tolled, lamenting Crown Mage Jehanne's death. Xelle quickly realized—she did not believe Jehanne had really died.

Without time for Kern to maneuver without risking his Spire position entirely, Pelir ascended to Crown Mage, and an unexpectedly young Mage, Nar, was given the open spot on the Arc Spire.

On Xelle's return to Ever Tower, Crown Mage Avail told her she could not stay. And while not confirming explicitly, he seemed to agree with Xelle that Jehanne (his former lover) was still alive. After contemplation, Xelle asked Avail to quietly assist her on being admitted into Grand Tower, to stay there for a while. And then, on an assumption, asked how to enter Ever Tower via its Back Desk.

With her new openness and the previous encouragement of her friends (she's not sure they thought she'd really do it!), Xelle also decided to call herself Mage. Mage Xeleanor Du'Tam. She presented herself as such at Grand Tower, and convinced them, for now, to let her stay.

Xelle is nervous about what the future holds for her, especially in this new, unfamiliar place, and she now holds to the anchor of her friends: Helia, the Arc Mage with whom she has now shared both intimacy and trust. Rayn, the newly pledged Ever Mage from distant Sharre, with whom she found an immediate connection. Kwill, a Breath Study from the famous family of the Seven Mages of Satta with whom Xelle feels able to talk without tension. And Thunder, the young dragon with whom she shares a telepathic connection via the sigil on her forehead. More than three months have passed since her arrival at To'Grand.

StormTree

To'Grand
Wehj
To'Breath
Vattam
Satta
Iyero
To'Frond
Savanna Sheer

To'Arc
To'Ejer
Mytil
Tam
To'Charm
To'Dust
Sharre
Alyssia

01 - Something Happens

No one expected this. Except Xelle, who had seen these pers up close, and now put nothing past them. It didn't take long to assess a heart of greed, nor to understand the contracting yet boundless nature of its audacity.

She laughed. To herself. Perhaps a more proper (though that was definitely not the word) immersion into the magesphere was making her Magier than ever. "How long until they're here?" she asked the Staff Mage as he escorted her into the room.

"A half hour," Mage Dram replied. "And only that because—"

"Time is pressing," Spire Mage Beleg interrupted, his normally sonorous voice sounding strained. "What will they want, Xeleanor?"

Mage Beleg had omitted her title, but in this context, Xelle did not mind. For the most part these last months, they had let her be, affording her most privileges of a visiting Mage of low rank. While she knew she couldn't let her guard down—after all, somewhere in this huge Tower she knew a Mage was covertly under control of the same Lunests who now walked up the wide road in a moveroom caravan she could already imagine—she felt a certain comfort and trust around the Grand Spire Mages. They did not, she had learned, enjoy games.

Or, she should say, games they'd not elected to play. Xelle felt the same.

"I believe they want to take at least one dragon under their control. However, as I am the only way they know how to locate dragons without attempting to directly approach and assail them again, they will want custody of me."

Another thing Xelle appreciated about Grand culture. No one

here would gasp, or belabor the ethics of such an obviously unethical suggestion. Instead, they parsed it.

Spire Mage Shan gripped the hilt of her wand against her primary side table. "They have no standing in custody for well-being. And custody for transgression would take you out of their reach."

Funny, that. An irreparable transgression, if they could argue or bribe their way to it, would take her directly to Frond Tower, where having a turned Mage in the right position could put Xelle directly under their control. Yet last Xelle knew (or believed), Irla had specifically wanted to stay away from Frond, Dust, and Ever Towers. Xelle also had contacts at Frond, something Irla would have to know. Well, barely contacts. She could hardly remember the names of the pers she'd worked with there, it had been so long ago and such a confusing whirlwind of a time. Yeah, they probably wanted her out of the Towers entirely. Then, who would know why she suddenly disappeared one day.

"Which leaves the distinct possibility they are here to convince you that I must not be allowed to reside here, to open their options." Much had changed for Xelle to state such a thing so plainly.

But that's the thing. Much had changed.

"I'd prefer to stay here with the Spire during their visit." She did not want to say that she knew, somewhere (still potentially including this room) that a Grand Mage was turned, working for the Lunests. She stared directly at Spire Mage Sandaba. Of them all, she trusted him the most. (And not just because he boldly framed his bared cleavage in much the style of Firana, Stalker of Night, but also because of one of those connections that felt even beyond the understanding of Arc Magic. Not that she was going to broach either with the tall, confident Mage. She'd sound like an admi.)

Sandaba had noticed her gaze. "I concur," he said. "I think your presence would be valuable." With a glance to Mage Dram, he continued. "They arrive, uninvited, with immediate concerns regarding a Mage, they have no right to dictate who remains in our chamber."

As Dram nodded and left the room, Xelle did her very, very, best to not react outwardly to Sandaba calling her a Mage. And it was clear not everyone thought this was a good idea. But none enough to argue with Sandaba. Or at least, not in front of Xelle.

Soon, an indistinct, yet comfortable, padded chair was pulled to the side and offered to her. She sat in it, not noticing the weakness in her legs until they finally let go her body's weight. She ran her fingers against the worn but soft upholstery as she waited, tracing out little loops and vines into the short pile next to her legs.

Four ceremonially-dressed attendants entered first, in layers of red velvet and golden fringe, with an embroidered L prominently displayed. Between them, a hu of Irla's make who was specifically not Irla. She stepped forward, her voice clear and unwavering. "You are in the presence of Este Irla Du'Lunest and Este Mark Du'Lunest." By the time she'd finished the proclamation, Mark and Irla had indeed entered, standing just enough in front of their attendants that instead of looking at petitioners before a Spire, they were two groups of seven, facing each other. Xelle had the image of herself as a puck between them.

Irla looked starkly ahead, not in the aloof off-white Xelle had first seen her in, but in a tailored red suit, brighter than but coordinating with the attendants. The matching slouchy cap convinced Xelle that she had a cap made to match every outfit. Which . . . meant she had different pants for every shirt? Anyway, this was not the point.

Mark looked much the same as before, in another configuration of shiny black and titanium accents. Somehow the coolest clothes made to look less cool simply because he was wearing them. Again, he wore a different set of tinted glasses, though these more muted than the last. His Tower look, she thought with almost a giggle.

It was at that moment she realized that her anxiety had taken a different form. Her pressure had increased. Her fingers shook. So, she was clearly upset. But she did not *fear* them. She wasn't sure if that was . . . wise. More to parse later.

Crown Mage Da'Selin did not rise, but bowed forward in her chair. "We were not expecting your visit, and our clerks said the details could only be spoken to us directly. Given what must then be a matter of sensitivity and urgency, please proceed with your petition."

Oh. Now Xelle really had to keep her calm. But, of course. Mark and Irla thought they could stomp in anywhere. And, yeah, here they were. And while the Spire Mages must know the two were best not dismissed—not holding the power that they did—they were still Spire Mages. Xelle sat up a little. Mark was now looking her way, though with the tint of the glasses, Xelle couldn't quite meet his eyes.

"I see that you are aware of the source of our mutual trouble, yet there is no need for her to be here." Irla barely flicked two fingers in Xelle's direction.

"Agreed," Crown Mage Da'Selin answered. "Now, please proceed with your petition."

Was Xelle . . . supposed to leave? With gratitude, she saw Spire Mage Sandaba looking her way. A subtle shift of his eyes told her clearly. *No. Stay.* She tried to sit straighter.

Irla paused, her displeasure apparent, then with whatever calculations she had made, continued. "Xeleanor Du'Tam trespassed onto our property and used a slash of illicit magic to threaten and harm us. In her lack of skill of such subjects, she forcefully broke through one of our skylight windows and left through it, terrifying our staff with a shower of glass shards. As she was alone, we are certain Ever Tower did not receive the truth of what occurred from her, yet they gleaned enough to expel her, as Arc Tower had before that. We are concerned that you also have been given a ruse." Irla paused to reach for an unstoppered drink of water held out by an attendant. She needed water already? So, like, she was pausing on purpose?

Alone. Oh, Fira. This was a test. Kern was probably trying to repair their relationship, but Irla was worried Xelle had compromised him. So if Xelle agreed she was alone or made up another story, the Lunests might suspect the truth—that she'd gone there with Kern on purpose, to see what they could learn while forcing a more direct relationship and higher stakes for the Lunests. It had gone poorly, and she'd, you know, sort of attacked him with time, and she hadn't talked to him since. She had the feeling that was fine with Kern, that he'd agree that distance was needed. But she didn't want anyone to know any of this; keeping the Lunests believing that the Arc Spire Mage was loyal to their plotting was not an advantage she'd want to toss.

She didn't have time to be clever. Mages had been there, to tell Mark and Irla what she'd cast. Kern would have had to explain it, or at least explain that it was 'illicit' and thus unexpected. And the Lunests would never have come up with a story using *that* magic unless Xelle had really done it. Yet, if Kern had really captured her and she'd escaped him, wouldn't she tell the Mages immediately of the threat? She was good at truth. Not stalling. Truth. She tried to divert.

"Yes, I went there. I . . . didn't intrude. They let me in. And I turned the magic to get away." She whipped over to face the Spire. "They said they'd keep me there; capture me there. My emotions overtook me, and I snapped time. With Arc. It echoed, in my mind. When I think of it, that's what I see. The slice." Without more time to consider what she was saying, she was terrified to make a mistake; something she couldn't take back. The best she could do was throw Irla off her game. Which . . . with a glance she realized she was not doing.

"Secrets," she managed to cast, directly into Mage Sandaba's ear. "Help."

He stood and snapped toward her, his face furious. "You should have told us. That is dangerous magic, Xeleanor. No wonder Avail showed you his door. Do you know what a cast like that can do to time in a moment? To your mind?" He sat down, his head shaking. "I do not meddle in the affairs of Arc, but a cast like that done improperly can snap in both directions, taking with it the memories past and ahead." He looked back at Irla as though considering it. "Ever found her soon after, wandering around the Arc Village, muddled and asking anything she could learn."

"She doesn't remember it," Mark said, his voice tense.

"That could explain why she told us none of this," Sandaba replied, sitting back with a frustrated sigh. "We could revisit asking more."

"No need; it doesn't matter," she snapped. "Any loss of memory happened after a series of transgressions, to which she has just admitted. We request, for the safety of those in Grand Region, that Xeleanor Du'Tam be permanently renounced by and expelled from the mage-sphere, immediately."

Normally quiet, it was the eldest Mage, Spire Mage Ghalen who spoke. Also, Xelle could not help but remember, the one who had made the wall of magic when she arrived. At the time it had seemed patronizing, but she'd come to see it as a bit . . . grandparently. Antiquated. Almost a sign of respect from his view, to let her show them who she was herself with the directness of Grand, rather than with the acuity of Arc or the patience of Ever.

His gruff voice was measured and low. "Do you also petition for finances, for the damage done?"

Irla's lip twitched, but it was Mark who answered. "We don't need your coins; I make glass. I could order a thousand of those windows made without a scratch to my ledger."

"Mmm. Could we offer the assistance of Frond Mages, to evaluate and help treat any trauma to your staff?"

"They are fine," Irla snapped.

"I'm glad to hear that," Spire Mage Ghalen said, leaning back. "I can have a statement drafted, codifying our regrets at—"

"We don't want your apologies; we want your action against a clear danger, which I have just explained and *she* has just confirmed." Irla thrust an arm her way.

Crown Mage Da'Selin raised a hand. Xelle knew it. The informal gesture of 'this is over'—when a Mage decides it's time to remind you one is a Mage. "If you are without damages or plans," she said, "then there is nothing I can offer on your petition. And with regard to general safety, we share this concern—yet we do not discuss the handling of

Tower issues. Now, could we offer you the hospitality of a meal with some of our diplomatic Mages before you start back?"

"With respect," Irla answered, "harboring a transgressor who has posed a direct threat to the pers of Grand Region is no longer a Tower issue."

Crown Mage Da'Selin rose and stepped forward. "As the Crown Mage of Grand Tower, Sacred Prong of Alyssia, I decide what is a Tower issue. And as I see your lack of understanding in that structure, I will state, with clarity and intention, that Xeleanor Du'Tam is under the protection and authority of Grand Tower. Now, you will leave."

Xelle was trying to absorb far too much at once and didn't quite catch what the pair murmured to each other, but they did leave, their entourage trailing, and Xelle was also pretty sure the Mages were doing some sort of secret message thing between each other.

She also couldn't quite describe the new feelings that were bubbling in her tummy, so she looked a bit aimlessly toward the Spire, waiting for some instruction.

"Xeleanor." It was Sandaba. "I was in the midst of enjoying racketsports, as will be noted by the unfortunate posterior sweat mark when I rise. I request that you go do something you find relaxing, and return to discuss your visit to Highponds with me at a time when you are feeling in more solid mind. You will not leave the Tower until then. Understood?"

It was more than understood. They'd stood up for her. She was only starting to process that. "I will schedule it with the Front Desk shortly, Spire Mage Sandaba. And I will not leave the Tower. Also, thank you." She bowed deeply.

Xelle sat on an outdoor stone staircase watching the wide field of spring flowers make waves in the breeze. They didn't really do gardens here, but they more . . . coaxed nature. No hedges or trellises, but vistas and nooks. She always had the sense here of more, often literally more: tunnels and chambers, and who knew what the massive trees hid. This had, of course, shattered her previous knowledge of the older construction of Arc Region, another one of those 'learned from Arc' embellishments she was going to have to get better at questioning. Maybe more like, everyone had their old and new, and the difference was the display. And those flowers were beautiful. She stared again, letting the waves calm her.

Oh, yeah, so she figured not leaving the Tower meant its oversight and protection, not like she couldn't go outside. Every Study learned their first year what Mages thought of saying 'on the grounds' wasn't 'in the Tower', she thought with a mix of anxiety and fondness.

That on top of the weird feelings she'd had up top, ones she was still parsing. No, not fear or repulsion, but . . . The Spire. They'd backed her up. They'd known she'd been hiding something and trusted (for now, she still had a meeting to set up) that there was reason behind it.

Despite her attempted bravado, Xelle had felt small here ever since her arrival. But, as Mara had told her on her way through Vattam, saplings were not unimportant to the forest. Oddly, instead of all the pressure to be more, show she was more, here . . . she found some comfort in being a sapling. A thirty-year old sapling, she groaned to herself.

With all she didn't know about what continued to churn outside these walls, she'd had to push herself to let things settle after she arrived. That was slower-going than she'd hoped. Being generally tolerated as a Mage did not help her fit in, she'd found with frustration. Even as an Apprentice, she'd had a place that could be understood. Now, no one knew what to do with her. How to treat her. She could not, would not, spend another year this way. So she'd sat. And thought. And realized she needed not only to stay here—but to live here. For now.

Once she thought about herself, someone no longer with a future life to build, but with a right-now life to nurture, her pressure had lightened also. In the same perspective Grand took toward the forest, she'd realized no one had enough energy for the world, so she had to find her role in it. The dragons were back in the lower mountains. Her inkbloom were well; she could sing to them through the pathways now. And, she realized, she could not keep moving. Cultures required familiarity. Familiarity required trust.

And so, she'd taken the space to think. To adjust.

To rest.

Grand had kept her on a tether of its own, checking in frequently, not offering her opportunities to learn Grand Magic, but offering opportunities to help in other ways around the Tower, an implicit urging to stay close. In the daytime, she'd immersed herself into getting to know To'Grand, along with spending many evenings getting to know Vi'Grand, a booming and unabashed place of colorful light-pods and rich nightlife of which she was growing very fond. And so, instead of resisting their tether as she tended to do with tethers, she had accepted it. Done her best to relax, and find herself again. To be more ready when something happened.

Now something had happened.

And, finally, Xelle felt ready to face it.

02 - Trust and Water

The Staff Mage was flirty. Xelle, her mind on remembering what she wanted to say to Sandaba and hoping she didn't forget anything, had mostly ignored him.

Fine. She hadn't asked him, what was his name, Dram, to stop; the attention wasn't totally unwelcome. Xelle didn't know if that was bad to think, or whatever, but right now, she was focused on this meeting.

"Mage Xeleanor," he said, extending an arm forward. Leaving Dram back in the corridor, Xelle walked into Mage Sandaba's office.

Now this was an office. Were they all like this here? Tall ceilings, natural light, an outdoor patio. "Can we sit outside?" she blurted out. "Spire Mage Sandaba," she added with a more awkward chuckle.

"Alone, San is fine," he said. "Unless you prefer the formality. My answer is yes, and also thank you for not allowing me to neglect such a perfect spring day."

Soon they were situated on two imposing looking but actually quite comfortable lacquered wooden chairs. As he set out (amagically, she noted) a small table and a large pitcher of clear, delicious-looking water, Xelle took a moment to glance his way.

Here, in the open light, the Mage reminded her less of the caricature of Firana, but more like a friend's really cool parent. Or a favorite teacher, remet in older years.

She was making him sound ancient. If she had to guess, he had to be at least mid-fifties. With the radiance to feel any age, but the composure to remind you he was not.

Sandaba joined her in the second chair, met at friendly angles. Pulling a lever beside him, a long footrest unfolded from under the chair, and he rested his legs on it, his delicately bordered split skirt lolling off to one side, exposing a set of muscular legs. She quickly turned to meet his gaze.

"Why did you go there? And why do you not want to say with whom?"

Decision time. Normally she'd grumble about the unfairness of putting her on the spot, but he'd specifically not done that. He'd given her time to think about what he might say, might ask. And she had. She was going to be truthful.

She'd considered he was the turned Mage. The one working for the Lunests. But she didn't *think* so. And if he did, he wouldn't have helped her in the Spire, with them. If they just wanted him to deceptively earn her trust, they would have done so without going there and angering the Spire Mages. At least, she thought so.

"I went there with someone who'd pretended to have captured me. To find out whether they were behind the attempted thwarting of Crown Mage Pelir's Ascension, and the attempted capture of a dragon. To the best of my knowledge, they have four Mages working for them. Specifically, against the magesphere or at least, not alongside it." Mages could take side-jobs, so she needed that to be clear. "The one I went with did not want to become one, but was threatened into it, and now is trying to use that positioning for good."

Sandaba's curl of disgust would have been *very* good acting. Should she tell him, then? That there was one here? Yes. She would. "I believe one of the Mages is Grand." She didn't say the other Towers, and was glad he didn't ask. The per she went with, of course (Spire Mage Kern Du'Arc) could just as easily have been from To'Ever, as she was living there at the time. Or Breath, where she'd spent a month previously. Or Frond, where she'd once studied. Anyway.

"So, to state the obvious concern, I don't think the Grand Mage is you."

He pointed, but without amusement. "Excellent intuition. Though it worries me also. If we are truly in a time when Mages are turning, your trust puts you at risk. As it sounds like it did at the Lunest Estate. So, tell me nothing about your companion, or hints of xyr statements or magic. What did you do?"

"The rest is as I said. They wanted to keep me, as a 'locator' (they called it) for the dragons. I had the evidence I needed to convince me they really were behind this, and I wanted out. I fought the Mage, who had me . . . tethered . . . and knew it would have to be convincing. So I turned the magic for the first time, and in the shock of it, bolted out and traveled quickly away. I did break the window."

Xelle kind of wanted to be proud of that, but she also *did* still think about the ethics of the spell she'd cast, *did* still think about her lack of total surety she was even going to fit through that frame. It didn't feel nice to think about.

"Are you coping with all of that?" San's voice was kindly.

Xelle nodded.

"Why is everyone always concerned about my trust?" She felt like a child saying it, but if Sandaba—San was a bit of an extremely cool mentor to her, maybe this was the place for that conversation. A conversation she didn't want to have with her parents, her friends, anyone else.

He smiled, a bit sadly. "Because we are questioning ourselves, Xeleanor. How you've been through quite a bit lately and yet you hold to it more steadfastly than ever. While the rest of us have learned the hard way that trust . . . hurts."

Instead of a wise reaction of contemplation, Xelle felt her mind oddly blank. Trust was necessary. She tried to explain it. "Without trust, I don't have a handhold. Without a handhold, I might fall. I . . ." She'd been about to add she didn't know what that meant, didn't know why she'd said it. What piece of her mind already believed that to be true. "I don't want to stop trusting," she managed to say.

"I don't want you to either," he said, though there was hesitation to it. He seemed to be working through something himself, so Xelle sipped the water and took in what, especially from this height, was an absolutely stunning view.

"Is that the sea?" she heard herself asking. "I've never seen the sea."

He gazed out with her, at what felt like a mountain range of treetops. "Not that way. But you can see it from here. There, that triangle of deeper color. That is the sea. Spire Mage Beleg used to have this office. It is rare for a Spire Mage to move without an Ascension. The offices are equal; you take the space and make it your own. But this is the only office with an unaided view of the sea, however small. Beleg knew I would treasure that, and so he moved."

"That was very nice of him," Xelle said, gazing out at the little patch of water. She loved her daygarden, but she would never have a view of water.

San chuckled. "I know how he comes across, but his secret is the softest heart of us all." San took a drink. "And now you have seen the sea. And then, another day, you can visit it. Which brings us back to you. Your caution. Your goals."

Again, he winced oddly. When she was young, Xelle used to imagine that Spire Mages grew their unfeeling, unreacting expressions through years of training and change. Like the weight of their roles pulled away diversions of joy. That didn't even make sense to say (to think) but something like that. Now she was starting to see. The Spire Mages were among the most emotional, the most affected hu that she had met. How heavy must that mask be? Was it truly necessary? Would, by the nature of—

"Our adherence to a single prong of magic teaches us the value of focus." The seriousness of his tone drew Xelle immediately away from whatever she'd been thinking. "And surely, specialty is necessary for expertise. But we absorb this foundation: that stability is in carrying one thing, and carrying it well. When one is juggling, they are unstable. They are overextended. Something might drop. And a Mage, a Spire Mage—holds too much weight to let something drop. They say," he quickly and perhaps subconsciously added.

Xelle wasn't sure where this was coming from. She didn't think he'd brought her here for a lecture on her not pledging. But they'd barely discussed the Lunests, so what if—

"The magesphere exists on a state of steadiness; I don't need to tell you that. To trust as you do also requires a state we don't quite have a word for. The ability to trust deeply, meaning—" he paused, pointedly "—to *love* deeply, lowers the wall of caution, eases the strain of vigilance, amplifies the radiance of spirit. But then, what must also be carried is a basket of tools, and the willingness to use them. Fortitude. Agility. First aid. The willingness to accept the possibility of profound pain in exchange for the ecstasy of profound connection. To carry all this, is not stability. But it is power. What I consider might be a higher power—power unbound by the limitations of our structures. This terrifies a Grand Mage. Arc Tower bends the closest to such a thing, and I sometimes think because of that, they are the most guarded against it. Yes, Arc will change. But always within the structure. Change the structure when needed. But always with it."

That was way more than Xelle was able to process. She felt a bit like she was jumping at catching leaves to remember what it was he'd said, and ended up with: *Trust brings instability. Grand is scared of that and Arc protects against it. Trust is love?* This was of course, an inadequate summary, but she hoped it was enough to parse through and reconstruct later, and so she repeated it to herself.

When she took a breath, San was watching her. He leaned in, and Xelle tried very hard not to watch the gorgeousness of his cleavage as it squished gently. "I will tell you another secret," he said. "In addition to Beleg's soft heart." He laughed a bit mirthfully. "Grand Mages find Arc Mages unsettling. Not out loud; never out loud, but as a bit of a freethinker myself, it's something I've noticed. Yes, all Mages exist on stability. But Grand especially. Stability is essential. Even our Spire, with a gathering level open to the winds, is possible, because it is in a space so stable, so permanent, so protected by our own magic, that no harm could ever come to one within it." He leaned back.

"Then," Xelle said, working through this while navigating the increased spin of her mind, "is it a false wind?" She cringed, though not certain if it was because she might have just blorbed out something unforgivably offensive or because it sort of sounded like a fart joke.

San breathed in sharply. "What I am hoping you will hear from this is that Grand is a place of stability. Growth, not stagnation, but still, stability. This is not Arc Tower. Yet, Grand Tower has given you trust. Real trust. Understanding that. And you providing every stability you can—including staying—will be critical to your continued welcome here." He turned toward her, eyes flaring. "This is not a threat, it is a reality that I am exposing to a Mage that for all eir talk of Alyssia, is very, very much an Arc Mage."

She felt her face twitch. "Thank you. I don't totally understand yet, but I'll work on it. Thank you." Quite true on the understanding, she was busy keeping up with herself, let alone parsing the Ways of Grand.

"So," he added, "I'm going to get you into a lab. Not under my name, but I'll make it happen. One suited to your knowledge, that will offer unique perspectives of our Region. And we'll see what you do from there."

She had no idea what that was supposed to mean, but she knew how much trust this Mage was putting in her, right after she'd said she trusted him, and— Oh.

"May I offer you a pledge of some kind? A statement of my own stability? That I won't lie to you; that I won't betray you or Grand Tower?"

For a second, she worried he'd cast some sort of freezing spell. Again, that wasn't a thing (she hoped not) he just was sitting real still. Then he broke into a tilted, sly, broad but sincere looking smile. "A water toast?"

She didn't know what that was but it sounded gross. Then he raised his glass.

"It's something from my home in Charm Region. When finery is magic, simplicity is power. To toast with glasses of water is a toast of sincerity." He held up the glass, the liquid within it clear. "Transparency. A toast of fine wine is for diplomats, lovers, and thieves. A toast of water is . . . more." Seeing her confusion, he nodded. "For all the structure of Grand Tower and Grand Region, there is one place I think we might be ahead. We see relationships in a greater context, in that we do not try to label all the facets of closeness; it would be like labeling all the angles of light in the forest, when you could instead let them warm you. So, if you consent to my water toast, it offers—a relationship. It offers honesty."

"What about trust?"

Sandaba shook his head. "Don't Arc Mage me out of this."

Xelle laughed. She just . . . liked him. And raised her glass. "To our relationship."

"To our relationship," he said. And their glasses clinked, before each took a small drink.

She looked up. "With the ritual complete, may I ask you a question?"

"Is this a test?"

Xelle grinned. "Possibly? I'm curious why it was so important to you to have a view to the sea. Only if you're comfortable answering, of course, if I can add that to our water pact."

"It is mutually added," San confirmed. "Grand Tower allows the diversion of rainwater throughout the Tower. It is plentiful, flowing, and clean. I could have added a fountain here in my office, even a pond. But as much as I am drawn to water, from my childhood, the sea is something more. It is a mystery. How far does it go? How deep does it reach? Why, so focused on Alyssia, do we not ask such things? The sea—humbles me. Calms me. And gives me spirit. All at once. Now, I meant to discuss your goals here, but maybe we will save that for another day. Thank you for answering my question about the Lunests. I will not share that answer, except to tell the Spire I am satisfied with it."

Xelle was so awkward with goodbyes, and whatever short time they'd spent here on the porch felt sort of special. But she was spared the worry, because San practically rose and left, soon replaced by the Staff Mage.

"Have a good meeting?" Dram asked as they moved back into the main corridor.

"We did. Sa . . . Spire Mage Sandaba seems really cool."

"All the Spire Mages impress me. But I was asking about you."

Oh? "What about me?"

"What's your team?"

"My team?" This could not be appropriate.

Seeing whatever expression she was making, he chuckled. "Your magipuck team."

Oh. "I don't have one? Honestly, I don't even know what the teams are."

He leaned back in mock, and whistled. "I'd heard other Towers had a feather in their pants about it, but I didn't know it went that far. Honestly, Xeleanor, it's fun."

"Huh. It's Xelle. And . . . I've never seen a game." She would have said that to almost anyone, but Xelle had spent a lot of time alone, and the quirks of his smile and lightly muscular arms showing from rolled-up sleeves were not something she was going to miss.

"A travesty. Want to see one sometime? The two of us? No big deal, just magipuck? In Wehj," he clarified.

"Sure," she said. "Let me know when. And," she said, pointing a bit playfully, "make it a good game."

Suddenly the confident Mage seemed a bit at a loss for words, and Xelle found herself back alone in the lift.

The lab was on the second floor of an adjacent building. It was a pretty enough space, as the ability to use and preserve ample hardwood along with access to a small quarry did provide an easy aesthetic to the grounds, but still, Xelle knew what the location of the lab meant.

Yet, she felt grateful. Light. After her talk with Sandaba, he'd offered her a step forward. A way to really live here. (Staying here indefinitely was not something she was ready to think about so she settled more on the idea of at least staying here in full.) And unlike some of the games, however well-intended, at To'Ever, here she did not think To'Grand would send her anywhere unpleasant or without instructional merit.

She poked her head into the door, to find a small, windowless room. Again, impressed by the ability of Grand to maintain their aesthetic whether one was in the Atrium or a storage closet, she marveled a bit at the pretty little space. The walls were coated in a whimsical floral wallpaper (!) framed on every edge by smooth wooden trim. The hardwood floor stretched into the room, leading to a series of Post-style desks, with little cubbies and a sliding cover. And in the center was one rounded table surrounded by tall chairs. This lab needed a few cushions, she thought. But. First, she should find out what it did. Two hu leaned against a wall, sipping cups of coffee, and another hu rummaged at a desk to the side.

"Hello, I'm Xelle, she or e. I've been assigned to assist here with your work."

Xelle, she reminded herself. "Mage Xeleanor Du'Tam, but please, Xelle is fine." The coffee drinkers greeted her warmly and explained they were analyzing forest health at different levels of density. One went on at length about the implications, especially in the context of balance between the needs of phyta and anima.

It was an assignment that did not require the casting of Grand Magic (though surely the Mages would use it), yet one on issues close to Xelle's heart: nature, happiness, helping life thrive. So she settled into a desk and resolved to make the best of providing useful assistance with the lab's activities, many of which resonated with skills she'd learned co-leading traffic analysis for To'Arc.

At some point, it became impossible to ignore that the third per, the only one marked as a Mage, had made no motion to approach. He (they'd told her he was Mage An'oar, their lab lead) sat buried in his work. If there was fizz in the jar, she might as well crack the lid.

"Hello, Mage An'oar?"

He turned around and curtly nodded. "Yes, hello."

Weird vibe, but no hostility? Well, some pers needed time to adjust. Which reminded her, she hadn't checked in with Thunder in several days.

That night, she did.

Hey, Thunder. It's me.

So first things. The Hurts actually showed up here demanding I get kicked out. The Tower, this one, stood by me. That was nice. However, I've learned a lot more about how pers operate here, and I need to stay in place for now. Other hu are working on learning what's going on and what we can do about it. I'm sure you'll let me know if anyone tries to come near you up there. In the meantime, the Hurts are going to have to make a decision. If they keep getting more aggressive about what they want, at some point they won't be able to keep it a secret. But that worries me too.

Well anyway, sorry, I don't know how much these messages strain you (a question I will ask) so I'll keep it short for now. I need to stay in place a while longer. I'm making connections. I'm learning new things. I'm ready to try and see if I can even learn some of the magic of this Tower, maybe just at least a level of understanding. I think as long as I keep practicing my Arc and Ever, that should be fine.

But, soon, we'll move forward. And yeah, I wish I knew more. When to stay, when to act. At some point, I guess I have to make a decision, and then trust myself.

So for a bit longer, I'm staying here.

03 – *Taking*

Xelle enjoyed her project, which involved a great deal of forest hiking and measurement, as the summer progressed. The forest here had curves of natural breezes to it (e had stopped wondering what was Grand Magic influenced and what was purely natural or even if there was a difference) and it cooled the air from the late summer heat. New smells, new sounds around every bend. And here, with taller trees and more distinct layers beneath them, the rain fell as music—in waves, patterns, and songs. She found herself composing tunes to the uneven but patterned rhythms, smiling in moments she didn't realize that she was.

This wasn't Xelle's forest, but it gave her a sense of comfort, especially in the moments when she remembered how alone she still felt.

She still thought of her old lab partner, Ay'tea, in moments here and there each day. Here, she told no one. Certainly hu would find it strange, to still think of someone she hadn't seen in, what, a year and two-thirds now? So much time, passed. Yet she did think of him. Missed him.

And she kept it inside.

"Xelle, I heard something. In staff."

"Hmm?" Xelle had almost forgotten the young hu was walking alongside her. Te'lon, one of the two Studies who'd first explained the lab to her (the other had moved along mid-summer) had become a solid friend. Not a close or likely lasting friend, but someone whose presence did not drain her mind greatly. Someone she enjoyed chats with, about their homevillages and such. Te'lon was from a Grand Region foothills village that sounded so different from Tam, yet, with similarities that often caused the type of laughter only unexpected solidarity could bring.

"An'oar is trying to get you removed from the lab."

Well that stopped her in her tracks. She'd practically done back-flips (even *with* Arc Magic, Xelle did not do backflips) to be nice to the quiet, self-appreciating lab lead, who barely said much to her at all other than an occasional 'hmm' or pleasantly-worded remark.

"On what basis?"

Lonny shrugged. "He . . . doesn't seem to like you."

Working dynamics could be a reason for pers to mutually agree to an adjusted path, but what didn't he like? They'd barely talked! So, it wasn't that. She almost blurted it out. That it was because she was unpledged. Or because she'd made improvements to the processes here. Or, probably both. Because of his standards, or his jealousy, or some such thing. But Lonny had seemed to accept her as a Mage, and she wasn't sure she wanted to give An'oar the kind of satisfaction of dismissing that. Ash, she was a Mage, and here was a perfect moment to act like one.

"Who does it go to?" she asked instead. "His request?" She didn't call it a petition; she didn't think it would go *that* high.

"Mage Tatock, she," she answered. "Head Laboratorian."

Xelle almost squinted, but, no, she needed to get that Magey face down if she were going to keep this up. "I'll talk to her," she said casually. "And no need to worry about it; we've got work to do."

By the unease in Lonny's eyes, Xelle wasn't sure that had been the right thing to say.

Xelle stared at the wall. Staying put and getting known had been a necessary first step here at Grand, from everything Rayn had told her, and everything she'd seen herself. But if she'd been here long enough to have low-ranking Mages campaigning against her, she'd been here long enough to show them who they were messing with.

She still had her pod. Yeah, this pod had been inside her a *long* time. Since her last stop at To'Arc, since the Ascension. Having had no training in inkbloom other than from the inkbloom, she'd had to rely on them. And they didn't speak hu.

Instead, they'd given her, well, a tummy ache. Enough so that she felt the distinct feeling they were trying to tell her something. At first, she wondered if she'd just have to travel to the village and walk back, just to use it up. But then she really would be stuck here; there was no way she would attempt to rune-travel more than a short distance. She knew Frond Mages did it, but they must have some greater sense of the connections of the world, something through Frond phyta, the way the inkbloom helped Xelle. And no, she wasn't randomly going to start rubbing ferns and see which made her sense the world.

Huh. Why didn't Frond Mages have to *eat* the phyta?

She wondered briefly whether she really needed to *eat* them, like, perhaps she could carry around a jar of pods, like with runepaste. Briefly, because at that thought, she'd cramped and nearly doubled over.

No jar.

It had only been after writing her first set of letters, using her new wax seal, that she realized something about the discomfort. The inkbloom pod was not asking to leave, it rather felt stressed. Stress was something Xelle knew, so she wondered if there was a technique to setting it aside. Relaxing from its presence, temporarily. So that it could relax from hers, she also now understood. Xelle could not relax from a stress for so long at a time, but Xelle was also not inkbloom, with their own sense of space and time.

When she did this, settled it, rather than tried to ignore it, the discomfort went away. She learned as quickly that feeling for the pod stirred it, somehow, and the discomfort resumed. As if she could let it sleep, but once awakened, it reached back for its place of origin. The garden.

Over the summer, she'd grown better at letting it sleep. Not sleep, but there was no word, really. Dormant was too soft. Needing a word so that her mind would not spin causing her to think about it which would then awaken it except she wasn't calling it awake either, she settled on rest.

She'd let it rest.

Well, she certainly tried to. At first it was constant wrestling, like someone telling you not to think about something, which made you more likely to think about it. Then scolding yourself not to think about it, which of course caused you to really think about it. But she had a life to live here, and work to do, and she tried to focus on that. It really wasn't long before she realized it wasn't any sort of discipline to technique that was making it easier, but simply familiarity. Acceptance.

Not fighting the thoughts that arose, but just going on with other things.

And whatever doubt she'd been trying not to consider regarding whether its potency would remain in that state, that was immediately made moot by the force of need within her when she finally reached for it. Hurling her in mind, but perhaps also in body, back into her nightgarden, where her hands pressed against the now-dusty tiles, her breath heaving in harsh gasps.

"Hey, all!" she said in some abandonment of cheer, as she rolled over onto her back. "Good to see you too."

Well, and it was. The unseeable yet not fully illuminating blue filled her eyes, filled her spirit. Like air she'd forgotten to breathe.

Her mind felt foggy, her body exhausted. She forgot why she was here, what she was supposed to be doing, why she hadn't yet bought a *blanket* for this space, and just curled over into her swiveling chair, closed her eyes and sang.

Sang whatever. Melodies. Emotions. She fell into them.

And in the presence of comfort, she realized how much she'd missed it.

These were a lot of feelings all at once. And like the inkbloom pod itself, she now understood the only way to move past them was to sit with them, acknowledge them, and then return to things. Doing them, she meant.

She didn't need to ask the inkbloom for a pod; one had already pushed forward. Assuming that meant it would be safe to go, so soon, she reached into the world and traveled it, to the place her sigil guided her.

The dragons had accepted her presence.

This did not cause the ease or joy she thought it would, because apparently dragon pers were much like hu pers in their caution around Xelle. Either staying at a distance, gathering in clusters, or staring her way, or even leaving as she arrived. Not Thunder—zhey were thrilled to see her, and kept trying to maneuver around to block the other pers' view of Xelle. *It doesn't help,* she thought to zhem. *Might as well let them look.* Of course, this was layered with Thunder reading her own thoughts of frustration. That just being here, being open, being herself—what *was* it that made her so different? She really didn't feel so different. So what *was* it?

A lack of one pledge? Her choices of friends? That she had proven to've done some things well, and didn't use that to try and wedge her way back into the structures that had shunned her entire approach?

Or was it her? The storm in her mind? Was she doomed to be stared at or ignored forever, always alone?

Thunder's puff of hot breath made zheir thoughts on that clear.

"No, not alone," she corrected, placing a hand on zheir snout. "But so often, feeling alone, waiting for a moment when I can be around others, and then finding I am more alone there. Even us, here, it's always fleeting. I have reasons I can't live here, and you can't live at a Tower, and so." She leaned in against zheir skin. "I don't know if you understand," she murmured. An uncharacteristic lack of response from Thunder showed perhaps zhey didn't.

And Xelle could not hide how that made her feel.

"Hey," she tried, taking a breath. "I'll be able to visit more now. I had to show To'Grand I was serious about their trust, or tolerance, or whatever it is. And if I've not earned that by now . . ." She shrugged, unable to complete that thought, as it ended in a jumble of confusion and churning she didn't know how to parse.

Xelle was tired of confusion and churning. Including on this.

"So, here's where we are," she said, preferring to talk aloud as the vocalization apparently muted her thoughts somewhat, hindering eavesdropping, or wherever, in the absence of eaves, a listening dragon might linger. "I'm going to root in at To'Grand for now. I just can't keep moving around." She rolled her eyes. "And since that came out insensitive, I'll get to the thing I wanted to ask you. Well, no, first, I just want to say that I understand there was some treaty between hu and dragons, or probably Mages and dragons, and none of the Mages are allowed to talk about it, at least not to me, so if there's anything you shouldn't tell me, just, please let me know that and we'll work something out. I don't want you to be nervous. So. My question is, I have the sense you haven't always lived here, in the mountains? Is that true? Oh, and mild meddling—are you able to convey your age? Only if you're comfortable! And also, do you know where dragons used to live? Everywhere? A specific Region?"

She had a lot more questions, but she'd already asked at least three when she'd said she was starting with one, so she stopped and watched Thunder's pondering gaze.

Zhey nudged her gently with zheir snout. Xelle and Thunder had signs now for yes, no, ready?, and shrug, but she wasn't immediately sure what this meant. Well, they'd used the ol' process of elimination before.

"Are you asking me something about how to communicate with me?"

Yes.

"Do you need something from me to communicate?"

Yes.

Xelle considered. The first time they'd communicated, she really hadn't done anything except roll around and feel sick. Basically, she'd just agreed to it and— *Oh.* Do you need me to agree to the communication?

Yes.

Xelle was confused. They already had the 'Ready?' sign, they could— Oh, Thunder looked upset. There was some nuance of language here she wasn't understanding. "Do you want a different sign to open dragon-type communication?"

Yes.

"Sure. Why don't you give me your part, and then I'll give you my part. And maybe . . ." Xelle was getting a gut sense on this. "Maybe this one should be less visible, in case we don't want hu to know what we're doing." She had a sense dragons would know either way, and Thunder didn't seem to disagree.

Thunder tilted zheir head. While this normally wouldn't seem a very reliable signal, it was a specific tilt that somehow didn't feel natural. Xelle wouldn't have thought this if she hadn't spent some time with Thunder; it was a subtle motion. But seeing it, she realized—this was a motion she would recognize. She nodded.

And was suddenly inspired to come up with something similar. Something a hu would find normal, but Xelle herself didn't normally do. Not exactly sure why this came to mind, she reached toward her knee and tapped it twice with her fingers. Like, pa bum. Thunder nodded. Zhey took a step back as if clearing the slate, then gave the subtle tilt to zheir head.

"Oh, wait!" Xelle interrupted. "Let's try a single sense again. Since we haven't done this in a while." Single probably wasn't the right word, but as it conveyed the idea of limitation and she didn't think dragons were necessarily hearing the words anyway, she'd worry about it later? Maybe. From that first jumble where she had felt far too many things at once, Xelle had the concept that dragon senses weren't quite the same. But, still, the idea of light and sonic detection seemed clear, and somewhat separable. The idea of smell and taste were more similar in the idea of internal sensors, and not divided into two. Touch was the most different, as a dragon feeling vibrations felt more like hearing, temperature felt more like sight, and to them, touch seemed to indicate patterns of everything reaching the body. And a sixth sense. To dragons, e suddenly realized, emotion, feeling, was a sense in itself. Not the result of thought processing physical light and sound, but the sensors of being, something . . . bigger than hu perhaps put into words. Except, she thought with sudden surprise, poets.

Thunder was sitting and watching her think with what appeared to be great interest. Anyway, zhey clearly knew to limit what zhey conveyed. For now.

And Xelle suddenly realized she didn't even really need a signal, since she could answer in thought like she'd been doing extensively, but oh, well, they'd set the double-tap and then it would be clear. "One thing first? Given the treaty situation, are there any topics I need to avoid with you?" Thunder dipped in zheir sign of no, seeming unconcerned by the question, and then, again, Thunder tilted zheir head, and Xelle—tapped eir knee. Twice. Pa bum.

Dragony concepts flooded eir mind, and Xelle was probably rolling around again or something. This time, e tried not to dwell on it. There was vision only, yet it felt unrealistic, nearly drawn. Now that Xelle understood Thunder could convey thoughts that were imagined or constructed, not actually lived, Xelle could feel with certainty this was not something Thunder had seen directly.

Green waving hills. Indistinct dragons flying and landing, rushing through brilliantly reflective ponds, diving in and through and into the air, rainbow sparkles of water following them and splashing back into the beautiful landscape of greenfloor and small fruit trees, and—

"Oh, ashflame," she blurted out, jerking painfully back into the real world to find herself curled in a ball and shaking against where Thunder had reached out a claw to steady her.

"You lived in the Highponds." The most coveted land for hu. The largest estates, the most cherished inns and resorts, and—

Thunder was nudging her harshly, as if prodding. "What?" she scratched out, waving her hands immaturely like swatting off a blanket for an unwanted rest. Again, zhey nudged her. And tilted zheir head.

Whimpering a bit, she tapped her knee.

And the next thing she saw—wasn't real at all. Nor could she even see it. It was the touch of colors, the concept of treat, the impatience of rest. And the distinct concept of counting. Loud counting. Nothing she could track, but just follow.

"Seventy-six," she said aloud, coughing and sputtering. The sensation was loud, as loud, almost as a toddler stating their age with a vehement 'and a half' with some additional emphasis after that. "Oh, you're seventy-six years old?" So much for turning thirty.

Thunder looked as pleased as zhey did offended. Another tilt. Well, this was going to stop soon, but she, still not caught for breath, tapped. Again. Just that last feeling again, the punctuation. One.

Xelle lurched a bit, waving her hands frantically. "Ash, Thun! Give me a second. Seventy six was right. But also one. One year?"

Thunder nodded excitedly.

"Well, so we met a year ago? So are you seventy-seven?"

This made the dragon spout a burst of flame, to which Xelle threw out a quick travel shield. "Thunder!" The idea of being seventy-seven was deeply offensive, but the question about being seventy-six had certainly gone poorly also.

"Seventy-six and one," Xelle mused.

Thunder ran around her in circles, stomping in what she recognized as happiness.

"Is that your age? Seventy-six and one?" She considered this. "Seventy-six years when you met me, then a year since?"

Yes.

"Ok, ok, got it. Well, I'm thirty as hu say it, and I suppose, then, twenty-nine and one as dragons say it."

At this, Thunder seemed slightly less pleased, but gave no indication this was inaccurate.

And Xelle was done with this for now. Her fingers felt like curd casings, as Na Foose would say it, which she just realized was quite an unappealing phrase, but also reminded her. "Oh, yeah, I meant to ask you. Do my messages to you strain you at all?"

Thunder shrugged, the dismissiveness of the 'no' actually irritating. "Fantastic. Then I won't stress. However, this *is* wearing on *me*. I want to go find the others and sit down a while." Xelle was also worried about the look of her only visiting with Thunder. She glanced at zhem sharply. "We are friends; I'm here to see you. But it doesn't help us if they don't get used to me; learn to trust me."

With dramatic swagger, Thunder lowered zhemself and nearly dragged off toward where several pers were lounging around a series of fires and food bowls Xelle had previously seen chipped into the stone.

"Wait, one more thing, first. If it's ok with you. Do you have the concept of a birthday? When you were born?"

Tilt. Tap.

A rush of cold hit Xelle, and Thunder disconnected, as if there were no more to say. Xelle sat now, shivering, even though it was quite temperate here on a lovely day of summer *just* holding on a while longer, here in the lower mountains.

"A day in the winter? Or born generally in winter, without a day attached?"

Thunder clicked down two talons.

"Born in winter. Hey, me too."

Thunder seemed . . . *thrilled* . . . to hear this.

And this time, without the dramatic pout, Thunder, seventy-six and one winterborn, walked off next to Xelle, thirty on the penultimate day of the year, toward where several dragons sat, passing a few meanderers on the way.

Xelle paced around the edges of the Grand Atrium, doubling back at times to avoid the traffic route between the Front Desk and main corridors. The Highponds. From one view, it seemed quite the coincidence that the dragons wanted to live in the area the Lunests lived in. From another view, it seemed obvious that what was broadly considered the most desirable land in Alyssia would be, well, desired.

But who could she talk to? She'd realized by now that pledged Mages clearly had made some agreement not to talk about the treaty, but she had no idea how far it extended or why. Kind of hard, when they couldn't talk about that either. She rested her hands against the sides of her cap as she paced, taking that opportunity to stretch her elbows back, not really caring who was watching her or what they thought about it at this point.

Progress in life, she thought with a grin.

Xelle went through her options. With her pledged friends, primarily Helia and Rayn, it wasn't a matter of trust, but of risk. What predicament might this put them in, even more than they already were being close to the unpledged dragonfriend Mage? She didn't know Rayn well, but she'd already be seen as close; Xelle had been the front-row guest to her pledging. She and Helia had been discreet ever since Thunder had first been seen at To'Arc, but Helia had met her in Mytil for the new year. Anyone could have seen that, at least anyone in the Enchanted Forest. Still. Too much risk.

Then, what about Kwill? If she was reading em right, Kwill was nearly looking for an excuse to leave the magesphere. But what would Kwill do with the info, now? Without a plan. Besides, Kwill had a certain . . . guilt to em that Xelle would want to consider first. Having come from one of the most prestigious families in Alyssia, she wasn't sure she wanted to give em another reason to despise the very structure of hu. And, sure, she could talk to pers in her homevillage, or casual friends she had made here. What would that do?

No. She needed to keep this close for now. Get a better handle on what the Lunests were really doing. Have more in depth conversations with the dragons—who were going to have to stop being referred to in a lump in order to do that, she now acutely understood—and make plans when she had more to go on.

As for the dragons, she was starting to understand that sharing thoughts did not make the dragons a united, or even open, society. It seemed easier for them to withhold thoughts, which started her down a road—of how they must see mind-babbling hu—that she didn't want to go down right now. Which also meant, she would probably have to start talking to various pers without Thunder right there. After learning Thunder was seventy-six and one, she'd introduced herself to a few other dragons as thirty and zero (she figured Thunder would appreciate zheir extra edge) and while she'd not communicated with them directly, she had the impression the others were not just a bit older than Thunder, but perhaps even by hundreds of years.

Trying not to be intimidated by *that*, she'd sat and made herself comfortable amidst the larger groupings of dragons (casually knowing lots of dragons still did not feel totally familiar, though at least now it did feel real). They now seeming interested enough in what she had to say, Xelle had let everyone know how things were going in the mountainside areas of Alyssia, to her knowledge, and also made sure everyone knew that they should be keeping watch for anyone approaching. Of course, Thunder could have conveyed this, and perhaps already had, but this felt like something she needed everyone to hear from her. Her pers, her actions, her responsibility. And so she told them clearly that while there are many hu who could be trusted, right now, she was not aware of anyone who should be approaching. And, frankly, any Mage who could be trusted would surely have a way to make that case. And—they were welcome to reach out to her anytime. Now, she had a way to travel directly here. (Preferably through her nightgarden if she wanted to get back afterward, but they knew that.) And she would do what she needed.

Not just through obligation, she told them. Not just through guilt or justice. Not even because every per should do what they can to take care of each other, but because, well, she *liked* them. Xelle was in no way planning to start sitting naked and chewing her own nails, but there was something in the sharing of minds, the lack of covering—the lack of caps!—that made Xelle feel . . . calm.

Keeping up with most hu was exhausting, she'd begun to realize. Not that she didn't want to be around them. Of course she did. Naked, even. But those rare *(Xelle, don't sink again)* moments when she could sit with Helia, or Kwill, or Rayn, and just be emself . . .

Precious.

Absolutely precious.

Pacing alone still, in the Atrium, she decided to go get some lunch.

04 – The Gatekeepers

Enough pers were going from To'Grand to Wehj to see the game that there was a mix of vrooms lined up at the front walk.

"Desk clerks got tired of managing gameday reservations and requests," Dram explained, pointing her to a specific vroom several down the line. "This one; it's smoother."

There were about twelve pers on the mid-size vroom, all talking so excitedly about the game that Xelle had no need to feel uneasy. She sat quietly, listening and taking in the sights. Dram didn't have much to say, and it was odd to see the per dressed comfortably in stripes of dark gray, with no sign of being a Mage except a hint of his chain peeking out from a front pocket, overtop what looked like paper tickets.

Xelle, having not really thought this through as a Thing with Customs, was wearing her usual black, though, she admitted, with a little extra lace and fluff. Look, she hadn't been out much.

"It'll do," Dram said with a grin, seeming to read her mind. "Not quite Gatekeepers without the stripes, but at least you're not in the gold and white."

"Gatekeepers?" Xelle scrunched her face.

"I keep forgetting you genuinely don't know. Yes, the Gatekeepers are the team of Wehj." He gave her a apprizing glance. "Extra toppings; we're starting from the start here, aren't we."

Xelle waved this off. "I understand the concept of sports; we had all sorts of them in the forest at which I was not terrible. I just don't know about magipuck teams and such."

Dram, who dropped all enthusiasm and suddenly took on the air of quick notes to a fellow Mage before a meeting, started in: "A game is won after nine scores through the opponent's guard. Each team fashions their guard differently; it's core to the origins of the sport: pers messing with fuelstones in the vroomlots, hiding what they were doing with things like banners or draperies. So the Gatekeepers are fashioned around the corecity aesthetic. Their guard is constructed like large metal gates. Hence, the Gatekeepers."

"It's a terrible name," Xelle heard herself remarking. Not thinking this made for good company, she quickly followed on, "So who are they playing? Who is gold and white?"

"The Nightcurtains. They're—"

"Mytil!" Xelle had rather called it out, causing the entire vroom to turn and glance her way. Whatever. "I mean, I'm assuming so? The nightcurtains are a tradition in the night market of Mytil. They—"

"Yeah, normally Mytil doesn't have much chance, but this year they're hot as flame." Dram cocked his head. "You said you wanted a good game, I held for one. If you're a Mytil admi, sorry you'll have to see them lose to the Keeps."

Oh, it was like this now. "After that, consider me an admi. Also, I assure you, if this team plays anywhere near the art district, their colors are not gold and white, but stone and gold."

Dram made a sarcastic face, but at least this one felt more cute than dismissive. "Stone is not a color."

"In Mytil it is," she replied, then relaxed against the seat's back. Thoughts of the city were making her feel a bit galecaught, and this Mage barely knew her. It didn't seem the time to explain all that. He looked about to ask more, but this was not a good path for her right now. "You made it sound like there was just one Wehj team," she prompted. "Even Mytil flies the banners of a few, and in Vattam it seemed there might even be several."

He nodded. "Oh, sure, there are several in the area of Wehj. I suppose to an outsider it's all sort of 'Wehj' but pers here are fairly serious about outvillages, supply towns, even neighborhoods. Only the Gatekeepers are Wehj."

Xelle stifled a snort, not thinking Dram would get it. He seemed quite serious about his team.

As the vroom began to reach the outer areas of the city, Xelle began to see what Dram had meant. Despite the immense diversity of the areas of Vattam, all had proudly boasted they were, indeed, the City of Progress. Here, there were hardly signs for Wehj at all. Streets were marked differently even from one center of pers to another, and as they approached the large arena, the signs all bore the insignia, she supposed, of the home team. Team, not teams. It seemed clear that, however many other teams were in this area, they were not based here.

As they piled out of the vroom, Xelle realized she didn't even know who, of the other passengers, were Mages, Studies, staff, or friends— what she did know was they were all here for the local team.

Well. When had Xelle played along?

Dram had begun to nearly waft toward a food stand. "I'll be back real quick," she said, patting his arm. This because Xelle had seen, next to the huge painted building labeled "Gatekeepers Gear", a large traveling cart with the artfully-lettered signage: *Nightcurtains.* Beyond it were an array of tunics, fans, cap covers, and other items in familiar shades of Mytil stone, with gleaming gold-toned accents.

"Hello," she said, to the young shopkeep, who gave her a broad smile. "What's the nicest, oh and also flashiest, thing you have?" Xelle didn't like to squander or wave wealth, but she was, in fact, a Mage, she did, in fact, have Essie stocked with coins, this was a place dedicated, literally, to waving colors, and this would definitely . . . definitely not be squandered. "And nothing that will make me sweaty," she appended.

As the shopkeep pulled out what looked like a long piece of softly-combed stone (color) fabric embroidered lovingly with metallic gold that Xelle immediately recognized as a nightshawl (she almost cried!) she assured xem that she knew how to wear it and barely heard the price as she held out a rather heavy coin. "With whatever's left, give something to a child wearing the colors," she said with a wink.

"Will do, Bon," xe said, returning the wink, before moving to another customer.

Bon! The irony that the cutely offered title intended to flatter would actually demote her was almost as much of a shock as the idea of Xelle, regular old Xelle, being called a Bon at all.

"Bon Xelle Du'Bon," she muttered to herself as she wrapped the beautiful fabric around her cap, and twisted around her arms so the ends could be tucked, gathered, or—waved, as she gleefully did, seeing Dram nearly salivating as he paced impatiently.

"Oh," he said. "We're doing this?"

"We're doing this," Xelle confirmed. "Now, what's good to eat here. Is everything breaded?"

He grinned. "Pretty much. Unless you have an allergy or aversion; there's a cart three wedges over for that."

Whatever he'd just said was a bit overtaken by the sight of a tissue basket of breaded pickles walking by. Probably held by a hu. Xelle did not notice.

"It's on me," Xelle said. "Since you got the tickets."

"Sure," Dram said. "In that case, a dark beer and a warm pretzel."

Xelle found balancing her own warm pretzel, a tissue full of breaded pickles, and a berry-brewed beer (not sweet, the good landy kind) while walking up the stands to her seat without her usual reliance on travel magic a bit more complex than expected. Given her relative freedom throwing Arc magic around the last several months, she had to stop her own instinct to do so here. Admonition or some such thing regarding the rules of Studies was no longer her concern, but, she suddenly realized, being a self-proclaimed Mage, she'd need to make her own. And she just thought casting without need around the populace was rude. Some pers were sensitive to shadows; others superstitious. Just didn't seem polite. Besides, she was here for the experience.

She wondered if Dram was carrying a wand. Oh, there was no way he was not carrying a wand. She glanced over, not trying to consider where it might be. Which didn't mean that! She was just saying—

"You didn't spill one drop," Dram noted, licking a splash of dark beer off of his hand, a gesture Xelle was unable not to notice.

"Um," she stumbled, "Arc stuff. Balance. I mean, I didn't cast." She'd better stop, but luckily she wasn't sure Dram could hear her over the pleasant chatter of the crowd as they made their way to their seats. He pointed to two, each with a table and a bit of space on the side.

"Oh! I don't have to sit next to anyone?" She realized she'd said that a bit loud, but Dram just laughed.

"Couples seats. Doesn't mean anything, of course. Just two pers choosing to enjoy the game together."

Xelle hadn't talked to Dram much at all, certainly not about her anxieties around unknown pers, but she was intensely grateful to sit into the not too uncomfortable seat, set down her beer and snacks, and finally take a look around.

"I didn't know if we'd be climbing up or down," she said, really not meaning to say it.

"Same thing in the end?"

"Mmnnm." Xelle shook her head. "Up and then down is not down and then up." She realized immediately why the concept came to mind. This place was huge. Xelle had often played games, but not so much spectated them. She supposed the place would have to hold a lot of pers. Like a theatre. But, no, even the theatres of Mytil were not so large.

A slightly slurred voice called over. "Mytil chews ash!"

Suddenly realizing she was wearing a brilliant shawl, whose bright and metallic colors caught in every beam of light, amidst a sea of gray and black (ironically, her normal colors of preference), Xelle considered her options. Shrugging away an annoyed look from Dram (no matter how serious one was about one's team, one couldn't be the literal Spire Staff Mage and not have some sense of propriety) she stood, instead, letting her shawl flutter around her. (And thanks to the seating, only flapping in Dram's face, and then only slightly.)

Issue was, she had no idea what one might say in support of a magipuck team, though with the last remark, her bar was at least set low. She ran the new fabric through her hands. Xelle didn't want to say something rude as a guest in this city, but she also didn't want to simply sit. All at once, the musicians of the night market sprung to mind. She didn't think of them. It was as if her mind thrust the idea at her—here, this.

No harm in song? Just a line or two.

> *Blessing of the moons upon you*
> *Blessing of the lights beyond*
> *Blessing for the ones who guide you*
> *To Mytil, to Mytil in song*

There. Showed them. Just as she was about to sit, her voice rather small among the now turning spectators, she saw another stand. Xe was wearing the colors of Wehj, and waving off a larger hu, likely a partner, to xyr side. Xe had joined in that last line, and was smiling her way. Together, they nodded.

> *Lampposts of gold paint our paths through the market*
> *The criss-cross of moonslight the skip to our step*
> *Baskets of treasures to carry to sunshine*
> *Hearts full of memories forever kept*

Now look, the song was a bit of an advertisement for the night market, often played near the entrance ways, especially during festivals and holidays. But anyone who had frequented knew the bit, from the merchants, to the citypers, to the visitor who looked forward to a long-awaited trip. And here, that wasn't as many pers. But there were enough, now, joining in, that the words were fairly well carrying over the section. Well, then, best to finish. She took a breath.

> *Blessings, oh blessings, of the moons here, upon you*
> *Blessings of the farlights that twinkle beyond*
> *Blessings for the lights in our lives; they will guide you*

To Mytil, to Mytil
To Mytil, *dear* Mytil
To Mytil, *in art, and in song*

A small cheer erupted as everyone sat back into their seats. A few pers yelled "Boo!" while a few others, caught off guard, had applauded.

Dram was laughing into his beer. "Xeleanor, do you enter every new place this way?"

Well, she kind of did, but he didn't have to point that out.

"Pers are trying to see what's going on from all the way over there. Look, the glint of magnifiers." Again, he chuckled, and then resumed biting into his pretzel. Which, Xelle realized, was a very good idea. Oh, but she also had pickles.

Sitting here felt surreal. Not only the entirely new surroundings, but if Xelle had ever imagined going to a magipuck game (she honestly hadn't given it much thought) she certainly would not have imagined watching one with a Grand Mage. (The point being, with a Mage at all, but on top of that, why Grand?)

There was no magic involved in magipuck. Fuelstones, which were actually amalgamations of deceased plant cells hardened over time, naturally repelled each other when charged with sunlight. These unique objects had been used to cause motion and automation ever since the properties had been discovered. (The history books in To'Breath had centered the magesphere, but certain populace innovations were fairly integral to Alyssia's history and given some level of due.) And while concerns over conservation of the stones, which could be recharged, but not manufactured, had traditionally kept them to regulated usage, the use of chips or shards to infuse into the 'magic' puck, the sticks used to guide it, and the gear of the players had long been overlooked by such regulators.

Who were probably admis, she realized with a chuckle.

Xelle was thrilled to see a band come out and play, surrounded by hu twirling shiny sticks and banners. She even recognized two of the songs; one, "Long Parade of Little Ducks", had been a favorite of the brass band at To'Ever and she didn't know the title of the other, but knew the last song they played was a tribute to Heart Lake. The Lake was so revered the song was played lovingly before many ceremonies and events, as far from the Lake as Tam, and certainly as close to it as Mytil, where it took even more significance. She wondered how the Mytil team, presumably somewhere closeby, was reacting to hearing something so dear to them. Wondered if Wehj understood that connection.

They were even farther from the Lake here than she'd been in Tam, though not quite as far as at To'Ever. The only Tower on the Lake was, of course, Charm, but To'Arc had a deep affinity to it also, with the Lake forming from the mountains and essentially right underneath Arc Tower. A sensation, almost like a cast, she thought with a bit of surprise, ran down her arms at the thought of Arc. She sighed.

"You love music," Dram said.

She had forgotten he was there.

"Yes," she said with a smile that she hoped made up for it. The smile was a little for Dram, but a lot for him seeing this about her. "You know, when I was at Ever, I found a band I really loved watching." She felt a pang at realizing she hadn't even looked to see if such a schedule was published at Grand. But of course it was. There it was again, that depression of absence. "I need to look that up. Concerts, I mean. At Grand," she clarified.

"There's a— Anyway, yeah, you should. Look, here are the teams."

Two teams of seven hu each (oh, the magesphere must really dislike that) nearly floated out onto the field. Floating was too gentle. Something in their footwear gave them a walk almost like a vroom, yet combined with their own. It was fascinating—unlike any motion she'd seen. As they moved into an evenly distributed pattern, two sets of posts were carried out and clipped into place.

As Dram had described, they were . . . decorated.

One side had two elaborate metal gateposts, with decorative swirls to the outside edges. The other were gleaming gold lampposts, with protruding arms, again, to the outside, where large, stone colored curtains fluttered as they were moved into place. Familiar herself with traffic patterns (her main research at To'Arc) she quickly noticed a region around each gate where no players stood.

"They're avoiding that section? Something happens if you go in it?"

"Mmm," Dram confirmed. "The nozone. But nothing happens; you just don't do it."

That seemed ambiguous. "What if you fall into it or something?" Even in tall ladder competitions, which were jovial enough, there were penalties and disqualifications, meant to prevent a winner from being embarrassed by an unintended breach of guidelines.

"Shame upon your family for a thousand years."

Xelle cut him a look. "A reasonable question; some sports have penalties?"

"No, seriously, no penalties, it's just a bad look." He watched her reaction for a moment, then grinned. "I forget, like, all the backstory. So the sport has always been seen as a bit of rebellion, right? Against the order, the magesphere, the regulators. So there's a lot of honor involved." He hesitated at that. "Spirit over letter. Is a better way to put it."

"Funny thing for a Staff Mage to like?" She hoped that wasn't offensive, but he didn't really seem like the sort to be disturbed by much. She was getting that impression quickly.

"Hu are funny," he shrugged, picking up the last piece of his pretzel. "I should have got two of these."

"You could have some of mine," she offered. She didn't really want to give up any of the delicious pretzel bread, but, you know, sharing. And she had just scarfed down the pickle bites.

He laughed. "Sorry, that's sweet, but that's always what I say after I eat one, and never what I say after I eat two."

It wasn't sweet, it was generous, but her attention quickly moved to the players, standing still in what definitely appeared to be a moment of note.

A highly sparkly puck suddenly went flying out onto the field, and in an instant, stillness broke.

Xelle didn't know if she should be laughing, but never having seen the sport, she could immediately see its appeal. Players and their sticks went after this puck with the force of angry lumberjacks, but by the force of the fuelstone powder, or whatever they used, nothing touched each other. The players bounced around in a sort of brutalist ballet, and the sticks nearly met, and then separated like children playing at sticktouch, and the puck glittered and bounced and sparked, and then whooshed, as if drawn, right through the gate. The dark-colored gate. The Gatekeepers gate.

Xelle stood, cheering, flapping her shawl wildly. This is how it was done, right? Across the way, she saw an entire section of pers wearing the stone and gold, standing and cheering. She waved their way.

She'd barely sat and taken another drink of the beer (if Wehj arena beer was this good, she would need to try more beer from Wehj) when Mytil scored again, similarly. Not wanting to make too much of a show, she stayed seated this time, but did lean over to Dram, who was grinning at her.

"What if the game's super short? Won't pers be disappointed? Who traveled all this way, paid for tickets?"

Dram snorted. "A little two-oh confidence going, Mage Xeleanor?" He paused, taking a drink of his own beer. "First, no, they'd just go move to the grasslots and the vendors would stay open. Second, don't check your bootlatches just yet; Somh's just getting the feel of the play."

"Somh?"

Dram looked decidedly smug. "Yes, Somh Du'Wehj, hometown kid turned best magipuck player in Alyssia. That one," he said, pointing down to a rather small, wispy figure. The teams both wore the same, standardized gear, but with caps of the team colors, each marked with a different symbol. That part, Xelle figured, was for the crowd. "She's got keen strategy, delicious aim, and a quality I think you might actually appreciate."

"Incredible charm?" Xelle offered, extending her hands outward. One accidentally rubbed up against Dram's moving arm, but he didn't seem bothered. So much for her joke.

"Perhaps; never met." He raised his beer as if he didn't mind the idea. "No, she never, ever, gives up. Eight-oh on the final flip, doesn't matter. Everything is winning the game."

Xelle thought about what he'd said about honor. She didn't think he meant it that way, just, well, what he'd said first. Never giving up until it was truly over. And sure, enough, Somh went zipping down the field, nearly spinning as she used the leverage of the fuelstones to leap nearly horizontally and back again, solidly whisking the puck through the gold lampposts of the Mytil team.

Now she was in an arena. The placed roared with such intensity, Xelle threw her hands over her ears, then ducked below the edge of the seatback so that pers wouldn't think it was a sour gesture. It was just loud. Very loud.

"You're well? Need anything?"

"No, just not great with volume like that. Don't worry," she quickly assured him. "I'm fine here; just didn't expect it to get that loud that quickly." What she didn't add was her attempt not to cast; otherwise the quickest wisp would have traveled the sound away from her ears. Remembering that she used to carry little ear plugs in Essie, she rummaged through and found they were still there, little foam wedges a bit squished into a side pouch. She fit them in, feeling much more comfortable at the dampened cheers.

"Always prepared, I see. Reminds me of an Arc Mage."

Xelle was glad to see Dram wrapped immediately back into the game, as she sorted away both the simultaneous shock that she seemed an Arc Mage, but yet he didn't think of her as one, and the recognition that as Staff Mage, he probably knew the Arc Spire Mages better than she did. No, not better. Just more time around them. That wasn't at all the same.

She very much did not want to twist in the nightpaths over a worry that she'd spent the game angsting and not watching the game itself, and so she tried to focus on the field, finding that the mention of Arc Magic had put her in a different place about it all. The game was strength, power, and momentum (in the senses of team and crowd morale, which did make Somh's approach very interesting for her to think about later) but much more, the game was travel. Patterns. Seeing where things were, where they could go. And up here, from a bird's eye view. As if assessing a map. Seeking data patterns from an overhead perspective.

That? Was something Xelle *loved*. And she started to see them develop. The keenness of strategy of the players and the teams overall. The setups, often resembling a game of diamondboard but with independent, physical pieces. The artistry of a glittering object bouncing and curving and never touching anything but the floor itself, and then with near defiance and survival with the speed with which it would again be aflight.

Dram was right about Somh. And not just Somh, but her rapport with her team. They played hard, and at the time Dram went to bring them both a second beer (was he really going to drink two dark beers, despite his wisdom with the pretzels?) the Gatekeepers were ahead with five points, and the Nightcurtains now at three.

Yet Xelle saw why the Nightcurtains were having an unprecedented year . . . season? Whatever. Point was, they were *skilled*. Any edge the Gatekeepers had in aim, coordination, and perseverance, the Nightcurtains matched it with strategy, adaptability, and nuance.

Enough that she forgot even to cheer when they scored again, bringing the match to an even eight to eight.

"Good game?"

Xelle knew there were layers to the statement, but she waved off whatever he was going on about. "Yes! Awesome. Just one score to end it, right?" Seemed an obvious, friendly statement, so she was surprised when he shook his head.

"Can't win on the flip after a point."

"Do they just keep going, then?" Seemed to take the juice out of the nine thing.

"No, after eight, the score doesn't register right away. If the other team matches a point on the next flip, it stays at eight-eight. If they don't, then the game ends."

"Huh." Wasn't perhaps the most involved commentary, but it was her first game.

Back and forth, around. She was, admittedly, mesmerized. Barely forgot she was holding the beer. But did continue to sip; it was delicious, and not heavy at all.

And she nearly missed it when a roar erupted around the arena, but realized immediately that the puck she'd seen flying toward the iron posts, or whatever they called them, was no longer visible. Mytil had scored the . . . almost ninth point? There had to be terminology, but at this point it was much too loud to ask.

Last play. Sohm glid right out to the center, looking like she was going to wreck anything in her way. And then Mytil lined up. A huge gap down the middle, protected only by one player, daring her to try it.

The Mytil Bridge Problem! Ha! She sat up in her seat. "Oh, Mytil's got this," she said into Dram's ear.

"Want to bet?"

"Absolutely. You pick. They're going to win."

He laughed, but before he could offer a bet, the hu a bit behind them broke out again. "Mytil still chews ash." The voice bellowed from behind her.

Alright now, enough of this. Xelle whipped around, determined not to miss the play. "Then apparently the Gatekeepers are ash, because it appears you're about to get absolutely devoured." She waved at the hu's companions. "Watch this play, then get xem some water."

A laugh from the crowd caused the pers to shuffle, but Xelle wasn't paying attention; she was back to the game. Or trying to; now everyone was standing, and Xelle, not being of tall stature, could not see an ash-burned thing.

"Hop up?"

Hop up? She realized Dram was pointing to his shoulders.

"Isn't that rude?" she asked. With the volume increasing he was pretty much going to have to guess what she said. Shaking his head, he gestured again.

Well, fine. Once she did so, she realized many other shorter pers were doing the same thing, at least outside of what appeared to be a seated-only section across the arena and also in some glass-enclosed spaces, both high and low.

Any musings on arena design did not last long, because as Somh rushed forward with the puck, the hu in the middle broke the center position, leaving a path to their own gates completely clear, pulled the puck away with xyr stick, and sent it banking off of a Wehj player's midsection, and angling back around to slide firmly into the Gatekeeper's goal.

With excitement and trying to wave her colors, she instead wavered in place, and reminding herself not to cast, grasped on tighter, her thighs now pressing firmly against the Mage's strong, like very strong, shoulders, and her fingers running along the soft fabric of his lightly-padded cap and onto his slightly sweaty neck.

Oh, no. This was . . . sexy. With a realization she should hop down, she started to, but Dram misinterpreting her intent, she served only to wobble her thighs against him until he did realize she was trying to return to the floor, at which point she had tried to steady herself, and ended up sliding around, nearly falling until his strong arms pulled her in, resting on her sides.

Xelle, she scolded herself sternly, *whatever you do, do not sleep with the Spire Staff Mage.*

05 - *Impure Thoughts*

Xelle slept with the Spire Staff Mage. Not just once, but, well, about ten times that week. First in a Vi'Grand Nook & Bunk, then again in her room at To'Grand, then the next morning, well, again in her room. Then, on a bed of falling leaves in the forest when they went to walk and talk about what might be going on, then again in his room, and—

Well, you get the idea. And, this continued, though not quite with said pacing, over the next couple of weeks, during which Xelle also tried to get out and enjoy the fall weather, and try to schedule an appointment with Mage Tatock about the lab situation, and occasionally see Dram in the hallway and suddenly not be in the hallway anymore.

Frankly, she still hadn't gotten to know the Mage. He wasn't really funny; he kept a lot to himself. But also he was funny, he had a sharp wit about things, and a default of joy? Or, if not joy, rolling with the situation? He had a rather busy schedule in his assignment, and as neither of them wanted to rock Xelle's relationship with the Spire (what a word choice), they weren't really doing much in public, and—

Her mark pinged. (She didn't know a better word for it?)

A distraction sounded great right now. She grabbed Essie, rubbed on a bit of lip balm, and made her way back to the nightgarden.

Actually. That had not been nearly as difficult this time. Like . . . muscle memory or something. She told Thunder to hold on, as her inkbloom deserved a song, and frankly Xelle had realized stopping emself to do so was vastly calming, especially before a second travel, and then, the inkbloom happily gave her a pod, which she ingested, before holding on to their offered vines (figuratively, as in, in the magic) and whisking to the site where Thunder waited, arriving nicely on her feet and without much drama.

She'd learned to take the victories.

Seriously. So much of the time she either didn't think she was pushing enough on her goals, or too busy to think about it, so when a thing that had been previously difficult now flowed like a casual glass of berried water, she'd learned to note the moment, pause on the gratitude, and then get on to the next.

Thunder was alone, and didn't seem pleased that her two initial thoughts were beaming about her own work and thinking directly about Thunder not being around the others. To Xelle, that was natural—conversations to be held with or without pers were a thing. But when she was a teen? Even that first year (fine, especially that first year) at To'Ever? No, she would have taken it as wondering at her lack of supervision, or unwillingness to include pers of authority, or, anyway.

At least zhey seemed pleased—*sort of*—to hear that.

Back to things being easy or difficult. Right now, communicating through Thunder's mind, or magic, rather than via perfectly normal mind-reading and big dragon sign language, was something they'd have to meter. The attempts left her pained, and weak, and less able to be alert.

Xelle tried to always be alert. Frankly, it was one reason she'd been enjoying the last couple of weeks. The company was nice, and the sex better, but not being *stressed* all the ashed-out time was an unfamiliar feeling. You know what was a good feeling? The reactions Dram had to her presence; the flare of his eyes, the hardening of his muscles, the moment of reaching to feel the shift in his pants, to confirm the speed and strength of his reaction; like who cared whatever else needed her, he needed her, and—

Thunder roared like a hundred stampeding elephants who'd just had their cookout canceled.

Oh. Burn it, mind-reading dragons.

Thunder stamped.

"Well I am allowed to have a private life, Thunder. And I am working on—"

Well, what indeed had she been working on? She'd been thinking about what to do with her new knowledge about the dragons, whether to check-in with Kern, her new lab lead was already trying to oust her, and she was still fairly new to Grand Tower and everything really wasn't supposed to be on her.

Talk? Thunder signaled.

Xelle sighed and tapped yes.

By the inaccurately large size of the Thunder that she could see before her, she knew this was not a literal memory of Thunder's but something zhey were imagining. Look, Thunder didn't even have memories seeing zhemself, outside of close reflections. Sure, it could be someone else's perception, but she'd not had any indications Thunder could share someone else's vision. And she actually hoped that while she was like this, Thunder couldn't read her thoughts (she had a feeling that was the case?) because she could almost ignore the surges of pressure and panic threatening her at the introduction of the dragon vision, because Thunder had made zhemself, like, kinda swole.

Swole Thunder, ok fine, she'd stop, was strutting toward a series of hu, that all basically had the build of Xelle, but with more dragony faces. So. She didn't think this was a lizard-per thing, despite her sudden craving for such a development, but probably the fact that Thunder still hadn't seen any other hu up close. Zheir only model was Xelle. Hmm. She'd have to think about that.

So. Thunder, who she realized rather had the design of a flipbook animation, roared at the hu, but then the hu came up and threw a huge canvas sack over zhem, covering zheir body.

Triggered by remembering the sack over her head, she stopped the vision immediately, wrenching to the ground and waving Thunder away, before remembering she could just think things, at which point she quickly thought, *Give me a moment!*

Zhey did, sitting back politely.

Xelle knew the bag thing had happened; it wasn't that it couldn't ever be mentioned. But she didn't like thinking about it, and this had been thrust at her without warning.

Already knowing this was an idea rather than a memory, it didn't take her long to realize why. *So you want to be captured? No!*

Thunder breathed enough fire to char the rock in front of zhem. Noting it, Thunder kicked the charred rock, sending it rolling off a bit until it thunked to a stop.

"Ah," Xelle said, quite out loud. "I know, I don't tell you what to do. But I'm allowed to say I don't like it. We aren't at any level of need for that kind of thing." She saw zheir expression. "Yeah, I went, and I flaming left as soon as I could. You haven't met these pers; their hearts are twisted into empty peapods. And, look. You're already at risk here, as a group, but at least you're together and not under their control. Just, let me work it. I'm still thinking through options."

The echoes of Thunder's mind within her own gave quick images that were rather lewd, and she glared back, yanking away the connection to give her a moment, but not before also hearing very clearly that zhey were seventy-six and one and Xelle was twenty-nine and one.

"I don't think we want to do that, buddy," Xelle nearly growled. She sat back against a rock. "Look, sometimes I've been kind of condescending, and I don't want to be. It's not that I don't trust you, I just feel the same sort of impulsivity in you that I had at your . . . stage of development."

Thunder nearly screeched.

"I get it," Xelle almost shouted, lowering her voice immediately. "We're friends; I don't control you; you don't control me. Let's just . . . work together." Thoughts now swirling, she realized how absurd her own ideas were. Impulsivity *then*? Impulsivity *now*. And both simmering in a thick broth of sitting the flame around, getting more knowledgeable, getting more situated, but doing what? Yeah, she was in a better position now. To do what? Wait more effectively? **Argh.**

And yes, Thunder could read her thoughts, but zhey knew she

knew that. Did others know that? Did the Lunests know that? Fine, so that's why zhey wanted to get captured. To read the minds of everyone in that compound.

Consent issues flashed through her mind. And forget the Lunests, what about around other pers? Or was that like telling a bird not to note the lean and direction of another per, just because the other per didn't know what senses the other possessed. Could per hide their thoughts from dragons? She rubbed her head.

Firana, what had her plans done so far? And maybe that last bit, yeah, that was it. This just wasn't Xelle's call. Then why'd zhey called her? To bounce it off? To help? Both? She stared into Thunder's eyes, wondering what it was zhey saw in hers.

"Ok, I understand. I see it. But I think you need to get permission for this. From the others." By the tilt of her head, if not a hundred other ways, Xelle knew zhey'd know what she meant: from the dragons. The leadership. From the broader group, however that worked.

She didn't have time to think about it.

Thunder did not roar or stomp this time, but straight-out glared. Having never truly been glared at by a dragon, Xelle found herself . . . Not afraid, she'd never be afraid of Thunder. But it was a sick feeling. A crack.

Xelle felt the whole hillside dropping out from under her. "Wait," she called, using Arc Magic to sling after Thunder who had turned and was leaving. "Wait, can we at least talk about it?"

Thunder turned, gave the most exaggerated form of the no crouch that Xelle could have imagined, then flapped off.

She began to sling forward, to follow, then stopped. A sudden image in her mind of flying out of her parents' house and into the outside tree. But Na Vuia, she had followed.

Na Vuia was her parent. Did that matter? Should she follow now? She wasn't as fast as Thunder, but she knew where zhey were, from the . . .

She didn't know. It was . . . quiet. In no way did she think, even for a second, that it was severed. She didn't really think that was possible. And she sensed no anger. Just, well, it felt like *leave me alone.*

The sick feeling only growing now, Xelle scanned, abstractedly, and finding a tuft of leaves, lowered into it.

Hey. Thunder. I'm sorry.

She had to have more to say than that, but declaring them equals or some such thing sounded as bad as considering the thought in the first place. She was sure zhey were not listening to these thoughts, now. So a dragon didn't have to hear. Or maybe it was more like, closing one's eyes? She took a breath.

I'm used to the magesphere, she thought with direction, right into her sigil. *Even among labmates, or Mages, someone has rank, someone has command. I . . . maybe it's a hu thing. Or just a Mage thing? I don't know, and I'll need to think about it. Even my sibling, he's like younger, but in charge of his curas. He doesn't have a partner. I had one, well, we worked together, but we were both kind of different. I thought I had a partner, but see how that . . . Fira, Thunder, all I can say right now is I love you, and I'm sorry I upset you, and next time we talk I'll try not to be such a prod.*

She rocked forward, starting to reach for the inkbloom to take her back. Then stopped.

No. There's more. You're absolutely right, friend. It is completely time to go.

A particular coffee shop in Vi'Grand in mind for a good place to go think, she fell gently into the pathways, and back to her nightgarden.

06 - *Looking Good and Feeling Grand*

Dram looked surprised to see her.

"Mage Sandaba should be expecting me?"

He cocked his head in an expression that perfectly balanced his work and personal persona, she couldn't help but think. "You can just come on up now?"

Xelle chuckled. He wasn't wrong. "A certain mystique," she said with a shrug. It was true. A Mage from another Tower couldn't just walk unattended to the Platform (the local slang for the open platform plus the Spire floors below, and, Xelle presumed, above it.) But somehow Xelle showing up uninvited, being allowed not just to stay, but allowed to call herself—*be*, she reminded herself—a Mage gave a lot of pers pause about what could or couldn't be questioned.

She knew not to push that. But, when she'd scheduled a meeting with San, as she had here, she felt fine strolling her way up and nodding cheerfully to those along the way, who made no move to question her.

He leaned closer. "Speaking of mystique—" As Spire Mage Beleg suddenly appeared, whatever suggestive thing Dram had been about to whisper disappeared just as suddenly. "Spire Mage," he said with a bow.

"Ah, excellent, Xeleanor. I see you are immersing yourself in our hospitality." For almost a moment, Xelle thought the remark was meant innocently, or referring to her lack of stewardly escort. No. Dram looked *almost* rattled. Almost. Ha!

"Yes, Spire Mage Beleg." She bowed deeply. "Your Staff Mage is attentive, flexible, and consistently dedicated to results."

"Well, yes, Mage Xeleanor," Dram said, a tiny bit off of his rhythm. "Mage Sandaba is expecting you? Let's not keep him waiting."

With the look Beleg exchanged with Xelle, it was all she could do not to laugh. But the fact was, Dram did take his, um, position here seriously. So, she nodded with a mostly straight face, and followed him along.

The door to the balcony was closed, and San, looking uncharacteristically strained over a stack of papers, made no move to invite in the mid-fall chill. She felt certain he knew a cast for warmth, but Xelle understood why a Mage who treasured the tiniest view of the sea would not normally use it.

She took a seat in the direction he motioned her, and waited quietly for him to complete a clearly mid-way path of thought.

With a sigh, he pushed the papers aside. "Xelle, I fear for these times."

A bit ominous. Was it a message? No, she had to stop thinking everything was a message, even with Mages. Actually, he just looked stressed.

"I stayed around the Tower until I felt the weight shift," she said, wondering at her own honesty. But, then again, their agreement over water felt stronger than magic. What he'd said on that had really found her in a true place. "Recently, I've gone to talk to my friend twice." Something rested on her tongue. Something she'd never said.

"It's alright," he said.

"Thunder. I call zhem Thunder and zhey said zhey like the name."

She'd never, ever told anyone the specific dragon. But, also, it was a little funny, now hearing it aloud. How would another hu know which one was Thunder?

"Envy is a curse, Xelle," he said, oddly dry in tone. "But what you have. It is so rare, so special."

There. That uneasy look. There were clearly things Mages weren't supposed to talk about. Well, he knew she went there. He hadn't said don't. So. That wasn't actually why she was here.

"I am interested in truly learning some Grand Magic. More than the feel, the whiff, the magical equivalent of hello and how do you do. And, it's a little awkward to go directly to you, in your position, but . . ."

He waved her off. "If we are going to trust, then we cannot expend ourselves on such caveats. Are you here for permission, or to discuss?"

"To discuss," she said without hesitation. "Despite my travels, it took a great amount of effort—months and months essentially alone, really, to balance my Arc with a strong grasp of mere pieces of Ever. I used Frond, early on it turns out, without even understanding it, and still I'm always just swinging the hammer behind my back. Dangerous. Yet, here I am, in Grand Tower, the only Tower right now not just issuing me residence, but making me feel . . . welcome." That was true. Grand did not feel like . . . her place? But she did feel welcome here. She felt easier. Calmer. Less worried about walking into a group of Mages, or a foodshow, or even stopping to say hello to a group of Studies whose feet dangled off of a garden wall.

It was a bit of a borrowed life, but compared to the last year plus, it was . . . a relief. "So, whatever that time of residence turns out to be, should I not be learning—or at least better understanding—the core of the place? Or am I treading too roughly on a roof of thrown sticks?"

"What is a Mage?"

If (almost?) anyone else had asked her that, it would have felt like a quickclicker, but San looked quite serious.

"A Mage is a per who casts . . ." Not true, her Na had cast and had not been a Mage, surely others had too. ". . . within the structures of the Seven Towers." Well, had she just called herself not a Mage? Or was her own structure different? "No. A Mage is a per who learns magic, and casts it under a structure of ethics and support." She paused. "I don't know why I said support. Maybe it's just ethics. I'd have to think about it."

San only nodded. "Then that per, who learns Magic under a structure of ethics and/or support, would need to balance those questions. Perhaps you could answer them yourself, perhaps you need to ask someone like me, who has witnessed the lives of many Mages and the consequences of their choices. Or perhaps, if you are making your own structures of ethics, the structures of support are inadequate for your questions."

"Well, is that a failing on me, or on the existing structures?"

"I don't know," San replied, dryly but not disengaged. "It's a good question."

Xelle thought a moment. "Then, why do Mages only practice the prong they were a Study in? Because of centuries of developed under-standing, or because of centuries of unnecessary restriction?"

San tapped his wand to a bundle of dried herbs, which gave off a pleasant smell. "You're walking untrodden ground. So perhaps it is a question to you: whether, how did you say it? Whether you are treading thrown sticks or fine hatches. And it seems to me, if you are here to ask the difference, I would advise caution. And perhaps some renewed consideration of a system born of centuries of experience that knows its own foundations."

Her arms prickled. Was he defending it? Poking her? Or just chal-lenging her ideas? Or . . . challenging her to challenge her ideas? Or . . . She was reaching that point where she wasn't feeling secure on her footing. Here in the now, forget the hypothetical. Whether she was really someone of capability, or an untied banner, smacking around in the trees and annoying the pers doing the real work.

"What about confidence?" she blurted out. "Does a Mage have confidence?"

He stared. "A Mage must always acutely know when they do have confidence, when they do not, and when they must act to the contrary."

Huh? Xelle couldn't imagine being confident but not acting like it. Or was that what she was doing now? This water was getting too deep.

"What about a wand?" she asked. The way it came out, it sounded like one of those 'confident when not' scenarios. "Making a wand doesn't mean using a wand." She knew this from her discussions with Rayn. "But the effort to learn it, commit to it, execute it might show my loyalty and belonging here, without my pledge."

San burst into laughter. "I like you! And, oh, my friend, if I already confessed that an Arc Mage unsettles any proper Grand Mage, I cannot fathom the reaction to a wand-bearing one." He seemed to be wiping his eyes.

Xelle made a playfully annoyed face as San settled his little laughy spell down.

"I think it is a fantastic idea. You will make it under our supervision, then, which means you will swear to its use and restrictions. Correct?"

She nodded. That was totally fair.

"I will consider the best way to enter you into that process."

"I'm planning on meeting with Mage Tatock on a new choice of lab," she added. "My welcome in the current assignment is complicated and, while it's been wonderful, I think I am ready to contribute in new ways." And leave An'oar to his pettiness. She really didn't need to deal with him. Perhaps a lesson from Fepa, a small voice added. She brushed it away. If she could forget Fepa existed, it would be a life goal met.

San was exhaling slowly. It was a familiar gesture, one Xelle saw in herself when she had just considered something bold. Ah.

"Perhaps combine the two," he offered. "The wand lab itself. Researching and making, an open exchange of ideas around time-tested techniques."

"I'm up for it," she said, thinking that actually sounded really exciting.

San chortled in an involuntary but rather annoying way. "It would be throwing you into a fire."

Despite the language, there was a sparkle in his eyes, one that connected with Xelle's own. "So, a Grand Move, you might say?"

Now, he bellowed, delightfully and intentionally. "They won't know what they are in for! Now," he waved. "Don't mention me in this, it'll only hurt your chances. Go to Tatock, and make your case." He grinned her way. "Xeleanor, your sincerity is rare and beautiful."

She tilted her head. "I mean, pers here are generally honest."

"Honest is different!" He tapped his desk. "You have direct access to a Spire Mage, and you really just want to learn. Get advice. You're not here for status, or favors, or even the power of personal knowledge."

Personal knowledge? "I love magic. And want to help."

He shook his head, slowly and deliberately. "The water led us well. Let me ask you something. Do you know the shape of the prongs?"

"The prongs? As in the forms of magic?" Of course he meant that, but she didn't understand. What shape would there be?

He nodded, and held up his hand, as if Xelle could nestle a small spirits cup within it. "The seven prongs of magic, holding within them the gem of Hallinia. I only have five fingers," he added. "Imagine seven. Whether a secret, a myth, or a fabrication depends on the teller of the tale." He lowered his hand. "May I blaspheme?"

May he what? "Uh, sure." Go ahead. Blaspheme.

"They are all correct. One Tower per Region, yes, reaching up toward its gem. But, not equidistant from the Lake. Not set for a brilliant cut, but for its own reality, which perhaps someday you will learn."

There was no question in his choice of words that whatever followed about the actual city of Hellina (or a metaphor it stood for) was not going to be told today. But, what he was going to say was clearly something fascinating and new, and so e sat, drinking in every word and every inflection and microexpression as best that e could.

"When it comes to the core of our structures, we do tend to talk in absolutes." He was now rolling his wand between two fingers, atop the desk. Casually, though, as if it were a fidget toy, and not a magic instrument of tremendous power. "A gem, A crown. A rule of our own, not of another." He shrugged. "The world is much more a parure; the *choices* are our own."

Apparently seeing Xelle's expression, he flicked the fingers of his wandless hand. "I am delving too far. What I wanted to tell you is that the setting, the prongs, would much more accurately be called a chain, made from its process as much as its design. Once pinned. Then linked. Then inspected from within. Another pin. Then, inspected from without. Another link. And then, a final pin. A flexible diadem to set its gem. Yet the Mages who oversaw this surely thought that a diadem of chain did not import the permanence of stability they desired. And so, they made themselves its Crown, septagonal and set. Now," he continued, without pause to signal no questions would be asked about any of that either, "Which prong is which? To what are we all pinned?"

A slight rise on one side of his lip told em this was a lure. So e looked right at him. "Arc."

"Yes. The connection of space and time. Perhaps this is not the best pin to hold our weight, but it's the one that we know. And what is the essence of Arc Magic?"

Now this was funny. When e was at Arc, considering a pledge, e would have said 'travel' or 'connection' or both. And that would not have been wrong. But now e'd felt the pathways. Heard what San had just nudged her way. "Access to the pathways of space and time," e answered.

"Good!" he nearly shouted, smacking his palm on his desk. "And an advanced Arc Mage, in collaboration with another Mage, can add that Mage's casts into those pathways."

Oh, Holy Firana. E was going to have to think about that.

"Don't feel too special yet—there are three pins."

Three pins. Could access . . . pathways? Kwill had never mentioned pathways. Nothing at Ever or at Frond had suggested such a thing. San had a look Xelle knew well. Pride for one's Tower. "Grand. Grand is a pin. The pathways of . . ." Oh, this was simple. "Life. You can see the pathways of life?"

He grinned. "Close enough. Then, the third pin?"

"Death? To . . . To'Dust?"

"Yes. And close enough. Now, the watchers."

Ever. Ever had to be a watcher. "Ever," she answered. "Permanence."

San nearly giggled. "And what do we joke as fleeting?"

Xelle nearly snorted, one of Na Foose's sillier sayings coming to mind. But 'beauty' was not the answer. Not quite. "Charm Tower. So that leaves Breath and Frond. The links?" She knew how Frond Tower would take to that characterization. Well. Did she? She'd never really found herself fitting in there.

"I am telling you much more than most would say I should, so I'm going to say this once, and you'll remember what you will."

Quite unfair, but it wasn't like she was going to complain. Besides, this she would remember. She had a feeling San knew that and was adding the caveat to appease his own inner qualms about sharing the information.

> Arc, the pathways of world.
> Breath, the perception of states.
> Charm, the awareness of transience.
> Dust, the pathways of spirit.
> Ever, the awareness of permanence.
> Frond, the perception of bonds.
> Grand, the pathways of life.

She'd never, ever, heard it like this. And despite her hope she'd remember, she was repeating it again and again in her mind.

"Now I feel like a jerk," San said, raising his wand as if in question. She nodded, whatever it would be, and suddenly, the words had been passed to her, in San's voice. She let her repetition stop. "Thank you," she said.

"We view ourselves here as guardians of our pathways, while you view yourselves as travelers of yours, and Dust would say they honor theirs. They are not separate. None of this is separate. So, back to your original question, how much to learn, how much to explore and expand, these are questions of life. Unification, they called it. But really, it was more organization. Bringing those together who could amplify each other's research and works, ensuring all aspects of magic as we knew it were given due. And safety. The use of magic was . . . fraught. They don't like to talk about it." He was gazing toward his sealed patio door. "Towers are places we connect, but also where we hide."

"Like Frond and Breath."

He glanced at her sharply. "Exactly like that. And it consternates me as much as it amuses me that you, a former Frond Study, found no connection in that place of connection, yet pass between Towers as if made of spores yourself. The Towers are not the same. The Towers are not separate. And if you try to understand everything, Xeleanor, you will lose yourself. You remember what I told you about trust? And love?"

She nodded.

"Mages will admire the depth of your trust as much as they will fear it. But trust is not trust if it is given to everything. That is simply—falling. So, I tell you, Mage Xeleanor, you ask me where to go and where to focus. And my answer is, sit with yourself. What you are, what you do, and what you want to do. In that, find yourself."

He stood. "No more talk. But, perhaps you will indulge me."

"Sure," she said.

"It's a bit of a test," he said. "I want to know who I'm dealing with, and in exchange, I will show you."

"Ok," she said, thinking this sounded . . . very Magey. Who was she kidding? Whatever this was, she was here for it. "What do we do?"

Now, his smile was huge. Playful. Not sexual, but with the energy of engaging a new partner. And, she supposed it was. Arousal and intimacy. Of magic. Vulnerability. Risk. Change. He held his wand steady, yet Xelle had nothing to hold. Finding that actually cool, she stood, shrugged, and put her hands in her pockets.

San laughed, a big joyful laugh. "Your return pod. Don't use it up, but use it to connect to your inkbloom." He stopped suddenly. "No inkbloom in this Tower, right?"

While unable to hide her cringe at the open mention, she answered only "None," truthfully. Just what was in her belly, and he'd indicated he knew that. "How do you know how they work?"

"I don't," he said. "You're the Arc Mage. I just didn't want to strand you here. Now, ready? Talk to your inkbloom and meet me in the pathways. Let's go."

She had no idea how to do anything he was suggesting. And he was not moving his wand, not swishing it or pointing it, just holding it. Yet, she felt a power within it. A power channeling through it. As if suddenly realizing a waterfall raged behind a wall of stone, but she could only hear its echoes.

Xelle closed eir eyes. E should probably get used to not closing them, but it always felt better on a first connection. Eir stomach lurched as she reawakened the pod inside her. *I don't want to go back, yet. I want to join my friend in the pathways, just for a while. Can you help me find him?*

Eir sigil pinged. Thunder could feel what e was doing, but now was not the time for a conversation about it, or learning how to better control that connection. The feeling of the sigil wavered a bit, then receded, and Xelle knew not by eir own doing. E concentrated on eir garden. How many times had e done this now? They knew em; e knew them. "Can we show a Grand Mage how it's done?" she thought with an echoey giggle. A shared giggle? The thought elated her. This was not a struggle. This was the vines climbing the tree and the tree nurtured by the vines. This was eir magic. Eir place. Emself.

E swept through like exiting a changing room in the most extravagant finery, and feeling the pathways all around em, e saw San. He had dressed in his own finery! Or perhaps that was eir doing. Eir own suit, e realized, was arcblack, a sleek suit with a lace cape? Lace gloves. The more it made em happy, the more e embellished. And as San came into view, e saw his gown, glowing and shining in the richest form of grandgold, a long v accentuating his shape, and bare arms wrapped with satiny ribbons of black, as though in jest.

To eir suit, e added gold. A stripe down the length of each pantleg. E reached for his arm, and they began to dance. As they danced, Xelle felt a new sensation. Life. All around them. Insects in the air, the reach of the forest, and the roots, and it was more overwhelming than all of space and time itself. But what would they do here, in such a place? He'd said it was a test. A measure. So e couldn't just dance here, and admire a well-tailored suit. Could e travel the life around them somehow? Connect the pathways?

San continued to dance. Clearly he could do more, but he seemed comfortable here, watching Xelle adapt and puzzle. And e felt a wave of safety. San would not let anything happen to em. E was safe here, if e was careful. Considerate.

Surely he didn't want em to try and move them, somewhere. Then, what of time? What of the forest? What had the forest seen? E flowed into it. It was too easy. This was the power of Spire Mage Sandaba. Xelle was small. Xelle was nothing, compared to power like this. No, not power. Experience. Understanding. Flow through restraint. A musician, metering the soft vibrato of a horn into waves of dynamic climax, not blasting it to a breathless end.

Eir awareness flowed into the forest. Not far, e was already feeling tired, like holding a thousand weights for a thousand years. No, don't think about that. This tree. This first tree. E climbed it, a forestper from Tam in the joy of a tall tree. And looked out, and saw—no Tower. She saw a time before the Tower existed. The tree saw it. This tree was here, then. There was a clearing. A gathering of small buildings. And among them, what was that shape? Dragons! E saw dragons, but not living here, visiting with what were these, fledgling Grand Mages. Pre-Unification. E could climb higher. These were not heights; this was life, e could—

It was not a jerk, but a swing. A dance partner swinging em over a patch of mud at a night festival and gliding them back to the platform.

Xelle was in San's office. He was holding eir arm. E was dizzy. He guided em into a seat, brought a cup of water. Then swept from the room.

Moments later, Dram entered.

"Whoa, you ok? San said you were doing a bit of magespar in here, but I'm not used to him leaving in quite such a wind." He glanced at the door, then put a hand on the back of her neck running it back and forth softly.

The motion calmed her.

"I'm ok. But I think the meeting is probably over for the day. I'll see you later. I think I need to go to my room. Rest. And think."

For a moment he looked like he might offer a soft kiss. But this was a Spire Mage's office. He did offer her an arm, and make sure she got back in the lift.

"You're ok?" His smile was warm.

"I'm fine. We'll talk soon." She gave him a wink.

07 - *What She Wands*

Xelle had a scheduled shift in her current lab, and she wasn't going to bail on the Studies. Hopefully, An'oar wouldn't be there, and she could work for a nice day, then get that appointment with Mage Tatock, wish her friends here well, and move on with her life.

Of course An'oar was there. She gave him a pleasant smile and sat at her desk. Normally, if he were here, she'd head immediately to the forest, rescuing a Study or two with her. But if this were, hopefully, her last shift, she'd rather be responsible and catch up on her reports and filings so that the break would be clean and leave no reasonably ruffled sleeves, or more importantly, no messes for An'oar's least favorite Study to clean up.

Speaking of the properly cordial Mage, he worked for a while, ignoring her, then standing and looking about for a bit, wandered her way. "Glad to see you're catching up on your papers," he said. "Let me know if I can help in any way."

"Thanks; I appreciate that." Xelle offered a small smile, then shifted her chair to return to the papers.

"It must be difficult not having a chain." He pointed to his own, as if it were not important, yet ensured the few charms on one end jangled before letting go. "When I worked in Diplomatic Management, I was awarded three separate times."

Xelle rarely passed up an opportunity to use 'thrice' but An'oar didn't deserve that, so instead she looked up and managed an, "Oh, wow. That's great." She wondered who got him into the diplo lab. It was one of the most coveted assignments in any Tower, because you got to be a hero to harried, stressed, high-ranking Mages just for doing your job, while reaping the benefits of all those connections, and yet without the actual stresses involved in the rather complicated intricacies of diplomacy and negotiation. She couldn't imagine An'oar in a negotiation. Maybe his skill would be just making everyone else want to leave.

She didn't enjoy any of these thoughts, especially as they felt so unnecessary. The Mage probably felt completely justified in campaigning against her assignment here. Felt bad for her, even. Maybe? She looked up at him, still standing there, as if mentoring her work. He did mean the offer to help. Thing was, that was his issue. Not quite as unpleasant as someone like Fepa, which meant there wasn't any spirit even in the rallying. It was all just sort of . . . sad.

But, she also reminded herself, not just sad for him. Sad for the pers who didn't get the opportunities he'd had. Sad for the pers who maybe didn't have Xelle's . . . um, self-assuredness? And had to sit here and feel lesser because he jangled his chains like little signs of his virility.

She snorted, then held up a paper, pretending there was something amusing on it. Issue was, it was a paper she was filling out, so then she acted as though she'd made an error, quickly erasing some lettering that actually had come out fairly nicely. Ugh. What was it about pers with narrow spirit that made everyone squeeze through their little hoops?

She'd have to parse that another day. "Oh, An'oar?" She said it as he was finally walking away, but if he was here, might as well ask now. She'd hoped to finish the papers first, but he was here, and come to think of it, the idea of her waiting around if he happened to wander off was not pleasant either.

"Mmm?" He turned back.

"I was thinking about talking to Mage Tatock about a new assignment."

No real reaction, though she could almost hear his gears turning. "If you please. There are always Studies looking for a spot here."

Wonderful. "Yes, I figured that as well. And I need a ranking Mage to sign off on the appointment. I was wondering if I could use your name." Not really *ranking,* but Xelle didn't know Mage Tatock at all, and she would rather have a lab lead signatory than risk it on her own. Not with this Mage. From her own experience, she knew that a Head Laboratorian tended to have a specific personality type. Which made sense; it was a tremendously powerful (to the pers it affected) but also tremendously difficult and thankless role.

He almost cracked a smile. "Oh, well, we'd miss having you here, but if it would help."

"Thank you," she said. "It would help."

An'oar crinkled his nose and gave her a friendly (for him?) nod. This didn't make her feel better; it made her kind of sad. She'd had some really good experiences here. He was taking something from her, even if she was making better plans from it. She felt sad. And uncomfortable. And, suddenly imagining the hand she wished she could squeeze for the tiniest most assuring moment of comfort, and knowing it was not Dram's, felt . . . empty.

Xelle took a breath, and tried to focus on the papers.

Whatever clearance Xelle had been given on wandering toward the Platform did not apply to approaching the Head Laboratorian. After politely explaining to a third steward (explaining thrice!) that she had an appointment, and that it had been submitted by a laboratory lead, she finally found herself being walked through a rounded corridor to a set of double-doors. (She'd done all the submitting under An'oar's name, and while that distinction might carry significance elsewhere, in labworld, she knew it did not.)

Mage Tatock was every bit the part, which actually meant Xelle took to her immediately. Look, she had a definite fondness for a hu being what was on the tin. Tall, a fitted, plain robe, a prim cap, and steely eyes that looked over, and not through, spectacles on a loopless chain.

"What should I call you?" the Mage asked, gesturing Xelle toward a chair, without rising.

"I prefer Xelle. But if you mean in terms of formality, then Mage Xeleanor Du'Tam."

Her lips tightened the smallest bit. "It is my fortune in this ever-changing world to not be an adjudicator of your titles. Just my labs."

Xelle nodded. "I would like to request an unusual transfer of assignment." Well, that sounded weird. "Unusual coming from me, I should clarify."

Tatock leaned back in her chair, as if waiting even to react.

"I would like an assignment to the wand lab."

No reaction.

"I have no experience and no skills in wands, wand-making, or research. I've only . . . never had a wand." She'd almost slipped and said she'd only touched a wand once, but as Grand Mages never allowed others to touch their wands, she didn't know how that would reflect on Rayn.

The thought of Rayn jarred her. She wondered how she was doing, at To'Ever. She needed to continue. "I think I would have a lot to offer in the lab. I have different perspectives, I'm good at thinking about problems and seeing patterns, and I could do more tasks on my own, without required supervision."

"How would I possibly think that was a good idea?" Tatock was looking toward the door. "How do you think you can walk in here and do whatever you want?"

"Please, I'm sorry, I don't think I made my case right," Xelle hurried to say. "I . . . don't do whatever I want. I'm here, and that's why I'm asking you. I think it would help me understand To'Grand. I'm not a Grand Mage. I'm not going to be one. I'm not going to pledge here. But I'm also here for the foreseeable future, so I'm asking your help to allow me to be part of something. To help me understand. I'll follow whatever guidelines there are, and I'll offer my insights."

Her fingers tapped the desk. "The Wand Laboratory is nearly the most sacred environment in this Tower. How can I trust someone who is neither under the constraints of an exchange, nor has not moved through our structure, been observed by our Mages, been understood? Generated any level of trust beyond whatever dazzle you offered the Spire on arrival."

Nearly? Dazzle. No time for that, now. She was asking why Xelle could be trusted. Xelle could be trusted, couldn't she? "I hope to be worthy of trust. It's . . . what matters most to me. Well, friends. Then trust. That's—who I am. It's my core. I'm . . ." She wanted to say more. She wanted to explain how her mind spun and things that felt clear in her thoughts were difficult to say to others. She suddenly felt tired. Why was she here? Why couldn't she be in her lab with Ay'tea, making jokes and telling stories, and passing little notes to smile. Why didn't she appreciate what she'd had? Why did she have to let things get so complicated? Why had she let so much fall apart?

Mage Tatock rapped her desk. "Why does An'oar want you removed?"

Her mouth hung open as a stream of pleasantries flashed past her thoughts. How to speak to ranking Mages. How to stay away from conflict. This was one Mage in her path, what if they were friends? What if they held the same connections, used the same connections?

Trust.

But trust for whom? Grand Tower? Or Mage Tatock.

No. For herself. Wherever that led.

"Whatever An'oar's motives, I believe the issue is his own, not related to my performance or presence."

"Is that why you want a change of assignment? To evade this risk? Or . . . this situation?"

"No," she answered. "It solves that problem as well. Especially if the transfer is immediate, which I'd really prefer. Again, if this is possible. Which I hope that it can be."

Mage Tatock leaned forward. "Did you speak to anyone else about this idea?"

Ah. Xelle lifted her chin. "If I did, it was privately."

"Why do you want this?"

"I believe it will help me understand the essence of Grand Magic and culture without entering into its formal study. My outside perspective may add some benefit to Grand Tower, which will help me give back for your hospitality and trust. Also, secretly, I kind of want a pocket wand."

She cringed. Did she really just say that out loud? It was not a . . . retractable or repairable comment, so she just stood there.

Mage Tatock looked like she was holding in a fart.

Xelle waited.

"Mage Xeleanor, for that, I will grant the assignment with a note to Mage Ollia that said assignment should be treated as an ongoing trial. And I look forward to hearing all about you using that phrase around Grand Mages and watching their expressions. And perhaps at some point, someone will tell you what it means."

Holy Fira. There was nothing to say to that. "Ah," she tried. "I will . . . watch my language. And look forward to the opportunity to learn. In many ways. And thank you. For this opportunity. I won't let you down."

Mage Tatock looked like she had a retort. She pressed her lips together, and gestured Xelle to leave.

The wand lab was so much more than Xelle had imagined. She hadn't really known, like, the idea of everything from some pristine holy space to a storytale workshop to the roughest, most demanding Mages on Alyssia had crossed her mind.

The place was a joy. Sure, everyone worked really hard and more hours than she'd ever seen put into a lab, but there was an atmosphere of celebration in the work. Mage Ollia knew everything backward and forward about wand-making and kept everyone on task, and then would surprise Xelle by taking everyone out to a lunch, or for a hike and picnic. Labs as a rule watched that sort of thing. Being an environment for everyone, it was important to ensure the comfort of all participants, including in light of power dynamics. But wand-making turned out to be a very group activity; even the most personally-designed wand benefitted from a community of Mages, infusing their own elements into it like backup vocals for the most thrilling solo. And so everyone worked together, they found ways to mesh. They had to, or it simply wouldn't be the same place.

Was this what it was like just being around Mages who could enjoy the work together? She and Ay'tea had been like this. But had they? Always the tension of the unspoken. Here, she just felt . . . content. And excited—excited to see what new technique there was to learn, what new help was needed.

Ollia had been in place for at least twenty years, Xelle learned. There were about eight other Mages, none of whom had been shifted to allow Xelle's entry, making ten Mages total. And there were Studies! But they were not treated like Studies in the same way. It was a comfortable, familiar mentorship here. The four Studies were all senior, and to Xelle's surprise, two were here on exchange. One from Charm, and one from Breath. The elements of wand-making were not only celebrated, they were shared.

She did of course ask about Rayn. Rayn had made a wand, she hadn't even really placed this was probably where she'd done it. Two of the Studies, from Breath and Grand, had worked here during Rayn's exchange, and they and the Mages spoke fondly of her, happy to hear about her pledging at To'Ever, and generally seeming pleased and surprised Xelle had been at her pledging ceremony. The two other Studies, including the Charm Study, had rotated in at the same time Rayn had left.

"Rayn Du'Sharre?" Jalahaja had asked. "As in, the heir of the Spice Lord?"

Xelle had almost dropped what she was certain was an expensive vial of finely ground pin'nut powder. "The Spice Lord."

Jalahaja waved a dismissive arm. "You'd have to be there to understand. In Sharre. My uncle was from there, we'd visit sometimes. Of course you know of the salt mines, but given the unique climate and drastic variations in growing conditions, they were also the main suppliers of spices to Alyssia, until other places figured out how to do it. But, still, you want the best? The rarest? The most complex? You go to Sharre. And the Spice Lord, it sounds silly, but they mean it as an honor. It's the oldest family of growers. No matter who tries to best them, decade after decade, it's never done. I had heard that the kid chosen to take over the business had left, but you're saying she's a Mage? An Ever Mage?"

Xelle had more to unpack than was going to be done while clinging to the tiny expensive vial, but the first thing that bubbled into her mind was (ok, other than 'Spice Lord') that the entire, what, *Region* knew about Rayn leaving, but not about her absolute excellence at Ever Tower? Xelle felt weirdly annoyed.

Not wanting to express any of this right now, she walked the vial over and set it back into the small gridded drawer, not trusting herself to measure or tap anything out right now.

"So you two are friends? Well, of course you are, if you were at her pledging ceremony! Who'd you go with, a Metal Baron of Wehj?" He giggled, amusedly.

"Actually, I went with Study Kwillen Du'Satta," she murmured, now rubbing her temples.

Now everyone was looking at her. Including Mage Ollia. This was getting way too intense, and she wanted to take a step back before asking (or saying!) more.

Xelle looked around the room and grinned broadly. "Well, the dragon wouldn't fit in the seat!"

Oh, these were good pers. Because, taking that exactly the way she'd meant it, they dropped the subject entirely. And no one asked Xelle for the powders she'd been asked to mix, instead Flav beckoned her over, asking if she'd help wash some shelves he'd just cleaned out.

Right now, washing shelves was something she could do.

There was a lot of connection between Grand and Ever. Thinking about it, there was a lot of connection between Arc and Ever. What had San called Ever? The watcher? Certainly the concept of being or unbeing would apply to any magic, anything, really. Did the Mages understand the level of connection between prongs? And did that strengthen her case against pledging or weaken it?

The more Xelle understood, the less she did. Not a really comforting thought in an already uncertain mind.

Wands were really . . . enchanted objects? Mages would insist not. An enchantment was for an unliving object cast upon to perform some task. A wand, first, did not feel unliving at all. In fact, the wood used to make them was taken fresh from a tree, not from a fallen branch. With life still in it, life somehow used in the cast itself. Then, the object was not set to perform a task, but to channel its caster. To make a Mage more capable than the Mage would have been before. But not alone. Through a ceremony that felt like all the prongs at once. The permanence of Ever. A ritual glazing that reminded her of a Frond rune. The elegance and ceremony of Charm. The subtle infusions of Breath. Even the concept of Dust, the little she understood of it, as the living branch carried some element of life through the cast, but the wood itself did not live, did not grow.

Only Arc she did not see in the making. This unsettled her. But she did not tell the others. Did not ask. At least not a question for her first few shifts! But maybe, even, that was an excuse. Ugh. Xelle was tired of thinking of things that way, of qualifying her own instincts. This wasn't a question for this lab or this team, and with all the things to track in her own mind these days, some dividers were needed.

Unmet goals did not store well in her mind, but she tried to tuck this one away. To understand what Arc and Grand meant to each other. Or if they were just seven Towers, each imperfect, and not everything offered its reason.

"I know Kwillen, from the Tower," the Breath Study said, as they were both practicing a technique called 'stranding'. "E's always seemed so unfriendly." Xelle wasn't sure how to respond to this. Kwill was in many ways, her closest friend. She felt a moment of guilt, thinking of Helia, but that was the thing with friends. It was a single concept describing a multitude of relationships. Helia would lift her from the depths of the sea; she knew that. And she hoped she would for her too. But Kwill and Xelle—they understood each other. In speech or in silence.

And so she found herself, again as often in this lab, unsure of what to say. Kwill was not unfriendly; e was tired of being cared about only for eir family, or eir connections, of some perception of skill, or even comportment, that would never match what eir strengths truly were. Nor did it seem right to send the senior Study back with a charge to go find and reassess her friend, who had perhaps grown a little prickle as a ward.

Kwill had been raised with a daily bath of niceties; she tried to think what e would say. Ha, on this, probably 'I am unfriendly; thanks!' Well that was no help.

"E's lovely," she managed to say. "And I'm grateful for em, just as I imagine you are for your friends there. Do you miss them?" she tried, hoping to change the subject.

"Sure, but I'll be back soon." The Breath Study adjusted the metal magnification device they were using to create threads of bark so fine, they could be woven into a nearly invisible fabric, one that would both protect the casts of and yet absorb into the wand during its birth. (She did find it interesting that rather than cast or enchantment, Mages here referred to wands by their 'birth'. Especially since to create the item, they'd removed it from its source of life.) "I'm, uh, I asked for this exchange because I thought they wouldn't take me. My pledge, I mean. I thought if I did something bold, got good notes, it might help my chances."

Oh. Xelle felt . . . kind of jerky. She hadn't said anything hurtful, but just her existence felt rude. Here she was, navigating the boldness of doing her best while refusing to pledge, standing next to someone who was worried no matter what she did, it might not make a difference.

Xelle had learned in her lab, when pers needed help, to lend an ear, but also to extend commonalities. And one came immediately to mind.

"Uncertainty is a weight that many pers don't understand," she offered. "Excitement or anticipation, many call it the thrill of life."

The Study either didn't dare take her eyes from the device or was glad for the reason not to. "It feels cruel. If pers like contests, they can enter them. But when they want something nice in their life, just . . . tell them if they can have it or not."

There was much, much, more in that than Xelle had the capacity to parse. And so, the two concentrated on their task.

08 - *Oh, Oh, Xelephone Line*

"Hi, excuse me?" the steward said, nervously peeking into the lab. "Someone here to see Mage Xeleanor. Someone important," he said in an ominously loud, sort of . . . whisper. Now, what was this about? Her first thought was simply annoyance. She'd been trying really hard to just be Xelle this first week. Get to know the team. Learn how to do things, at this point, fully amagically, that she'd never before even heard of. Besides, the last time she'd had an important guest, oh, fine it had really been the first time, it had been Kwill, being doted over by unabashed Front Desk clerks. Which they could just tell her without all the drama.

Though, she didn't think Kwill would just show up here. Helia and Rayn were Mages but not of any rank to spark this sort of nerves in someone used to dealing with dignitaries? Kern, then? No, Kern wouldn't show up. Honestly, she didn't think they'd be talking for a very long time.

Oh, ash. Not the Lunests. No, they wouldn't make her meet with them?

"Are you coming?" The steward was staring at her like they were both watching a balloon float away.

"Oh, yes, sorry." They hurried into the hallway. "Who is it?"

"Spire Mage Nar Du'Arc. She's here to see *you*."

Ignoring the rather rude inflection in that, Xelle instead considered her own surprise. Nar? She'd literally never met her. Not before the Ascension; not after. She'd been a surprise pick to replace Jehanne (or really, Pelir), much younger than would be expected, and rather . . . modern in her approach. Again, Arc Spire was more receptive to change than any other Spire, but not so much to suddenly pluck the local radical onto its top board. Well, radical for a Mage.

Except, apparently, they had.

And why on every crossroad, stream, and treebridge of Alyssia would she be here to see *Xelle?*

At least she was dressed for the lab. Now that she wasn't tromping through the forest, Xelle had been wearing some of the finer clothes she'd had made in Mytil during her shifts. They weren't gala wear or something, but they were tailored, with nice fabric, and artful touches of black lace that made Xelle just feel better in her own skin. It was hard to feel confused and lonely, even when making new friends, and feeling cute sometimes, even if in her own mind, just . . . didn't hurt.

Spire Mage Nar was alone, no entourage, no stewards. Xelle felt pretty sure she'd just inkbloomed on in. Well, certainly not into the Tower uninvited but perhaps just outside the grounds. She wore a layered skirt over black pants, and a flowing blouse. It all suited her, and was of nice make, but also with the fabrics and fit that could have been made by a community co-op tailor. Xelle had the sudden certainty that it was. Not to say it wasn't as fine, but that it was comfortable, not trying so hard, while still with enough frills to pass as a Mage reminding you she was a Mage. Her cap matched none of it. A white beanie of sorts with stripes of lavender, gray, and a pop of a light green.

Xelle was intrigued. She bowed deeply. "Spire Mage Nar Du'Arc, it's my honor." She almost said 'to meet you' but maybe the Grand Front Desk pers didn't need to know that.

"With me," Nar said, motioning her along into the Atrium as if she were fully welcome wherever she wanted to be. "I've reserved a room," she added, as Xelle realized she was following her.

Oddly, it was not a diplomatic meeting space, or even a nice space at all. It was an old-style lab office apparently under renovation in a back section of the Tower. Xelle kept having to remind herself this was a Spire Mage, and Xelle did not need to have her first impression be a lot of incredulous faces and questions. And so, she followed, waited until Nar had closed the door, and watched as the Mage quickly closed the room in a wrap of Arc.

Oh, this felt like sex. It had been so long. Well, no, there had been sex yesterday, but— Not like this. She pushed away thoughts of Dram and instead focused on the feel of expertly pulled Arc Magic around her, breathing it in like the steam from a scented bath.

"I was going to let your ogling of me in the lobby pass, but as I see you are now overtaken with lust for our craft, let's be clear. I'm not going to get involved with you." She leaned in. "Physically."

That was a weird thing to say. And Xelle wanted to rebuke it, consider this some form of harassment, until she realized the Mage was extremely hot, really good at Arc Magic, and Xelle was right now imagining that which the Mage was telling her was not going to happen.

"Alrighty," Xelle said. What the ash was she supposed to say?

"How do you like it here?"

An interesting question that Xelle could give an interesting answer. "Way more than I thought I would. I was told repeatedly pers weren't welcoming here, or that there was some sort of arrogance, or I'd surely be rebuked. But I've been treated so well. You know, it's never perfect. I'm working, I'm learning, I'm making friends."

"Yet it's not home."

A bit personal? "It's home. In a way."

Nar's eyes flicked over like the answer had been childish. This was actually getting annoying. Now that she was seeing her, the Mage actually couldn't be too much older than Xelle? Late 30s, maybe?

"I'm 41. I can't read minds. But you're like a walking broadcast. Might want to learn to wrap some of that."

"Hi, why are you here?" Xelle squinted.

"We'le thought you'd want to learn call casts. She seems to think you're ok. I offered to help."

Oh. "Yeah, wow, actually that would be extremely helpful. Thank you. If you're still willing to. I mean, I'd really appreciate it."

Nar's lip twisted up on one side with sarcasm Xelle didn't ask for, but nothing that made her annoyed. "I was starting to wonder if you were up for it, then I saw how hot you got for Arc Magic, so let's make this fun. Do you consent to my teaching, however it goes?"

What the ash was happening. But, then, Avail had been open about his relationship with Jehanne, and then she was pretty sure there was some San / Beleg ship going on. Were Spire Mages all horny?

No. She could not think of Kern as horny. She would not. She cleared her throat. "I know your time is valuable, Spire Mage Nar. I'm really interested to learn, so yes, I agree to follow your instruction. What can I do?" It seemed a rather blanket arrangement, but she did trust We'le. And We'le had sent her. (A small voice told her she did not know this for certain, countered by an immediate thought that anyone who crossed We'le would live to regret it.)

Nar hopped up onto the table, the one piece of furniture left in the ragged room. "The cast itself is simple, the consequences are not."

"Meaning?" Almost about to sit on the floor, she decided otherwise in this one particular case, and so she hopped up on the table, taking a cross-legged seat there beside the Spire Mage and her dangling legs.

Nar kicked off her shoes.

Not to be outdone, Xelle kicked off her own.

"Oh, thank Jehanne," the Mage said. "You're someone I can work with. Now, consequences. Do not underestimate this piece. The Call relies on a certain relationship with phyta, which I'm assuming you have—and please don't tell me how—or Mage We'le would not have sent you my way."

Inkbloom. Of course. Xelle only nodded.

"Then you know the power that they hold over the pathways. What you apparently have done, though, is like diving into water. Pretty ash-burned foolish without training, but here we are. You probably thought what you were doing was advanced, but mentally, the phyta was gravity to your mass. They pulled you in. Once you established their trust, their love, you were diving into a sea without breath, with a devoted friend always at your side to watch for obstacles."

Xelle . . . did not expect that to be the explanation. But, yeah, she could see it.

"Sight, hearing, well, not to that today. What we call the call, is like skimming a rock across the pond and having it land in a specific location. Very different. You're from mid-Ever?"

She nodded. Yep, she got it. Forest analogies worked. Suddenly, though, she wondered where Nar was from. Her affect. Her name. Wehj, she realized. Well, probably not Wehj proper, in either the literal or metropolitan sense. She's from here, from Grand Region. "You're from Grand Region?" Xelle risked asking.

"Vi'Grand. Not Cu'Grand," she clarified.

Ah. Growing up around the Tower but not in the Tower. Interesting. And quite the distinction for someone who had rather trounced in here and somehow known some old room she could use. Of course, Xelle reminded herself a bit forcefully, she was also a Spire Mage. She didn't need connections or familiarity to be accommodated. Even here.

"So we're going to start in here. And no, the distance doesn't matter."

This actually raised a question in Xelle's mind about Frond Runes, where she was pretty sure distance was important, but this didn't seem the right time or place to ask it. Actually, just the idea of asking an Arc Mage about Frond Magic was silly. But then, if distance didn't matter, why start in here? She wasn't going to ask that. There had to be some obvious answer.

"Hold my hand," Nar said, reaching outward.

Xelle did.

Nar took her other hand, and caressed it overtop. Xelle bemoaned for a minute why We'le, who was lovely but quite old, had to send the hot young Mage for whatever this was. After a quick glare from Nar, she hurriedly took a breath, and watched her for whatever might happen next.

"There are few forms of familiarity," she said, pointing sternly during the pause, "that we'll be doing here—that are greater than the meeting of hands. It is personal. It is mutual. It is intentional. It is vulnerable." Nar tossed a small object between them, but Xelle's hand firmly in her grasp, her other hand was not quick enough to maneuver around and catch it. By instinct, she swept it instead with an Arc cast, guiding it back to the table, next to the Mage. The other Mage.

"Yes," she said as if expecting the action. "But now you've exposed yourself. Your prong. Your cast. Your skill. Over my candy wrapper." She continued now to caress Xelle's hand, now with both of her own. "This little bump. The pattern of your veins. The ridges atop your nails."

Xelle suddenly realized she was giving this total stranger a lot of personal information. A way perhaps to find her always. Part of the lesson, she realized. And so, she reached her free hand just over Nar's, who smiled and then nodded. And so, they caressed each other's hands. Nar had an old cut on her thumb, sealed over and not magically repaired. Then, below it, what was that? Some sort of implant? Like metal left inside the skin? Or maybe an accident? She wasn't going to ask. She didn't want to know.

She was feeling completely and totally overwhelmed by the intimacy of this experience. And of realizing that not only did this Mage now have a permanent link to Xelle, but she was learning one back. Then, she'd better learn it.

E closed eir eyes. E figured Nar would tell em when enough had been done, and so e simply explored her hand. The roughness. The smoothness. Not just skin and structure, but poise. How it was held, how it responded. Down a little, onto her wrist, the bumps and hairs, now standing on end at Xelle's touch.

It was Xelle who released first. Not sure what to say after that, she raised her eyebrows and made what was supposed to be a friendly face but must have come off strange.

Nar ignored it. "I am hungry and going to go find some food. You, talk to your phyta while I'm gone. See if they're willing to take this step with you. Want anything?" she added.

"Um, some water would be nice," Xelle managed to say. She'd eaten before her shift, and was fine for now.

"Citrused or plain? Never mind." Nar left.

And Xelle realized something else. The break wasn't just to convene with her inkbloom (who weren't anywhere near here but she did have a pod?). It was for herself. To reset. To consider what she'd done, the very lack of Magic in it.

She calmed. And she knew why. San's warning about trust. She'd let this Mage in, let her take her into a wrapped room, let her take something of immeasurable value. But she'd traded, for her own. She'd left, for Xelle to think.

A thought occurred to her in that moment.

Trust was love. Trust was risk.

But trust was not random.

Xelle needed to think about the same clues that had led her to understanding Nar was from Grand Region. What had led the Old Vattam bartender Mara to know the make of her cloaks. And what led her to understand, as best she could anyway, the intent of a heart.

She wanted to trust Nar. Was that the same as trusting her? She thought of Thunder, of their last parting, and grew sad. Trust was not perfect. Love was not perfect. Xelle was not perfect. But to follow the joy, not hide in its absence, this was life. Avoiding it was *more* of a risk, she realized.

Running her fingers up into the sides of her cap, she thought to herself, when had holding a hand caused this level of thought?

Then, she thought, when was the last time she'd held a hand?

The sadness overwhelming her and no longer wanting to follow where these thoughts led, she took the other path Nar had offered her.

And found the inkbloom.

Hey! I'm here with Spire Mage Nar. She's going to try and teach me the calling cast, but she said, it's up to you to decide whether to help me do it or not.

Xelle suddenly had a question.

How do I know you want to help me? I seeded you. I planted you. I helped you grow. I feel like everything you've done has been your choice, but how do I know you want to help? That you'd rather not just be left there, or somewhere, to simply exist?

Xelle toppled off of the table. As in, literally fell. A quick travel cast was all that kept her from bruising, or breaking something, and she swung herself back to the table, her arms now shaking.

E closed her eyes. Sat still. And listened.

One cannot put the sentiments of phyta into words. But as words are what is here upon this page, and Xelle wants you to know what it is that she felt in this first moment of genuine communication, we will try, here, together.

Solitary existence is only an end. Anima must create copies of themselves, then protect those variants, if the anima would survive. Phyta grow. They seed. Beings larger and smaller than anima and phyta can comprehend, variations on our world and others, exist on connection.

Without connection, there is void.

In void, all falls away.

Solitude is different. It is of essence. In solitude, the hu must learn to value itself. In solitude, a hu can value the world around it. In solitude, a hu can live in connection. But a solitary hu is a machine, an instrument of physics. A ticking of temporary instructions, invisible to space and time, because, without impact to space and time, they never existed.

Only in connection can we reach.

Only in connection can we grow.

Only in connection can we truly be ourselves.

The inkbloom showed Xelle their joy. A garden was only a means, a seeding a gift. They did not live in a cramped, dark space, under an old ramp for hu transport. Their roots, there, fed from the soil, and the moisture that crept in from the outside. Their leaves and vines were let to grow, multiply, and fade, in the glow of the softness from their own petals and the lights from their own blooms.

They lived in a world. They felt the world around them. Through them. Spinning. Staying. Lasting. Fleeting. The essence of life was a myriad of pathways, an endless exploration. A place to slide, to climb, to leave or gather weights, an endless space to leave behind what could, and seek remedy for that which could not.

Nar walked in, holding two cones of fries.

"Want one?" she asked, holding out the same hand Xelle had caressed.

A trick? No, these were fries.

And they were really good.

"What did you season these with? Why do they taste so good?" Xelle managed, a couple tree-milling their way through her mouth.

"Arc kitchen seasoning. Carry it in my purse." Nar winked. "Grand uses a good herb blend, I'll give them that. But it's got nothing on the black pepper heavy mix of the Arc kitchens, with the good garlic."

The inkbloom, through her connection, laughed! They laughed. As if to say, this is what we meant—we cannot keep you from pain, but through connection, there is endless joy.

Nar was staring into her eyes. Seeming satisfied, she nodded. "Now, we begin."

Xelle recounted everything the Mage had taught her. And again, found her inkbloom. She thought about Kwillen Du'Satta. Eir room, a space for a Mage, given to a Study, because of who eir family was. Eir couch, upon which she had a few times fallen asleep. She thought about the closed door to eir bed and armoire, the beautifully polished furniture, and the long striped couch with its mismatched pillows. E thought what it felt like, to lean forward and hug eir friend. The hug not of romance, not of heft, but of familiarity. Of comfort. How e had never held eir hand, but now longed to. To know. To feel.

E could see Kwill's room.

Sort of. It was blurry. Moving. The edges rippled in and out, and sometimes showed the guest space where Xelle had stayed there at To'Breath, which thank Fira, no one appeared to be in at the moment, despite an unmade bed covered in books.

The danger now was clear. What if whatever visitor this was walked in to see her unauthorized pathway? What if her hold slipped and her face appeared in the corridor? She did not need To'Arc receiving angry communications from the Breath Spire. Or if she appeared on the stairs, and startled someone, and they fell?

With a shiver, she held closer to her inkbloom, asking them for help, apologizing for not being stronger, more guided on her own. Resolving to understand, to learn.

And Kwill, would e know how to answer? To grant permission to the call? Was e even there? To do this, wouldn't they have to establish some kind of schedule, or sign? There were enchanted pairs, for signaling, but they were very expensive, and very regulated.

A wave of relief almost knocked her back as Kwill accepted the reach. There, in eir room, which she knew e would have just wrapped. In fact, the connection along with the wrapping both and then together seemed to help her hold steady, and the space came into clearer view. Xelle felt like she was holding a tent line against a ravenous storm. The connection wasn't moving anymore, but fira, she would have to hold on tight. While talking.

She sure hoped this got easier.

"Kwill," she managed to say. "Can you hear me? See me?"

Kwillen, with a twist of eir mouth, applauded. "I almost asked if you're holding a rope, but it's not real, I can see that. You're in a room. Style of To'Grand. Ok, I see your plushie forest tree. So it's your room. You're still at Grand. And, is this your first call? Are you really making a first call into a Tower? Xelle, that's even Xelle for Xelle."

"Not my first call," she managed, trying to lean into the rope, which apparently was taking so much of her focus it was actually visualizing for Kwill.

You know, ropes were hard to hold. She changed it. Or tried to. The best she could manage was a long measure of soft cloth, which at least she could wrap around both arms. Still, it pulled on her. Enough for now; she couldn't risk letting go.

"Not my first," she repeated. "The Mage who trained me did some practice runs, but they were all when I knew exactly where she was. And in a zone."

"Could you tell I was in my room?" Kwill asked, looking curious.

She wasn't sure, actually. "Let me think about that later and when I'm not keeping this . . . curtain from blowing away." For a moment, she considered anchoring it, like hardware to the wall, but she wasn't confident, and . . . No, this had to do for now.

"Yeah, first real call, you can have the honor," she managed to get out.

Kwill curtsied. "I am honored, Mage Xeleanor. So, probably need to keep this brief. I wish there was a Breath way to help this, I'm just . . . Anyway, not now. Are you well? What's going on?"

"I'm well. You?"

E shrugged. "Sorry, I shouldn't be ambiguous. I'm fine. So what's up?"

Grateful, Xelle knew e was not intending impatience but was probably recognizing the strain in her features. Or whatever silliness she was currently projecting across literal *Regions* of Alyssia. (Not a good thought for right now!) "All in confidence?" She trusted em, but needed that to be clear. Maybe they could come up with a code for that. Another day!

"Absolute," e said.

"Well, the dragons, at least this group of dragons, I have no idea if there are others and haven't asked," (The thought had crossed her mind Thunder might not know either.) "used to live in the Highponds. I don't know what happened yet, but some part of whatever agreement was reached with the Magesphere, or maybe even the populace, is what caused them to move to the foothills." (After seeing the high mountains, it was much more difficult to call the areas where hu occasionally wandered 'mountains'.) "So even now, back, and with whatever we learn about the Hurts, they're not where they want to live."

"Ga Kwilloura on a pool raft, Xelle." Kwill was hard to shock, but that seemed to have done it. "That layers it, doesn't it?"

"But I don't think the dragons just folded, in whatever this was. No Mage will talk to me about dragons except under extreme distress or caution, so there's got to be something in the pledge, about not talking about it. And obsidian and . . ." Trust was different than compartmentalization, and Xelle wasn't going to explain inkbloom to a non-Arc Mage, and certainly not on a wavery call. "And related Arc Magic, that has great import and risk to dragons. It's all massively guarded."

Kwill looked off at a corner of the room. Eir tell of truly deep thought, she remembered with fondness, feeling a sudden urge to let the inkbloom take her there and give her friend a hug. *No, Xelle!* She lurched, and the connection made a terrifying buzzing, and Kwill's eyes grew wide as e snapped back her way and then slowly drew back. No. She could not pull through. Even if it was easier or even safer, it would use her pod, and she'd have no good way to leave. The Grand Spire would not be happy. Or Breath!

Grunting loudly, she imagined the distance between their Towers, and the lengths of the cloth she was holding. She was *here*. Kwill was *there*. She steadied on her feet, sort of. Her stomach felt sharply unwell. But, oddly, the image of holding the cloths was no longer as strained. She could feel her hands and arms being pressed, still, under them. Again, no way was she letting go now.

"Are you wearing jasmine?"

She had been, sure. *Oh. Fira.* She grimaced.

"Yeah, you let some of your air through. Arc Fart."

Xelle burst into laughter. "Firana, do not make jokes!" She held the pathway firm.

"Ok, ok. Let's close this up. If you die in Mage Limbo because of that joke, I would—"

She glared, amusedly, but firmly, and Kwill stopped.

"Business. Fine. Business. So we need to learn more about the agreement. First, no, first things first. If you can't hold this, can I let you know when I'm here? When it's safe to try again?"

That was a great idea. "Yeah," she said, hearing breathiness in her voice. "Only from your room, until we decide otherwise. I've gotta get used to it. What do you have that you can hold or put on, something familiar to me?" What would that be? They hadn't ever really exchanged gifts. Why hadn't she given em some trinket? She should be giving pers trinkets. Kwill had turned away from Xelle and was reaching over something.

Standing back where she could see em, e held out . . . a floofy pillow with a large embroidered rose. One of the comfy ones. "That first time? When you ported here. You drooled on this while you crashed on my couch."

"I mean, you washed it?"

Kwill made a side-scrunchy face.

"Fine, you didn't wash it. Actually, it's not the effect of my, uh, drool on it. Well, maybe that helps. But yeah, that was a really big moment with my—" *Xelle, don't say inkbloom!* "Arc Magic. What had to be going through my mind and body and, um, drool, while I was crashed out on that thing. But it's cute. Are you ok if it's mostly put away?"

Eir face answered that question also. E tended not to be attached to eir possessions, many of which were gifts from various relatives. But, come on, the rose one was pretty. "Fine, keep it in a drawer; don't let guests touch it. And when you're holding it, I'll know you're here and want to talk."

"Right then?" E looked surprised.

"No, I don't think it will signal me or anything. Not with what I know now. I'll need to check. So, what's a good time of day for me to do that?" She answered her own question. "Before lunch. You always go to lunch at the same time, and you always drop your things off first."

Kwill nodded. "You look strained, let's hurry." Eir voice had intensified.

Kwill did not have either the interest or the skill, or maybe the first was more relevant, in magic as Xelle, but e'd spent more time around it than anyone she knew of eir age. (E was about seven years younger than Xelle, she remembered.) So if e was concerned, she would listen.

"The agreement. Mages won't tell you. That tracks. What about the dragons, do they have a way to tell you?"

Ash. "I just realized. My friend, with them? Zhey're younger than this 'treaty', I think. So zhey might not know . . . Oh, ashes, what if the dragons—ugh, that always feels so dismissive; I am going to have to ask them if there's a better thing to call them—can't talk about it either? What if Thunder has gleaned or overheard, and zhey're the only one allowed to talk about it." Xelle had tried to give Thunder some space these last few days, but maybe this would provide a good subject on which to reconnect. "I'll talk to zhem. In the meantime, I think I've got a base here. Some friends and a tenable situation. I need to stay because . . ."

She should tell em. "The Lunests came here in late spring." A quick look at Kwill told her that not only did e already know about their visit, but everyone knew it, and that there was more. She stopped.

"You haven't been out much?" E winced. "Whatever you said to them, whatever Grand said to them, they've not taken it well. Irla has barely been seen or heard from, while Mark is all over the place. No one made a speech, led a celebration of any significance all summer without him on stage to cheering crowds. They have a new logo for customers."

"Not the script L?"

"That's still their logo, but that's only for them. No, this one looks like a glass knife. Pers are sewing it onto clothes, stenciling it onto windows. And . . . Xelle's there more but you look like you're going to combust . . . Know a Mage Dram?" E grimaced.

Every element of Xelle's being that wasn't already strained by her awkward cast of magic across the land was now exploding like flavor balls in sparkling water. "I'll . . . get out more," she murmured. "And . . . how do we . . ."

Ash. Suck on ash. It had absolutely been eating at her that she hadn't been doing anything about them since their 'visit' but it had been made clear to her that she needed To'Grand. And specifically, To'Grand, because even if there were another Tower that would give her the amount of protection, respect, and access she'd been granted here, leaving Grand Tower now would cause a permanent rift.

Xelle'd had enough rifts. She'd been trying to acclimate, she thought . . . She tugged again at the cloth she held, trying not to think about its strain and discomfort.

Kwill sighed. "We need to start working on their power and influence, and the nuances of what they're trying to do and its implications. That's a longer discussion, and you look like you're about to faint. For now? Flame-toss, Xelle, you need to go. Listen. For now? Think about the potion's ingredients. What do they need? And what Nenn can we put in their way?"

Laughing at the unexpected joke, her arms slipped against the cloth. She staggered back, and felt something like a flash in her eyes. *Do I let go?* she asked the inkbloom. *Can you help?*

It was wildly unclear which had happened, but Xelle fell staggering back, smacking one arm against her dresser before landing unsoftly onto her bed, without even the coherency to cast against the fall.

She felt ok. Not her arm. Herself. Her material.

She hoped Kwill wasn't worried. They hadn't said goodbye.

For reasons she didn't understand but probably linked to this new and tense experience, Xelle started to cry.

09 – *Unpermitted Acts and Musings on Balance*

Xelle actually knew (or thought she knew) much of what the Lunests needed. It was a long and formidable list. But then again, some of these things she'd accessed on her own, and she wasn't the two richest pers on Alyssia.

Firana, she hoped they were the richest.

They wanted to open real estate into the mountains for 'dragon views' and travel to the moons. Yes, the moons. Xelle made a list of what any of that would take. A literal list—writing things helped sort her mind.

A sizable growth of inkbloom

Someone who knows how to use inkbloom

A sizable amount of obsidian (at least for the inkbloom, probably for other magic too)

At least one dragon assisting with magic

A way to persuade or compel the dragon(s) - - - RAGE

A way to persuade or compel the inkbloom (?!) - - - RAGE

Someone to assist with Grand Magic

This probably wasn't the full list. She only knew Grand Magic was involved from what Kwill had heard through the chatter networks: that the main plan was to somehow combine inkbloom travel with Grand Magic to send pers to go, what, hang out on the sacred moons of Alyssia.

Oh, that was another one for the list.

*Somehow convincing pers that sacred moontromps, and only
for the super wealthy, was remotely acceptable.*

Something else pricked her in that. What was it? She thought of
Kern. *Ohh.* Not just the wealthy, but the bribed. Pers in power, offered
a chance to walk on a moon. On their own moon. Xelle was reverent
of connections and the unknown, but she wasn't structurally religious
about the influence of the moons the way many were. For healing. For
luck. A blessing. There were pers who would do *anything* for that.

Not a reason to deny pers potentially nice things, but certainly a
reason not to want the ability to grant them solely in the hands of total
prods and without consideration of impact.

She groaned.

Well, where could she start . . . Culture felt important, but also
what would she do now? Go around telling pers what the Lunests
were planning? Weren't they already doing that themselves? And their
capturing dragons, oh, she really didn't want to get to any point where
that was normalized even in discussion.

She'd just had her monthly meeting with San, which was a generous
schedule for a Spire Mage, but she wasn't sure opening up about all of
this was in his best interest, and besides, the ability to cast together
with someone of such skill was precious when she had other friends
she could ask for advice if she needed to.

Xelle winced, not yet knowing what they were saying about Dram,
presumably in their subscription letter. She couldn't pretend this
hadn't been a continuing factor in her caution. She was nervous to
talk to her friends because any time she was around them, they were
further pulled in by the Lunests, punishing the pers who stood with
her. And see, that was it. It was so vicious, so unkind. In contrast,
Xelle was cautious to do too much, go too far, to lose support too
early. The gentle friend of the benefit of the doubt turned into an invisible monster by pers without hearts. Her caution suddenly felt cold,
dangerous. Nothing could be a good thing, a nice thing, that required

sneaking up on her friends, that required trying to capture Xelle, that required turning Mages. But then, what could she do?

Her finger rested over the word *inkbloom*. After realizing she probably shouldn't be writing it either, and quickly blurring the word with a travel cast and a little shh sound, she considered how difficult it had been for her to procure the seeds. But she had done it. Could she get in the way of that?

No. Inkbloom access wasn't really something she could work to restrict. The system already restricted it. But maybe she could warn the pers trading in them? She could . . . *What, Xelle? Go send word to the supplier or suppliers not to take the money of the pers with the most money?*

As silly as that sounded, it was sort of how Xelle thought. She'd justified her own rulebreaking because she meant no harm with it. But clearly. Clearly. Not everyone followed that code. A righteous speech wasn't going to stop pers from getting their hands on whatever they wanted. And she wasn't going to start threatening pers either.

It was clear. The Lunests were going to need an Arc Mage at some point. A skilled one. Even Xelle wasn't some randocaster. Her ability to use inkbloom had been part years of dedicated, passionate Arc training and self-study, part luck, and part the inkbloom deciding to help her. She couldn't block all inkbloom seed sales. Even if she could, she certainly couldn't block all Mages, including ones with access to their own phyta. Even if she focused on discerning how close the Lunests really were . . . What even then? The next week they could turn the right Mage.

Was she really back to: Just go tell everyone what was going on, and tell everyone they needed to stop them?

Xelle had always thought of herself as a good problem solver. When she worked with Ay'tea, they'd operated with such confidence: there wasn't a need that pers had that didn't at least have a partial remedy. But those were in cases where everyone wanted to make things better?

She threw her head into her hands.

Trying to solve a problem where some pers only wanted to make things better for themselves made the whole thing a lot tougher. And more frustrating. And more asinine. Pers should just be good!

She let out some longish sound that, once hearing it, sounded like Na Foose trying to lift a heavy box.

If there really were pers that wanted to make things better for everyone, and pers who wanted to make things better for just some pers, and pers who didn't really give it much thought, wouldn't there be more of the first group? And couldn't those pers just all get together and tell the selfish pers no?

Maybe they did just need to be told. Including the ones who hadn't thought it through? Pers were mostly kind. Xelle believed that. Xelle had to believe that. Would putting it out in the open make a difference?

Then, that was her decision. Xelle didn't yet have a solution, but she did have an idea. Tomorrow, if Mage Ollia would allow it, she was going to Vi'Grand.

"Balance," Mage Ollia had said. "I know who you are, Xeleanor. I didn't approve the assignment because I was looking for another hand." She moved over to another table, where she was arranging some kind of dividers into rows on a large, heavy tray. "You may sometimes feel like you're taking on the whole System, but if it has not yet been made clear to you, you are not. The minute you bounced out of bounds, the mage-sphere had a million ways to make sure you never bounced back."

Hey, good morning. That was ominous.

"And a million ways to help me. I understand that too." She hadn't actually given this enough thought, but now wasn't the right time to go through that. So she nodded sagely.

Ollia cut her eyes over slightly. "There is a thing in ecostudy called the X Factor."

Sure, Xelle had heard of that in her last labwork. Cures no one understood. Mutations. Appeal and disregard and all levels of crouch, stand, or jump.

"A lot of us sit here and think, what is it about her? Why Xeleanor Du'Tam—causing all this stir?"

Xelle herself had thought about this, though more in the vein of why she couldn't just behave and be normal and go back to her lab with her friend, and, ugh, anyway. "I'm just me," she offered, trying to push the other thoughts aside.

The ever-composed Ollia let a snorty giggle at this that was nearly explosive. "Hellina shelter you." Then the expression disappeared. "Yes. You are. So my advice? Stay with that. Be you. Yet, as critically, also be us. This lab is not an affectation. It is one of the most coveted places to be in the magesphere." Her eyes lit a tiny flame. Just a moment. "So, be here. Now, with that, are you a Mage?"

Xelle started to answer the question. Then, as if she could see Helia suddenly there, shaking her head, she stopped.

"Mage Ollia. If it doesn't trouble any timelines or intended instruction here, I have matters to attend to in Vi'Grand. I will be back in tomorrow."

Ollia nodded, barely looking at her as if this had been the entire conversation. "No issue here. Live well, Mage Xeleanor."

She was almost growing used to 'live well,' rather than 'travel well' but somehow a twinge on that made the point better than anything else could have. In some weird sense, Xelle was unable to say either. So she tipped her head forward, and then left.

Xelle did not call a vroom, but enjoyed the windy fall day, thriving to the point of glowing on the exhilaration of an occasional sling cast, winding her up and around and through the trees, which were plenty around the road to Vi'Grand, unlike the sparser, more rolling paths from To'Ever or To'Arc.

There was no desire for suspense in Xelle's world, and so the first thing she did was head to Post and ask if they carried the horrid subscription dedicated to 'exposing' her and her friends. Last she'd heard it hadn't grown past Arc Region, but, they were now apparently going after Dram. Of course, she'd been at Grand Tower a solid ten months, and she'd majorly flamed off the Lunests twice since then.

And in a flash, what Ollia had said about Xelle being so different pricked like a thorn. Xelle was not special! There was no X. She was just there and . . . authentic. And messy. And angsty. And she'd given up a lot in not just trying to protect other pers, but in not stopping when it got hard. Saying what needed to be said. And what did she have for it? She was lonely. She was upset. She carried the ever-shifting weight of unpredictable choices they all tsked away as somehow easier than the compact burdens of expectation that they'd chosen. These other Mages acted like they couldn't stand up too. As if their continued grace with power gave them moral authority to 'protect' or 'defend' her when they wouldn't stand up themselves.

Maybe if other pers put themselves out together, a few wouldn't have to bear the wind alone.

"Not alone," she nearly growled. "My friends. I have my friends."

But did she? Her friends except the one she missed the most? The one who had left for no valid reason whatsoever?

Xelle roared now more in intensity than volume, and she didn't regret it. She roared again. And again.

And then stopped, because this would get covered in this subscription too, and she preferred to keep her growling to herself.

Xelle walked into Post with a pleasant smile. "Hello. I'm Xeleanor Du'Tam. I'd like to transfer Basic and all notices from Vi'Arc to this location."

She saw the clerk's eyes dart to the side. Clearly a reader. "And while that transfers, I'll take the most recent copy of my subscription."

"Which subscription?" the clerk tried.

Xe looked like a really nice per. Just the vibe. Xelle tilted her head with the kindest version of her 'you know' face.

The clerk made a noise sort of like a party whizzer, then cringed, and grabbed some paperwork. "Please fill this out, sign here, and rub over your coin here—" Xe pointed. "And I'll get that paper straightaway."

It turned out quite straightaway, as the paper was in a bin in the exact direction the clerk had glanced and xe just had to reach for it, but Xelle nodded politely, completed the form and pushed it back.

The clerk pushed the paper over, with a sympathetic nod.

Xe didn't get it. Xelle knew that. If Xelle looked distressed, it was because this was the first time she'd transferred her Post since first arriving at To'Arc. During the visit to Breath, the stay (though brief) at Tam, her year-ish at To'Ever, even the almost year here, she'd never cut that last tie.

No, not the last. But a very symbolic one. Not wanting to explain this to the politely sad-facing clerk, she gave a tight face expression, said her thanks, and took the paper outside.

Oh, she'd forgotten how vile this ash actually was.

Here goes.

Protectors of our Populace

Confirmation found: Her body for power.

Loyal Protectors. Even the cold, unfeeling reaches of the Ever Tower could not bear the heat of Xeleanor Du'Amberborn after the unexplained death of the revered Jehanne Du'Arc. With such transgressions unable to be swept under even a Tower-sized rug, and Xeleanor to be cast from the magesphere in bleak finality for we, the populace, to finally confront and contain, Xeleanor did what she had done at Breath Tower—used her sexuality as a weapon against the weak. Seducing one Mage Dram Du'Grand, a young Mage futilely positioned to protect his Spire from such villainy, she stuck a forest-booted foot upon the chest of Grand Tower—

Actually Xelle did not have to read this. She really did not. If in the 'revolution' someone should, what if it didn't have to be her? She rolled the thing into a pocket and paced back and forth.

Someone could read them. Sure.

But why? For what? It seemed important to know what they were saying about her, especially if they accidentally dropped hints, but it seemed really unfair. Why could pers with lots of money say whatever they wanted about you, say it nearly anywhere, and you didn't have a chance to, well, she wouldn't respond to this sort of thing, but even put out one's own messaging. Once one had a handle on what that should be.

Xelle wished there was a cast to make a piece of *her* paper appear on everyone's desks. She thought of the paper in her pocket.

That wasn't a cast. It was a subscription. There were mechanisms to do this. Money. Coordination. Safety. There were many obstacles. But it was something to think about. After she was back from Vi'Grand. Here, she was going to talk to some pers. Sniff the breeze as they said back in Tam. Then go put all these pieces together.

She didn't go the tavern route this time. Always good for getting the beat of the local music, but that's not what Xelle wanted this time. She remembered a print shop, and walked that way.

They charged a little more than she was hoping for, but soon she had three sturdy cardstock signs, each lettered with:

Open Plaza Discussion

With Mage Xeleanor Du'Tam

Meet at Daylight Balance Bell at Festival Stage

She tacked them to the announcement boards at the three main entrances to the festival loop, and then went to have a coffee. One thing she gave pers out this way a lot of credit for was, in general, they read body language on whether a per was looking to be approached. And, so, Xelle, leaning over a piece of paper with her stout cup of steamy foaming deliciousness, was not interrupted as she considered what topics to start with, which to avoid, and a few more to keep things moving long enough to not be embarrassing if there weren't any questions.

And, as the daylight balance bell rang throughout the village, Xelle made her way to the festival loop, surprised to see a sizable group forming up and around the stage.

"Hello," she said, waving, sort of half-jolted and half-delighted as several of the pers responded a mix of "Hello" and "Good Day" in a mushy but discernable rumble.

A hu was walking up the side stairs, and Xelle turned in worry. Xe was wearing a village vest, but still, Xelle held herself alert.

"You need a permit to speak here."

Hmm? It was customary for Mages to use the village stage if the schedule was open. And she'd checked. Beer Market had ended, and the Squash Festival didn't start for several days. Was this a challenge against her title? She glanced at the hu, who gave no signs of direct confrontation. She considered what xe was looking at. A well-dressed but casual hu. No sash. No chain.

And that was what everyone else saw too, she suddenly realized. And whatever happened here would spread through the village like that paper she'd been considering. She had, uh, set herself up pretty good.

She'd been in the Tower most of the year. Whether pers agreed with her welcome there, whether they didn't, or whether they acknowledged her self-given title or not, they were used to her. Or at least—they let her go about her business.

Here, it wasn't just about her, but pers' relationships with the Tower. She had thought through all the things she wanted to say, but not whether she'd be allowed to say them.

And everyone was looking at her.

Well, if this was going to be the populace's introduction to Mage Xeleanor, she hoped she could get it right.

"I'm here from Grand Tower, hoping to leverage the hospitality of Grand Village to discuss items of mutual interest."

The hu, who looked more bothered than perplexed, nodded with forced noddage. "I, uh, usually a Mage is recognized, and um—"

Xe waved vaguely toward her chest, where a chain might be worn.

She was not going to say, 'I am a Mage.' But then, how could she establish that without show, without stomping down, or force. What made a Mage a Mage?

Ack. San had asked her that, and she'd meant to go consider it. She'd said something about using magic, and having ethics, and something else? Being confident? Or was that with Ollia? She looked around at the audience. She was running out of time. She was just Xelle, and she used magic, and wanted to be able to help pers, and the structure wouldn't let her just say and be that. But, see, that felt silly here. Those things were what made a Mage a Mage to a Mage. She was just like everyone here.

Ash. Ash ash.

Except, she wasn't. The Lunests were after her. And they'd be after anyone else who stood in their way, even if these pers didn't see that yet.

Her neck tingled and a new spirit shot through her like a drug.

She cast to amplify her voice, and looked back and forth between the village worker and the crowd. "I apologize for not getting a permit; I assumed and I shouldn't have. If I may, let me introduce myself. I'm Xeleanor Du'Tam, she or e, a Mage who is staying at Grand Tower under their generous hospitality, and here in your village under yours. Some of the things you've heard about me are true." (Flying with a dragon.) "Much that you've heard is untrue and/or intentionally misconstrued for bad purposes."

"What bad purposes?" A voice called out.

"If you'll let me stay without a permit, just this once," she turned back toward the worker, "I'll address these questions. And next time, I'll ask at Post about the process. Perhaps you could join us?"

The hu had clearly not been directly invited before by a Mage or someone purporting to be one, and looked a little stunned. But also not like xe was leaving, so she leaned toward the front group. "Can we make a little room here?"

As xe moved over to the quickly cleared spot, pers began to take thin cloths out of their bags and baskets, and set them down onto the greenfloor, which she just realized was neatly kept and full, despite the amount of pers walking over it on a regular basis. This was not the joyfully trodden stone paths of Vi'Arc nor the wooden paths and seats of Vi'Ever. But no matter where Xelle stood, she was still Xelle, and she would address them as that per. She caught herself from laughing. She'd be terrible at being anyone else. Well, then.

"Hi, I'm the real Xelle. And I see that you here also have been hearing about a lie given my name." She pulled out the crumpled paper and waved it a bit, before shoving it back into her pocket. "So I think it's time to just be open, isn't it?"

She twinged inside, hearing herself. But surely pers understood that being open was not the same as sharing everything. Oh, these last years had got to her.

"We are reaching a decision point as the hu of Alyssia. And as dramatic as that may sound, it is worse that we are doing so, as we'll see it, without warning. 'Everything is fine. Things are getting better.' In many ways, this is true! Yet the pers behind this bulletin, whose names will be spoken by me when it's time, are siphoning from your trust. Your goodwill. The culture of aid and spirit that centuries of work and failure and sweat and pain caused us to forge together. They think we won't notice. And what is it they want?"

She paused. She'd thought through this. Information was power, and there would be times to keep it close, but— She'd thought through this. She was doing it.

"They want to control things that don't belong to us. Or at least, that belong to all of us, and that means not just hu. And why? The more they control, the more they can charge you for. The more they can manipulate pers. They are taking a system of open trade and turning it—" she took a breath at the use of the loaded word then kept going "—into a violence of greed. And they're not stopping there. When they couldn't get enough through a violence of greed, they moved on to a violence of lies. A violence of control."

This didn't feel like enough, but her mind was starting to spin and she was worried she was rambling. Fortunately (she hoped), a hand was waving from near the back of the crowd. By the glimpse she caught of the stout aproned per, xe looked like a blacksmith who'd stepped away from a shop. "Who are we to say what other pers are supposed to have?"

Someone with a louder voice called out from the other side. "Besse's just saying that because she's charging twice the metal for garden bugs."

Her worry about starting some sort of confrontation spiked fear in her chest, but settled when she realized everyone was laughing. The city worker, up in front, was smiling too. "She makes these forged bugs on sticks for the garden that move in the wind. Can't keep them on the rack, everyone's so into them."

Ah. The slippery slope. Xelle and Ay'tea had dealt with this when working with local officials on replacing old structures, and such. Someone would inevitably ask, if the Mages want to tear this down, why won't they tear down insert sacred thing they'd never tear down. It wasn't that Xelle didn't believe in the slippering of slopes, it was that the question was whether someone was slippering them. Her normal analogies to bridge routing wouldn't work here, but another version came to mind, and she went with it.

"Let's say your Ga makes sticky casserole." If this were her own story, she would have said pinebread, or if she'd been at Vi'Arc, definitely samosas, but she had learned pers out this way were extremely serious about their casseroles. "No. Sticky noodle casserole." The crowd looked like she was about to tell erotica. "Is it bad if one per eats more than everyone else? Also, if anyone would like to speak, I plan to use a little magic to amplify your voice. Please signal if you don't want that."

One nice thing about a Tower village, they were used to casting, so no one so much as flinched.

There was, however, some muttering regarding her question. It was the city worker who first spoke up, waving at the same time he started to speak. "Hi, I'm Clof, he, work for the Grand Village Festival Grounds." Xelle nodded dignitarily, while weaving a thread of Arc to his words. "I don't think that's as simple an answer as you might be expecting."

Xelle hadn't said what she was expecting, but she let him continue.

"Maybe someone is allergic to something in it. Or they ate too many rolls. Or everyone knows how much someone likes it and don't mind if they chomp up a bit extra." He stopped, his expression quite serious.

"Well, I agree with that," she said. "Now, what if the annoying sarent says that she owns the casserole dish that Ga used, and holds up the matching spoon in her hand. And she takes half of the casserole for herself, and then another sarent is nervous he might not get any if he says something about that, so he takes the spoon and dishes some, then hands it to his spouse, so he can get some too, and then there's just a tiny bit left, which someone else scoops up while everyone else is thinking, well, I can still eat my roll and cupcake, since those were divided up front, and who knows what she'll do if I say something."

It really interested Xelle the patience with which a Grand Village crowd would contemplate. (And not shout out.) Pers were still pers anywhere, but it marveled her how distinct the small things in a culture could be, never even noticed until different somewhere else.

Someone raised a hand. Xelle acknowledged xem, and threw a cast that way.

"And someone who would be that much of a prod at their own family dinner would not stop at the casserole."

Firana. Xe made that sound really ominous. Well, it was ominous. And Xelle wasn't going to start getting into the sarent turning family members and taking bribes and trying to capture pers, but yeah. In fact, Xelle had a flash of thinking anything she'd add to that would probably diminish or confuse the point.

But then, who was Xelle. Where did she fit into this? What was she, the Lord of Casserole? She was just some per who—

Oh.

"And you can think of me as a per who's been disinvited from dinner for asking questions about it." And not the first, she suddenly realized. Pelir. This had all started with discrediting Pelir. But she still didn't know if that was because of Pelir's self, or because of just wanting to put Kern in. And she wasn't going to get into Mage business here. "And that's really the question I'm here to ask. Are there any other family members who, if they find out Sa Greedy is claiming control over dinner, will want to do something about it?"

A voice called to her. "You're not really saying anything."

Xelle stared ahead. Was that true? She thought the dinner thing had been effective? Maybe dinner wasn't a . . . What was she here to say?

She raised and steadied her voice. "I'm saying they are hurting pers." Several glanced around uncomfortably. "If you haven't felt it, it means either they haven't reached you yet, or you'll be a tool used to hurt someone else."

"We know who you're accusing!" Someone spoke up, their voice strained. "How do you know all this?"

Easy answer. "Because they've hurt me. They've hurt my friends. They've hurt pers I don't know. Look, I'm not different than you. I just found myself in their path already, and when I was offered a chance to get out of their way, or continue to oppose them, I picked . . . that one. And I guess . . . that's what I'm here to offer you. Look, I didn't get it either. I couldn't understand why they were hurting pers. What was the motive? And then we learned, they just want more stuff. And they don't care who's in their way to get it."

She took a breath. "So I'm here to ask you, of course, just one group of pers, but a sample to start with, if a group of us could work to determine and spread accurate information on the harm we believe these pers, or any pers like them, are causing, would anyone here want to do anything about it? Would pers, in general, risk helping that effort?" The words, 'How alone am I?' sat on her lips, but she breathed them out, did not ask.

Everyone was now speaking to each other in a growing rumble anyway, and Xelle let them. She moved back to the stage's benches, sat a moment, and unclipped the water flask she'd filled at the coffee shop. Not with coffee; couldn't get that taste, and not the good part of it, out of a flask. But with citrused water. She only wished it hadn't been quite so cold; it was an uncharacteristically chilly day, even for mid-autumn. She shivered a bit.

"Hey, there," a voice shouted louder than the rest. "He says what you're proposing is some kind of attack club."

Ash, she didn't want to parse attack and defense and all that, but she also wasn't here to mince words. She stood, clipping the flask back. "I'm saying that if pers are out hurting other pers, then instead of just accepting this, I think we should do something about it. And I just can't do too much alone. I do have some pers of my own to run all of this past. But it shouldn't rest on them either, and frankly, I don't trust the magesphere to understand the mood of the populace, so I'm asking you. Would you want to know? Would you do anything about it? Especially if you knew that they might come after you too? When it shakes out—and I'm certain it will—would pers like to be standing against the wind, or sheltered by the ones siphoning them to make the storm?" That was way too dramatic, but once she started in with the metaphorical wind thing, she'd kept going.

On cue, a gust of literal wind whipped by and pulled a large-brimmed sun hat from its wearer's head. With a tiny flick of her fingers, Xelle cast. Arc. Beautiful Arc Magic. She caught it with ease, and guided it back into the outreached hands of a per crowned by a halo of late afternoon light reflecting off of a shiny white undercap, until the sun hat was ribboned back into place.

"That was magic!" a young child called out. Xelle grinned xyr way. "But she doesn't have a wand!"

An intense wave ran over Xelle, like invisible ice water had been thrown on her. "I don't have a wand, because I'm an Arc Mage," e heard emself saying. Loudly. Boldly. Amplified on the breeze and the wind, and probably to the lingering fall vendors on the outer edge of the ring.

She stopped, expecting a heckle. An admonition. A declaration that without a pledge, this could not be possible. But there was nothing.

"Yes," she confirmed trying to sound more normal so that her weirdly spoken declaration would not bracket the silence. "I don't have a wand, because I'm an Arc Mage."

Again, to this there was no outcry. No gasp. Just a stretch of murmurs, and then a voice. Not a voice Xelle had casted, but it rang out plenty loud and clear.

"Why us? Why are you asking the populace? Mages don't want to get their hands dirty?"

Her skin prickled. This was going to be noped right now, and wherever it came from. And she could answer, because in a lot of ways, it's all she'd been really thinking about these past years.

"The answer is we're going to need pers everywhere. Mages. Studies." She started to think about things like Tower staff, Post workers, festival groundskeepers, print shops, but she was not about to start giving strategies in public, a thought she really just had in that moment. "Something I've had to learn about is balance. And the biggest question about balance, is who is asking for it. I now know something you've all known forever. Which is if you're going to leverage the mage-sphere, your easiest route is understanding and sometimes playing to their structure."

A whole lot of pers nodded at this.

"But that doesn't mean that if someone tells you y'have to do things a certain way, that you do. Not when they are using ingrained biases to limit your potential."

Someone had raised xyr hand, and Xelle signaled for xem to wait a moment. "So I want to make this clear. Pers in the magesphere are at least as complex as anyone else." That came out wrong. "What I mean, is if they seem more complex, it's because they're twisting themselves into knots over things like the positioning of the charms on a chain." There were several snorts at this, and Xelle was pretty sure one of them was actually a Mage she'd recognized. Ash, she had to remember that there were probably lots of pers from the Tower in this crowd. But that was fine. For now. Just . . . more to remember. "I'm trying to say that the magesphere will continue to be involved, and what good would it do anyone to use what I might know about it to earn your trust?" She was not sure she was making sense. What was her point? "If it's about to get as bad as honestly I feel that it is, we'll need everyone who's willing."

That last point seemed to at least land. Until another per rather shouted out, "What is it about you that makes you some sort of leader here?"

Some little burst of resentment bubbled at this, like a painful burp. It was a reasonable question, but she was tired of the An'oars of the world talking her down when she was the one up here ashburned doing something. "I'll answer that in a moment. This per had xyr hand up earlier."

She pointed to the other per.

The per stepped up on something; Xelle couldn't see what. "I was going to ask, about your musings on balance, who decides which balance is advised and which balance is harmful? You made it sound like an answer, but without that, there's no solution."

A number of oohs and twitters sparked around the crowd, and Xelle silenced them with a rather stern, fully amagical swipe of her hand. "The solution is to know it's hard. And to understand what you're balancing and what you're not, thinking about whose advice you should trust and whose you shouldn't, for a whole lot of reasons, and then making sure you are the one making that final decision on balance. If the hill says no sledding, maybe it's not a big deal to take a nighttime ride. Maybe it's dangerous. Maybe it's fine, but not worth risking the ire of the nearby shopkeep. My point isn't to introduce logic and decision-making, it's letting you know that if we're going to have any power, it's got to be together, and together is going to look different for different pers, so we've got to stay thoughtful about it."

This was getting too complicated and her points too muddled, and she wanted to pull it back. She pointed over to the interrupting per. "And why am I a leader here? Because I got smacked in the face with it, and simply couldn't look away. So I could either work to fix things for myself, or try to fix things for other pers too. And I'm a we kind of guy."

The wind blew through again, and as the light also dimmed, it really was getting cold. "Hey, it's cold. Let's go on our way, now, and all think about this, but if you want to let me know what you think before you go, I'll be sitting over on that bench. It's got a heater."

At this, Xelle saw her first smile from Clof.

"A really nice heater," she added.

He beamed.

Xelle made her way over to the bench, slowly, as a number of pers looking to be on their way quickly (and all starting with "Real quick") caught her and said they'd like to hear more. A few grumbled at her, ominous sounding things about minding her business or watch what you ask for, or something akin. By the time she made it to the bench, there were just about eight pers left waiting to talk.

It was well into sunset when the last per walked forward, a younger hu, looking like she'd been hovering a while. "Hi. I just wanted to say one more thing. You're not random. You didn't pledge. You're the dragonfriend. So, there's something about you specifically."

Xelle smiled kindly. She'd thought about this a lot. "I did sled on a few marked hills."

The hu grinned. "As long as you know that too. So. Was it worth it?"

Oof.

She thought of Ay'tea. Of losing him. Of moving again, and again. Of having experiences no one else had had, of knowing Thunder, of what it meant like to fly. But all those days alone. All those days that were so heavy. All the feelings of what it meant to really be alone. Not alone, but . . .

"I have one regret," she heard herself saying, and with a polite nod that hopefully signaled the end of the conversation, she rose and stepped away.

10 – Interference

Xelle hadn't heard from Thunder. She'd had plenty going on these last days, and wanted to offer zhem space, but if she didn't hear soon, she'd have to reach out. Seventy six and one or not, Xelle knew what it was like to get in your head at that age, and yeah, with her thirty-first birthday just a couple months away, she was starting to solidly feel . . . thirties.

Unrelated, Xelle was seated on the throne of nature outside the wand lab when a familiar ringing sounded in her ears. This was absolutely a surprise—

It was Kern, she could feel that. She did not actually think they would be talking *anytime* soon. And how did he find her here? And *why here?*

Xelle walked into the sink space, washed her hands, and gave permission for the call. She thought about casting for additional privacy, but washrooms were sound shielded and the door was locked. A little passive Arc magic emanating from a washroom with Xelle in it would not be of note, even if anyone was out there detecting it, and a quick, faint swipe of a travel cast told her the hallway was quite clear.

Kern was controlling this call, so she didn't have to worry about any stone skimming or cloth holding. She considered trying to block the view of where she was, but no, he was going to call here, he could enjoy the experience.

The Mage's figure stepped into view, and then as if showing off, sat down on the small couch, well, just a little above it, as clearly whatever he was really seated on was a bit taller. "Your butt is floating," she said. "Also welcome to the washroom."

He peered in. "They haven't changed a thing," he said.

Xelle cut this off with a wave. "How did you know I was here?" She'd almost asked 'Why here' but she'd really just worked through that.

"Better," he said dismissively. "Yet still disappointing. You're aware there is a Mage at Grand in the employ of our associates; I asked this Mage for your schedule. Apparently your rhythms on lab days are still predictable, even with your change of labs."

Some Mage was tracking her here? She'd deal with that later. No, one thing, first. "The Grand Mage. One question. One time. Or I cut this off. Have I been alone with xem?"

Kern's eyes flared a bit.

"Please."

"I won't answer this again, after this."

Xelle nodded.

"No. Well," he waved off a bit, "the corridor, et cetera. Not alone together in the way that you mean it."

She could have fainted. Not San. Not Dram. Not Ollia. Not wanting him to see the depth of that reaction, she tried to smile politely. "Thank you. So, are you going to walk through this time? It's pretty fragrant in here."

Kern's lip curled slightly, and not in amusement.

"I eat healthy?" She shrugged, trying to keep her hands from shaking.

"Xeleanor, I need you to be aware that by agreeing to this call, you've given me a sense of where you currently stand. I will also let you know that, without the locket, I do not have a strong enough connection to find you anywhere."

"Thank you," she murmured. It sounded sincere, and that was a small comfort to know. And a good understanding, too, of the power in answering a call, perhaps even more than making one. "Do we know," she asked, "what it takes for that type of connection? Is it more trial and error? Does it depend on the per?"

He shook his head, looking slightly less annoyed. "No time for a lesson here, but there is something I think is critical that you understand. The difference between a Mage and a Study is not primarily the acceptance by a Tower. It is having the structure we've spent years building under you kicked out in an instant. Of a Tower's trust that you will survive that fall. That there is much we do not understand about this world and our connections. Even here at Arc. A Study learns the structures of Magic. A Mage understands that they are vapor, a thread of truth, in the ways that hu can understand them."

Xelle had so much to ask about this, she wanted to—

"I'm not here to chat," he said, his tone plain but firm. "There is a dragon, who, for the last five days, has made zhemself seen around Arc Tower, though not within its grounds. Playing ball in the empty fields. As of yesterday, I detected shadows of magic around the dragon as I took watch. No clomping machines or visible movement. Much more sophisticated." He held a tight face for a moment. "And, by the lack of shadow otherwise, I suspect some kind of enchantment." He rubbed his forehead. In that small gesture, Xelle felt almost a softness. Of not presenting himself as Mage Kern, but Kern. Sure, many other Mages had now dropped that veil, but she and Kern had plenty of reason to hold distance.

Then she twinged. "Do you think they have someone at Ever?"

Kern turned in his seat, a jarring vision against the couch he was not sitting on that reminded Xelle he was very much not here. He wasn't calling from a washroom, was he?

"Think of the pathways, Xeleanor. Binaries allow communication, but all things are infinite." He looked like he was trying to say something.

"I know Irla has an issue with Ever."

He glanced sharply. "Yes. And my suggestion is she doesn't have to influence an Ever Mage to get an enchantment. There are many ways to turn and not turn. Not just magic, of course, but power. Influence. Intent. There are many pathways to get an enchanted object." He stared at her like he was trying to decide whether to say something.

Then he did. "I don't think she fully trusts any of us. The 'team' she assembled has had some cracks, our own situation included. I don't think you'll see her operating in that manner again unless she has to. Smaller pieces. Smaller influences."

This was making Xelle's stomach churn. Everything felt harder, now that they'd gained some insight. Like instead of tossing a rotten log, they'd hit it, allowed it to splinter.

But that wasn't their fault. Ugh.

"Take the lesson from her, Xelle. Don't take on everything at once. Not alone."

He sounded almost kindly, almost parently. Until she met his gaze and it glared like a pointlamp. "I need to know right now if you know anything about this dragon."

This was way too much to process sitting in the wand lab bathroom. Speaking of which. She'd have to tell them she'd been meditating or something. After a bit of travel cast to clear the air. Or, no, she didn't have to tell them anything. Anyway. Kern seemed to be open with her. And Thunder, zhey hadn't even waited for Xelle to reach back out, zhey were doing it anyway.

That was actually a little cool.

Xelle turned toward the seated Mage. "I need to thank you. I see the ways now in which you've been trying to guide me. I am grateful for anything you offer to me, personally. And something in the weird, disjointed way I feel right now is really affecting me. I knew I didn't know things, because I'm not as experienced. Because I keep wiggling my way out of more direct avenues. But it's not just me. We're all trying to figure it out. The way you spoke earlier, you're working with a Breath Mage."

That got him.

She nodded. "And I don't expect you to tell me who or how. It wouldn't be wise. We share what we can, when we can, but Firana, Kern, now you're connecting to my lab's washroom. Magic. Shadows. Detection. We've got to stay away from each other. This is way too risky."

"I agree. I had no intent for conversation, but then your dragon started making ball fields of the——"

"Zhey're not my dragon. Zhey're my friend. You already figured that, since zhey were seen by half of Arc Tower, even if from a distance, by a whole lot of Mages, something zhey have to also realize. Or I don't know, zhey're impulsive, and zhey see things zheir own way." She steadied her voice. "I need you to leave zhem alone. Completely alone. If . . . zhey are taken, monitor it. Learn what you can, but do not intervene without talking to me first. I will let no harm come to zhem, even if it means calling you for help."

Kern really had very little reaction to any of this, including the vulnerability of the fact she had just confirmed. He was mostly quiet. Then, he spoke. "Agreed. For now. But this lock needs a key. If there is a time when a communication occurs, and it is not safe to speak plainly, not safe to cast, we need a way to convey that to each other."

Ugh, Xelle did not like Magey riddles. But it did seem important.

It had to be something plausible, unless needed to blow everything up, and they probably needed that too. So, how did they unlock this? Just an agreement to talk? Warning that they were lying? Needed help? She wasn't going to make up a whole secret language in the washroom.

Quick, Xelle, think. So she needed to at least bin what the critical messages could be. Danger? Untruth? Help me? Total disaster? The first two seemed linked. And maybe even the last two. But what could they say to each other that would raise no suspicion yet be clear to the other? It could not require magic, or visualization, or tone——it had to be conveyed in any way possible.

Well, first the 'blow everything up' one. What would be credible but unnecessary? Irresponsible, even. "Betrayal," she said. "If we need help, if we are in danger, if everything has gone awry and nothing holds, we speak of our disappointment in each other, our betrayal of trust."

To her slight while nervous delight, Kern raised his eyebrows slightly. "That's a good one. But too limiting. So I propose an affirmation of trust works the same. And then, also a warning?"

She nodded.

"That's the one I went for first, so I'll offer my idea. I did consider being nice to each other, but we might need that for show. So, if there is a warning, a warning of danger, a warning that the words we speak are false, and no way to convey more—double-back. Once for an alert, twice for a clear warning.

Her head snapped up, despite her attempts not to look impressed. Well, that was clever. And so very, very Arc. The double-back signal, the tiniest squiggle to apologize for imperfect calligraphy, but not take the time to correct or re-do it, would probably not even catch the eye of anyone but an Arc Study or Mage. Nor would the related gesture. An intentional twitch of the end finger pers used with a similar flub of words. Xelle loved getting calligraphy right, but she'd practiced very hard to stop doing what always felt like an apology for non-perfection. And in her speech; she was always stumbling around, so she'd never developed the habit. Kern must have noticed. Yet, if they were under duress in the presence of Arc Mages, she would not have to fake the nerves to double-back a couple or few times.

"One more." He raised his hand. "In private, or in safety, we do not have to hide our codes. In private or safety, we will always greet with this." He traced a shape, sixth of the planar basies. "So then, we will stay apart. If the need arises, mind your signals." It sounded like a silly joke, but he wasn't joking. And she could feel the call loosening. Controlled, calm, but ending.

This all felt too imperfect. Too fast. A risk poked her, an uncertainty. "Kern, what is the deal you made? To stay in the graces of the Lunests?" The last part seemed clear to her, but then Kern was probably having to make more than one deal.

The call solidified again, and he stared at her a long time, longer than she quite liked. But she waited.

"To discredit you. Not as they tried with Pelir. Not seeds of doubt, not blathering ribaldry like this subscription of Mark's. But poison in your very name. To see you expelled from the Towers. To stain you so uncomfortably the populace will not risk your presence."

Xelle was still processing this when he added, "And to help them capture a dragon. This time, no feint. That was a card played once. So Mage Xeleanor, it seems much rests on you."

He nodded in departure, and before she realized she'd done it, she'd nodded back and the hu had already disappeared from the room.

Xelle leaned into eir sigil.

Hi, it's me. I was going to ask to come see you but it sounds like you're moving around a bit. I'm really struggling with what to do here. And no, I don't mean it's my call. It's not. But I've also confirmed that the Hurts are trying to capture a dragon, and it's pretty clear you've directed their attention your way. Which also means if I come to see you, which I did consider as some catch sounds great around now, I'll confirm it's safe for us to communicate. I'm not sure how many hu actually know that you communicate, let alone with hu. I know, that's insulting, but we also don't need to reveal any advantages we still have until we have reason.

There is a Mage, Mage Kern, here I'll think about what he looks like if you can see that, who likely suspects your plan. He has agreed to leave you alone, but in dire need, go to him. The way she sent that last thought punctuated how dire she thought the need would have to be.

I'm not totally comfortable with your plan. Yeah, I can't tell you what to do, but also if we're friends and we're working together we should talk about things like this, which yes, I realize that you did and I kinda stomped on it. So the thing is, it comes down to my advice, and I just don't know. I don't want to give these hu any chance to hurt you, via manipulation, confinement, or anything else. But also, maybe I've just been too careful. They're not being careful, not really anymore. I'm certainly not going to use their measures for myself, but I'm starting to feel like a knockball player watching for a sure move while the other team haphazardly wins.

So I guess here's what I have to say. You've clearly made your decision, I mean it seems that way. So if you're comfortable opening your location back up to me, it would make me feel better. And I won't intervene. If you change your mind about the plan, that's ok too. If you don't, I promise you something. I will always be with you. No matter what happens, no matter how long it takes, we are together. Always.

Xelle lurched back onto her bed, suddenly glad she hadn't decided to message inconspicuously from the Atrium, which seemed a rather surface thought to avoid the fact that she had lurched from her own thoughts.

No, not hers. Thunder's. Shaking now, she drew in a strong breath, and let something, something that had been blocked, bottled up, burst through her in a terrifyingly vulnerable way. Not painful, but uncontrolled. Sensations in 'places' (that wasn't quite the right concept) she didn't even know she could feel.

For all the strength of it, what came through her sigil was not just the return of full connection, nor words, images, or senses, but the smallest flash, a push of certainty. The message, a pact. Thunder would be there always, also. They'd said it before, they'd said always, but now it was sealed. It would be always.

Xelle had no other words right now, she only felt. And the connection ended, not suddenly, but like a woodsper gently unhooking the last rope loop.

Her sigil. Her room at To'Grand did not have a mirror, and she had not bothered to get one. And so, hoping she looked somewhat normal, she stumbled into the nearby washroom, fervently glad the front room was empty, and leaned into the large, old mirror there. The sigil no longer looked like the ink of a grayscale tattoo. It was black, a slight shimmer in the dark lines as she moved.

And Xelle understood. All this time after the bond had been offered, it had finally been accepted.

Three Mages walked into the wand lab. One Xelle recognized as part of Grand Tower diplomacy, the other two she did not, but by their chains they were all of reasonably, but not particularly, high rank.

Everyone in the lab stepped back, except Ollia, who strode forward. "I was not informed of this visit."

"Mage Ollia, you are aware of the protocol." The diplomatic Mage did not look upset, but stated the response as though she'd expected Ollia's. She turned toward Xelle.

"Mage Xeleanor Du'Tam, you are retained by Grand Tower on transgressions of magical trespass and magical assault."

Firana. One point Irla. Maybe she should be more scared, but she didn't feel scared, she felt annoyed. There were just too many pers who wouldn't want her secluded off in Frond, or wouldn't want to risk her being expelled. Especially knowing her regard for the rules, ha. But, retained by Grand Tower . . . Xelle had lived at Frond long enough to know how the transgression process worked. A per wouldn't be detained unless they were dangerous. The charges must say that she was. Any host Tower would not want to deal with a potentially dangerous hu: caster or not. They'd love Frond to take that per out of their hands and responsibility. So if Grand Tower had laid claim to her retention, that was solidly having her back. She gazed up at the waiting Mages thoughtfully.

"I dispute the transgression in its entirety, but not the retention. I will abide by whatever terms Grand Tower imposes, and ask for your help in navigating the process."

Diplomatic Mages didn't really have 'expressions' but by the side-glances of the other two, Xelle felt pretty sure she'd just passed some sort of test. That not everyone there had thought she would. She also noticed no one was holding onto a wand. (Something she would never have thought to check before living here.)

"Then the terms of your retention are that you may not cast or leave the Tower without being in the presence of a Grand Mage. You have already accepted these terms." That last was said in a slight tone that perhaps Xelle should have at least asked the terms first. She thought about San and the balance of trust. And also that he, knowing more of what had actually happened than anyone else here, must have asked for trust from the rest of the Spire Mages.

"I am Mage Frealonn Du'Grand, she, Diplomatic Tenure and Society of Thirteen Banners. I have agreed to serve as your counsel, under the premise, as assured to me by the Grand Spire, that you have not done as accused."

Huh. 'Accused' was a specific word choice. Transgressions weren't just thrown around, their filing required evidence. So what Frealonn was actually saying was she believed the transgression itself was fraudulent. And that was a major, major transgression for whoever was behind this. Maybe Frealonn wasn't in this just for Xelle.

Oof, though. Kern, he'd said she hadn't been alone with the turned Mage. It could be any of these three, though truth be told she would be much more worried for the one who tried to turn this Frealonn. This one probably slept with the code books. Still.

Never be alone with anyone new, she reminded herself.

I despise that, she thought. "Thank you," she said. "So, um, what do we do now?"

Frealonn glanced over at Ollia and the two seemed to communicate. "You are relieved of your shift. And you're going to come tell me what happened."

Without enough time to think that through, she nodded. "I request Mage Ollia accompany me. She could not perform mentorship without an understanding of this situation."

They had not formed a mentorship, but Ollia should understand—it wasn't a lie; it was a request. And even though it felt fine to call someone like herself or An'oar a 'lab lead' the term felt inadequate for the hu in charge of this sacred wand-making space. But, who wouldn't want to hear this story.

Mage Ollia nodded, and the five went on their way.

Xelle had thought about what her story would be, if pressed, not in the sense of planning for something like this actually happening, but in her spinning and worrying about blocking off the things in her mind that she would *not* say.

And so she told them (Frealonn and Ollia, she'd requested the other two not be there and Frealonn had no objection given Ollia as a witness), and repeated the story again, however she was asked. Different questions, same answers.

The Lunests had invited her to the estate and arranged for her travel. She agreed to go because she had heard the rumor that they had been behind the destruction of the dragon habitats in the mountains (these events known now by all Mages), and she hoped she could confirm involvement by going. But then, when she stepped from the custom vroom, which she could describe in reasonable detail including their fine materials and the remarkable quietness of their fuelstones, she was escorted inside by hu that were clearly Mages, no she could not describe them, and led through a long set of corridors and halls. Then they told her they were going to keep her captive because of her dragon sigil. She said no and tried to leave. She was rushed at, and so she cast as strongly as she could, resulting, as she'd pieced it together, in something she'd never done before: cast a thin slice of Arc into the pathways of world. And, in that distraction, she must have broken through a window to leave, given the cuts she ended up later healing on her skin. Not expecting her to use such a level of Arc Magic, neither the Lunests nor their Mages were able to catch her.

She repeated that anything else she did or didn't remember doing before or afterward was irrelevant to the transgression, and kept to herself that without being certain what information would be accessible to Irla and Mark—the actual transgressors in this act, through this process—she would not provide any additional information.

"No, I do not know if I was addled by the cast. I couldn't tell you something I don't remember."

Xelle was sure glad these were two Grand Mages examining her.

Breath Mages didn't read minds, but without casting herself, they'd sense the parts she was concealing and push for more detail in those places. Charm, well, she wasn't totally sure what they'd do, but they were known to read subtleties of inflection like large print.

And Frond, phew, she had no idea if they would sense that she'd arrived, connected to someone, not on her own, and she was glad not to try that out. If she did have to appear at Frond, she'd have to consider that more.

And Arc. Arc Mages would have asked about the travel. When did she get on the moveroom? How did they arrange the invitation? What did she remember about the cast? Describe which direction you cast and why did you cast that way? By what cast did you leave?

At no point did she worry that her omissions were deceiving these Mages. The Lunests had done this. They'd tried to force her into proving her lack of memory, in which case their own version of events might hold, or into admitting she'd gone with Mage Kern, any version of which could knock over a whole bundle of still-important sticks. Everyone here was now a victim of their plot. She'd spoken no untruth, only withheld facts that would put many pers in increased danger to reveal.

Mage Frealonn finally breathed out, about as much reaction as Xelle had got from her the whole time, and pushed her notes shut with a prolonged pat. She paused there with her hand on the notes, and the pause was a bit long. Then she released it, and looked right at Xelle.

"From what I know of hu, a Mage who would ask a well-ranking Mage to accompany her to document an act of self-defense would not have accepted an invitation from pers with a reputation such as the Lunests as an Apprentice with that sigil without a companion of witness or trust."

Oof. Well, Irla had handed her this one. She didn't even have to evade it. "The transgression states that I was alone," she said, flatly.

"It does. Hypothetically, as our going in presumption is that their story is untrue, if that point also were an untruth, knowing who you are both covering for could better reveal the dangers that we, and that per, are facing."

Xelle had a million retorts, some quite clever, on her lips. Yet, no question had been asked and unlike the pathways, she couldn't see where any reaction on that could lead. So the one she chose was silence.

"I hope you know what you're doing." Frealonn didn't appear to be looking for an answer to that, and as she stood and left, Ollia, looking troubled as well as exhausted, rose and followed her out.

Thunder had stopped playing ball in the fields near Arc Tower. From what Xelle could piece together from a stream of emotions Thunder had sent and then repeated for clarity, zhey had spotted a hu, approaching zhem. Well, kind of reverse, the point was that the hu had come close and Thunder had been seen looking back, so zhey could not pretend zhey hadn't. It wasn't Mage Kern (communicated more as a question wondered and a quick no) but once seen, Thunder had to convey some kind of reaction. Zhey'd chosen to screech and fly away in strongly acted fear (the emotions Thunder conveyed to Xelle was that the small hu did not scare zhem, which actually worried Xelle, though who knows, maybe it was someone innocent). And then Thunder had flown slowly over that spot a few times on other days, as if nervously looking to see if anyone was there, and then retreating.

Xelle really should have given zhem more credit. Or at least an open ear. No, she wasn't going to keep kicking herself about it, but she was sure to let Thunder know this felt like a clever plan—a way to continue to lay out a potential capture while also giving everyone else a little more time.

For the next several weeks, Thunder would fly a little closer, or edge around, then if the hu were there, appear startled and fly off. Xelle sent zhem messages every day, frustrated beyond measure that she was stuck here, unable to access her inkbloom (she would not break her word to Grand) or start working on her ideas for sharing information, while who knew what advantages the Lunests had been able to gain with all the delays. Their delays. Frealonn responded quickly to every step of the process and then the Lunests took their maximum allowed time to appeal, argue, debate, whatever they were doing.

The fact that a process meant to protect pers from instances of unmitigated danger could be turned into a weapon filled Xelle with a new rage, and she could only hope for now that someone at Frond was feeling the same and could do something about it.

Thunder seemed to have felt as thwarted by the oversimplicity of zheir own plan and the complications of being believably captured, and so the two shared nightly emotions that felt like stomping on over-ripe fruit.

Meanwhile, Xelle considered going to Arc Tower to let them know what was going on, but she would need to be accompanied by a Mage. When she raised the idea to Frealonn, she actually thought that was a very good idea, but refused to approve Xelle's travel. "You're acting like an impatient squirrel," Frealonn said, the words quite irritatingly *undiplomatic*. "But if you believe your relationship to Arc Tower is that strong that you would go there even in the midst of *this*, I am willing to send Arc Spire a petition."

This is what Frealonn couldn't understand. This reliance on waiting was unbearable. Ever since passing up her chance with Ay'tea, then wasting all that time at Breath when she could have been preventing harm at Arc, she had wanted to act. But Xelle was an Arc Mage, an expert on logistics. She knew the need for proper planning. Yet she'd tied herself into her own confinements, at least to some extent. First that year at Ever, feeling like she couldn't do anything, then when she'd finally done something, she'd had to leave. Then she arrived here, now ready to do *anything*, but took the advice that acclimation here was essential. Now she was moving again—she'd had that whole audience in the village, and suddenly she was trapped, confined again. Having to ask one of her labmates to watch her like an infant while she practiced her routine of Arc and Ever casts, not daring to try anything more experimental or time-consuming under the watchful gaze of a junior Grand Mage who just wanted to leave.

Even worse! Dram said it would be 'inappropriate' for him to go out into the village or back to Wehj with her. She said he was a Mage, she needed a Mage, surely they knew how to close that loop if it had been a concern. He'd said, "How do you know they didn't close it because they trust me or some such thing," and as a result Xelle hadn't felt like being around him here, either. The worry rested in her mind that she could not push someone away again—would not, but fortunately, she was reaching a point of nearly being of use in the wand lab, and so she put her energy there, learning so well, that she was often finding herself reaching out to help or mentor the two Studies, even the younger Grand Mage. So well that she barely heard the news that Arc had sent a statement in her defense (!) but definitely heard that she was not supposed to send them any note of thanks because it might work against her.

And all the time in the back of her mind was when would this ash-singed transgression be resolved so she could get back to business and drama and normal things like dating and saying thanks to pers who looked out for her.

Even moreso now! She couldn't imagine whether Irla actually thought Frond would sanction her over the protests of both Grand and Arc Tower—she surely hoped not, but using the sanctity of magesphere traditions and protocols sure was proving to be an effective way to slow her down.

And, she thought, cutting a yellowroot right down the center with a single strike with a shared knife from the kitchens, there were only so many times Xelle was going to be slowed down, before she never— ever—would be again.

11 – Mage Counselor Keisaren

"They are hearing our case today." Mage Frealonn was standing in her doorway in full Mage regalia.

Today? At Frond Tower? She was dressed as if going. "You can get there in time? I'm sorry, you're Mages, I'm sure you have a . . . Can I, um . . ." Was she supposed to go? Offer something? She'd barely woken up.

"A quick decision, Xeleanor. Go or not. If you go with us, you will be open to questioning. If you do not, you will not be available for questioning. What is your preference?"

Didn't seem like much of a choice. Of course she'd go. Defend herself. Get out of this Tower for two minutes. "And did they just tell you?"

Frealonn shrugged. Xelle wasn't yet sure if she liked that the Mage had dropped all pretense of diplomatic formality over the weeks this nonsense had taken.

"You have ten minutes to dress and meet us outside." She barely moved her wand in some sort of circle. "I am reading your casts. Consider it an escort."

Well, that turned out to be good, because there was dust all over the robes she'd bought in Mytil, and Xelle made quick work of it, and straightening them out, with careful swipes of travel. Her crownhair looked like a lopsided nest, but no one would see it under the matching cap and undercap set. With a quick check to Essie, a quick run to the washroom and her washcloth hurriedly tossed into her laundry bin, Xelle slung herself out, flying over the stairs to the irritation of a group of Grand Mages, and swinging herself out through the Atrium and past the Front Desk with a wave to the irritated desk clerks, and lowering to a soft landing (comfortable shoes in all cases) next to Mage Frealonn and two other diplomatic Mages.

Seemed a lot for just Xelle. But, she remembered, a self-proclaimed Arc Mage being held at Grand Tower on a transgression likely forced by the two wealthiest hu on Alyssia because she was a dragonfriend was no standard event.

Xelle really wasn't awake yet.

And a very odd . . . not vroom? . . . was sitting on the road. It had four seats like a vroom, and a glass windshield, but otherwise was made of a lightweight material—a painted wood, it seemed. And it had no feet, but instead was sitting on some sort of glossy cushion. And there were four doors, one aligned to each seat.

It appeared Xelle was going to learn how Grand Mages traveled across Alyssia.

She watched, eyes admittedly wide, as Mage Frealonn sat in the farther of the back two seats and motioned Xelle beside her. "Mage Kowra, he, and Mage Kesta, he." She did not note their obvious affiliation to Grand Diplomacy or any accolades, which Xelle felt like was both a compliment and a reminder of place all at once? Maybe she was overthinking it.

Noting she had not been introduced, Xelle did not get into the . . . moveboat? Flying log? She hoped they were traveling by sky! If this was somehow used to navigate on actual water, Xelle would . . . No, she didn't need to worry. However they'd have to get to the water was surely how they'd continue. Anyway, she turned toward the two Mages and bowed. "My gratitude for your assistance. I am Mage Xeleanor Du'Tam, an Arc Mage under the shelter of Grand Tower." She slowly rose, happy to emanate respect, especially before whatever they were about to do. Seeing the hu shift but each in turn collect themselves and bow back, Xelle stifled a grin, and, without opening the little door, swiped an Arc cast to lift and lower herself into the rather comfortable seat. Seeing what appeared to be a safety harness, she gladly fastened it, trying not to think too hard about why Frealonn was not wearing hers, or if fastening it was some sort of slight. Well, they were used to this.

And they had wands.

The two in the front appeared to be co-running the, um . . .

"I've not been in something like this before, Mage Frealonn. What is it called?"

She did not look surprised, nor did she look Xelle's way as she responded. "A box."

Oh. Alright.

The two raised their wands in concert, and then lowered them as the box rose into the air, and continued to rise, at least half the height of the Tower as Xelle found herself clutching onto the safety belt with both hands. They moved slowly at first, then faster. A light snow began to fall, or of course she should say they traveled into a light snow. While the box was clearly not enchanted, nor did she hear the sound of any fuelstone heater, someone was casting a shield of air, and some kind of heat source, as the wind and snow did not affect the passengers and Xelle felt a calm warmth as they sped on, faster and faster.

At some point, the snow abated (again, meaning they passed through it) and with clear skies around her, she realized she could look and see Alyssia some distance (didn't really need to know how far below) beneath her. Perhaps there would be a day when Xelle would look over the edge to see what she was passing over (she really rather yearned to), but with open sides and nothing but a bit of wood and a glossy cushion under her bottom, she chose not to look this time, instead closing her eyes, and thinking through what they might ask her at Frond, what she would respond. What she wouldn't respond. Or, would they ask her at all?

Xelle got a bit lost in her fretting, which for once served at least two useful purposes, and when she opened them, she saw Mage Frealonn's were now shut. The two Mages in front, ash, she'd already forgotten their names, were however fully alert.

She made a small noise, so as not to startle Frealonn, who may or may not have been availing herself of a power nap. "So then," she said, trying to speak softly. "Where are we about now?"

"Well into Breath Region," the one on the right said, which was good because with the other one's back facing her, at least this one could somewhat turn her way. "Coming up on Satta below, if you'd like to take a look."

Satta. That's where Kwill was from. She knew from maps it was quite large, and she knew from Kwill that pers who lived there also called it a city. So then, they should be nearly halfway to Frond. The idea of that somehow felt more amazing in this fast-moving box than it did traveling in an instant with the help of eir inkbloom.

"No, thanks. I actually really would, I've never been here at all, but I'm still grappling with what would happen if we fell."

Did she really just say that out loud? Xelle.

The Mage actually chuckled. "We go through that too. Always have at least two Mages in one of these, this high up and this fast. Would take all of us losing capacity at the same time, same as if we were swimming."

That didn't make her feel better?

She wished she had brought a book or a notepad or something as all she could see were clouds whipping past, but then, she hadn't been given much time, nor been told they would be going like *this*.

Eventually they began to slow, and lower down, until they were resting on the ground off to the side of what Xelle, with a hard, hard, pang of emotion, saw was Frond Tower.

She gazed upward.

Unlike the other Towers with a single prominent peak, Frond Tower rose in patterns and shapes. The main section rose highest, with wide subsections at regular intervals. Other buildings rose up several floors, interconnected by open pathways, each balcony or walkway covered in thatched awnings of local phyta, never having to endure the weight of snow, or ice. Peeking through the layers of dried greens, browns, and sands were walls of deeply etched stones, their lines and swirls so deep they could be seen from a distance.

She took a breath. This was really it. Frond Tower.

Xelle sometimes had a hard time believing she'd spent a year in a place so far away, so different. She'd run to it, in a sense, she knew, and though she'd left for reasons she knew were right, she also knew to others it gave the appearance of running again.

All these perceptions; they grew so tiring.

Using the door this time, and nearly tripping because she was not used to wearing robes and she had acquired a bit of a stride, she was surprised to find herself gripping Mage Frealonn's hand for support, as though she was used to catching teetering forestpers. Xelle straightened herself, risked a bit of an Arc cast to smooth her robes and look formal enough, and held her expression calm and chin level as she walked more carefully up the path, reminding herself this was very much real, despite the warmness of the air, the unfamiliar scents.

There was no conversation at the Front Desk; they were clearly expecting the group. Instead, a ranking steward met them and began to walk slowly through the huge, huge, round Atrium, its own thatched roof distinctive enough to be of legend. Again, she resented walking quickly through a Tower Atrium, even one she knew, but this was not the time for requests.

Still, she ignored the pers staring her way—let them look, let them see she was hu—and gazed upward at the immensity of detail, cut by sharp lines and sharper empty space. Morning light streamed through the windows, but she could see the faint presence of glow plants. This was the only space in all of Alyssia where interior glowplants were allowed, and it was a spectacular space at night.

Xelle was rather hoping she wouldn't still be here at night.

"Enough wandering," Frealonn said sharply, and Xelle stopped looking around, but gazed rather numbly ahead as the group moved through the Atrium and into the Loop (as she suddenly remembered they called it here), a wide, curving corridor.

The lift did not lift long enough. Which was to say, they weren't apparently going before the Spire in the Spire's spaces. But, of course not, transgressions were held in a separate building, through a walkway to a shielded side-structure. Shielded magically as well as from view. Not hidden, per se, but only viewable after traversing the interior of the Tower complex in one manner or another. Now, she wondered if everyone was allowed to walk here through the Atrium.

She passed through a door bearing a rather large rune. And then the door closed.

Three Mages sat behind a curved desk. They were, in fact, all Spire Mages. She'd not met any Spire Mages when she was here, and couldn't remember their names. Then, they were treating her as a Mage. She felt grateful, but her nerves now fully engaged, she also felt her stomach tightening.

Four seats with four separate drink carts and a choice of water, light juice, or tea, were set out next to four comfortable-looking chairs. Looking for a cue from Frealonn, Xelle calmly took the seat the Mage subtly pointed her wand toward. One of the two middle seats. Frealonn took the other.

She was glad for the seat, as now her legs truly wobbled. Every hu, no matter how dangerous to oneself or others, was given comfort and dignity at Frond Tower.

Interestingly, the Frond Mages were not announced, but announced themselves. No stewards, no Staff Mages. Only these three.

"I greet you in hope. I am Spire Mage Ba'kea Du'Frond, e or she." An older Mage, which a look of vague familiarity, spoke.

"I greet you in hope. I am Spire Mage Gillehem Du'Frond, she." This one, clearly tall even while seated, very Frond Region in dress and speech.

"I greet you in hope. I am Spire Mage Mykhaila Du'Frond, she." Soft spoken, wearing less adornment than the others.

Wait. Xelle just realized. Four chairs. The Lunests weren't here. She glanced around the room as if expecting them to bust through the walls.

Mage Ba'kea seemed to note the reaction. "How would you desire we address you?" E was looking right at Xelle. Not sure if she should stand, she did anyway, glad her legs held strong. "I am Xeleanor Du'Tam." Fira, she hadn't said Mage. Well, she wasn't going to add it now. Burn it. "You may call me Xelle."

Like Spire Mages tended to do, they showed no reaction. But Ba'kea continued to speak. "We have reviewed all materials submitted. Xelle, do you wish to review the accusations made against you in the transgression?"

"No," she said easily. "They are false, submitted in bad faith, and without averment. Are there questions for me?"

Xelle glanced to the side, where Frealonn stayed very, very still.

"Did you, in any way, trespass at the Estate of Irla Du'Lunest and Mark Du'Lunest?"

She looked right at the speaker. "I did not," she said, having resolved to not offer additional information, for a wide variety of reasons, including giving them a chance to delay again for a need to verify.

"Did you, in any way, assault any per at the Estate of Irla Du'Lunest and Mark Du'Lunest?"

"No." This one she did want to clarify, but she'd practiced the words. "I used a cast of Arc in self-defense that no one has stated hurt xem, physically or mentally, but allowed me the surprise to escape their stated intent to confine me, at that time, a marked dragonfriend, and Apprentice under the protection of Ever Tower, now an Arc Mage, under the protection of Grand Tower." She remained standing, though she thought she didn't need to.

"Do you have any other testimony to present?"

"No," Xelle answered. She felt almost a shift in the mood of the room, though she could not place it.

Ba'kea's expression, stolid and firm, revealed nothing. "Then, before we review, we will allow any witness testimony. Is there additional testimony from the representation?"

Frealonn stood and answered. "There is none."

The Mage nodded curtly. "There is one witness who has self-presented for testimony."

What?

Frealonn actually twitched. What could this be? Had the Lunests turned so far they would openly bring a forced witness? Was it a Lunest? A worker from the estate, paid or threatened to tell a sympathetic story? In alarm, Xelle forced herself not to crane her neck to see who it was who was entering the room. Feeling shaky again, now she did sit, Frealonn matching the motion.

A Mage. Frond chain. Simple cap. Flowing robes. Something . . . slightly familiar. Who was this? Why could Xelle not remember? Surely, surely, this Mage was not involved. Xe walked before the three Spire Mages, and silently drew a shape with xyr hand. "I am Mage Keisaren Du'Frond, she, Counselor. I assisted the instructor of a first-year class that Xeleanor Du'Tam took here at Frond Tower, when e was a Study. I did not know em before, and I have had no contact since."

Xelle had to force herself to listen, to not be distracted. Yes, Keis. The name popped into her mind, tumbling out of one of those side-room mind cabinets. A quiet senior Study, it also told her. Not even the instructor, but, she'd spend the whole class walking around and assisting the junior Frond Studies. Including Xelle. Had they interacted much? It was all so long ago, such a blur. And Counselor? A Frond Counselor had immense expertise and credibility regarding the minds of hu. Where was this going? She peered in alarm, but Keis did not look her way.

"I will say one thing that I remember clearly about Xeleanor Du'Tam. Whatever e is now, whatever e will be—you can believe every word that Xeleanor Du'Tam speaks. And you can trust every word that e does not. That is my testimony." Still without looking at Xelle, the Mage bowed at the three Spire Mages and left the room.

Was there a reason to not allow for questions? But who would ask them? Why would Xelle question this? And Keis, she was a Frond

Counselor Mage! A Mage not under suspicion and not presenting facts of the case would not be questioned except for clarity.

What she'd said had been pretty clear.

Xelle felt dizzy. What had she done for such a per to remember her? She'd honestly been a bit of trouble when she was here. Barely in her twenties, out of sorts, more than a little full of herself.

A prick hit her arm. Had Frealonn just magically poked her? Oh, well, the Spire Mages were talking. "Any final remarks?"

"No," Xelle and Frealonn said at the same time, with Frealonn adding, "Spire Mages."

"Wait in the adjacent space. You will be notified of our decision shortly," Mage Ba'kea said.

Everyone stayed quiet as they made their way to the box, where Frealonn opened a little case and offered everyone a mix of candied berries.

"Only ingredient, berries," she said, with the tiniest lilt that for her was nearly giggling. Xelle realized then, what it meant for a diplomatic Mage to be eating sticky candy in shades of dark colors. Sure, any Mage could clean their own skin or garments with a simple cast, but the symbolism of eating something messy and stainy, as Na Lleyx would have put it, had a bold and childish quality that did make Xelle smile, as much as the idea of this being a diplomat's rebellion did.

"Thank you," she said, not bothering to clear the sticky candy from her mouth. "Not just for the berries, but all of it."

That really didn't seem adequate, but while Frealonn was jamming berries didn't seem like the time to list all the work the Mage had had to do these past weeks.

"Truth endures," she said.

But did it? Didn't seem like a good point or time to argue.

And Xelle was exhausted. Not tired, just, she didn't realize how much weight she'd been holding until they'd told her the entire transgression was dropped. And she'd be best off having no further contact with the Lunests. There was clearly more behind the scenes on that, and maybe questions she'd need to ask later, but now she felt—well, a lot of things, but first—exhausted.

She slept the whole way back to Grand Tower.

12 - Not in Love

"**Don't.**" Owin's voice rang out from across the room. "Don't put them up. I can't see right with all those colors, and I'm finally getting somewhere with this."

Tenne had thought the colored pods would be bright and cheerful to celebrate Night's Bell, but then Tenne had always made art where he was and where he could, so maybe Owin's art took more—specificity. Anyway.

He took down the display, not wanting to hurt Owin's feelings by telling him how long he'd spent making and welding the brackets for the little lights. Well, he hadn't welded them, but he knew a per that worked the market sometimes who had a little forge. He'd been there guiding it, even with drawings of how it was supposed to connect. Maybe next year would be a better time for them.

Owin was doing super lately, better than he had yet. There were constantly pers by their new home, buying Owin's art, getting Tenne's signature, or another one for a friend, and seeing what new techniques Owin was practicing, so they could buy the latest of that, too.

Tenne hadn't been making his own art lately. Well, just these experiments with lighting. He liked playing with lighting. Pers were fussy about lights at To'Arc, too, so he'd not really had a chance to play until now. He pulled down the last stand. Thing was, Owin was generous with all his success. He gave Tenne plenty of spending coin, and in some superstition or whatever his Ma had instilled in him, Tenne always slid half of it away into his trunk.

Which, apparently, was where these podstands were now going. Tenne didn't want to get rid of them. He liked them, and maybe there'd be a chance to use them, even before next year. Maybe at their wedding. His mouth twitched up, involuntarily. He could picture it. The community gallery, maybe. Decorated in bright colors, scented with iris oil. Tenne loved irises, most of all. Ma had, too.

He glanced over at the artist, stretching down to relax his often-aching shoulders. There was no wedding, not yet. Tenne had brought it up twice, and a third time just seemed sad. Some pers needed more time than others, he knew. Not Tenne's fault he was the less-time sort.

With a sigh, he walked to the window, enjoying the early dark-ening of the end-year sky, and the twinkling of the many lights of Mytil over the low-rolling hills. He wondered what Da was doing. His old friends, at the Tower. But here, here, he had everything he wanted. Art. Freedom. And the per he loved more than any of it.

Xelle cradled the card in her hands. She opened it. And then closed it. Ran her fingers over the smooth, matte-coated front.

Sent in advance, the card contained lovely, hand-inked wishes for Xelle's upcoming birthday. Sent early, because Helia said, as much fun as they had last year, she had a slew of cross-Tower travel and events, all falling around the new year.

There was a separate note too, handwritten with swirly calligraphy on paper that looked like spun sugar. Updates on life at To'Arc, about Helia dating someone special, about Bear's new game of hiding Helia's socks so ae could sleep on them. It was all very nice, very lovely. Like Helia.

She sat both down on the small writing desk she'd bought in Vi'Grand, as soon as her restrictions had been lifted. Xelle had very mixed feelings about starting to make Grand Tower feel more like a home, but the beautifully-painted restored old desk with its backpiece of small drawers had caught her eye, and she was glad she hadn't passed it by.

Dram was waiting outside, his outer cloak covered in fluffy snow, not yet getting into the vroom he'd called. Such formality; it was charming. Xelle would have been sitting in that warm vroom. Maybe she would have even scooted over. Given her date the butt-warmed seat.

"Hey," she said, leaning in for a quick kiss. The conn didn't seem to be looking.

His kiss back was not so quick, and Xelle encouraged it to stay; the feel of his slightly rough, cold lips with a dusting of snowflakes was unexpectedly arousing, and she shivered, not at all from the snow. He stepped back, with a slightly proud grin she found endearing.

They each walked to a door, and opening them about the same time, scooted in. "Hello," Dram said to the conn. "Just to the village, drop us off at the festival loop."

Had this been a standard vroom, Xelle would have expected a cheery "ah, to the lights" or some note of the snow, which was very pretty in the darkening sky and the glow coming off of Grand Tower, but, being Tower staff (and Xelle reminded herself perhaps finding the Spire Staff Mage and the dragonfriend holding hands in xyr vroom a bit of new territory), xe simply started the fuelstones, and pulled gently away toward the village.

"Heard the final paperwork was sealed this week," Dram said.

Small talk, as surely he knew that. "Yeah, I was kind of hoping they'd go after the Lunests for a transgression in filing it, but sounds like Frond thinks it'll be more trouble than it's worth."

"You'll never really know," Dram said. "Towers like to keep things in their pockets. Pers would be shocked if they knew how much the Spires did and discussed behind the drapes, and this had to have torqued off the Frond Spire something fierce."

"Not just Frond, I imagine!" She'd seen how much of Frealonn's time had gone into this. And not for Xelle's company; she hadn't even seen the Mage since.

Dram shifted uncomfortably. "Xelle, you know I can't discuss that."

"Discuss what?" She looked over at him. "Oh, the Grand Spire? I wasn't prying. Seems pretty obvious they'd be extremely concerned about this whole situation, especially being in closer proximity to the Estate and, you know, sheltering their enemy Mage here."

"Well." He shrugged a bit.

It irritated Xelle when he did this. Were they dating or not? He didn't have to tell her anything, but he also didn't have to talk down to her or constantly remind her he wasn't telling her things.

"Well, thanks for still being seen with me." That sounded . . . harsher than Xelle meant, so she tried to correct. "Sorry, I just mean you must have heard the latest from the village."

Xelle was referring to the 'news' that she'd threatened to command the dragons to burn down Frond Village, but by the look on Dram's face, there was something else she didn't know? Firana. "Ash, let's change the subject."

"Sounds good to me. How about this cloak?" He pointed down at her charcoal cloak. "That is . . . top."

"Oh, yeah." She was very proud of her cloak. "I made it myself. I mean, I didn't sew it; a tailor did. But I designed the look I wanted, and the enchantment was fully mine."

Dram nearly shivered. "I mean, I could use an enchanted object if I had to, but to keep part of it inside yourself?"

Well, Xelle thought keeping your ability to cast entirely outside of yourself was a bit cold, herself. Or, she used to think that. Her understanding of wands had grown a lot these last weeks. And speaking of which, she knew better than to ask to see a Mage's wand, but now that she understood composition, she was curious.

"I'm curious what your wand is made from. If you're willing to share." Seemed an annoying addition to someone who had, well, you know, shared a whole lot else, but she knew it was a sacred subject.

"Xelle," he said, calmly, "have I ever asked what color your crown-hair is? What colors have grown into it?"

Was he scolding her, she'd only—

Seeing her expression, he reached out a hand, and rubbed it on her knee. "No, it's fine, I'm just trying to explain how personal that is to me, especially in my position. I'll think about it. About sharing that."

Yeah. Well, Xelle had been thinking about her own wand composition a lot. No, Ollia had not approved this yet, but it seemed to be within her reach. Now she didn't know what to say. What were they allowed to talk about? Was there a list?

"I really like you, Xelle."

The words from the Mage were unusually vulnerable. She reached out and held his hand. Suddenly, she felt without words. So she squeezed.

"Careful," he whispered, moving close to her ear. "Wand hand."

Not sure what to say about that, she hadn't been crushing him in any way, she instead unfolded her hand and rubbed it atop his, until, not too much longer, the vroom was pulling through the streets of Vi'Grand.

"Here you are," the conn said, and wishing xem a good evening, both Xelle and Dram got out, each taking nearly the same cleansing breath in the chill air, then laughing together at the similarity.

Oh, what a difference from the last time she was here! The fall chill now a crisp winter night. The pathway lightpods had been dimmed just to what was safe for walking, and new, small lightpods hung from every post, every sign, every tree branch, in a multitude of colors. Between them, little mirrors and crystals dangled, catching the colorful light, reflecting it, diffusing it. Like the world was a wind of colorful lights, a village of pers invited to fly through it.

"You really aren't cold?" Dram was shivering. Xelle grinned. Not that his being cold was funny, but it was a huness she wasn't used to seeing in the Mage, whose whole job was to look and act official enough to command authority but yet still blend into the background.

He had never put it that way, but she'd been thinking about that.

"No, my cloak adjusts to my needs," she said. Feeling odd about saying it so flippantly, she wanted to add it had taken her months and months of study and practice to even attempt this enchantment, that on top of her many years of Arc knowledge, but what purpose would that serve to say it.

It felt like they were winding up into some sort of competition and Xelle had no space for it. She tried to take this all down a notch. And grinned. "Well, I'd offer it to you, but it only works for me. And it doesn't grow or shrink or anything like that."

She'd meant the last part as a joke, but he nodded as if that were something possible.

"But here, I've got a little warmth." She tapped her lips.

For a moment, it felt like time was irrelevant. A side light of a warm green danced across his eyes, and a purple glow highlighted his cheek, and all the warmth of the world rested in the look he fixed on her, a look not of passion or laughter, but the look of a hu caring for another hu, the look like maybe, he was seeing something beautiful also.

The kiss was not even the best part. Under her cloak, his strong hands slid around her waist, steadying, stable. She could stand like this forever.

Soon, they were walking down the path, glancing both ways at the holiday vendors set up, selling hot drinks, lightpods, decorative banners and hand-held sparkles. "The thing with Frond felt like a timewarp," she admitted. "Feels like forever ago I was here. I was feeling urgency before. Now, it's clicked back on. Just, a need. To get back to it." That was very true, she realized. If all these stops and starts were going to be part of their plan, she was going to have to find a way around that. She was ready to *go*.

"I heard you had some sort of public talk?"

"Yeah." She nodded. "I keep having this feeling like we're letting these pers do all this harm, but there aren't very many of them, and there's a whole lot of pers who just want to live and be nice to each other, and do we really have to just let them have all this power over us? Like, what are we doing about it?"

Dram didn't respond at first. "I'm nervous about you running crossways with the Spire," he finally said.

"The Grand Spire?" Fine, that was obvious in context, but she didn't like feeling talked down to. "I think we're in a good place. I've abided by anything they've laid out, I've worked pretty well in the wand lab, and I kept my head down during the transgression, like they asked me to."

"You made yourself a Mage, but it's like you don't know what that entails."

"Excuse me?" She stopped in place, barely noticing a parent ushering away a group of children. "I have spent years around Mages. I . . ." No, she wasn't going to explain this. "I'd like to know what you mean by that."

"Being a Mage is being part of a system. You don't just do what you want. When you got here, I admired you. I still admire you. But it feels like the answer to being careful not to cross the Spire would be an obvious, yes, thanks for the reminder."

No. No, she was not listening to this. She cut him off, with a wave. "Doing any single thing that not everyone agrees with is not doing what I *want*. I know all about systems. I have taught and mentored Studies through one. I have been dragged into an Alyssia-wide conspiracy of turned Mages and use of transgressions for threats that lost me my best friend, is keeping me away from my other friends, and is causing you to talk to me like I'm the problem. I've been directly attacked thrice. I sat for a year under the thumb of some pompous ash-hole. I've been here nearly a year waiting, acclimating, building trust. I went out and got immediately slammed back in my room. That's done. Finally. And now, I can't, what, talk to the populace? On my own? I need an escort? Or a lecture?"

His voice did not change tone, but there was an edge to it now. "You're taking this the wrong way, Xelle. I'm trying to help you. Do you not know who you are? The dragonfriend? Maybe pers don't know what to do with that, even Mages. But I'm trying to give you good advice, and I cannot protect you if the Spire decides—"

"Whoa." Xelle cut him off extremely rudely, knowing next he'd accuse her of losing her cool and not caring in the slightest. "First, a dragon sigil does not belong to the magesphere. It belongs to the dragons, and then to those they choose to share it with. I do not need your permission for my relationships. Speaking of which, if you are implying in any way what those vile papers are saying, that I am using your position as Spire Staff Mage to—" Seeing a few pers slowing as they passed, she lowered her voice. "To get leeway with the Spire, I assure you I am not and if that's how you view me . . ."

She really didn't know how to finish that statement. Dram was watching her with that Mage look. That measured Mage face. Nothing, nothing could irritate her more in that moment. But this is who he was. She tried to take a breath.

"You're right," he said softly. "I would never think that, and if it came off like a lecture to you, then I was out of line. Here, let's just enjoy the lights for now. I think some pers here are a bit too interested in our conversation anyway."

Now annoyed by that also but not really wanting to show all the ways she was annoyed, especially here when she was finally out of the Lunests' latest trap and hoping to enjoy some ashburned holiday lights for a few flameseared hours, she instead dropped it all (metaphorically) and reached out an arm jovially to Dram, her breath releasing in one big *whoosh*. His face switching immediately to a broad grin, he took it and they strolled together, with the confidence of Grand Tower's newest power couple, until finally, they found a little hill behind some trees and sat, sighing, onto their respective cloaks.

"Hey. That was fun," he said. "All these years here, I'd never actually walked through the lights."

"Oh," Xelle responded, surprised to hear that. "Well, I'm glad I could share them with you."

"I've got to get back though," he said, the true and honest look of a Mage with Tasks on his face. It was such a familiar expression, Xelle felt a burst of affection toward the Mage. "I'll walk back with you?"

"Oh," he said, glancing her way, a visible puff coming out of his mouth. "I'm freezing, and I have so much to do and really, I'd just like to enjoy the night for what it was here in the village and not be seen getting my wand out on the way back or anything like that. Let's get a vroom."

Xelle had a compelling urge to walk.

He leaned in toward her, and she felt that familiar sparking in her limbs. She kissed him, but, what, they weren't going to do anything here in the middle of festival crowds.

"I'll catch up with you soon?" she offered.

He smiled, running a hand over her jaw. More tingles. Can't ignore those tingles.

"I'm super busy all week, I had to put some stuff off for tonight. I mean, I'm glad. But I probably can't go out until after the new year."

"Mage Dram Du'Grand, are you giving me the old 'see you next year'?"

He chuckled. She was glad to hear him laugh. "I look forward to it," he said, leaning in for a long sweet kiss that Xelle savored like a warm mint cocoa. "The per that you are is beautiful and amazing," he added, softly. "Anything I've suggested otherwise is me not knowing how to handle that."

Xelle felt warmed and calmed, if a little uneasy but not in a bad way, by the sentiment. And she wondered, should she tell him about her birthday? He might change his plans if he knew. He didn't seem to know. She did not. She watched, calm, and warm in her cloak, as the quite handsome Mage stood, swept his gloved hand around him to brush off the snow and needles from his finely sewn cloak, and bowed in her direction, touching his lips to send her an imaginary kiss.

She sat there, just a while longer, taking in the lights and holding that little kiss in her hand, as if it had sunk through her own glove and into her palm.

The walk back to To'Grand was no longer chilly, but cold. Xelle was glad for her cloak, and talked to it, not about Dram or the night, but about the lights. How pretty they were. She imagined herself walking through them, and then as she reached her room and started to pull out of her whimsy, realized the face she'd been imagining next to her was no longer the tall Mage, but the awkward Study, Ay'Tea. Surely by now, a Mage himself.

"Ash burns," she muttered, and closed her door shut.

13 - Thirty-One

Xelle sat up in bed. Thunder? Her sigil rattled like it never had. Not a message, not distress, but almost like an overflow from whatever was happening on the other side. Forcing herself to have the discipline to go first to her night garden, she sat on the rather dusty floor, remembering she really needed to make those improvements here and visit more often for cleaning. She sat to sing to the inkbloom, but was flooded with a new emotion, one she'd never felt and couldn't name, as the inkbloom responded in gratitude yet immediately produced two pods, without her request, and urged her to go.

They were helping her now. They'd always helped, this was their magic, but now actively helping her in the pathways. There, there was Thunder, and here, here was a safe place, away from *them*. Xelle appeared, delicately placed onto a wide tree branch. The sky was dark, but she could easily make out Thunder's shape below. Zhey were screaming—screeching, in a tenor so uncharacteristic of the moody but self-confident per. So, an act? She could sense magic now, reminding her she should not cast and reveal her presence. Thunder would know. The connection was open; Thunder knew she was here.

Can you show me, real quick?

Xelle held onto another branch with both hands and steadied herself. A quick, wavering vision came into her mind. Five hu shapes appeared to glow in the darkness. Two glowed differently, oh, those two were Mages, Xelle suddenly felt sure. She almost tried to break the connection and respond, but no, if Thunder was going to get captured, then zhey would. Xelle would monitor it. But, since they'd discussed this, she also knew Thunder now realized zhey had to try and escape so that Thunder's motives were not suspected.

Thunder was pulling against something. Zheir leg, a back leg, was angled awkwardly, attached somehow. But Xelle did not sense much magic; she didn't need to convey any of this to Thunder, as it seemed Thunder could sense the use of magic around zhem, at least its nature if not its cast.

But of course, this area was heavily monitored now. If the Mages didn't want to be noticed until the dragon was in hand, they'd need to minimize any shadow and move quickly.

Her fingers wrapped too tightly around the branch, pressing the bark into her skin. Xelle had not been scared landing here, because she had her magic. Their magic. But letting go of her control atop the branch felt much different and so, unfocused on herself, she only hoped she was hanging on. She forced her focus—the sooner she could assess, the sooner she could be herself again—trying to make sense of the wavering, unreal dragon vision, her gaze landing on Thunder's unmoving leg. An enchanted object. A rope or chain of some sort. She didn't think she'd be able to sense a mild enchantment this far away, but Thunder could see it, see some distortion of the view, as if zhey were seeing more in the line from zheir leg than Xelle could understand. The distortion did not lead directly back to a hu; it was anchored, perhaps around a boulder, or into the rocky ground.

An enchantment, then? Did they have an Ever Mage now turned? Had Irla changed her mind? Of course, as Kern had emphasized, there were many ways to get an enchanted object without literally turning an Ever Mage to your employ. Perhaps this object already existed, it could be any age, for any purpose. Forgotten, saved, there were so many possible stories.

She also realized with urgency, this was another reason to get organized. They could not get by on guesses, old information. Her arms prickled with the need to move, to do something, compounded painfully by her helplessness here, the sharp bark marking her fingers, perched on a branch and seeing, perhaps, through Thunder's eyes as zhey could not leave.

The hu were closing in. Thunder could not just lift up, could not try to break the chain, not an enchantment of any reasonable quality. Zhey screamed now, even louder, screeching with dramatic effect. Xelle had to remind herself that even though Thunder was not projecting zheir emotions to her, zhey knew she was there. If zhey really needed her help, zhey could tell her. She hoped this was a dramatic performance, and any real fear was managed, or not felt, by the young dragon putting zhemself in harm's way.

Fira, Xelle loved this friend.

Then, silence! Silence all around her, a muffled calm, as if sound forgot to exist. A powerful Breath cast, no, not just Breath, she knew Grand was involved. Like the smell of a familiar kitchen, this was simply the place she'd spent the last year. Breath and Grand. Perhaps, then, two of the turned Mages. And, she realized, not Kern.

Then, they must be ready to act, to risk the shadow of magic and be gone before it was noticed and investigated, which might be soon given that any transient, huge wrap would leak some signature—and the ability of an Arc Mage to appear in a second. Well, if they could transport to the signature, but surely inkbloom could help with that. Unless . . . She couldn't think about this now. The hu were moving in quickly. Thunder stayed calm; zhey were so brave! Xelle knew enough now to know that dragons had their own magic. But, to her understanding, and she really thought she would know, Thunder was not using any.

She didn't know if zhey had magic that could influence the enchantment, or at what point zhey'd think about using it. But, oh! She quickly broke the connection, willing away her extraordinary disorientation and staying only in the moment, other than unwrapping her fingers, now stinging from the pressure. She sat up.

Thunder! The enchantment was not likely built for living things, and certainly not for the strength of your mind. I do not believe enchantments are sentient, but they can bend to will; it is their whole design. If you don't want to go now, not this way, then try telling it. The rope, or chain, or whatever they've held to you.

She could no longer see, in the dark, without the lights of a village or Tower. Suddenly, breaking through the sound shield, she heard Thunder's victorious screeching, as zhey flew quickly away. The Mages, they could follow, but then, what? They knew where Thunder was likely going.

Ironic, she realized. If Thunder had told the chain to release zhem, then a strong-forged metal chain might have worked better. She didn't know enough about what dragons could or couldn't do, or how prepared these Mages were to deal with dragon strength, speed, or potentially magic.

And Thunder, zhey would not want to harm the land below, or the hu. That would work to the Hurts' advantage.

Quietly, with the softest of travel casts, Xelle made her way toward the clearing. The hu were arguing, in postures of anger, though she could not hear them or see the features of any Mage present. Then, they were inspecting something. Xelle had to see.

She pulled the tiniest bit on the pathways to see closer, knowing the risk and begging her inkbloom to keep her from tears or snaps. There, she could barely make it out. A ball?

Then, to her surprise, one of the hu tossed it into the air, and before Xelle could make out anything else, they gathered together, and moved quickly away. Likely in a box, from Grand?

She had to know. She glided to the ground, and asked her cloak to give her the shape of the trodden, uneven weeds, to ripple the snow to hide her, and she pulled herself forward, moving with her arms against the very, very cold ground. Then she saw it.

It was a ball. A play ball. The one Xelle herself had made, from twigs in the high mountains, but now stuffed and coated. She dared not touch it, but it gave the sense of light resin and a springy moss. Like something Hall would do for durability and bounce. The Mages, they'd done something to it.

Not wanting to add the pattern of crawling back again, she used the first of the two pods her inkbloom had given her, and appeared immediately and directly into her room at To'Grand.

As she laid down to sleep, knowing there was not more to do tonight, she thought to herself, that thought—she'd had about the solid chain, the other Mages had probably had too.

~

She awoke to a knock, and immediately remembered that today was her birthday. Her thirty-first. The least remarkable of all birthdays, except in this moment to Xeleanor Du'Tam flopped out over disheveled sheets, who was now *in* her thirties. Her point being, Helia was busy, Dram was busy (and didn't know it was her birthday), her parents wouldn't have something delivered (though if she showed up in Tam something would appear very quickly). Kwill would have arrived surrounded by trumpets.

Xelle sat up. Maybe there was a problem. Oh, or something with Thunder. Or an emergency. She rushed to the door, and snugging on her undercap, she opened it.

It was Rayn. Rayn! Mage Rayn Du'Ever, she reminded herself. "I just woke up," she murmured. "Had some stuff happen last night."

The guardrails of safety that the Hurts had yanked from Xelle's trusting mind pinged with worry why Rayn was at Grand Tower and how it had related to— But no, she trusted Rayn and also that was nowhere near here. Thunder had been closer to Arc Tower than anywhere else.

"The caverns echo the tragedy of your awakening," Rayn said, an eyebrow raised. "Would you like me to come back?"

"Hmm? No. No! Please, have a seat." Awkwardly, she realized she'd pointed to her wildly rumpled bed, but just as Xelle remembered this was a decent-sized room and she actually had a table and chairs even if no one used them, Rayn had kicked off her shoes and was leaning back against the bed's pillow with her eyes closed.

"Get comfortable?" Xelle offered.

"Yes, thanks," Rayn murmured. "Sorry, just feels nice."

Xelle found herself gazing at the Mage she'd once met in the vroom and then only a few times since, lying across her bed. Looking so calm like everything was comfortable and here on Xelle's kicked off sheets she could just ignore how odd this was. Like maybe her first year of being a Mage had been harder than she'd thought. Like maybe . . .

Xelle had the sudden urge to kiss her, and she quickly turned away. Xelle was going to have to go dunk herself in ice. What was she doing? She couldn't just be hot for everyone, could she?

The unfairness of the thought snapped back like a drawn bowstring. That was so unfair. And inaccurate. All those years at To'Arc, other than a casual date here or there, the only one she'd ever had true feelings for was Ay'Tea. She'd let that go. She'd . . . ugh, she couldn't cycle through that again. She and Helia had always had good energy, but Helia was off doing her thing now. Dram? Dram flirted with her first and how was it her fault that he had such hot, muscular arms and unique—

She was thirty-one, and she'd barely dated anyone, and maybe that was the issue. Or maybe, maybe Rayn was— No, she couldn't wrap Rayn up in whatever angst Xelle was going through.

"Are you here for my birthday?" she blurted out.

Rayn's eyes opened, but she stayed in place. "I had no idea when your birthday was. Is it soon?"

Xelle scratched her head. "It's today."

Now Rayn sat up. "Oh! What timing. No, I had no idea. Do you have plans? I must be intruding!" She rose as if to leave, but then sort of turned in place, as it was a nice room but not a large room.

"No, please, stay. Here, I have chairs. If you want." Xelle gestured awkwardly toward the table. "And I haven't cooked anything but I can have something brought? Or we could go to Vi'Grand."

Rayn slumped down on a seat at the table. "I'd love to go to the village, but I'm just overloaded with pers right now. But it's your birthday. So, let me know. I'll go."

Xelle understood that. All of it. She pointed. "I can place an order from the best brunch place in Vi'Grand and have it brought here. Birthday treat. For me. And even better with your company."

Rayn grinned. "Do you, um, need to get ready or something? I could wait somewhere?"

This was the point where Xelle realized that she had very much slept in, and she was standing in her room wearing a sleep shirt, an undercap, and underpants. Did she really answer the door without pants? What if it had been . . .

She gestured at herself. "What am I hiding now? I trust you."

Rayn looked away as Xelle pulled on some pants, grabbed a shirt and cap, and some new underwear, and headed off toward the washroom. Her soaps and cloths were stored there, and when she returned, she hoped she looked presentable.

She stopped in the doorway, suddenly realizing she didn't know how to politely ask why Rayn was here. She was glad she was here. They were friends, right?

Rayn broke out laughing, and quickly waved away any questions Xelle might ask. "No, don't try. I understand. I'm here because I've just been to Breath Tower, and I figured I'd keep on out this way. But first, that brunch?"

"Yes, give me a minute. Um, stay here. Or, I mean, you don't have to. You're welcome to." Realizing everything she was saying now sounded ridiculous, Xelle wiggled in some sort of apology (?) and hurried out of the room, to head down to the Front Desk to send a delivery note to the diner, with advance payment and a sizable gift.

"A joyful birthday to you, Mage Xelle." She spun around, surprised by the voice coming from the Front Desk. What was not affection, or extra effort, just the basic respect of a clerk who kept track of Mage events. Including her own. Mage Xelle.

She felt, in that moment, the worst thing she could do would be to invalidate this treasure by letting the clerk know what a treasure it had been. She stopped, gave a slight bow, and said, "Thank you, clerk. Hoping your day finds joy." She added the sign of the Grand, done slowly and deliberately, and waited for the clerk to return it before turning around.

However, the idea did not hold to the friend lounging in her room, as she burst back in with, "The Front Desk wished me Happy Birthday!" She didn't want to add 'because I'm a Mage', but Rayn jumped from her seat and rushed at Xelle with a huge hug.

"You did it!" was all she said.

Xelle, however, felt like her being had been shocked by a combination of lightning, ice, and fire. The hands on her back felt stable, comforting, like she'd just met comfort for the first time.

It was a pretty normal hug. What was getting into her? *Xelle, I know you're repressed or whatever this is, but pull yourself together!*

Still, she let her own hands reach and rest, just briefly, on the smooth fabric of Rayn's back, and felt a nearly physical pain in drawing them away.

Rayn had already turned from her, which was good because Xelle needed to change the subject. Or, start a subject. Firana. "So, what's it like being back at Grand? Oh." She remembered something else. "You said I wouldn't like it here."

Well, that came out ruder than she meant it, but when Rayn turned around, her face was Mageily blank. "You just seemed so at home in your, forest place, and here . . ." She glanced around the room as if there were something to see in the starkly undecorated space. Well, she had the one pretty desk.

"Grand felt like too much pressure to me. Every moment here, I was not one of them. Doubly so. I mean, I'm used to feeling out of place."

Xelle hadn't realized the Stu— Mage felt out of place. She always seemed so comfortable where she was.

"But here it wasn't even my magic. And the culture is so strong. I mean, I loved working in wand lab, they were all so awesome to me, but I always felt like a visitor. Ever just . . . feels more open to more pers. I don't know if Arc feels that way or . . ." She trailed off, and sat down at the plain worktable slash eating table slash . . . Xelle had a sudden desire for a home. A suite. Her own washroom. A bedroom. Somewhere she was allowed to paint the walls.

She wasn't going to say that. She tried to think about what Rayn was saying. The question about Arc. "What I've learned about Grand Magic is that it takes a certain strength of character. No, that sounds terrible, not strength or character! I mean, a need to push through some things. The cultures of Towers are different, you know that, you just said it. And there is something of a dedication here. Like, the way a tree is planted, it stays. It stays a long time. It shelters the plants underneath it. It knows the signatures of the wind, the wind only in that spot." Xelle had no idea if this was making any sense.

Rayn stared thoughtfully. "My mind is spinning," she finally said. "Does it take the transient view of an Arc Mage to understand the flow of our own Tower cultures? When you put it like that, I feel . . . a warmth toward this place. A security. Not of permanence, but of staying. Of how much I did feel that when I was here." She dropped the Magey expression and just leaned back. "Or who knows, maybe I just didn't want you to leave Ever."

Xelle felt a sharp sensation at this, and sat at the table with her friend, feeling now a bit overloaded. "Well, Avail kicked me out, so." The mention of her daygarden had stirred her, also. "Haven't been back to my place either. Figured it would be there, but yeah, time is sort of whizzing by." It felt like it was going faster all the time, like a rope was slipping from a treebranch and she kept noting she should grab it but her hands were always holding something else. It was burning her up.

Rayn made a rather rude noise. "Avail got you in here, right? It was the best thing he could have done." She wasn't looking Xelle's way. "You needed distance from the high rim, a harder yank from Arc. Some separation, to learn to be yourself. My sense of Avail is that you'll have a friend there if you need him."

Noticing the casual reference, Xelle looked her way.

"No, I'm not friends with Crown Mages. As I'm presuming you're not with Crown Mage Da'Selin." She spoke the Mage's name in the standardized, serious-sounding, monotone voice she always used.

"That's funny. And correct. Anyway, just Spire Mage Sandaba." At this point, Xelle just wanted this conversation to go another way. "So, you're here at Grand. Could I ask why, or is there a super-secret Magey reason?"

At this, Rayn beamed. "Actually, one can thank the revolution."

Xelle leaned forward. "Oh, do tell."

"In all this time, I am finally, slowly, wriggling myself from under the saltbags of the 'New Mage' situation. Not just workshops, and more workshops, and not even just Tower assignments, but almost—*almost*—my hand in them." She made a stirring gesture. "I had reason to be at Breath, so I slipped aside to have a lovely evening with young Kwillen." She pointed at Xelle. "See, we should own the age." She paused. "Just turned twenty-nine. And by the face you just made you're probably now thirty."

"Thirty-one," Xelle murmured, resisting the urge to add 'it went fast'.

Rayn waved a dismissive hand. "Ancient. So Kwill is not in a great place right now. I think e needs to leave the Tower, but e's not ready to make a decision like that yet. Plus, honestly, someone who doesn't really care about eir status in the magesphere and yet will be given as much leeway as anyone knows how? E's in a bit of a perfect position for us at the moment. In fact, the idea of it cheered em up considerably."

Xelle could see that. "You know about my transgression?"

Rayn about snorted. "Xeleanor Forestper, *everyone* knows about your transgression."

She felt certain her face was a bit childish, but whatever. "Fine. My point is, I have been a bit constricted here. But, right before that, I had a talk, I guess you could call it, in Vi'Grand at the festival stage. Got pretty good turnout, too."

Rayn was smirking.

"Why are you smirking?"

She shrugged. "Just keeps flying my flags to hear you call it Vi'Grand and not 'the village'."

"Well, did you hear? I'm an Arc Mage. Mage Xeleanor Du'Tam works fine, but I am an Arc Mage. I may not be claimed by Arc Tower, but it is still the Tower of my heart, and Vi'Arc is my village." Xelle grinned.

Rayn cocked her head. "How did that feel? Deciding it? Saying it?"

Uh. Guess the grin didn't hide that part. "It felt scary. It felt like I deserved to be a Mage, but didn't deserve to claim a prong that hadn't claimed me. And . . . it also felt right. Like a wobbling board whose notch finally worked into place. I didn't want to leave there . . . And please, don't say 'go back'."

Xelle was surprised to see visible pain on Rayn's face. She leaned forward. "I need you to believe me that I would never say that. I'm not an Arc Mage, but I know a thing or two about permanence. You'll do what you'll do, but a decision is never the same as when it was made. *Never.*"

That made Xelle feel a new pain. Something inside, a splinter she didn't know how to pull.

"So, in Grand Village?" Rayn's face had brightened, forcibly, Xelle presumed. She was really good at that.

Xelle ran a finger under her cap. Small itch. "Yeah, so I asked pers there. What they thought about the stuff the Lunests were doing. If they'd be interested in learning more. Ash, I don't even totally remember all I said, everything has been a lot."

Rayn nodded. "So that's what I was discussing with Kwill. Turns out, e's a writer."

"A writer?"

"Mm hmm. Has kept journals for years on Breath Tower. E wouldn't say on what, but my guess is, they're pretty good."

Xelle had already been thinking about some kind of publication.

Seems Rayn had too. Then, she supposed, in the face of well-funded lies, getting the truth out did seem a logical step. "So does Kwill want to write for the revolution?"

Rayn grinned, and Xelle could only imagine she was remembering some rather clever joke of Kwill's. But, then, that was it. Kwill wasn't just famous, e was clever. Witty as all sunrise.

"E does. But e said if we're going to influence sentiment, we need a lot more than a writer. We need at a minimum organization, publicity, eye-grabbing art."

"Eye-grabbing art would not be me," Xelle thought, not liking the other two at all. She was good at organization, but didn't enjoy the mental strain of taking on others' as well as her own, or the feeling of getting stuck doing it. And publicity? Ugh.

"Nor could I join that dance," Rayn said. "And, look, I can organize, but I quite resent always having to be the one to do it."

Xelle laughed. "I was just thinking the same."

"We'll have to divide it up somehow. Kwill felt strongly that the leadership should stay, for now, in our initial group. And I don't even know how to start finding a publicity per, but you have substantial notoriety mountainside, and I have substantial notoriety sunward."

Xelle's eyes widened. "Ash, I forgot. You're the Spice Lord. I completely forgot about all that."

Rayn groaned with guttural release. "And thus we begin. I am not the Spice Lord. I am of said family in Sharre, and I do love and have exceptional talent with spices, but I dated the mayor's hot cura, decided she and her whole family were a glob of nope, got in a bit of a brine over it, and ran off to study Magic." Her eyes narrowed. "I know you're dealing with dragonfriend, Xelle, and I can't imagine what that's like, honestly, but I also can tell you, you don't know what it's like being born with it." She looked like she had more to say, but whatever it was deflated into a long sigh.

"I know you didn't run off," Xelle said, softly. "It feels that way, but it was a catalyst. To a change I think you needed."

Rayn's face scrunched even further. "Now look at you, Mage Gives Advice She Could Use Herself."

Xelle thought about Ay'tea. Why? Why then? She hadn't thought of him as often lately, but she thought of him now. About their lab. He'd called her good at organization. Good at analysis. But he'd never pushed it on her. They'd worked together, picking each other up when the other tired. Oh, she couldn't think about this now. But. Oh.

"Why don't we work together. What do you say, about the roads take us to the same place?"

"What? Not that. But go on."

Xelle saw something new in her eyes. A little light. Maybe this would work. Be a good way forward. "We could be partners. I used to co-run a lab. It can work so well if the two pers . . ." Now how was she supposed to finish that.

"Let's try it. We're doing this for a good cause, so it's not like we have to worry about someone being a stink. If it doesn't work out, company reorg. Deal?"

She looked nervous. But how to seal it? Of course. Xelle slowly made the sign of the Arc, and held it.

Looking like she'd been awaiting the gesture in the process of a well-known ceremony, Rayn stood tall and made the Ever, somehow in the most elegant way Xelle had seen, fingers not curling toward herself, but curling as if aware of all things, all at once. She felt a shiver.

Rayn lowered her hand. "So we still need that artist. Know any trustworthy yet equally famous artists who could use a gig?"

Xelle snorted a bit helplessly. "So you know I'm from Arc Tower. Or, spent some time there. Once upon a time I made the acquaintance of a certain Bon Tenne Du'Mytil."

"Why on Alyssia would he——" Rayn stepped back, bumping into Xelle's dresser. It wasn't that big of a room. Then, she knew. She guessed. Well, if Xelle didn't have a story for it, she'd probably know. Xelle let her. Their eyes met.

"You're comfortable contacting him?"

Xelle nodded, silently.

"Hey, you have a full load today? Well, not on your birthday?"

Xelle was supposed to be in the lab today. She hadn't asked for it off, because she'd anticipated feeling blue and wanted the distraction. But she hadn't slept well. She was distracted. Doubly now. Tripley. Triply? Anyway, she'd be no good there. "You'll be around?"

Rayn ran her hands over her Mage chain, new and without charms except for one green-bejeweled pin, marking her Tower. "I should be heading back. But really, as long as I'm there by morning, what would they care?"

"I just need to send a few notes. And check on brunch? Feel free to wait here, or, whatever you want."

Xelle stopped by the wand lab, told Ollia she'd had a difficult night and at the same time an old friend was here, but only for today. Ollia asked if she needed anything, and then told her she'd see her after the break. "Mage Xeleanor?" she added.

"Yes, Mage Ollia?"

"Thirty-one doesn't feel as long ago to me as it was. Make them all count. For you, also."

Xelle sort of bumbled out of the lab after that, and hurried down to the Front Desk, just as the order from Vi'Grand was arriving. "I've got that," she said. "No need to deliver." She flipped out a small packet of hash-browns, with a mark on it. "Roots, spice, and oil?"

The clerk nearly giggled, taking the warm package. "Thank you!"

Xelle winked, glad to see the clerk smile like a regular hu.

And soon Xelle was setting out the items she'd picked across the room's plain Tower-issue table. A soft scramble with a mix of finely shredded green onions, seared roots, a spicy sausage, and a thick, peppery, garlic cream. And a sealed bag of fresh green juice—the actual green kind, not apple juice with a leaf or two in it—which she poured into two waiting cups.

They ate for a while in contented silence, Xelle amused to see that Rayn also ate in reverse order, and they both saved the sausage until last. Rayn tapped her fork against her last one, before spearing it. "What's in this? There's something I can't place. Me."

Xelle was pleased to know the answer, because once this summer, she'd eaten there and been so overwhelmed by the quality she'd near-annoyed the chef (oh, he was delighted) over it. "Two regional things, I'd never had them either. One is in the filling. It's made from a specific tree nut that only grows in the Grand Region forests. Sounds like just a nut, but apparently it's got its own . . . nuttage." Rayn's eyes cut over, squinting a bit. "The other is something they call sharpleaf, but I've had sharpleaf, my kind of it anyway. This one only grows in the under-cover deep in the forests here. They aren't rare or anything, just a local taste. Makes you wonder how many other secrets Grand is hiding."

"I don't even wonder," Rayn said through her last few bites. "This place is loaded with secrets. I got that right away. All Towers are, but here, I don't know, there's something different to it. The secrets aren't even secret."

"Yeah," Xelle agreed. "I know what you mean." The Mage's chin was drooping. "Are you ok?"

"Mmm. Sorry, I'm just so tired. And full belly. They've kept me going, and then travel, and then—" She yawned, rather hugely. "I've got a full teaching load when I get back. Not sure how much use I'll be for this partnership."

"I've still got my place there. I can travel." Seeing Rayn, thinking of her daygarden made her yearn for it, actually. Suddenly, Grand felt like less of a home. But, she needed to stay here. She knew that. For what could be quite a long time.

"We can figure it out."

Rayn's speech was nearly slurring, and Xelle decided one thing. Business partner or not, this Mage needed a nap. To Rayn's mild protests, she hurried to find a change of sheets, remade her bed, and tried to fold it over like an inn host. "I'll check in. Make sure you get back tonight. Do you need transportation?" Xelle wasn't sure she had the clout to get Rayn flown back to the Tower, but Rayn said no, she had borrowed an enchanted seat, and she'd be fine flying it. Just needed a rest.

"Thank you for the rest. I'm sorry, we should be—"

Awkwardly, Xelle folded the blanket over the now sleeping Mage, who was quite a bit too tall for Xelle's compact bed, so Xelle tried to wedge a pillow under her feet, and hoped it wasn't too uncomfortable.

"Hallina bless me," she worried. Then, wanting to give the Mage her privacy, Xelle stepped out, deciding it was a good day to work her laundry and organize her books. And yeah, a whole lot of these needed to go back to the Grand Library where some librarian Mage was undoubtedly tapping her name on a list.

Just before sunset, she walked in to find Rayn sitting groggily on her bed, pulling her cap down over her undercap. "Did I really just sleep?" She sounded distressed. Xelle knew it. Disorientation after a nap. The hangover of life.

"You needed it," Xelle said. "But, you also need to get back?"

Rayn stood, wobbling on her legs. "I do."

"Are you sure you'll be fine?" Xelle worried at the wobble.

"I promise you," was all she said.

That was enough for Xelle. "Well, then, we'll be in touch?"

"Yes," Rayn said. Turning around, just in the doorway, she added, "The paths wind heartward."

Huh? "Sorry?" Xelle was trying to figure the meaning.

"It's a Sharre phrase. You muddled it earlier. Just thought you might want to know."

"Oh, yes. Travel safely?"

One side of Rayn's mouth curled. "I will."

14 – Expensive Tickets to the Wrong Show

The new year came and went, and Xelle, having a week with all the labs closed, decided it was time to pay an artist a visit. "You've really not been to Mytil?" she asked, pulling Dram's arm close in the box as it skimmed over the rocky land approaching the city.

The two-Mage rule was for flying higher than was safe. As long as everyone involved were Mages of any prong, a low flight only required one Grand Mage. "Never. I've been to all seven Towers, all throughout Wehj, and quite a few trips to Satta and Vattam, but never been to Mytil."

"Well." Xelle felt nearly giddy. "You are in for so many delights. Mytil is a city of art. It feels the passing of the seasons, and enjoys them with equal passion. It is sewn of monochromatic patches, layered together with all the colors of nature and creation alike."

"Let me guess. We're headed toward the big art gallery first."

Xelle had to cast out a piece of spit that lodged into her airways, causing her to cough violently. Dram looked over in concern. "Sea dive, Xeleanor, are you well?"

"Yes, sorry. I mean, thank you. I, uh, the art gallery is off limits for a bit still."

Now he actually looked concerned. "Is there something I should know about?" He didn't sound to be joking.

"In your position? No. But, anyway, Mytil is filled with art, no need to visit a gallery. Indoors and outdoors, it's our love."

"At the new year? Isn't that a bit cold?"

"Yes, but you've dressed appropriately." She hadn't wanted to hear any further whining about his cloak, so she'd made sure he wore his good outdoor robe set. "You'll be fine. It's barely colder than Grand, you won't feel the difference."

"Sure than Grand Tower, but much colder than Wehj."

Why did this matter? He was dressed for the cold. Anyway, they were getting close and she needed to figure where to go first. She wasn't just going to spring Tenne on him. She'd thought about the Enchanted Forest, but somehow . . . Not today.

"See there, those streets that look like a quarter-rune." Apparently Dram never took runes. "Just here, follow my cast." She threw out a directional flag in front of them, knowing he could easily follow its shadow, and guided them down into the old part of the shopping district.

"Everyone has the fry, right?"

"You mean fried food?"

Xelle stared at him a moment. He was serious. Come to think of it, in all her time in Vi'Grand, she had not been to a fry. *Hallina.* "Oh, you're not ready." He did not respond to this, as she led him to a bright red door surrounded by garish, wonderfully joyful (to Xelle) signs. "So first, we go through here and buy the food we want to cook." She lowered her voice. "It's all marked down because of the cooking fee."

Dram looked at her skeptically.

"Come on, it's fun." She led him through the icy trays of sliced curds, presses, mushrooms, roots, and onions, recommending the ones she liked the most. "No, really, it looks plain, but that's the best one," she said, pointing at a white curd. "Get some of this sauce. Now, here, you pick from these dough squares and/or batter bowls. See, the ingredients are listed here. I mean, you don't have to take any of either, but then you can roll things up and eat them together. Every bite an adventure."

Perhaps realizing that everyone else was perfectly calm and not paying attention to him at all, Dram finally relaxed, ordering them both a spiced spirit, and watching with interest as Xelle showed him how to select an oil and a pot, adjust the temperature, and then lower a skewered piece of battered sunpetal into the now-sizzling oil. "Or watch this," she nearly giggled, carefully lining up a gorgeously fat green onion segment, the white curd, a pickled pinkroot, and a drizzle of brownsauce onto a dough square, folding and pinching it, then lowering it in her grated ladle until the perfect amount of gold bordered its edges.

"I ate too much," Dram finally groaned, leaning back. Xelle liked this side of him. It was fun to see the proper Mage leaning back and nearly burping fry oil.

"It's a sometimes thing. You'll be fine." She grinned.

"I thought this was a city of sophistication," he said, lightly.

Xelle's eyes surely flared. "There is nothing. Nothing. More sophisticated than the fry. And on that note, I do have an artist I need to see."

He was attempting to wipe his face with a checkered napkin. "Why are we visiting an artist again? A custom purchase?"

Oof. She hadn't really thought through the reasons for this. But she didn't want to make anything up either. "Oh, I just want to offer an opportunity. Something related to one of my friends, so I thought I could do it in person plus show you the fry. He won a big prize here and has mega connections to Arc Tower. So, like, all in the family." She smiled.

They made their way across town, Dram still groaning whenever other pers weren't in view. Had he eaten more than her? Xelle felt fine. "This should be it," she said, looking up at a lovely small home, plain in design but surrounded by a colorfully painted fence, which had nearly its own glow in the golden hour light.

She stepped up, and knocked on the door. A tall, muscular (don't judge; she noticed) hu answered the door. "Hello, I'm looking for—"

"Tenne," the hu cut off. "An admi." Without giving her another look, he (she assumed this was Tenne's romfriend?) walked inside.

Suddenly feeling a bit Magey and not needing to be left on a porch, she boldly strode inside. Dram followed. Funny, for all his knowledge of protocol, he trusted her here. Actually, that was sweet.

Tenne stopped, stunned, walking into the room. His mouth opened and closed.

"Hello, wonderful to see you again. I'm here to talk about an art project. Maybe we can step away?"

"He hasn't even been making art," the hu said.

Xelle was tired of this already. She turned to face him. "Hello, I'm Mage Xeleanor Du'Tam. This is Mage Dram Du'Grand. You are?"

He made a pfffty noise, and then bowed. Sort of. "Honored. I'm Owi'neil Du'Hubo, he. Call me Owin. An artist. Sounds like you know Tenne here."

Xelle did not like this hu. She felt guilty thinking it. Hadn't Klein said Tenne was in love somewhere? With this hu? Hopefully not this one? She looked around. This hu was definitely at home. She bowed, deeply and stately, "Bon Tenne. Perhaps we can step aside?"

"Uh, yeah," Tenne said.

She shot Dram a look. The hu was practically a diplomat, he could work that here.

To her relief, he engaged immediately. "Owin, is this your art? We're always looking for new pieces for our exhibits; would you show me what you have?"

Xelle gave Tenne a rather piercing look, and the two walked back into a room. She leaned in. "Does he sense casts?" Tenne shook his head. Xelle reached into her fry-augmented material and cast a quick swirl around them.

"They can't hear us now. The Mage, he could break in, but he won't. I trust him."

"The Mage? I've seen the type. He didn't come here on business."

What flame-seared nonsense was this? "So? We're dating. Same as you, right?" Not the same, why did she call it the same?

"No, not the same. We're in love." Tenne stood taller, which was a bit of a feat given the hu was already huge. Well, tall. Owin was both. And that was a sting. Should she argue? No, she was better than this.

"I might just leave, actually."

"You came here."

Damn it. "Look, I'm not a diplomat. I'm an Arc Mage who is real tired, ok? I have a chance to help your Da. Help all of us. And I'm not going to grovel to you. It just, seems like a you thing."

Tenne plopped down on a stool, knees flopping to each side. "What's a me thing?"

She at least didn't have to worry about secrecy with the young artist. Not with what she knew. Not a threat, just a reality. "We're fighting back. Against the pers who hurt you and your Da." That said, she wasn't going to tell him who yet. Not here, not like this. Not until he demonstrated he was in. And probably more beyond that. If he guessed he could guess. She looked at his expression. He was not trying to guess.

"They are issuing a publication dedicated to spreading lies about me and now my friends. It sounds like, who cares, but I've started to understand the harm that can be done by words and lies and weirdly devout followings. Why us? Well, I just happened to be the guy who's friends with a dragon and also the kind of per who helps her friends including when they are dragons, so here we are."

"What?" Tenne made a rather rude gesture. "Do you hear yourself when you talk?"

"I do," she snapped confidently. "And I think I'm pretty cool. And what I am here about, is we are going to start our own publication, dedicated to the truth." She almost said 'wherever that falls' but that wasn't entirely true either. They had to hold some cards. Ugh, that was something to parse through later. "I don't want to play a power game, but I also don't want to lose one. And we've been reliably informed that in order to be a thing pers want to get, we need something extra. Like eye-catching art. A famous name attached to it."

"Mageshit. You're dragging me in."

No. This bothered her. "I'm not dragging anyone. I'm here *asking*. And if your answer is no, I leave. And feel pretty sure you won't have to deal with me again."

"What does starchy-pants know?"

What? "If you mean Mage Dram Du'Grand, he is not involved in this."

Tenne nodded. "Didn't think you trusted him."

Xelle was actually getting mad. "I absolutely trust him. You know how Towers work. He is a Spire Staff Mage. Do you know how absolutely trustworthy that makes him? He's one of the pers with the most influence in the world, and—" She wasn't sure where to take that.

"And yet you don't want him in your little club. Telling." Tenne shifted. "Look, I'm not trying to be a dip here. But you can't act like this is all business. What you're asking is personal. Big personal. And you, you're an artist. In your own way. The way you cast. The way you imagine. Your aura of angst, as Ma would have said. Mage Dram Du'Grand out there. I know his type. Solid. Steadfast. Like whole grain bread."

"Excuse me? Where do you get off talking about my romfriend like you're Advice Hu when your romfriend is the Bad Vibes Express? Let me guess. Always knows best. Won't let you do stuff you love to do."

All fires of eternity, though, he was right about Dram. Xelle knew it, but he'd been fun to be around, and *Fira.*

"No one has ever loved me like he does," Tenne nearly growled.

Well, Xelle was all off her balance now. Guess this was happening. "Owin? He's hot, I'll give you that. Probably cranks the engine pretty well. But your Da, *he* loves you. Look, Mages, they learn to close off. It's—"

"How are you a Mage? Du'Tam? That's not a thing."

"It is because I said it was."

Tenne, suddenly quiet, seemed to be gazing right at her and somehow not at the same time. Xelle realized her hands were shaking.

"Actually," he said, leaning back on the stool while holding its edges, "that's pretty baller."

Xelle actually threw her hands out. Then started laughing. "Well, we're starting a revolution. Want to draw for it or not?"

Tenne now sat still, and was slow to respond. Xelle waited.

"Devout following? I know something about those. Who are these pers, Xelle? I don't know much about you but I know this is going to be something."

Well, here was the one per not following her news. She took a breath—and changed her mind. "Mark Du'Lunest and Irla Du'Lunest."

"Shit."

To what Xelle realized was her own relief, Tenne didn't seem scared of that. Just . . . understanding of the gravity.

"Pers like that, I don't get them. Well, I do, I just don't want to. I know, the magesphere has its full quota of greedy bilebags, but at least they're limited by their own pretenses. These populace types. Lunests. The Landpack. Selte Du'Wohl. Trader Jay. Augalio Du'Satta. Lerf." He trailed off. "Who's the writer? You want an artist, so you must have a writer, and I'm guessing it's someone with name."

"Kwillen Du'Satta. E's—"

Tenne snorted. Loudly. "I know who e is. Wait, you're telling me a Mages of Satta kid wants to lead a revolution with a Spire Mage kid."

She hadn't actually talked to Kwill about which artist, but, not wanting to negate this rather lovely framing, she stood, and waited.

"Sure, I'll talk to em. Might be fun. Not deciding yet." He pointed at her. "But I'm interested."

Xelle sighed. "Well, I don't want to be back here too long. I told Dram I had an opportunity to offer you. But nothing that sounded like a big deal."

Tenne raised an eyebrow.

"Keep it clamped. We need a story why we're talking, in case anyone gets too interested before we figure this out." Xelle was terrible at excuses. She really just liked the truth. "And also why we're talking to Kwill. My situation at Grand is also a bit sensitive right now," she admitted.

"That part's easy. I'll go talk to em. Just on my own. Super easy for me to want to meet em. Sort of thing that happens all the time. Front Deskers will gawk like they're watching birds mating."

Like what? Better to move on from that. "E lives at Breath Tower."

"Oh. Yeah, that's helpful to know which one. As for you, I found out that the per who I got in trouble at Arc for visiting me at the Gallery was actually the dragonfriend, and so I asked you to come back. Thought it would be cool. You took the opportunity to ask me about what you'd meant to ask me for in the first place—a commission for one of your Arc friends. If I don't join your thing, it fades away, and if I do, you want to use my name, anyway, right? Can't just be for my skill."

Two things in that. One pushed its way to the front. "Using your name would risk someone exposing what happened."

Tenne laughed. Not a happy laugh. More of an angry snort. "I wanted to tell pers, remember? So if they know, they know. But it sounds like as long as Da is still involved, they won't. And if anything, they want to keep us apart. Now, if Da gets out, like out of the situation, feels like Ol' Tenne's art prize would be the least of the cans to catch then, right?"

That all . . . made sense. "Do I want to know how you're so quick at coming up with things like this?"

Tenne just shrugged. "Growing up in a Tower. I'm an expert on mageshit."

What did he call it? Gross. Anyway. One more point needed clarification.

"Did you paint this?" It was a large trunk, covered in whimsical little animals wearing all sorts of fun outfits, playing and running atop splashes of color. It matched what he'd said before, about painting playgrounds.

"Yeah. That's just my trunk. Doodle stuff." He glanced at it awkwardly.

"Then I need you to know I am absolutely here for your skill. These friends of yours," she leaned in, "they are delightful. I feel joy looking at them. I am absolutely here for your skill."

"Oh," Tenne said. "Thanks."

"So how did it go?" Dram finally asked, as they turned a corner of the night market. Between Xelle's own distractions and feeling a lot of overwhelming emotions being here, in Mytil, with many of the holiday lights still dancing through the market, she realized she'd been pretty quiet.

"Turns out, he's a lot," she answered. "One of my friends at Arc was super excited about having something made by him, and I finally got an invitation back."

That part didn't feel very honest, and she didn't like the words falling out of her mouth. But she felt too tired to come up with anything other than what Tenne had planted there. Besides, Dram really didn't need to know.

And yeah, she was thinking about that, too. What Tenne had said. Rude and unnecessary but he just . . . wasn't wrong. Forget love, when would anyone love her. Was she really thinking this Spire Staff Mage, someone who acted every bit a proper Mage when he wasn't out at sports or, well, in his underclothes, was going to be fine when Xelle started organizing? Outside of the magesphere? Sure, he was pretty tolerant, if a bit wimpy at the fry. But Xelle could be a Mage because Grand Tower had accepted her as a Mage. But a whole revolution? Dragons as friends? Actually taking on the Lunests? What would happen the first time she actually had to cross the magesphere, not just irritate it. Balance was one thing, and she was grateful for Ollia's advice on that. She would be careful of the magesphere now, careful to find that balance. But that didn't mean she was going to slide back into line.

There was too much else at stake.

And the hu next to her, he still felt like a stranger. She shouldn't have brought him here. She didn't . . .

Burn it.

"I've never seen someone care about your friends the way you do," Dram noted.

"Thanks," she murmured, not sure where to stack that on top of everything else.

"And if you think your artist was a lot, you should have met the other one. Owin is marvelously talented, but I'm not so interested in calling back on a per that legitimately unpleasant. Seems to have your friend tied in knots."

"He's not my friend," she heard herself saying. "But yes, on the knots."

15 - *Fifty Ways*

She wanted him really bad. But she couldn't. Not knowing what she was here to do. "Dram, please, listen to me."

He stepped back. Now he saw it in her eyes. The very air in the room seemed to disintegrate. She was now a hu standing on a rickety stage, with a really important, well-dressed, handsome Mage standing in front of her.

"I need to end it, between us."

Dram, uncharacteristically, squeezed his hands against the back of a chair. "Look, I know I can be too reserved. It's a thing I do. I really like you, Xelle. I, you know, get funny about our positions sometimes, but really, it's cool. We're cool. And you're funny. And you see things a way I can never see them, and— If you need some space, that's fine. But we don't need to cut the rope if it just needs some slack."

A very strange sensation came over Xelle. She felt thirty-one. And the hu across from her was not a child. He was a full-grown hu, a Mage. In Mage robes, with a chain, and access to some of the most powerful Mages in the world. It was like, she had been in the pathways. Ever since, well since that day. And just arrived here. At a new part of the world. Older. Confused. And a hu, a very impressive hu, whom she quite liked, actually wanting to be with her.

Did she know what she was doing?

She only wanted to cry. She just wanted to cry. And she didn't want Dram to see that. Didn't want him to see her cry.

Oh.

"I can't do it. I'm so sorry, Dram." She wanted to say something nice, like he was a piece of her now. A part of her life. But, he wasn't.

As galecaught—as horrible—as she felt right now, she knew, in a year, five years, she'd not be thinking of him.

He looked awful. He looked upset. She wanted to comfort him. But she couldn't. She just wanted to cry. To be held. And that's why, she knew now, she could only leave.

It wasn't enough. It wasn't even appropriate.

She ran from his room, travel casting down the stairwell to her own. She closed the door, locked it, cast around her. And wept.

One could always tell a letter from Helia. Perfect writing, beautiful stationery. Carefully placed coordinating printed paper strips.

Xelle had been staring at it for nearly an hour.

She'd thought of Helia, this last week. She admitted it. Running off, to find her, to sink into her arms was all she could think about so very many times, as her emotions lifted, crashed, and lifted again. As pers whispered about her, thinking she wouldn't notice. As she found herself staring at a wall in the wand lab being tapped by a wand case by an impatient labmate, feeling at the center of all emptiness, and worse, that she had put herself there.

Those were the reasons she didn't reach out.

Thinking it that way, she didn't even really know which reasons she meant. The confusion. The emptiness.

She opened the note and read it again.

Mage Xeleanor!

I hope this letter finds you well. I have some exciting news that I would not want to get to you before I had a chance to tell it. I hoped for a visit, but I've already taken a hungry share of time off, and my task list is much less tidy than I prefer.

But – I hope that I will see you soon. There is something about an upcoming event that I would like to ask you myself. The event? Oh, this is the first time I have written this. I am engaged to be married. I don't think you know him, as he moved here from Ever Region for the employ of Arc Tower. Oh! He works construction for the Tower. His name is Drae Du'Estia, he, apparently it's a small village deep in the Forest. (He doesn't add the 'deep' but it does sound a bit more mystical to me that way.) Probably to you too.

We will hold a ceremony in the fall, when my current project is done, and I can manage to be away for a short break from Tower life.

I hope things are going well with the Mage you are dating, and I look forward to seeing you one day not so far from now.

With my love,

Helia

Xelle's heart was pounding and she couldn't sleep.

She'd made the right decision with Dram. She knew that, in the specifically painful way a right decision can fester around the edges of its peace. She felt even more terrible about herself. Terrible she wasn't strong enough to even comfort him, when she could see how upset he was. Terrible about everything. And she was thrilled for Helia. Xelle could have married Helia. She'd had that chance! She'd never thought of it in those terms. She'd just been . . . She didn't know. And she'd been vulnerable when she read that note. Maybe she'd been vulnerable down the branch lately. What was getting into her?

She tried to pull on the night ivy. But like she'd felt in the room, with Dram, it was like the pathways had shifted, just so, like she couldn't quite grasp around them. They were there, and she was here, but she couldn't connect.

She felt in between spaces, like she might just fall through.

She tossed, and turned, and wondered if she'd ever sleep.

Where was she? In her room, but not her room. Confused, she reached around in worry, and heard a whisper.

"I'm here. It's ok."

He was here. Emotion poured through her like a wind, a vibration, feelings that had no name, but she saw them, like wavy lines, passing through her, not leaving, but lightening. Dissipating.

He was here. She was so glad he was here.

He was here. He wanted to be with her. He reached for her. An arm, over hers, and what was left of her understanding melted. She released, she let herself be held.

He was here.

It was ok.

Xelle sat on her bed. Groggy. Confused.

She remembered the struggle. But then nothing since. A peace. Not just the passing of distressing nightpaths, but the sense of finding one, and sleeping in it. True sleep. A feeling of peace, and comfort. One she had not felt, since before. Before all this. Before her petition.

Whatever it was, whatever dream, whatever place she had found in the night ivy, or through which the night ivy had found her, she thanked the universe for allowing her any moments of it, even if the morning effect was more pain. More loss. Inside her, the inkbloom glowed. It was not them, but they knew what had happened.

Xelle still did not.

"So what was with those Mages, anyway? The one you left me with was as pleasant as murky cardstock."

Tenne chuckled. "That one that talked to me? That's the dragon-friend. From Arc Tower, though apparently she's off at Grand Tower now."

Owin turned back toward his canvas. "I still don't know or care a thing about these places or these pers. I assume Grand Tower is huge and Arc tower is curved. And none of them are anywhere someone like me needs to be. Your dragonfriend and cardboi did not change my opinion on that one iota."

There were days Tenne still couldn't imagine what it would be like to grow up completely and totally out of the magesphere. Forget growing up, Tenne still wasn't used to being out on his own. His own place. He looked around, at the art-covered walls of the spacious peach-walled room.

"Yeah, well, dragonfriend means she's friends with a dragon. I thought it would be cool to meet her, and talk about a project she'd brought up once, before I knew she was the dragonfriend."

Owin spun around. "You don't really believe that, do you? That dragons are real?"

Tenne couldn't help an annoyed expression at this. "An entire Tower saw her with one. Mages are real serious about stuff like that. An entire Tower did not make that up."

"They were probably all high," Owin said. "Half the stuff Mages do is drug hallucinations. Look, I grew up in the mountains. We used to sell the stuff to them."

"You sold drugs?" Tenne didn't care if it was up and up, but he did feel weird that hadn't been mentioned before.

"No not me, you lug, I was a little kid. But down at the main tavern. Mages were there all the time, feeling the spirit of the mountains."

Tenne's arms prickled a bit at this. "First, don't call me a lug again. Second, Mages being at a mountain tavern does not mean they are buying drugs. I'm not a big Tower admi, right? But you're just talking through your ass about all of this."

"Settle down." He wiped off his brush. "Maybe what you need is a good screw."

Well, Tenne was not one to turn down a—

"Tighten those loose boards in your head. Here, I'll be the dragon and land on you. Forget Grand Tower. They call mine Huge Tower."

Normally Tenne thought Owin's jokes were funny, but now he was kind of pissed off. And decided he'd take him up on the offer. "Come and get it, dragon."

It wasn't much longer until they were together, wrapped, wrestling through their own sweat, until they collapsed, each on their own side of the huge bed. Tenne looked up at the fixture. "I saw a cool piece of worked glass down district. Thinking about putting it in here."

"Mmm?" Owin rolled over. "Nah. I like that one."

"Sure, but this one would add some color to the room. It's our house, anyway."

Owin smiled. "It's my house, but maybe soon we'll go together and you can show me your light. Perhaps I can be convinced." He ran a finger along Tenne's jawline and then down his chest.

Tenne shivered. "It's our house. We brought people in together, a team, right?"

"Whatever makes you happy to think, but it's my art that's selling, and the only thing you own in this house is that patchy trunk and maybe a suit of clothes. Now, I've got a painting to finish. Don't mind the view," he added, rising up, all the lines and turns of his body in full view.

Suddenly, Tenne felt awful. Just . . . awful. "One more for the road?" he asked. And Owin quickly agreeing, Tenne took a new energy. One that had just awakened in him. And he loved Owin so hard, so well, that this time, the hu rolled over and fell asleep.

Tenne got up. He took a shower, and ate a meal. He rummaged through the wardrobe and took his best, coolest set of clothes, and a set of outerwear, and whatever underwear and socks he could cram around the items in his trunk.

He pulled the trunk outside, where it slid pretty freely across the sheets of ice alongside the road.

He didn't look back.

16 – Fight Moves

I am nudging my special ball. The hu shapes glow around the backs of trees and taste like dirty spirit; they think I cannot sense them.

Firefriend is wrong that I do not think enough. Everyone thinks repeatedly for years and years while so many beings feel painful emotions. All the homedragons think. Everyone should think. Not all hu think. We think. I think. This is a truth, but a partial truth is a snappy truth. I think many times, all the time. I also decide to do.

I make a happy sound, I flap my wings. I am nudging my special ball around, not yet playing, but showing how happy and excited I am to see it is still here. I do not show my anger that they spread dirty spirit onto my special ball that tells them I am here.

There are two hu this time, only the ones who fly on spirit. One who winds with a spirit stick, and one who tastes. This is not the hu firefriend knows. That one flies the pathways directly, and like firefriend, would taste like flowers.

I would step on that hu's little spirit stick if it were not sacred. Instead, I toss my ball into the air. Then, I catch it. I land on the ground and try to fly again, but the air is thick and smells so dirty, and—

From what Thunder had conveyed, a Grand Mage and a Breath Mage had worked together to poison her friend. Xelle had no idea how they'd moved zhem, how they'd not been detected or who they'd threatened or bribed not to be, but Thunder was now in a large, spacious yard.

Zhey showed Xelle what looked like food and water, and then a ceiling made of a steel cage. Thunder showed that when zhey breathed fire or tried to reach it, zhey were pushed away, and the pushing hurt.

Thunder didn't know if zhey could break out of it, but since zhey wanted to be there and were very clear about disliking the stinging feeling of the cast, for now zhey were not going to try.

Xelle hoped Thunder could not sense her crying (though certainly zhey could) when she saw zhey still had the ball they'd both made, and zhey had room to play with it. Zhey emphasized over and over that it did not smell bad anymore, something about zheir playing with it had bothered one of the Mages, who'd removed the tracking cast.

Xelle suggested that they should talk every day, at least briefly, and Thunder agreed, though sending her a poorly-constructed image of an egg. She'd laughed. *If it helps,* she'd said, *you'd do the same for me.*

Study Kwillen Du'Satta was really kind of weird. The hu oozed resentment for being a Study, despite having a room a lot nicer than Tenne had ever had, and e sure dressed the part, wearing some of the smoothest and somehow totally unstained clothing Tenne had ever seen. E even held emself like one of them.

Tenne had some seriously good clothes made for him when he was in the gallery, but they were always stained. And wrinkled. After Tenne wore them, he meant. Today, he was still wearing the one outfit he'd taken from the house, which come to think of it, was not real clean.

"I admit, every time I think Mage Xeleanor cannot surprise me more, she does. *You're* the artist she's suggesting."

Tenne didn't need to get pushed around at another Tower. "Look, she came to me. I can go." He stopped a second. "I don't have somewhere to go right now. Can we just talk? Are you able to drop the Mage act or is this you all the time?"

Kwillen made a loud rude noise at this. "Perhaps my act is somewhat of a consequence that you showed up, without Xeleanor, and I don't know you."

"Oh, Fira, like a codeword thing?" He hated this shit. What had she said about this hu? "She said you were starting a revolution. Kind of an intense comment, if that helps."

Eir eyes widened with interest. "Did she say 'her' revolution?"

What? "No, I think just 'draw for the revolution.'"

Laughing, Kwill pulled off eir head covering, and the cap underneath. Eir hair was mostly sandy, a little auburn. "Call me Kwill. No Mage act, at least until we leave this room."

Tenne's cap was kind of itching, so he was thrilled to whip it off. "Tenne. Just Tenne, please."

"I get it," e said. "Do you drink wine?"

"I do," he said, glad when Kwill pulled out a bottle and a couple of glasses. Not much later, Kwill was up sitting on the edge of eir couch, with one leg propped to the side.

"This room is wrapped, you probably know that."

"Yeah. I don't cast, but I believe you." He was actually pretty stoked that Kwill said nothing about this. Not why don't you cast, are you rebelling, have you ever tried. Just nothing.

Maybe this wouldn't be so bad.

"I've wanted to quit this place for so long," Kwill said, suddenly eir bright voice flattening like someone stepped on eir trombone.

Tenne, wanting to return the favor, did not mention that e certainly had that option. "So this revolution, what does that do to it?"

Kwill nodded. "I've been thinking about that a lot. For now, I stay here. I've got years before anyone gets serious about pushing me forward; I'm not that great of a Study, really, but no one will want to raise the issue. Maybe having some purpose will make me feel better about it, and I just keep reminding myself that if I can't take it here, I can leave. I just can't really come back. Xelle, she seems to keep coming back, but not all of us are her." E laughed, taking a sip. "None of us are her. Watch out if one of these days she realizes it."

Tenne had no idea what he was talking about. "I don't really know her, by the way. She broke into my place and yelled at me. Private issue, Arc stuff. Then nothing, until she dropped by my place about a revolution."

Kwill grinned. "Perfect. And you won't be disappointed, getting to know her. She's the best per. Kind. Bold. Funny. Doesn't take herself so seriously but cares deeply for others. Talks while burping." E turned seriously toward him. "I think for now, especially with worries of what Xelle will or won't do at any moment to torque off the magesphere, we can't let any advantage drop. If you're in to be in public, which, honestly unless you conceal your art style would be pretty necessary, then you've got to be Bon Tenne Du'Mytil whether you like it or not. And I've got to be Study Kwillen Du'Satta, with a renewed reverence toward Breath Tower and He to which I am guarded, retired Spire Mage Withrip Du'Breath. But, you said you don't have a place to stay. Arc is out?"

Tenne nodded, really, really glad when he didn't press it. "Complications with my Da."

Kwill nodded. "Would he intervene if you got a staff job here?"

Wow. That could work. If the job wasn't horrid. "I don't think so. Do you mean, like with you?" He would definitely need to know what he was agreeing to.

E let out a really long dramatic breath of air. "I'm practically calcifying where I am now, they barely notice me. I can meet with a mentor, express renewed interest. They'll be so happy to see my renewal of purpose, they'll probably trip over almost anything I want to do, or anyone I want to employ, as long as it's reasonable." E seemed to be thinking, so Tenne waited. Also, Tenne really only knew Arc Tower and not like, the labs, he had no idea how that would work here.

"There is one form of Breath Magic I could almost say I like," e finally said. "And it has to do with the creation of potions in the form of inks. It's viewed as sort of old-timey, so there's not even a dedicated lab anymore. Mages are much more likely these days to write with an ink then dust it, or just send a casted message, or a million other things that don't involve potentially leaky expensive pens. I assume you came here saying you wanted to meet, something like that?"

"Yeah." They'd almost given him a hard time about it until he mentioned Kwill, so apparently Big Artist Status played better in the populace. No need to dig into that pile right now.

"Sure, so we met. We hit it off. And we schemed. You just left your home, I've been hoping to start this lab, but didn't know how I could get staff. I don't think we need your Da at all. I'll get this set up."

Tenne felt major awkward saying this, but also, whatever. "I, uh, don't have clothes or stuff. It's kind of a situation. I did save some money that I can get started with. But, I'll be helping you with this lab thingy? And also Xelle's revolution? That will pay over Basic?" Basic was plenty to pay for regular clothes, at least to build them up over time, but Tenne had gotten used to having tailors. And soft fabrics. And looking good.

Kwill chuckled, though he didn't see what was funny. Didn't take it bad though, the hu seemed like a chuckler. Like a springy little wood elf. Kept that to himself.

"The less we tie in, the better."

What the ash did that—

"Here, give me a minute."

When Kwill returned, e'd counted out several rolls of coins, and then rolled those into a pretty ugly looking loose cloth. E handed it over. "Seriously. Pressure gifts from relatives. Feels like ashmoney to me. Keep your savings for when you might need them. Now, go make yourself handsome."

What in the Tower washroom was— Then he saw the glimmer. Some little funny wood sprite glimmer. "Adding clothes only detracts from my handsome."

Kwill smirked. "Oh, my asexual eyes fully appreciate the art of creation, including brutalism. So I am certain that is true."

Huh. But hey, something was more important right now. "You're agreeing to this, but like, you haven't seen my art. My real art." His old stuff, that'd all been trying to fit in. He got that now.

"You haven't seen my writing," Kwill retorted, raising eir glass. "My real writing."

"Oh." Actually that was pretty funny. "Good point."

Xelle believed Thunder must have communicated back to the others in some way, but her understanding was such communication would be what Xelle had starting calling pings, sensations of the mind, rather than the mental connection she and zhey shared. Nor could Xelle reach the others with messages, only Thunder, and so, she made her way to the cliff. It felt very odd taking the pathways to the spot of the buried obsidian, because it was not, this time, the spot of her sigil. Part of her ease of travel, the more that she worked with the inkbloom, was how much they wanted to take her to a place, in addition to how well she understood it. This was the first time she'd traveled to a place where dragons were because of familiarity with that place, and not her link to Thunder.

And that, which she'd been suspecting, was now confirmed. Her link only worked to Thunder. Thunder's feelings, Thunder communicating remotely, Thunder's location. But, she did know that other dragons could read her mind. And so, she wondered, could they speak with her as well, if in proximity.

Letting in a new dragon mind was not appealing to her, but knowing whether it would work or not work was definitely something worth knowing.

Lightning saw her first. She waved, hoping waves didn't mean something lewd in dragon-sign, but zhey did not seem worried about the gesture. Zhey, however, did not take zheir eyes off of Xelle, and so she walked directly toward zhem. She bowed, quickly.

Hello. I have been talking to Thunder, in zheir confinement, and wanted to present myself here. In case there are questions. Ways I can help.

Lightning appeared to understand, but seemed confused about something else. Breathing a quick, not totally friendly plume of fire, zhey began to walk away. Turning, noticing Xelle was not following, zhey stamped the ground. Well, then, Xelle would follow. She was rather hoping zhey were leading her to Windy, as she now realized Windy had some sort of personal relationship, perhaps even family or mentorship, to Thunder. But she wasn't upset to see that it was the lavender and violet dragon Breeze, as at least she would not be starting over with this dragon. In fact, she was going to try a risk.

Hello, Breeze. She bowed a bit more deeply. *I am here to tell you about my recent communications with Thunder. I do not understand the relationships here, but would it be appropriate for Windy* (she imagined the older, scratch-worn dragon) *to join us?*

Xelle could not understand what was said, but for the first time, she felt the presence of a communication between Windy and Lightning. Lightning squawked (it was a squawk!) and Breeze stamped a foot, and Lightning left. Breeze seemed to be waiting, and so Xelle did too—realizing that Breeze could hear these thoughts also if zhey chose to—until Lightning returned, with Windy at zheir side.

She kept her cloak on, feeling comfortable despite the rather fiercely blowing new year chill. One benefit of dragons, they didn't seem to need to see your skin or features to know who you were, and so staying warm did not appear, to them, as concealment. She waited as Windy slowly curled up next to Breeze, as if still resting. Then, not knowing how any of this worked, but with no one moving, Xelle went ahead.

I believe you know that Thunder intended to be captured. Zhey are being held at a huge estate which, I now understand, sits within the heart of your previous home. Zhey are being held in confinement, but zhey are not in more specific pain or distress, and we've agreed to check in together every day. Zhey are going to, well, be Thunder. (Lightning snorted at this.) And see what the hu reveal. We do not know if any of the hu understand that Thunder can hear them. And if their thoughts become blocked or if the situation changes, we will go from there. Either way, before Thunder is used for acts zhey are not comfortable with tolerating, we will need to intervene and remove zhem. We should all start considering ways to remove zhem, both at any cost, and in the case we want to make zheir escape plausible without revealing the feint.

I wanted to offer you that update, and also ask if there is anything I can do to help. But first, I have one more thing to discuss. Thunder and I believe it is worth taking action, any action that we can reasonably do at this point, to begin to establish a return of dragonkind to your lands of preference.

Windy uncurled, and rose next to Breeze. A few other dragons who had been pretending to idle nearby stood, and walked closer. And so, Xelle switched to her voice, knowing that it would not change how they heard her, but it would make her intended thoughts clearer.

"There is not a bit of those lands that is not claimed by a hu, a group of hu, anyway, by hu. I could talk to the other Mages but they won't talk to me about this, I'm thinking you know why?" (No reaction.) "There are some populace parks that we could potentially use, but they are small compared to the vast lands claimed by towns, manors, and other gatherings of hu. I do not know if you can communicate with me, or if you could tell Thunder, but if you have advice, I would be honored. This is a much bigger problem than me, but I am not willing to say there is nothing I can do. No way I can help. I hope that I can."

What Xelle felt in her mind was absolutely not the communication she received from Thunder. Nor was there an explicit question of consent, it was more the way a hu might speak openly. Except, not in words, nor in senses, but in concepts, images, a mix of which Xelle did not have language for. But, these first ideas, ideas, maybe she could call them? Came from Breeze.

Full and empty, share the rain.

It was not that phrase, but that was the best she could piece together the concepts in her mind. Like an object passing through the surface of water, she had the sense she was only seeing an edge here, an edge there. But yet, she could grasp a sense of pouring one into the other. Of sharing? The middle?

"A compromise?" she asked. Breeze nearly shouted something. Lightning jumped up. Windy pulsed to Xelle the feeling of warm berries. Joy? A treat? Hopefully something like that?

"What do you mean by a compromise? A small amount of land? I really don't think the parks would be adequate. And who could we ask? I don't know anyone there who could possibly . . ." Her head shot up. "Actually, I do. If I could find a reasonable, if small, but not *tiny* area, would some move to it?"

Hoping to help, Xelle thought very hard about the gestures she and Thunder had come up with together. The yes nod, the no crouch, the two types of ready, and shrug. (The second type of ready, the one for personal communication did not seem to apply, but she would think it and she didn't want them to think she was attempting to withhold something.)

"If that was understood, would some move to it?"

Breeze nodded. Then hesitated. And made the ready signal, the second one.

Xelle did not think Breeze could communicate like Thunder did, but she consented to whatever might happen. She braced herself.

No, it was not a direct communication, not like Thunder, but she understood why the request. Why the consent. The ideas, no that wasn't enough of a word, she would call them the . . . edges. The edges she saw were violent. Of pain. Physical pain, wounds. Of which being, she could not tell. But she thought she understood.

"Without harm to beings?"

Breeze nodded slowly. Windy closed zheir eyes, and laid back down.

And then time, the edges of time. "For now," she murmured. "Then I will see what I can do. And I will watch over Thunder. I promise," she added.

She didn't know if dragons had or needed promises, but it was a way she could express how she felt. Toward Thunder. Toward all her friends.

Feeling more emotions than she wanted to deal with now, she bid them farewell, and returned, landing softly in her blue-glowing nightgarden. Sitting in her swivel seat, she was glad to offer the inkbloom a song.

A snarky forest love song did not actually seem the most appropriate for the moment, but it gave her some feeling of ownership to choose it. She swayed side to side in her seat, not worrying as it swiveled. She knew it was motion and momentum and such, but she decided to feel like the seat was dancing with her. And the inkbloom along with her. And whether the blossoms were really swaying or she was just imagining it, she felt it just the same.

> 1. *Like you better than — ice cream.*
> 1. *Like you better than – my favorite chair.*
> *I like you better than – sunlight, moon beams.*
> *Darling, they're all around, when I'm solitaire.*
>
> 1. *Want you more than – hot fries.*
> 1. *Want you more than – soft underwear.*
> *I want you more than the air, sometimes.*
> *Because, unlike you, the air is always there.*
>
> *I need you more than sunlight.*
> *I need you more than water, food, and air.*
> *I need you more than every single night.*
> *And nothing else, nowhere else, no one else — will compare.*

Giggling at her own absurdity, and easily offered a small, rounded pod, she pushed through her exhaustion (she was simply not sleeping on this floor again) and found herself in the middle of her daygarden. How long had it been? All these emotions, all of them. They were so much.

Casting to clean any dust off her bedsheets, and turning on the stove in addition to another cast to give the room a head-start and warm her somewhat frozen water source, she did not linger in getting ready for bed.

She missed this space, wanted to absorb it. But she would be here in the morning.

And in the morning, she was going to To'Ever.

17 – When Moods Strike Me (a euphemism)

The locals would call it a Mage Bar. One of those taverns that, while not technically restricted, had a reservations desk and several private rooms. Besides that and the old, beautiful interior, unless you had Tower Connections or a desire to wait two hours for a seat, there were better places to gather and eat.

Xelle walked right up to the reservations desk, playing with the nondescript card in her fingers. A hu sat on a high seat behind an old, elaborate countertop, legs dangling. Behind xem were a series of stone doorways and arches. "I'd like to get out of the wind," she said, with a smile. Hoping to spare xem the awkward moment of asking who she was, she started to say, "I'm Mage Xelea——"

Xe stopped her with a sharp gesture. "No need. If you're just looking for a seat and a drink, go on through here." Xe gestured to a closed door on the side. Nodding, and handing the paper into xyr outstretched hand, she walked through.

Prepared for it this time, she found that through the door she was not in the tavern at all (she surmised) but instead in a lobby-ish room with a desk on the other side. A clerk barely looked up.

The stone archway still there, she closed the door and approached the desk. "Hello, I'm Xeleanor Du'Tam, she or e, hoping to see Crown Mage Avail."

The hu nodded. "Sec Sinan, he. Let me check his availability." He wrote something into a book, waited, and then said, "He can see you in about an hour, if it's not urgent. Could I send you to a waiting room?"

Not sure what the waiting room would be all about, Xelle agreed, and found herself directed to a nice, private room, with a combination of calming or stimulating choices. That sounded weird. What she meant was, the room was painted in calming colors, with comfortable seating and a beautiful enchanted painting that looked like the artistic version of a window to the outside, to a grove of beautiful and very snowy trees, an occasional bird landing or alighting. But in case some tired Mage didn't actually want to fall asleep and stumble groggily to their important meeting, there was a stack of short story books, and a rolled up mat with stretching straps.

About the promised hour later, a gentle chime played (Xelle supposed in case you were on the floor with your robes off and legs in straps or some such thing?) and at its conclusion, Sec Sinan escorted her out and into a lift. When the door opened, he gestured for her to leave, and Xelle hesitated, not sure of protocols. "Crown Mage Avail is expecting you," he said, without much inflection, and as Xelle stepped from the lift, the door behind her closed.

She recognized the door to the main office, and was glad that it was open and she did not have to guess if she should, you know, rap on it or just stand there. She had enough to do repeating to herself that she'd thought this through and it was a good idea.

Or at least, she was here now.

Avail's office had not changed much, and Xelle wondered that it felt like a long time since she'd been here, but also like she'd not left. The same green chairs, the same perfectly respected and respectable jumble of books—he wore the same flowing cap he had before. That said, the idea that she was in Ever Tower did not feel real, not having walked up and into the Tower. But, she was. She had pushed so hard for so long for the ability to travel quickly, and yet the concept of it was still unsettling.

But, she was here, a Mage, and a Crown Mage's time was not to be spent pondering. She bowed. "Crown Mage Avail, my thanks for your time and trust."

"Dear Xeleanor, please have a seat." The door shut behind her. A pitcher of water was out this time, no wine. She supposed, it *was* morning, and also, wow, she was getting overspiced. Should she demand a pastry service too? Glad unlike dragons, Crown Mages did not read minds, she smiled politely and sat.

"You are well?" he asked.

She nodded. "Yes, Crown Mage, I am. Grand Tower was a choice better than I understood."

Though Mages tended to be a bit territorial about their Towers, Avail seemed pleased by her comment. "Well, it seems it's worked out for all, as you'll be delighted to learn that Mage Fepa's productivity has not degraded in your absence."

"Oh, yes," she said, "but I'm not surprised. His reputation precedes him, which is why I'm sure you honored me with his mentorship."

"Mmm, mmm," he responded, finally sitting comfortably into the other seat.

"I understand now what it means to be a protector, like Grand. We all protect, but we are like a set of tools, each suited best for something."

"Ah." He leaned back. "Which is your tool, Xeleanor?"

"Perspective, I think. A benefit of knowing the maps as well as the pathways."

He smiled, more broadly now. "What have you been doing there?"

"I work under the mentorship of Mage Ollia in the wand lab. As a Mage myself, I can provide supplemental guidance to the Studies, including those on exchange." She thought about noting like her friend, Mage Rayn, but wasn't sure what Rayn's place was in the Tower or whether she might disturb it. Best to leave that alone.

"You're going to make a wand, right?"

She leaned in, "Do you have a wand?"

He leaned forward. "Not a magical wand. And I'd use care how you phrase questions of wands. They tend to be suggestive, to one not used to the culture."

"Oh, come on," she heard herself saying. "Sorry, Crown Mage."

"What?" he asked. "Oh, but surely you aren't here for wand jokes?"

"Crown Mage, I found out on my first application the confidence and openness and positivity of self I was demonstrating by letting pers know I was interested in a pocket wand, and I have stuck to the script ever since."

Avail nearly snorted. "You said that on application? You didn't. Oh. I forget who I'm talking to. You absolutely did." Whatever that little giggle he added was, was completely not necessary. "So, Mage Xeleanor, why are you and your positivity of self here today? Surely not only for the company."

"Not only," she said, smirking. "I am seeking funding."

"Oh, I've overspiced you," he said, tsking. "Surely you don't think that parting gift was from me?"

"Surely I do." She pointed, then lowered her finger realizing she was pointing at a Crown Mage. Though, in fairness, one insinuating dick jokes. In fact, he seemed rather animated. She wondered . . . But first, business. "But this request is not for me. It is for them."

Quite a shift in expression on that.

"I would like to work with someone in the Highponds to establish a small but autonomous dragon residence. I surmise there are things you can't or won't discuss, so unless it is explained to me why this is not a good idea, I am taking it on myself. I do have a healthy stash, but nothing near this scope. But Ever, the watcher, with purview over exactly such things, perhaps could justify funding for a project and then observing how it progresses."

"Presuming it is not your acquaintances, the Lunests, that you seek to approach for assistance, what would you tell me of your plan?"

"No. No Lunests." She could not maintain pleasantries for this comment, and she was sure her expression seethed in a very non-Magey way. "I will tell you exactly who I plan to approach, without subterfuge or parlance or any such thing."

"Intriguing," he said, only.

"There is a hu from my homevillage of Tam, well, you know where I'm from. His name was Rod Du'Tam, but it is now Rod Du'Highponds. He is a carpenter. A very skilled one. But also not a per I've enjoyed being around. Yet, because he was somehow the most famous per in Tam, in many cases, more than the waterfall itself, no one questioned his absolute . . ." She had to think of the word. "The extent of his pompously inflated entitlement."

"That's descriptive," he said.

"Yes. So he wasn't the worst, or of course, I would have stood up to him. Just more the per at every event being revered and uplifted, while he was treating kids like me with none of the respect he so enjoyed. You know what I mean?"

Fira, did she just ykwim a Crown Mage . . .

"I do," he said. "And you think that your village connection matched with your understanding of his egotistical needs will allow you to advance a cause without any form of deceit on your part."

Uh. "Yeah. I mean, yes. Crown Mage."

"While we do have the authority you note regarding the well-being of anima, and pers beyond hu, that would not transfer to agents of the populace. However, the projects undertaken by Ever Tower are, as you note, often of a natural bend, regardless. You, yourself, created an entire club and sanctuary for the observation of birds, I recall?"

Oh, that's right, she had stuck him with that. "I did," she said, telling from the tone of his voice that was still an ongoing and joy-giving thing. Which made her really, really happy.

"Then, if a carpenter were to approach Ever Staff with a request for a sanctuary of beings, perhaps without specificity, I could lean a bit on the scales of its adjudication, with perhaps the caveat of appropriate Ever Tower regulations."

All of the sudden, like a rush, Xelle just felt grateful. Grateful that a Mage of this import, this power, was open to her schemes. And suddenly, she wanted to ask. Wanted to know she was ok to speak. Or how much. Or . . .

She dove in. "Something else I've learned at Grand. My relation-ship with you, as it is, is important to me. And I realize there are things

Mages don't say about dragons, so I'd like to ask you—if I talk about them does it bother you?"

He tilted his head, actually taking a moment to consider his response. "I always find your theories intriguing, Xeleanor."

Oh, actually, that response made this next risk a lot worse-sounding, but he was a Crown Mage, he knew how to parley. If he'd given her an opening, he'd given her an opening.

"Perhaps we even think alike, if I could consider such an honor. Or perhaps starting here, as a Study, first gave me perspective on ideas of permanence that linger." She paused. "I think about old friends sometimes. My theory, by a slight bounce in your step, is that you do as well. Perhaps even reconnecting."

His expression flared, and Xelle's heart leapt. Too far. She shouldn't have—

"Yes, Xeleanor, you are correct. Meaning, of course, that I do also think of old friends. Old connections. You honor Ever Magic with your words, but knowing the power of Arc Magic, I am glad to honor that influence as well. May I say, Mage Xeleanor, I am pleased with your progress."

Xelle was nearly holding her breath. So, he wasn't mad, but that topic was over.

His face turned a bit serious. "And if I may," he continued, "to press also on personal matters. I learned that you had a connection of your own. My advice? A connection? A true connection? You never really let it go. Well." He waved a hand. "You're an Arc Mage, you know this best of all." Then he looked at her rather pointedly. "Oh, and, with regrets to your clear lack of privacy, I've heard you are somewhat of an item with Mage Dram Du'Grand. I've met him several times. Charming. Honest. Absolutely the sort I see on Grand Spire someday."

"I ah, just broke up with him. Nothing bad, it just . . ."

"Ah, stones do tend to roll when there's nothing to hold them. But remember what I said about connections. Love? The true kind? Once you find it, it will find you where you are."

She didn't know what he actually meant by that, but she felt some kind of warmth simply in being talked about like a hu. Like hearts and lives were messy and confusing and hard sometimes, and this hu—he knew that. And also, that last caught thread of guilt, or grief, or whatever it was about Dram let go. Released. Avail, he understood. And . . .

"May I ask one more personal question? I mean, about me, not you."

He nodded.

"How do you know if you're in the right place?" Ugh, she felt like a child asking it. But she kept moving, and finding things that were here, but the pieces never fit and—

"There is not a right place," he said, looking very stark and non-whimsical about his response. "There cannot be. Wrong places, yes. But right? Not one. And so, we think about the places that are a right place, the pers who are our right pers, the needs and joys that we can find, and we find a place." He glanced around the room. "Look at me. Power. Wealth. Stewards. A spacious office, a private bath . . . If I had to do it over again?" He shook his head. "I wouldn't be here. But then, what, worry every day about a life I cannot touch? No. I live every day, asking where I am today, is there another place I need to go. Want to go. Plan to go? *Can go?* If the answer is no, then I am in *a right place.*"

He let out a very normal hu sounding long breath. "I could tell you something silly. Something not quite becoming a Crown Mage."

"I'd like that," Xelle said, thinking it didn't sound like whatever he said would be silly.

"When moods strike me, it's a euphemism, I mean when I fall and my handholds feel weak, I consider that perhaps there are boundless possibilities in the pathways. And thus somewhere, different choices were made." He gestured. "Not always by me. By others, too. If those scenarios felt possible, in the past or in the future, or even both, then I think, that me could be living that life somewhere in the pathways.

I feel the joy, the comfort, the wholeness, for that hu." He had turned away.

This was something Xelle would have to think about another time. Her arms felt weak, her body suddenly tired. "Crown Mage Avail?"

He turned back, his face again placid.

"Do you offer hugs?"

"Oh!" he poofed. "Hugging a Crown Mage! This could be its own scandal! Are you quite sure?"

Relieved to see the sparkle back in his eye, she met it with her own. "I could try my chances with Crown Mage Da'Selin."

She was glad when Avail began to laugh, and continued to laugh. She was sure a Mage of his rank could hold from laughter if he wanted to, and it felt, nice, that he didn't want to. "Oh," he finally said, dabbing his eyes with a beautifully stitched clothie. "Compared to that, certainly no scandal will be found today."

He reached forward, and only then did Xelle realize what she'd actually just asked this hu. His arms pressed around her, and hers around him, and she was being held by a Crown Mage. It was not antiseptic. It was warm, and comfortable. Xelle . . . wished she could stay. Instead she stepped back, knowing her cheeks had blushed.

"Now, go on and get back to your tree." She started, thinking of her daygarden, but realizing (she thought?) that he meant Grand Tower. "If your Rod, pardon me, the gentlehu from your village, petitions Ever Tower, I will endure his presence and ensure the funds are adequate. Now," he pointed at her. "I expect this Rod Du'Highponds to be every bit as unoffensively objectionable as you have portrayed."

She chuckled. Not a concern. "Let's hope he doesn't let you down. And thank you. For everything."

"Mmm, hmm, now go on. I'm a busy hu." Some tension had returned to his voice, and Xelle realized, she had no idea what he'd been up to today, what he still had to do. What burdens might rest on the shoulders of a hu responsible for an entire sub-society without really having his hands in any of it. Then being pulled aside to relive and recount his existential moments.

She nodded briskly, and without bothering his clerk, leaned into the pathways.

And back to her nightgarden.

18 – Couch Pillow Magic

The Arc Tower steward was being extremely annoying, like Tenne was some visitor and not Tenne Cu'Arc. Surely the Bon stuff didn't reach the halls of his home?

"Bon Tenne." The voice was stern. "You will not proceed further or I will be forced to make your stay unpleasant."

Well, there that was some Cu'Arc energy. He didn't even answer, and plopped down on a bench in the corridor, irritated that another steward had appeared hurrying around a bend, then stopped, waiting.

"You got assigned to watch me?" he asked.

The steward didn't answer. A few minutes later, Tenne, no Da in sight, was being escorted back into the Atrium. Were they kicking him out?

Surprised, he noticed his Da standing in conversation with another Mage. Some new Mage. How were there new Mages that got to talk to his Da? He hadn't been gone that long, had he?

"Tenne," Da said rather loudly. "They just told me you were here. I presume you're not here to enjoy the blooms? The gloria are in full array out on the hills."

The steward turned and left. Ash. Maybe things were worse than Tenne had realized. "I'm here to see you. It's been a while. Thought we could catch up."

Da turned to the other Mage. "This is my cura, the artist Bon Tenne Du'Mytil, he. Tenne, this is Spire Mage Nar Du'Arc, she."

Tenne almost said 'whoa' but he hadn't been in a Tower in a while, and probably needed to do the Tower thing. It's just, she was a Spire Mage? She had the high-ranking gear for sure, but she was kind of young. And cool. Looked like she could be at an art rave, not running a Tower. But she was clearly here. "It's—" the first word came out in that Bon voice he'd been doing at the gallery, but that sounded silly now. He tried to just speak normal. "It's nice to meet you, Spire Mage Nar."

She nodded with that vague Mage expression they loved to do. "I must be on my way," she said, taking no time to whisk back toward a lift.

"I . . ." Da looked lost for words.

"I can leave if you want. Just . . ." Tenne worried about saying things here in public. But Da had a good, private office. Seemed on purpose he met him here, in the busiest part of the Tower. And with another Spire Mage just like, walking him down? That was bizarre.

Da put on his Mage face. "No, it's good to see you. I could use a break from the Tower, myself. What if?" He paused as though thinking, but it was like some fakey thinking face. Yeah. Some act was happening here. Tenne tried to go along. "We could walk to the village, get a dessert there like we used to."

"Yeah, sure," Tenne said. His new pants were scratchy. He probably should have washed them first. Or soaked them. He'd never actually washed his own clothes, so he should probably look that up. They both stood there for a moment.

Da swept his hand forward and did that thing where he starts to walk but makes it look like you both decided to walk at the same time. So, then, he guessed they were going now. And Tenne didn't think he was casting or anything, so he guessed no open conversation. A ball inside him formed at that. Resentment. Yeah, he supposed it was. What did he ever do in life to lose his Ma and now his Da. If this was what this revolution paper was supposed to help with, he suddenly grew a desire, maybe a need, to do it. And Xelle was definitely a lot, but seemed like the sort that knew her shit. He was going to trust her.

As long as she didn't go too Magey on him. Anyway.

"How are things with your partner?" Da started.

"Over," Tenne said. No secret in that.

Da didn't say anything. Actually, that was nice. No 'I'm sorry to hear that' or whatever. He wondered if Da had ever dated anyone before Ma.

"I'm going to be working at a Tower." Ha. That got him. He saw the twitch in Da's face.

"Not something I expected to hear," was all he said.

"Yeah. One of the Satta kids is a Study at To'Breath, and I'm going to be working on some magic ink projects with em."

Recognition seemed to be dawning on Da's face, but he didn't know what he'd said that was so interesting.

"Study Kwillen Du'Satta?" he asked, quite firmly.

How did he know that? But this was not going to be a secret. "Actually, yes."

"I cannot tell you what to do, but I should warn you that e is quite closely associated with Xeleanor Du'Tam." He looked at Tenne sharply.

Uh oh. He didn't know what he was supposed to say to that. They were clearly putting on some show here, while also maybe trying to communicate? That was Mage stuff. Except, when he said it like that, it was also artist stuff. Ok, so what would pers already know? Oh, yeah.

He snorted. Pretty real sounding, actually. "Yeah, she was the one I reported for trying to bust into my Gallery space. Thought that would be the end of it, but she showed up at my place a few months ago telling me her friend was looking for an artist. I told her to spin off and never come back, but you know, there's kind of a bond between Tower kids, and things fell out with, you know, so after thinking about it, I went to Breath. Turns out, e's pretty cool, and I don't have a place to go now, so I'm going to try it out."

Da lifted his chin in the 'give me a moment to process this' gesture. Then he spun around, venom in his voice. "Xeleanor is a poison apple. I told you this before, and you have the nerve to justify it to me? If you associate with her again, we will no longer be family. This is that serious, Tenne. Please, just stay away from her."

"Whoa," Tenne found himself saying. "I'm working with Kwill, at Breath. Like, an official thing. Breath Tower has agreed to hire me. Not because of you. Because of me. Because they like my art, and think Bon Tenne Du'Mytil is actually a firecursed force in this world. I am so tired of you telling me who I'm allowed to be around and not. I'm not involved in whatever your business is. I came here to catch up, but if you're going to threaten me halfway down the jerking driveway, then I don't need this. I have my *own* Tower now. Not Kern's. Mine. Get it? I don't need you and I don't need our family, or at least who's here left of it."

Suddenly, a wind wrapped around them both. A cast. An angry cast, with fury they could probably feel down at the village.

"We are firmly wrapped and we have seconds," Da said. "And until there is a change, a big change, we do not talk. Do you understand?"

Tenne nodded. He didn't like this. Why did it have to—

"Brace yourself for much worse. I will not be your friend, nor Xelle's." Huh, he called her Xelle? "Not until—" He winced. "I will think only of that day. I love you, Tenne. Always."

"I love you too, Da." He did. He missed him. The pressure was always too much, but not Da. Da was actually pretty cool. And his face quivered, so slightly. Tenne felt bad. He felt—

"Here," Da said. "We can't hug, but they won't see this through the cast." He held out his hand, an unclasped locket in it. Oh. Tenne didn't have to look. He knew it. He felt it. He grasped it and clutched it in his hand, until he could clasp it properly and without whoever was watching seeing.

"This makes it so you can find me?"

Da made a tiny sound, that stabbed Tenne somehow, like a needle. "No, love, no," he said. "I could always, always find you." He closed his eyes. "Whatever you do out there, be you. Go hard. I am with you. Now, let's give them the family show?"

Tenne grinned. Not happily, just, it just kind of happened. He really wanted to run and cry, but there was a defiant light in Da's eyes.

One that he hadn't seen, since— He rubbed the locket in his hands. "I think she's here. Watching."

Da, nodded, his eyes beginning to water. Then, he switched. All at once. Spire Mage Kern Du'Arc, Crown of Halina, Sacred Heart of Alyssia whipped the cast out from them, and stomped away.

"No! Da. Come back. I was just— This is *mageshit!*"

Kern did not cast, did not travel, but stormed back up the walkway. He said nothing.

"Da!" Tenne started to run after him, but after nearly slipping on some ice, he stopped. He stood up straight, and adjusted his cap.

"Burn the family," he yelled to the point it hurt. "I am an adult. I am a star. I am Bon Tenne Du'Mytil!" He reached into the snow and jammed up the best snowball in the world, the fully illicit kind, the kind his Ma had taught him to make, and heaved it, symbolically, toward his Da, toward Arc Tower, not caring where it landed, just that it hit hard. "Suck yourselves, all of you!" he bellowed. Then, stomping off himself, he did not stop until the village. He went to the best dessert place there, ordered a huge four-per stack, tipped extravagantly because he was taking the bowl and spoon, and marched off, waving a huge coin and demanding a vroom immediately all the way to 'his Tower,' To'Breath.

"You said it's wrapped here? Fully wrapped?" He glanced around the Study's room, his eyes landing back on the hu emself.

Kwill was like, cringing, but e'd asked him into this. Tenne didn't care.

"Yes," e confirmed.

"This pillow special to you?" He pointed at some ugly pillow that looked like it came off the back table at the Rich Ga shop.

"Not remotely," Kwill answered, taking a step back.

Tenne wailed. He cried. He slammed that pillow so many times that the stuffing flew out of it. He tore the fabric. He tore the stuffing. And when there wasn't much left to wreck, he wrecked himself, falling down on the pile of fluff and crying a lifetime of tears into it. Finally he remembered where he was. His eyes hurt. His body hurt. He felt so . . . alone.

"You got a potion or anything?"

Kwill nodded, silently. The last thing Tenne remembered was lying down on the Study's actually long-enough couch, his Ma's old locket warm against his chest.

As she'd realized at To'Ever, one downside to inkbloom travel was arriving in a place, and not to a place. The mid-spring had to be extraordinary around Breath Tower, and also in its Atrium, with plant life and decorations always matching the season. She closed her eyes and imagined the soft veils blowing in the glowing light and soft breeze.

But not today. She had to hold her cards for now. Until it no longer mattered, or until she had a better reason to nullify them.

Was there really a better reason?

She was getting in her head.

Kwill was not, this day as with any day, holding the rose pillow locked away in a drawer to signal e wanted to speak, nor did Xelle sense em in the hazy feelings of eir room. Yet interestingly, there was a second place Xelle could immediately feel through the pathways. It was not the lovely little room she'd stayed in for a month, or the Atrium, or her favorite library nook. It was a point of light. A point of warmth. A heartbeat. Not far from Kwill's room. And she knew what it was, without understanding why. It was Kern's locket. But, she did not think it was Kern wearing it.

That one, then. It was mid-day. All gods he was somewhere decent. She waited, watching it. In a closed room, moving about. Perhaps she should have coordinated this. But having taken the energy to return to her nightgarden, sing, and take a new pod, the last thing she was going to do was just . . . go home.

And sometimes trusting the spirits was, she admitted, a little exciting. *What do you think? Safe to go?* The inkbloom did not answer. Good enough.

Xelle appeared inside a smallish lab. Quickly, she assessed where she was and who was there. Tenne, next to her, as expected. Kwill! Across the room, grinning. And two more.

"It's ok," Kwill said, apparently to everyone in the room including Xelle, then hurried over. "We'll have to come up with a way for you to know if it's safe, but that can be a discussion for later. I presume you know Tenne."

"I do," she said, glancing at the artist, who looked a little stunned.

E turned toward the other two. "This is my dear friend, Mage Xeleanor Du'Tam, she or e, dragonfriend, and general menace."

Menace?

"This is Laenni Du'Satta, e." E pointed to a young, short, and stout per. Actually, Xelle recognized em from when she was here. "No relation. And Cher Du'Wehj, she or he, don't let her gentle nature fool you." This seemed to be a bit of a joke, as Cher looked like someone who woke up before dawn to go lift weights. "Met here. Personal body-guard." Again, this seemed to be some sort of joke, as everyone but Tenne was grinning away. "Both Breath Studies. No Mages assigned. I played it off like I wanted 'more opportunity' and they were exuberant about my newfound enthusiasm and basically gave me anything I wanted. Can't keep them out," e said, "but I've got a quiet sign on the door—can't rumble the ink—so they at least have to throw a light signal. At least, supposed to. Of course, they could do what they wanted, if we ever get to a point of that. But for planning, for talking we should be good for a while here. Some of the other stuff will need to move out. And backup plans and locations." E ran a hand back and around eir neck. "But I'm stretching my brain enough for now. And dealing with him." He pointed over at Tenne.

Tenne didn't seem to care whatever Kwill said either. Fira, were these two friends? Friendly? There felt like an energy to it. This whole room had an energy. What in the flames was going on here? Tenne was still staring her way, nearly glaring.

"Hello?" she offered.

"That is top Arc stuff," Tenne said, a little breathily. "Fast travel? And they let you go?"

Xelle didn't like the question. Frankly, the idea of Magey entanglements had her more puzzled than anything else and she wasn't ready to deal with all that yet. She shrugged. "I'm a free spirit. Now. Laenni. Cher. Did I get that right? It's nice to meet you. Kwill, I was hoping we could talk. And I don't have a lot of time. I've actually got something I need to do in my own lab in a few hours." Apparently Grand Mages really liked their wands to be completed in spring, so the winter lead-up was considered 'busy season'. Xelle had tried to respect that, and be as present as possible.

Besides, it was giving her a lot of ideas about her own wand, something she had absolutely not given up on.

"What are you grinning about?" Kwill asked. "Never mind. You need to get back. Let's go to my room? And as much as I'd love to give them ribaldry to write about, maybe we slip out a back way and try not to attract notice?"

Xelle pulled her cloak closed and the hood over her cap, and asked it to make her look nondescript. She glanced over at Tenne, not unhappy to see his reaction. But, he said nothing, except "I talked to my Da."

Thinking keeping the cloak pulled might be best, she said, "Anything you want to share?"

"I'm publicly disowned. He . . . still loves me."

That hurt. "Yes, he loves you very much. And I promise we'll look out for him, in whatever ways we can. Oh. I need to disclose. When you're wearing that, I can find you." She tapped her own chest.

Tenne paused. "Does he know that?"

"Yes. I mean, he has to."

The artist, leaning back as if tired, just breathed out slowly.

Feeling a wave of pain at the emotions written all over Tenne's face, she turned toward the Studies. "Very nice to meet you. I'm sure we'll be in touch." She offered the sign of the Breath, which they returned.

Kwill had clearly chosen the location of eir lab intentionally and certainly pulling a few favors, as there was a service passage that led nearly between it and eir room. Not precisely, but to the back of the Study quarters, easy to check first if the hall was clear.

"What is going on here?" she asked, as soon as the door was shut.

Kwill cocked eir head.

"Just— You all seem friendly. And like, happy."

E tsked. "Oh. Let me put this your way. We need to raise your first step. Something like that?"

"Rung," she answered.

"Rung," e repeated. "I'm simply saying that we have assembled a team of pers who actually work well together. Lift each other. Try to understand each other. Different but united in a cause."

"You didn't signal me," she said, needing to at least get out why she'd risked such a bold move.

"I didn't need to talk yet, and I figured you were off, you know, practicing that so I didn't have to worry about you imploding the universe to say hi. Oh." Kwill grimaced. "We didn't make a way for you to signal to me."

"Well, now we've got Tenne. Speaking of which?" She threw her arms up in a 'how's *that* going' kind of gesture.

Kwill laughed a bit explosively. "An absolute doof of a hu, but I admit there's a sweetness to him. Also, so horny. And no, I have not experienced this personally, but I think there's something to aceness that enables us, or at least me, to critique the art more clearly, if you will. I was fully unsurprised when it took him about two days to be recruited by the unofficial Dusk Club, you know the bulky dusk genders with an affinity toward open sexuality and a love of dance shows and game nights. I'm not even sure he remembers whoever he left."

Xelle shook her head. But was ready to not be on this topic. "But it sounds like you are getting along?"

"We are. Not without static, but there is a certain . . ." Kwill tapped eir lip . . . "negotiation one learns to do as a toddler in a Mage Tower. To cut through the fluff and figure out if something is going to happen or not. To not make it personal. When you're trying to get a cookie from some of the most powerful and bizarre pers in the Region, you learn how to focus on the path between you and the cookie and not worry if that path is strange."

Xelle could understand that. "So how are you parsing lab versus revolution?"

"Well, we were all open from the start. Working it together. I'm less interested in the ink part, but that's what drew Cher. I approached her because of her reputation of standing up for herself and others, but then I found out she's a complete darling, and the idea of ink research is exciting enough to her that she can keep our front up on her own. She'll be an incredible Mage. And Enni, well, e will as well. E's like, the version of me who isn't famous. Actually grew up in Satta, populace family. We've gone on breaks there together, seen what the city is really like when one's not surrounded by famous Mages. No relation of lineage, but e's really become my sibling. I suppose."

Aww. "That's nice, Kwill." She thought of her own sibling. Of her niblings.

She didn't expect this visit to dig up so much. And why, then, why did she have so much to dig. Anyway, to business.

"Dragon updates."

"Love it." Kwill did not yet sit, but walked around to rest eir hands on the back of a chair. Well, e'd been in a lab all morning.

Xelle asked her cloak to lighten, then plopped on the couch. Then realizing her boots were still on, hurriedly unlaced them, before throwing her legs up onto the couch unceremoniously. Ah, it was such a nice big couch. Her favorite rose pillow being presumably in the drawer, she reached instead for the one with the soft tassels. "No home pillow?" That one, pretentiously plain with the word 'home' on it, Kwill had only kept out for some sort of aggressive ambivalence.

"Had an incident," Kwill said.

"Hmm." She hugged the tassel pillow to her chest. "So I've confirmed that my link is specifically to my friend, Thunder. I can only know where zhey are, specifically. I can communicate with zhem in ways I can't with the others, and zhey can communicate over distance with me with clarity that zhey can't even with other dragons. Zhey have taken it upon zhemself to get captured by the Hurts, and are now being held outdoors at the Lunest Estate. Zhey're ok for now," she hurried to say at Kwill's tightened expression. "No experiments or anything. My theory is they're trying to make zhem comfortable. Get Thunder to trust them. While testing out if the dragon can escape their casted enclosure that shocks you when you get near its boundaries. So, it did not take too much acting on Thunder's part to not try zheir hardest to escape it."

She stretched her back and neck, arching one way then the other. "So I went to visit the others." (She still needed to learn a better way to refer to them, questions for later.) "And we can still communicate, in a different way. I mean, they seem to be able to understand me perfectly. A bit harder on my end. But we came up with a plan."

Kwill said nothing, but was clearly interested.

"I have a carpenter . . . acquaintance from my hometown that is now somewhat wealthy and successful in Highponds. I am hoping to convince him to make a request to Ever Tower for funds for the construction of an unspecified anima sanctuary. However, I find the hu quite . . . a lot, so I was wondering if you'd go with me. If you can take a break here, we could plan a day to go together, find him. I'll send a formal request by Post, marked as sent from Grand Tower, which I cannot imagine he'll turn down."

"I would never turn down a request to see you dealing with what sounds like a quite unique individual. What about two weeks from today? Plenty of time to send the note and get confirmation. And not so soon that it would raise any questions here. You'll send me the time and place?"

Xelle nodded. "You're not ready," she added with a grin.

"I'm always ready," Kwill quipped back.

She grinned. "Well, I'll see you then." She started to reach for her boots, but felt like Kwill was staring at her. Was something brewing? She looked up.

"I'm worried about you," e said.

She rolled her eyes, though not intentionally. "Worried about me? Why are pers worried about me?" She pulled her legs under her.

Kwill flushed a bit angrily. "We are worried about you because we care about you, and you work and work and dig and dig, but then are somehow surprised to see pers in a room getting along with some level of joviality. And Dram—"

"What? What about Dram?" What Mage thing did Kwill know. What new slop had she stepped in now?

"I'm sorry. It's not my business. Or it is? I'm not good at friend stuff, Xelle. I can get along. I can code switch. I can make almost anything workable. But I don't know when I'm supposed to say something, about pers' choices, about—"

"What is it about Dram?" Her heart was pounding.

"Nothing, except I could never see you sticking with someone like him. He's a good Mage, don't worry. I'm sorry. Nothing is wrong with him."

There was something e wasn't saying. What wasn't e saying. Look, they were friends, right? Good friends?

"What is it you aren't saying to me?"

"Aaaagh," e said. "Let's just drop it. I'm sorry, I shouldn't have said anything. I want you to have friends, and lovers, and have fun. Look, I'm sorry. And how about this. I'm just worried about you, because you seem so alone. Maybe I see it as like, an Alone Expert. Maybe it's because working in this lab has been the best thing that's happened to me in a while. I—"

"We're not even together anymore."

"Oh, I'm sorry. I just, mean, I know that must feel bad. And it doesn't actually change what I'm trying to say. Well . . ." For once, Kwill looked like e was sorting what to say.

E didn't have to say anything. Maybe e didn't know. It wasn't like Ever anymore, she was doing so much better. "It's fine; it really is. I have the wand lab! The wand lab is great. Actually they are some of the best pers I've gotten to know. It's a lot like what you have, just—less snarky. More smiling, less grinning. I don't know. It's really an amazing place. I've been *happy* there."

E pressed eir hands together. "And you're going to leave it, Xelle. You're not a Grand Mage, it's a temp assignment. And then, what, you'll crash again? I don't know how to help you. I feel like I should, but I don't know how."

"That's what we're doing, isn't it?" Xelle waved one hand around, the other firmly hugging the pillow. Which fell flat as she was somehow pointing at Kwill's bedroom with one hand while caressing a tassel with the other. Well, e'd know what she meant. "This revolution, this paper you're printing, this team we're building. You didn't feel right here, you know that. I haven't felt right—" She was not going to say when that went back to, actually. "We're doing something that could matter. With pers we like."

Kwill shook the back of the chair. "Yes, we're doing it, here. But you're not going to move to Breath. I know you. Ash, I don't think it would be a good idea either. So however many pers get involved, no matter how much good we do, I don't want you to end up sitting in a room, alone, at the end of the day, reaching for a potion just to calm the feeling that your heart is going to fall out."

"Ok. That's life. That's how it works. Won't you be alone at the end of the day, also?"

E pushed the chair against the floor. "I'm not you." E stopped, turned and walked away, sort of, it wasn't that large of a room so now e was facing the wall. E turned around. "I can't get involved. In other things. But I do have an idea. I'll get us books. Enchanted books."

She presumed e meant to communicate back and forth, the classic enchantment one thought of when one thought of a book. Still. Kwill had connections and money, but not that much?

"For the lab, Xelle. We're developing magic inks. I could send it up through the Laboratorian to the Spire. New lab, request for Ever Tower from the newly refreshed Kwillen Du'Satta. I think it could go through."

Xelle closed her eyes, wanting to think quickly on this. She didn't want to forget something and she didn't want to send a message like this via Post. She thought through everyone, everyone she knew. It wasn't the longest list, and that hurt. Ugh. Ok, ok, what did they need? The request, the request would have to go to Ever. For an enchantment. What about Helia? No, she wanted to protect Helia. Helia never asked for any of this. Besides, even if she did, it could endanger her rise at Arc. She was a good Mage. She'd surely go far. Maybe, maybe another day. But Xelle, she couldn't be tied to Ever. Three. Three was already way too far. But they could try it.

"Ask for a trio," she said. "Go big, go bigger, right? One for the lab. One for your research partner, Mage Rayn Du'Ever, to stay at Ever Tower. Oh, I'm glad she's a Mage, they'd never give it to a Study, well they would but only with someone supervising. But it's sensitive to a Breath project, so it must stay in her control. Breath Tower must add that specifically; shouldn't be a hard or suspicious sell. Then tell them you want a travel version. Ash, don't use the word travel. Say you want . . . Actually, use the word travel. Avail will see a request like this, and he'll know that's me. Even if Breath takes your name off it, which they might, thinking it'll come better from a Mage. And the travel version is to test, uh . . ."

"Oh, that's easy. Field tests. Distance, elements, what if the ink gets rained on, subjected to inhalants. In the presence of other magic.

Things they wouldn't want us bonking with in the middle of Ever Tower."

"Ok," Xelle said. "About me showing up. Is the lab always safe, if Tenne's there? I should tell you, it's him I can find. Don't want to get into why. And nothing weird," she added.

Kwill rolled eir eyes. "Xelle, you're a beautiful, charming hu with the sunlight in your eyes and the moonslight in your spirit. But I can promise you that neither Tenne nor the Duskies would be remotely interested in anything too weird with you, unless they were stuck with only you on the planet."

"What? Thanks?"

Kwill raised a hand. "No insult. That's just practical matters. I've already explained, they're quite horny with established preferences. Now, to your question. Once we get the books to communicate, our risk will lower. Tenne, he knows about this connection?"

Xelle nodded. Sounded like one risk lowered and another elevated, but not really the point. She started to lace her boots.

"Good." Kwill ran a hand over eir neck. "Then until we have better safety I'll tell him to leave if we get any visitors. He's not a caster, it shouldn't appear suspicious. Actually, it would probably look totally normal."

"Plans." That felt good to say.

"Yes. And hug?" Kwill smiled, and reached out eir arms in a way that made Xelle think, somehow, of little Loren. She didn't know if that was good or bad, or, anyway, yeah, Kwill was family.

She made a point not to end the hug too soon.

19 – Dancer and Carpenter

They met at a café in Wehj. She always marveled how much Kwillen Du'Satta could eat and yet stay a little wisp. "It's good your family is rich," she said, sipping her coffee. "They'd need to be just to feed you."

"Can't beat city food," Kwill said with a mouth full of syrup sausage. "At the Tower, they'd mold the ingredients into a log, wave a crisper over them, and serve them over endive. Here someone just smashed this out with their hand, and slapped it onto an oily stovetop that gets scraped every while."

That was a bit of truth. Xelle's own breakfast had spared neither the garlic nor the heat. Now, she hadn't ordered seconds.

"What's in that?" e asked, nodding toward the cup.

"Lavender oatmilk darkbrew coffee with a little froth." It was really good, and she took another sip.

"Ah, the drink to signal you delight in many genders."

Fira, she was trying to drink. "Oh, and what is the coffee of asexuals?"

"Oh, also dark with lavender. But then nutmilk and a toss of mallows."

She smiled. "I'll switch to iced in the summer, but with a little chill in the air this morning, I like cradling the warm cup in my hands." She'd specifically removed her gloves for this purpose, and asked her cloak not to let her lose them.

At least not being one for lots of staff and pomp, Rod met them at the gate. "Little Xellie Du'Tam! Big hug for Sa Rod?"

"Oh, I'm a Mage now. Mage Xeleanor Du'Tam. So instead I'll

offer you a bow." She bowed deeply, hoping she didn't have to get more direct about it.

"Fancy! And this must also be a Mage, then?"

A little rough, but she was at least glad he'd decided not to try and hug Kwill.

"Oh, I'm not a Mage, just a friend of Xelle's here. Call me Kwill, e. Well, don't I get a hug?"

She tried to control her reaction, as Rod didn't quite know where to put his hands on the lanky Study, who leaned in and controlled the hug with the skill of an orchestral conductor. E patted Rod's shoulder, then stepped back.

"You're not a forestper," Rod said, brusquely.

"You are insightful as well as charming! I am from the city, myself."

Xelle noted e didn't mention which one, probably happy to let Rod assume it was Wehj and not make any Mage-family associations. Just in case. Xelle didn't *think* he'd know about that, or care to, really.

"I am Rod Du'Highponds, a humble carpenter." He turned to Xelle. "Well, a Mage, then! Our little cura! Always knew you would be." He pointed at her, then turned to Kwill. "Xelle here is the pride of our village!"

Xelle . . . was not aware of this. What a holetalker. Oh, this was already bringing back all sorts of unpleasant feelings. She was so glad, so glad, Kwill was here.

Kwill moved alongside Rod. "I'd love to see the Estate!" e said.

Rod turned back toward Xelle, and so, allowing this one, she took Rod's other side, and walked up the path together. Still, no touching. She didn't have to, and she wouldn't.

The house was exactly as she would have imagined it. Unnecessarily large, without really taking on the airs of a manor. Beautifully constructed, with tastefully selected woods and joints, and then an interior laden with expensive folksy art, polished burls, and hanging beadwork.

"Hello!" A voice called out, and a hu in a neat, matching floral springsuit walked confidently into the room.

Rod turned to Kwill. "This is my spouse, Mik, she."

"Xelle! He said you would be here. You've gotten so old! But then, haven't we all? A hug?"

"She's a Mage! Mage Xeleanor Du'Tam, she says! She wouldn't hug me!"

Fira. If this was the way, this was the way. She turned and gave a slight, warmer bow to Mik, who was a lot but had always been basically nice to Xelle. "This is my friend, Kwill, e."

"Oh, it's so nice to meet you. Why don't I put on some tea and cookies."

"That would be lovely," Kwill said.

"Just tea for me, I had a large breakfast in the city." Xelle wanted to set that expectation now, before she had a stack of huge cookies passed her way.

"Oh, that's fine," Mik said, and turned, presumably into their kitchen.

Rod's gathering space had this rather exquisitely constructed set of furniture with polished wood frames that looked like it was built with an expectation of hu bone structure being a good quarter larger than any actually were, but not so bad once you found a way to sit on it.

"So this isn't purely a social call, as I mentioned in the note. I have a matter of business to discuss with you."

"Did you hear that?" Rod called back. "Our little cura is conducting Tower business!"

Yes, she could tell him to stop calling her things like that, but she'd be out of here soon, and it was at least giving Kwill the full experience. You didn't have to grow up in a gaggle of pompously disconnected Mages to have childhood stuff. Still, no touching.

"This is not Tower business. Not specifically."

"Oh." He looked disappointed.

"But, the project, if it's something you are able to lead, would be a Tower-funded project. Perhaps even one they'd want to make their business."

That got his attention.

"Rod, I am not only a Mage." She kind of wished she hadn't sat down now as this was a rather bold statement to try and make sound impressive with her legs up beside her. Though, having them not touch the floor would be worse. "I am a dragonfriend." She pointed to her sigil. "I communicate with dragons."

Rod looked like he was going to burst. "Really?"

But of course, that would be the reaction of a hu so disposed to impressing others with his innocently told but absolutely untruthfully embellished stories.

"Yes." She said it as seriously as she could. "They are completely real. They are not novelties, they are not heroes or monsters. They are pers who have not been treated well by hu. And, I have found out, they used to live here, in Highponds."

"Wha . . . What are you proposing?" Now he looked worried.

"That you offer your lands, all but this spacious house and work-shop, to a group of dragons. You would be funded to construct for them shelters and structures to their specifications, as a small offer from hu that could not make up for what they've lost but could accelerate their finding comfort here. You would otherwise leave them alone, unless they wish contact. They would not be an attraction. Passage on their lands would be unpermitted by anyone other than you and Mik and any close family."

For the first time in her life, she saw something other than Rod's glossy varnish. His eyes were nearly directly searching, for the point of her tall tale, the punchline, the true meaning of her words.

"She's quite serious, Bon," Kwill said quietly. "We didn't know anyone who could help, but then Xelle thought of you."

"I worked my whole life for this land."

"And you would not lose it," Xelle quickly said. "You would just not own it. And your legacy then, would include this. Being the first of our era to work a lifetime to reach for something that you return to those who have yearned for it longer even than that life."

Rod, still stunned, rose, and paced around the room. "Who else would you ask? People have more, some don't even work for it. They look down on me, but I'm here now. I . . . Who else would you ask? Does it need to be me?"

Xelle sat back. "Who? Who here would?" In his silence, she continued. "Who would not offer some laudable amount of resource, enough to amaze but not enough to miss? Who would say, I have a huge, more than comfortable house, and access to the world. What more do I need? Tell me, and I'll go there."

"No one," Rod said, though more to himself than Xelle. "But, let's say this were even feasible. How could such a thing work? Would we be safe? Who would enforce these rules?"

"Ever Tower," she answered, with a nod. "Mage Towers have a designated role with regard to the populace."

"They do?" He leaned in, looking almost hungry for a good story to not make him think about what Xelle was asking of him and whether she was really asking it.

Xelle nodded. "Yes, you know of many of these roles, though perhaps have not sorted it. Most familiar to you would be Arc, Charm, and Frond. Arc Tower manages maps and routes, Charm currency and trade, and Frond Tower transgressions and uncontrolled individual harm. In addition to those, Dust Tower catalogues and remembers the deceased. And Ever Tower specifically watches over the rights of personhood."

"Oh, like the sanctuaries. And, anima care facilities."

She again nodded. "You know how many resources Towers have. And so, they could fund a sanctuary here, yet for the first time, one administered by those who reside in it. If you are convincing, they could put it in control of the dragons, but under the protection of Ever Tower, and thus, of the Crown of Alyssia."

Rod looked about to overload, so Xelle sat back and let him process, as Mik brought out tea and cookies. She placed the cookies in between Kwill and Rod. Xelle was also pleased to see she'd taken the cue, and given Xelle a relatively small cup of tea. Oh, it was good. The right touch of floral without too floral. "It's delicious," she said, smiling her way.

"That's five. Five Towers." Rod stared at her like he'd found a clue in a game of Secret Visitor.

Xelle did let a grin at this. A carpenter always kept track of all the pieces.

"The roles of Breath Tower and Grand Tower are defunct, and not spoken of," Kwill answered, sounding uncharacteristically protective of eir Tower.

Whatever eir future held, Xelle liked seeing this bit of connection in her friend. One thing Xelle had decided during her weeks in the Breath library history section was that the role of Breath Tower, the covert gathering of information, was absolutely not defunct.

As for Grand Tower, their role was the administration of enforcement and order, in the rough days before the Regions of Alyssia had reached accord. 'Military' was a word some had called it.

From everything she'd heard, she was glad it was defunct. Yet, it was another reason Grand Tower felt isolated, or even, had the reputation of being unfriendly. No populace role, and never on the way to anything else, even by extension.

"Whatever Grand Mages would do, glad they aren't doing it," Rod said, with a bit of guffaw.

By the look in Kwill's eyes, e was both amused and frustrated that Breath Tower had not received the same comment. And probably, a bit satisfied.

Xelle understood now that while the other Towers seemed to think Breath Mages generally held silent irritation at their underwhelming reputation, for those who even gave it thought, the true nature of Breath Culture was an unspoken sense of 'go ahead and underestimate us.'

With what she knew now? Xelle would not. Never now, and never again.

Kwill catching the understanding in her eyes, winked her way. She grinned, then turned to Rod.

"I can only imagine, of course, all of this would cause massive interest here. From those with curiosity, or even harmful intent toward the dragons. And you'd need to deal with the increased traffic to commission your goods."

She noticed that Mik had not left the room, but was sitting in a far corner, listening casually while stitching within a hoop. Would Rod talk to her about this before deciding? Absolutely not. Xelle figured she was here to throw a penalty if needed. In fact, Xelle was now sure she'd been listening from the kitchen also.

"All my land." He gazed over at Xelle. "You really are serious."

"In Tam," Xelle asked softly, "how would you feel, if someone claimed our waterfall for their own?" She paused, then continued. "I believe the dragons would offer you and Mik passage on the lands, some access to the orchards, and such. Your curas and grandcuras. No one else without going through me. As a communicator," she clarified.

His eyes widened. "Do your parents know what you are doing these days?"

Actually, that was a good point. After a couple of days rest (working in the lab, just resting her mind and material), she'd fast travel to Tam for the afternoon and give them an update. "Not all of it," she admitted.

"Then, you're, at Ever Tower?"

Good guess. "No, I'm at Grand Tower for now, not so far from here."

"Oh." Rod stared at her without pretense now, trying to figure out if any of this was real.

"I know it's a lot to spring on you. If you need to think about this—"

He stood up. "I . . . I know you're a villageper and . . ." He seemed totally unable to express the power shift. Xelle didn't want to take satisfaction in that, but not noting it was beyond her capability.

An unexpected voice came from the corner. "Rod. This Mage walks Alyssia bearing the name of Tam. Look at her! Her clothes, her demeanor."

Well, that was a lot, but she wasn't going to argue the point. And she now looked at Rod. Bumbling and spinning on Xelle's every word. She cut a quick look to Kwill and then stood.

"I will not accept an answer today. It is too much to consider. If now is not the time, send sealed word via Post to Grand Tower."

Rod wheezed like an opened balloon, then turned her way. "What . . . what if I do. What . . . would I do?"

"In that case, no need to let me know. You'll need to petition Ever Tower, for whatever amount of money or any permits or other arrangements you think you would need. You surely know this, but I must warn you explicitly—this would be an unpopular development with pers of wealth and power here in Highponds. You would be at risk. You may wish to ask for security. Also, do not mention me in any form."

"Oh, I'm not scared of logbusters. But not mention you? They might think it absurd!"

"I must ask you to trust me on that. Again, only if this is the decision you make." She looked deliberately at Mik as well.

Xelle looked over to see the cookie plate empty. Kwill was chewing. "We must be on our way. Kwill?"

E stood, thanked them both for the hospitality (Xelle was always grateful but often forgot that part, thinking it was inherent) and together, they walked back, quickly enough that Rod could not regain his composure in time to insist on escorting them.

Once through the gates, and fully out of sight, they stopped.

Xelle finally took a moment to gaze around. It really was like a painting here. The flower-covered hills dazzling in the sunlight as if set with emeralds from the lush greenfloor below. She wanted to stay.

But she had to go. "I've got to get back," she said. "Very grateful for you being here."

"I am still in wonder at marvels small as well as large," Kwill said in a flat tone. "We'll talk."

"Yes, yes, we will." And she was grateful when e approached for a long, and so gentle, hug. She closed her eyes. And left.

The Independent: Issue One

First, an introduction. This publication is issued by Bon Tenne Du'Mytil with the assistance of a team. Each issue will feature his own custom illustrations, which may also be cut from the pages and framed, crafted, or used as the basis of tattooing with the full permission of Bon Tenne.

While Bon Tenne is currently on staff at Breath Tower, this publication is independent of any magesphere or populace government. Evidence may not always be presented in these issues, but all statements are believed to be true, and only issued with an eye to risk and responsibility.

We will consistently hold ourselves to a standard worthy, we hope, of your trust.

The goal of this publication is to communicate facts and needs in the interest of an Alyssia ideally without lies, deception, or harm—where all residents may not worry about the shadows of these in the sun or moonslight of our beautiful home.

[The illustration above depicts the sun as a simplified face that is smiling.]

It is because she is known as a truthspeaker that efforts continue to discredit Mage Xeleanor Du'Tam. These should not be believed. We want to disclose: Mage Xeleanor Du'Tam is a source to this publication. She is currently residing at Grand Tower, mostly working in her lab. She asks that hu consider the violations of privacy in discussing her relationships outside of any valid political context and how they would feel were such things made into fundraisers for thieves.

Mage Xeleanor Du'Tam is not affiliated with the Amberborn, has never been affiliated with the Amberborn, and believes the organization to not even exist. If the idea of being manipulated by a plain and unashamed lie is troublesome, perhaps it may cause more thoughts about the intent of such lies, and the tolerance of our society toward them.

Mage Xeleanor Du'Tam is a dragonfriend. This is true. She is in communication with a group of dragons who currently live in the low mountains near Arc Tower. These dragons are lovely beings, with complications of personality like any of us, who desire no harm to hukind. They wish the same in reverse.

[The illustration above depicts Mage Xeleanor Du'Tam as a stick figure surrounded by sparkles and symbolical hearts.]

This first issue will inform readers of two additional items of importance. On this first, there is discomfort reporting without more facts to present, but a need to report on the issue has been forced by the malicious filing of untrue transgressions against Mage Xeleanor Du'Tam.

Irla Du'Lunest and Mark Du'Lunest attempted to capture Mage Xeleanor Du'Tam because of her connection to dragonkind. She escaped and remains under the protection of Grand Tower. And thus, Irla and Mark filed a transgression (reversing the victim of their own assault) in the hopes of removing her from that protection. This publication will not use their titles of Este here not as a sign of disrespect, but a desire not to offer respect to those who would lie in the interests of their own personal wealth and power.

[The illustration above depicts what Bon Tenne imagines Grand Tower to look like, never having been there.]

In a project recently approved by Ever Tower, Bon Rod Du'Highponds is ceding the majority of his property to a sanctuary space for dragons. Yes, this means dragons will be living in Grand Region, amidst the manors of the Highponds. This sanctuary will be under the management of these dragons, not of hu, but will remain under the full protection of Ever Tower and all authorities granted under the jurisdiction of personhood and sanctuary granted to Ever Tower by all hu.

There is no danger posed to the populace by the arrival of these dragons. If you see them flying, wave your greetings; their eyesight will detect the motion and understand the intent. They will not land outside of the sanctuary. And no hu are permitted within its boundaries, except Bon Rod and Bon Mik, who will continue to operate carpentry commissions from their Highponds Manor, and who love to serve tea and cookies and tell stories of what they know.

[The illustration above depicts a dragon, flying freely, wearing a huge top hat and cape.]

The cost of this publication is as low as we could set it and maintain classification as a publication rather than flyer or billing. For those who can, it would be helpful to offer gift subscriptions at your Post, or to buy them by the stack and set them out in establishments loyal to the publication's goals of communicating truth, uncertainty, and ideas.

Unless an emergency need arises, *The Independent* will be published seasonally. A subscription now will provide the summer issue to your Post.

20 - *Of Blood and Spirit*

The Grand Spire wanted to talk to her. Honestly, she'd grown so comfortable in the wand lab and with her monthly meetings with San, she hadn't really thought about the rest of the Spire much. She was immersing in her work here as the spring rush continued in the lab, continuing to practice current and new Arc and at least keep much of the Ever she'd learned, and between that and checking in on Rod's progress, she didn't have a lot of time for much else.

So it actually felt a little like the old days when she received the note, meaning she felt kind of like a normal low-ranking Mage called before a Spire and what she meant by that was she was flame-tossed nervous about it.

She looked at herself in the mirror. Her best lace suit. Was it bad that it was really quite an arcblack? No, that was fine, she was an Arc Mage. No disrespect in that. She thought she looked good. Her cap was on straight. She grimaced, making sure no pieces of anything green had lodged in her teeth from the dried sealeaf crisps she'd munched down to settle herself. She'd found them in Vi'Grand and was going through a slight obsession with the unfamiliar snack, but they sure could leave some prominent flecks of green. Realizing that order of operations was not quite right, she went to the washroom and brushed her teeth another time, just in case.

Now looking in this mirror, a larger, nicer one, she turned, one side, and then the other. She felt pretty good. She'd be fine. She thought.

And Dram was on duty. She'd not really talked to him since their separation, and she'd gotten used to seeing him hurrying (without ever looking hurried) from this side of the Tower to that, but being escorted to an appointment did feel quite different. Meaning, she forced a glassy stare through the gale and hoped it didn't look glassy.

"Hi, Dram," she said. "Or, would you prefer Mage Dram? Sorry, I don't mean that in any way. I'm glad to see you. I still like you. I, uh—" She puffed out her cheeks and stared at him for a rescue. He didn't owe her a rescue. He—

"You may call me Dram in private, as we are. Titles in front of others. Now, please, this way."

There was no invitation to warmth here. But as the one who had ended their relationship, at least as it was, Xelle didn't feel like it was her place to offer it? Or maybe she should? This was really not a good time to consider this and all the sudden she was in front of the Spire. She turned to look for Dram but he had left. She bowed deeply.

To Xelle's sense of metaphorical horror, Crown Mage Da'Selin spoke first. "Mage Xeleanor Du'Tam, you have been operating on quite a scale without our consultation." Then silence. They all just sat there. Ash.

A painful shiver ran down both arms and a knot formed in her chest. She did not want these Mages mad at her. If she owed them an answer, or even if she didn't, and probably that first one, she would provide them one. "I am here in openness and humility," she hurried to say. "Is there a subject of pressing concern, or should I begin?"

No answer. All fires.

Well, she was the dragonfriend. So, then, dragons. "I have not consulted with the Grand Spire regarding the dragons for several reasons, the most notable of which being that clearly, pledged Mages are restricted in their conversations on these subjects for reasons unknown to me."

Holy Firana, now they all looked like she'd just farted and named it or something. What did they want from her? She was not going to figure that out? Maybe just keep going? She looked to the side for Dram's familiar face before remembering he was not there. The gesture was clearly not lost on the Mages, a couple of whom tilted their heads like a degree of a degree, which totally counted as Spire shade. Ugh.

She needed to go harder. "My friendships are my own, and not subject to Tower regulation by any measure. This includes consenting non-hu pers. The dragons, or at least this group of dragons, and no, I do not know if there are others, used to live in the area hu call Highponds. This setting provides fruits, land, and feelings of comfort in the low-rolling hills that are not present in the foothills. And so, I found a hu willing to offer them his own privately-controlled lands. He made a petition to Ever Tower, which was granted. Any discussions I had with Ever Tower were in confidence and not as a representative of Grand Tower, so if Grand Tower has issues to raise, they would be with Ever Tower. I come here in respect and immense gratitude, and welcome your instruction on where my reasoning fails."

There was no answer. Were they waiting to see what else she'd disclose? Sure, what else was there? Dram was none of their business and even any issues of bias were now moot. They didn't know about her nightgarden or daygarden to her knowledge and even if they did, they wouldn't be Grand issues and there were no Arc or Ever pers here looking to demand answers. Well, there was the whole revolution. Which, yeah, they probably knew about now, because of that publication. Which Xelle had agreed to put her name on, while urging Kwill's to stay off of it for now. Well, there was that.

"And yes, I am a part of the team publishing *The Independent*. I could not consult with Grand Tower about this or it would not be independent. I have made no secret of my desire to continue to act in the interests of the per of Alyssia, which includes exposing lies told to them and threats presented to them. I asked them to put my name in it, because if the Lunests are determined to drag my name into this at every turn, then I will put my name out myself, with my own words. If my role in that publication troubles Grand Spire, I . . . I do not know what options exist. I am nervous to leave the protection of this Tower. I am nervous what the Lunests would do. I do have places that I could hide, where I could move my base."

Ash. She worried about this. Worried about what Kwill had said.

Had e seen the paths she was taking before she even did? She did know it. That feeling, growing in her, the one she hadn't even noticed, and she saw where this was going. Where this must go. All at once she felt walloped in the gut, and disoriented, and her voice wavered. "That might be best. I am starting to see that now. I can't keep taking Grand Tower with me, you can't stay with me, I . . . I would like to finish my instruction in the wand lab. I would like to be granted my own wand with your full blessing and trust. I would like to ask for the continued protection of the Seven Spires of Alyssia, including Grand Tower, and I would like the Towers to agree not to discern where it is that I am staying."

What was she saying? What was she doing? She wished there was a way to tell them, to tell them how much she loved it here. How much it hurt to leave again, even if their bringing her here was to help her see she had already chosen that path. Could she just say it? She could try. "I really like it here. I am loyal forever to this sacred space, this culture, the pers here. It is not the pledge a Tower seeks, but it is my pledge." There was more. Her mind was spinning and spinning to grab it and then a waft, a something. She grabbed it and just started talking.

"We are siblings. Arc and Grand. And . . . Dust. Dust would be as well. Keepers of the pathways. If the others are cousins, we are siblings." That maybe wasn't right. Even the closeness of cousins felt too distant for the feelings she had toward Ever. The similarities in their birth, their ways. Her head snapped up. "Or if they are siblings, we are triplets. Life, Death, and World. This is why we quarrel, why we strive for our own images, distinct from the other. And so, I am always your sibling, your sameborn." Whew, she was really going in on this. But this was a Spire. An actual Spire. And for the first time, rather than feeling small before such a group, indifferent, familiar, or inspected, she felt . . . humbled. Grateful. Viewing each as a hu, but a hu who had worked, pushed, sacrificed, to be where they were.

She dropped to one knee, and bowed her head. Then stood again. "This is my petition, Grand Spire. Thank you for allowing me to see it. Thank you for allowing me to make it." She made the sign of Grand, slowly, and with gravity. Then the sign of the Arc, naturally and with the piece of herself that was always in it.

"You are dismissed, Mage Xeleanor Du'Tam," Crown Mage Da'Selin said. "We will consider your petition."

Spire Mage Sandaba, San, her water friend, met her eyes. And made the Grand. *With his wand hand.* Noting this, Beleg also made the sign, with his. Then Spire Mage Shan. The others did not lift their wand hands, but each in turn added the sign, last of all Spire Mage Ghalen. All except Crown Mage Da'Selin, who simply waited, waited for Xeleanor to leave.

She felt alone in the very large room, awkward leaving on her own. Then she saw him, Dram. He reached out his arm, in the way one would properly escort someone of unsteady steps. She took it, and walked out with him, arm and arm.

When they reached the corridor, he added one squeeze. A familiar squeeze, yet not intruding. She felt it, felt it in her arm.

They both turned, and left.

Lightning met her at the archway. She'd chosen to repeat the spot of her arrival, making it both more familiar to the inkbloom, but also as a message to the dragons. That she was here as a visitor, not meant to intrude. And so, she waited here, until Lightning approached, and though zhey still did not try and communicate with em, e walked alongside the striking yellow dragon with the thin back. Until, not just one leader or two, but a group gathered. Yes, she had the sense of a change. She was no longer appealing to one, but visiting as though with a group. They would know, as she was thinking of it now, that she understood this, yet she still made an effort. Or maybe that wasn't a 'still'. To think toward each dragon, no, each per, in turn, guiding her thoughts as one would their gaze.

This was taxing on her mind (Xelle understatement; she was reeling), and she let them know that, that her visit would likely be short, but she wanted them to know the latest.

There is a hu in what hu call Highponds who will be offering you back the land that is currently registered to him. Also to his spouse, but she does not think of her role as the where but more the how. It is their arrangement. He is called Rod and she is called Mik. Rod will maintain a home and generous yard that he continues to claim. He wishes to be able to walk, and also Mik, through your new lands without disturbance, and with any guidelines you wish for me to communicate to them.

Mages (she felt the rumble at this, but yes, she wanted them to know this), *Ever Mages have paid Rod a large sum of resources, basically allowing Rod and other hu to build whatever you need, or carry in any supplies you need to build, from other lands. I did not make this distinction to him, because I wanted to talk to you about it first. He is not my favorite hu—meaning, that is hu sarcasm for a per who may cause some harm without intending to—but he is also an exceptionally skilled carpenter, whose insights and designs have always impressed me. He has a branch from the forest, as we say.*

I need to tell you, this land is small, for all of you or even one of you. It may cause some frustration. But also, there are hills and orchards, and ponds.

I do worry that leaving the obsidian here may offer it more freely to those trying to mine it before, even with the protection of the magesphere. But I do not need to emphasize to Arc Tower the importance of the stone, so I hope that it will remain safe.

That was exhausting. A rapid fatigue; the new phrase came to mind. E stopped.

As e glanced around, with eyes this time, e saw that Lightning asked for eir ready. E nodded, knowing also zhey would have felt if not heard the piece about eir mind.

The concept of separation. But not of Lightning. Not alone, she felt the movement of shapes. But separated.

"You plan to stay here," e asked zhem. "With the obsidian. More than one of you."

Lightning responded with ideas of affirmation, rather than with the nod.

"I know that you are capable, but if you need my help, need to alert the hu of an approach, something I can do, do you have a way to reach me?" E was speaking now out of the utter exhaustion of conscious thought. Words did not come without effort, but they were plain, flat, compared to the intentional shaping of thought.

Skin. Skin skin skin skin. Lightning wanted access to her skin. She touched her face. Repulsion nearly shocked her, and feeling that disgust within herself she pulled off her cloak. Was she supposed to be naked for whatever zhey wanted? At least it was not cold? Surely, not naked?

Then Lightning approached, and without warning—zhey must have taken Xelle's earlier thought for a request, which it was, e hurried to think—zhey slashed at Xelle's arm, leaving two sharp cuts across it. Lightning pulled back, looking surprised by the thin lines of red that blossomed like shirt stripes, but then caught zhemself. And approached Xelle.

Through the sting, Xelle had the impression of stabbing. Of impatience. Understanding, e reached into Essie and pulled out eir small knife. Flipping it open, e hurried around to the back of Lightning's extended front leg, and not finding any area without scales, but an area where they were thinner, e stabbed. The small blade barely poked, sliding in between two scales. E winced, horrified at the violence. But it was done by request, e could heal. If appropriate? Was this it? Was it done?

Connect. *Connect.* **Connect.**

Breathing out rather audibly, for this was all a lot, e leaned in, and pressed eir arm against the small bubble of goo emerging from the scales.

It burned.

It burned like fire, and Xelle crumpled to the ground. Concerned, Lightning nudged em with zheir snout. Not loving, but not uncaring. Worry for eir survival.

Now, e laughed. Standing, the world an absolute blur of pain and exhaustion, e was too tired to ask if these wounds should be healed. Instead e cast over them both, just a cleaning thread, to remove blood from the surface, to remove any impurities. And from Essie, she placed a clothie (not the embroidered one), over the two lines. One of the dragons was pointing to a scratchy tall plant.

A mountain shrub, Xelle might have called it, not knowing a proper name. E moved toward it, and again took out eir knife to cleanly cut off two long leaves. One, e wrapped around her clothie, holding it in place, and thinking even if wrong it would not cause offense, walked to Lightning and wrapped one around zheir leg, securing it with a split notch.

Yes, e would always know where Lightning was.

And zhey em.

She did not have a bad feeling at this, but the unsettled, churning feeling of a new tattoo, however wanted.

Perhaps this was. A different kind of tattoo.

And even once back in her room, she did not cast to heal the skin.

She let it leave a scar.

21 - Spring Blossoms

A mere fortnight before the peak of sunlight to Alyssia, the skies darkened above with the shapes of winged dragons, silhouettes over the fluffy clouds.

One by one, another dragon landed on the soft green grass. Each with hues of jeweled color against a patch of flowers zhey'd chosen, each dragon, even those of considerable age for such stretches of old joints, rolled through the wide, jubilant, blooms.

Some rushed to an orchard, crunching into unripe fruits like the finest of delicacy. Others shook their heads like whelps into bushes of spring berries. They splashed in ponds, howled and giggled, and rolled again, into the grasses and down the soft hills.

Growing bunnies danced without fear at their feet. The birds landed, and joined in their song of reunion. And a hu, young as a whelp and awakening to the world—firefriend to absent Thunder, life-bonded to absent Lightning, and traveler of the sacred pathways—sat, and watched, silent tears pouring down eir glowing cheeks.

It was hard to concentrate on work after all that Xelle had seen. But work needed to be done, and so Xelle reset her breaths, and murmured the next steps to the pages in front of her.

Cataloguing. She never liked the actual cataloguing, Ay'Tea had taken that for her at Arc, and fortunately An'oar had been determined to manage it himself in her earlier assignment. But here, there was neither a Grand Mage nor a lab lead taking these tasks, and so it fell on her to sort the results of this year's curing points, compare them to last year's, and assess any differences that needed to be reported to Mage Ollia and perhaps beyond.

The work was tedious, but it did get her thinking about ideas of old and new. Time and change and other very Arc Mage things to think about something, she thought with an unsettled reassurance. Wands, for example. Wandmaking was such an old craft even its origins weren't documented. Yet every element was assessed. Every wand made, never the same. For every per who scoffed a new type of wand could not exist, there was someone inspired to try it, or someone who happened upon it.

The idea had her at least fascinated enough to endure the writing and checking and double checking and the checking again because she couldn't quite be sure she'd double checked, and oh, if she really was serious about not working in a Tower, the cataloguing would not be missed.

Work was one thing, and tedious tasks had to be done. But not all of them. And not all by only a simple forest per, ol' Xeleanor Du'Tam.

"Your ability to chuckle at your own thoughts astounds and delights me," said Piet, the Study from Ever who had replaced Jalahaja when he'd returned to Charm.

Xelle never got too riled at good-natured teasing, but even less so from this goofy, crinkle-grinned Study. He was as thoughtful as he could be bold, and would make an excellent Ever Mage when he returned home, something he referred to with increasing frequency these days. And Xelle hadn't realized she'd chuckled aloud, but believing Piet, plus feeling the memory still in her chest, she nodded.

"When you love yourself, you always have a friend," she responded, not wanting to take her eyes from the books. Until the door opened. Xelle simply had to look when a door opened. She didn't quite remember when she'd picked up the habit, but it seemed now to have stuck.

And she was not pleased, yet not worried, to see An'oar walking in with a carefully wrapped paper cone. He walked past Xelle like she didn't exist, then stopped, disappointed to see Mage Ollia's desk empty. "Is there a Mage here I can hand this to? They're quite sensitive."

Xelle kept her mouth shut and instead looked across the large room at Flav.

He caught her gaze, then saw An'oar and walked over. "Mage An'oar, hello. Oh! These are the petalcurled." Carefully taking them from An'oar, he touched his wand just barely in between the papers and closed his eyes. "Oh, absolutely perfect." He walked them over to the shelves. "Study, could you help me find an air case?"

"Right away." Piet walked over to assist Flav, leaving Xelle and An'oar alone. While Xelle had been content that the hu would have ignored her then left, he now, as he saw it, was obligated to bestow upon her some wildly condescending small talk. Xelle wasn't looking for a tussle. Before she could think of some phrasing that would end it quickly, he was strolling her way.

"Petalcurled stalks. For the flowers we need here. There's only the shortest window to pick them, in between when the petals begin to wilt but before they separate. Highest potency for a sap additive."

"That's interesting," she said. "I love the forest myself, it's cool that you can find the flowers so precisely."

"Yes, well it's no big deal," he answered. "I've been a Mage for almost fifteen years, gathered hundreds of specimens. Some commendations," he muttered, almost as if someone had asked him to mention it.

Xelle smiled. "It's wonderful."

"Well, I should be going," he said.

"Take care," Xelle answered. And went back to her catalogue.

Warning notices were sent out first through the city of Wehj. Delivered by carrier, as though in an emergency situation. They warned of the violent dragons, warned pers that they fought each other for survival in their mountain home, and they would treat hu the same way.

The next set went through Highponds. These said that Ever Tower took issue with Grand Tower after their sheltering of Xeleanor Du'Amberborn, and the Mages of Ever Tower were now planning to use their populace-given authorities to take pieces of Grand Region under their control, starting with those of most influence. That these huge dragons would never be satisfied with a small piece of land, they were already flying overhead other lands, scouting for more land, and that soon, every home in the Highponds would be taken by the magesphere, their residents pushed out to find new homes and live on Basic.

Xelle, already deep in wand creation, realized if she was not going to stay here, then she should take advantage of every moment left. And so, making sure Kwill knew this, and putting off her intended visit to Tam, she dedicated herself to private mentorship, reading through key volumes in the library, attending some shorter-length workshops, and learning what she could about the fundamentals of Grand Magic.

She did check in every day with Thunder. Zhey were no longer patient, but restless, and Xelle tried not to linger on thoughts that this was zheir idea, and knowing Thunder would find those in the strands, intentionally adding in that Xelle understood what that felt like. Deeply. To make an effort at something, take a risk, bear a pain, and then have weeks pass without any resolution whether it had even been a good idea in the first place.

One thing the practice was good for was Xelle's ability to understand (and not entirely retch over) the senses Thunder sent, even moving to two (they weren't really countable, but the concept of it) at a time, and then more.

And so, she saw the faces of those who visited, at least in the way that Thunder saw them. Never Mark, never Irla by sight. She could taste one or the other of them—oof, that meant Thunder could smell them—nearby at times, usually Mark, but they were never where Thunder could see or hear them.

Two hu interacted with Thunder. One was the Grand Mage. The way Thunder's senses worked (and Xelle also believed some clouding from the magic and wraps the Mage used), Xelle could not have described her, at least not with enough certainty to not accidentally accuse the wrong Mage. Thunder did not recognize a hu by the contours of a face, but by the entire sense of that per. So Xelle could not really see the Mage, yet she was, in many ways, getting to know her. She knew 'her' because Thunder could not repeat the Mage's thoughts, but could convey Thunder's own sense of her. She was . . . unkind. Slighted. Angry. Xelle did not think she had been turned under duress, but more, opportunity. She was not cruel to Thunder (beyond the inherent and obvious, Xelle meant) but she did not care for zhem. Did not marvel at zhem.

What she did do is try to coax Thunder to cast zheir magic in order to find treats: a new toy for the day, or luscious desserts. If Thunder used zheir magic to retrieve the item, then she would use her wand (Thunder was very focused on the wand) to try and change the nature of what was done. Thus, as was clear to both Thunder and Xelle, she was both testing what type of casts or abilities a dragon possessed, but also how her own Grand Magic interacted with, or could enhance, those abilities.

Refusing to engage could put Thunder at risk, and would also reveal the level of zheir understanding of the situation, and so Thunder balanced this. Sometimes, zhey admitted, a few of the treats looked too good not to break through whatever casts the hu used. Sometimes, zhey would pretend to look confused when zhey were not.

The strain of Thunder having to assess every action, and how to respond, and then remembering zheir previous responses was tiring zhem with increasing weight. Zhey were quickly growing miserable, but still, insisted that as zhey would do this exactly once (a new decision) zhey would not leave. Not quite yet.

As for the Mage's thoughts, again Xelle could only understand a limited and filtered version through Thunder's communications, but the Mage seemed focused on the tasks. On the casts. There was more, some mix of emotions and desires and fears. But if she thought of specific hu or specific plans beyond the day's tasks, it was not making its way to Xelle.

The other Mage was the Breath Mage, associated strongly with Thunder's sense of taste. This Mage had more emotions, but if she thought of specific motivations, they were beyond Thunder's understanding. Not greater than, of course, but something uniquely hu. Xelle tried to translate it. Jealousy, or pettiness? Profit. Revenge. A threat, or misguided love, as had been done to Kern. But as Thunder couldn't understand it, Xelle did not have enough basis to guess.

This Mage did not run experiments, at least not of the magic kind. This Mage was a groomer. Meant to earn false trust. Sitting, offering music, paints, or companionship. Thinking mostly of that, of gaining the dragon's trust through ease and familiarity. Of other things, too, but nothing that Thunder wanted to emphasize. Really, zhey tried not to tell Xelle as much about this Mage. Thunder found her actions, her feigned friendship, much more offensive than cakes hidden in puzzles, and Xelle had to agree. Xelle worried that the Breath Mage was using inhalants, or could be slipping potions into Thunder's food, but Thunder remained convinced she was not. Zhey would taste any magic, zhey insisted.

She hoped that was right.

Kern was never there, never around. So Irla's trust of him seemed to be limited. But, through the combination of Thunder's understanding of the Mage, and Xelle's own, they could tell he was still there somewhere, still involved, because traces of him appeared in the threads of thought of the Breath and Grand Mages. There were emotions with them. Conflict, confusion, maybe even dislike or distrust.

Again, Xelle had to keep in context that whatever Thunder was understanding of these hu's thoughts was not a direct transfer even to Thunder, let alone through Thunder's thoughts to Xelle's perception. Still, it was more than they had before.

Three Mages. Kern. The detached Grand Mage. The disturbed Breath Mage. Xelle thought then, which Tower had the forth? Charm.

Seemed that a Charm Mage would do the part of the Breath Mage. Sure, Breath was for subtlety, quiet, and core being, but the magic most closely tied to emotion was Charm. One could easily argue (if one was not being Tower-centric) that a turned Charm Mage would be the most dangerous of all. Persuasive. Compelling. Able to change the nature of objects temporarily.

But then, then Thunder understood. Zheir thoughts nearly tumbling over each other, Xelle asked zhem to slow down. The Breath Mage had thought this; thought she didn't want to be there. The Charm Mage, as Xelle had thought, should be there.

But the Charm Mage, the Charm Mage had left.

No one knew where the Charm Mage was.

What can you tell me? Anything about this Mage?

Thunder waited, and when zhey answered this was what Xelle could make of it: She holds (has? knows?) something important. Mark did something bad, related to her. At least, the Mage and Irla thought it was bad. Irla is going to find her.

Anything else? Even if it doesn't seem important?

Zhey did not have much else. But Xelle listened, asked zhem to repeat it, and translated into the way she could think of it, remember it, until Xelle did not think there was more to glean. And when they disconnected, Xelle repeated it again, to herself, not wanting to write anything down until she was somewhere safe, but remembering, clearly, for now:

The Breath Mage and the Charm Mage had not met, before the Lunests. The Charm Mage was there, first. The first of the Mages. Then the Breath Mage and the Charm Mage had been lovers, both together, and with Irla. (Xelle skipped some sensations about the sexual experiences involving the three, but would summarize it as effective lovers.) The Charm Mage left without warning. And the Charm Mage had a tattoo. An artfully placed series of blooms that Xelle did not recognize. Delicately petaled with a set of many more stamens, the stamens as pretty as a flower in themselves.

Xelle would never forget the image itself. The Breath Mage had touched it, traced it, licked it.

Xelle found the idea of sharing hu thoughts less appealing all the time.

She had enough of her own.

Xelle recognized the flutter of fabric in such a way, when the Mage sat across from her at the outside table where she'd taken her soup. Dropping her spoon with zero matching elegance, she looked up to see Helia grinning right at her.

"Beautiful day at Grand Tower," she said, clearly pleased with herself at whatever expression her arrival had caused on Xelle's face.

The first thing Xelle saw was Helia looking as happy and radiant as she'd seen her, which was saying a very lot. The second thing Xelle saw was her soft chest tissue peeking from layers of sheer peachy fabric under a minty green robe. The third thing she saw was an upgraded mark on her chain, signifying she was fully assigned to diplomacy at Arc. She commented on the third.

"Hellie. Diplomacy, already? You're doing amazing. I guess that explains why you're at Grand Tower, and why you don't have anyone trailing you around."

Helia grinned. "Yes, yes, and yes, and you forgot one. Why I'm here. Because I miss you, I miss your face, and Xelle—you have a whole new look to you."

"Huh?" Xelle didn't think she'd spilled soup on herself or anything.

"The lace. The Arc coding to the color and dress. Your demeanor. You're carrying yourself like the per I've always seen you as. And I must say, I'm delighted."

Xelle stretched back, curling her shoulders, over the old wood table bench. "Now, first, you've only seen me plopped at an outdoor table. And I can't have any expectations I haven't lived up to, here."

Helia shook her head. "Do you have time to talk this afternoon?"

"I should be in the wand lab for a few more hours, once I'm done with the soup." Xelle assumed that meant in private, or she'd just stay here a little longer. "Have dinner plans?"

"I do," she said, her eyes making her thinking face. "It's a late dinner, in Wehj, and we'll be taking the vroom from there, but . . . We should have a good hour or two, I think. Plenty of time to catch up."

She leaned in. "If you'll forgive my lack of diplomacy, several pers have informed me that you are no longer involved with Staff Mage Dram. Which is good, actually, because I met him this morning and knew better than to mention you."

A not totally subtle way of reminding Xelle she hadn't been writing. "Yeah, I should have told you." She shifted again, on the bench. "There's this weird thing about everyone writing and talking about you that makes you feel like pers know everything anyway. Like it doesn't matter. To reach out."

"May I?" She extended her hands.

Xelle nodded, and Helia reached out to hold Xelle's non-spoon-holding hand with both of her own. It felt really nice. Really, really nice.

"They are not talking about you, they are talking about an image of you. One they do not know, one laced with truth, untruths, and suppositions of both varieties. We're all weaving tapestries, Xelle. Some more ordered, and some more chaotic, and with looms less linear that we like to think."

Fira, it was nice to hear the logic of an Arc Mage again. Xelle just wanted to curl in her lap like a kitten and go to sleep.

"I also think that you are worried about my exposure to you, and while I may not be as system-bucking as the forestper from Tam, I am absolutely my own Mage. I am not concerned about our association being known." She looked down at the hand of Xelle's that she caressed, and Xelle did not pull it away.

Xelle, instead, felt something. 'Something'—that was ridiculous.

The blandness of her conscious thought was her way of acknowledging that in that moment, she wanted to burn the world down for anyone who cared as much about her as Helia did. No, not cared about. Would stand by.

Or maybe that was cared about. All Xelle knew is whatever happened in her life, whatever happened in Helia's life, they were going to be friends through it all. Solid. Loyal. Understanding. Honest. An absolute treasure.

She was not going to cry at the table.

"Meet me at the wand lab at social hour," she managed to say. "I'll introduce you and give you a quick show around, and then we'll walk to my room. I'll keep you unruffled for your dinner appointment."

"Mmm." Helia's eyes sparkled. She did have that eye sparkle down.

The rest of the afternoon felt like forever, even as Xelle gently added another swatch of freshly pulled bark fibers to the case she was using to gather them. One didn't have to pull the fibers oneself to make the wand their own, but the fact that Xelle had learned how to do it, in a way that seemed passable to the lab (at least in the making of her own wand) felt pretty special.

The idea of leaving the Tower, which she knew, at least for now, meant leaving all Towers, weighed on her more and more as the days had passed. She hadn't changed her mind on it, but in many ways, she was glad she had time this time. Time to think. Time to marinate. Time to really understand the blessings and privilege of working in a Tower, and absorb every bit of that exposure that she could, before leaving.

Gently, gently, so as not to cause any disturbance to the newly pulled fibers, she closed the fiber case. And the water case which kept her bark in a steady state for the work.

She'd distracted herself just to the point of non-misery when she saw Helia walk into the lab. Mage Helia. And she really looked and acted the part now, not just in her demeanor and confidence (she'd worked on that for years), but the ease with which she carried them. (Not implying it was an act; Xelle was simply proud.)

No need for Xelle to introduce, Helia was here for diplomacy. Helia spoke to Mage Ollia, and Xelle kept her distance, and then Xelle approached, walking the Mage around the lab spaces, introducing her and showing her some of the more interesting equipment. (Helia was always fascinated by the mechanical, especially when integrated with the magical.)

But, knowing their time was short, Xelle left much alone. And was comforted when Helia reached for her hand, as they walked down the corridors together, ignoring the looks and starts of the pers they passed.

Once in the room, once in private, and with Helia making her own cast to contain their conversation, Helia finally relaxed. "May I have a hug?"

It felt like a cast, without being one, like one that pierced through her chest. "You may always have a hug from me. Oh, Hellie."

Xelle was known to be a rather brief hugger, a reputation that she resented. And so, not sensing discomfort from her friend, she held her longer than before. She let her hands run over the soft fabric of the Mage's back. She pressed in, slightly, like a cat making sure one knew ae was there.

She drew back, reluctantly. "So you're getting married!"

"I am. And perhaps we can sit?" Smiling, clearly no slight intended, Helia walked over to Xelle's little table, sitting in one of the chairs. "Beautiful desk. No couch," she noted.

Yeah. Maybe there was something to that. Something in the reluctance to settle here, to know somehow, that it wouldn't last. Not with Xelle. Not with Xelle always—

"Love, don't spin. Here, sit, across from me." Helia patted the table, and feeling a bit disoriented, Xelle sat across from her.

"Brought this from the diplomatic suite!" Helia somehow pulled a large bottle from her purse, one that was stylish enough Xelle hadn't realized how large it must be. "It's an herbal water, infused only today from summer herbs foraged today. The kind of thing one serves to impress." She leaned forward. "Perhaps I wish to impress you."

"Done," Xelle murmured, casting to bring two water glasses from the wall-installed cabinet over to the table. Noticing they were a bit foggy, she also cast to clean them. "I'm so happy for you. You know that, right?"

Helia made a strange face that Xelle could parse better when she wasn't feeling galecaught. "I do." She looked like she had more to say, but Xelle wasn't in a position to press. "More about that later. I have something a bit more serious to discuss with you. Our conversation from earlier."

The mention brought her back a little. "About protecting you?"

"Mm. I had not used that word. I need you to know something now. However you view it, whoever has warned you elsewise, I make my own decisions. I always have and always will. I trust you." She winked. "Essentially. But, anyway."

What did that mean? Xelle made an annoyed face.

"Oh, don't pout, love. What I am saying is, anything that you choose not to tell me, or show me, is also your choice. But if you are doing it for me, in any context, then please, stop."

Suddenly she dropped the charm, and looked very . . . vulnerable. "I am not saying you have to or should tell me everything. I'm asking if I'm the friend I think I am to you. And what it is that you meant. Before."

Xelle sipped on the herbal water, which was one of the best things she'd ever had and she had complicated feelings about that. She resolved to figure out how to make things like this and stock them in her home. Her new home. Her future home. Water. It reminded her.

"There is a Mage here who taught me something about a water toast. Have you heard of it?"

Helia smiled. "I have indeed."

"Could we make one? With this extraordinarily delicious water?"

Helia leaned in. "Oh, I almost thought you said make out."

"You're getting married?"

"I am indeed. And I am looking very much forward to the two of you meeting and sharing your forest tales. But for now, I am thinking our water toast could be a bit unconventional." She shook one finger. "Just remember, no rumpling. I have an appointment in Wehj."

Xelle was getting tingly. "In that case, let's wait until the end for the toast. I . . ." Firana Stalker of Night she loved this hu. "I am leaving Grand Tower before the end of the year. I have two secret places I can hide, if needed. Most of the time, I will be at a home I built myself in the forests around Ever Tower."

Helia's eyes flared. "An interesting choice."

Whatever. "Sure. And I also have a growth of . . . inkbloom, at Arc Tower. A small space, but the phyta are happy there. I am willing to show you both, if you'd like to see."

Ha! Helia looked stunned now. Xelle couldn't help but savor this slightly. "I am also linked to a specific dragon. Zheir name is Thunder, and zhey are currently being held by the Lunests, who I believe to be, no sorry, I know to be, behind much of the difficulties of the last couple of years. Including the attempted intervention with Arc Ascension. Zhey are fine-ish for now, we talk every day but I will feel much better when zhey are out of there, and can rejoin those living in the Highponds, to a refuge I orchestrated with a carpenter from Tam that really irritates me but came through solidly on this one. And, yes, as you will know, the same Lunests who attempted to have me expelled from the mage-sphere (at least) twice, once by petitioning Grand Tower, and then by influencing someone at Frond Tower. Regarding the publication that came out this spring, with another issue forthcoming, my dear, dear, friend Kwillen Du'Satta is, for now, quietly behind it, using Tenne Du'Mytil, who didn't really win the E'lle Prize but has turned out to be a true ally, and one I weirdly trust, as the front. I am probably forgetting a lot of things, but I've been deep in work here taking every appropriate advantage I can of Grand Tower, while preparing to leave, and also preparing to make my own personal wand, with their blessing. I am so happy you're going to be married, I'm so excited to meet your soon-to-be spouse, and I love you forever, as a friend, a partner, and someone I am so glad to take a water toast with. I am surely, surely, forgetting a lot of things right now."

Helia sat for a long moment. "Xelle," she said, and for the first time ever, she saw her friend a bit overwhelmed. "I am ready for that toast. And what you said, it was fine. It was perfect. I am . . . glad you are outside Ever Tower, though for reasons I cannot get into now. Xeleanor Du'Arc, I am in love with you now and always."

Xelle didn't even know what was really happening at this point. Yet, they'd lifted their glasses, took a sip, and then kissed amidst herbs and withheld desire and a promise of friendship forever. They kissed—for the ages.

22 - Summer Blooms

Spring turned into summer, as it tends to do. And Xelle had gathered all the components e most wanted for eir wand. Each was being held, preserved, in specialty cases with protective casts casually named after natural elements, but once gathered, waiting further only introduced risk.

Xelle was ready.

The birth of a wand required three elements to plan, each in groups of three, which in a way Xelle couldn't explain, reminded em of starting a wave, like the threes would carry on from there. But, for eir purposes, three and three.

First, the materials. A base, a fabric, and a mortar, they called them.

The base was made of wood. In Xelle's case, a sprig, only palm's length, of two vines, one of yellow rose, and one of star jasmine, that had naturally twined around each other in the gardens outside of To'Arc, so tightly that the woods had fused.

This had raised some eyebrows, as the base needed to be a single wood, but Xelle was convinced, from the moment e saw it, this was eir base.

It was not dried, but still fresh as when alive, kept so in a carefully cast, custom-made (for the size) case, that in a gesture of respect, Xelle would be donating back to the wand lab. Everything e'd done and made would stay here, except for the wand itself, and the small pocket e'd sewn into the inside of eir cloak, on eir left side, to sheathe it.

The second piece was the fabric, pulled from fibers of a bark. In this case, a mix of bark fibers was standard, but Xelle had only used one. The bark of an oak tree from the forests outside of Grand. E had cut no corners, pulling the threads bit by bit, and layering them into the case. The weaving of the fabric was beyond eir skill, and so e was honored when Ollia herself wove the swatch, and cut it to the size needed, before placing it gently in another protective case.

And the third item, they called the mortar. There were similarities to the process of enchantments conducted by Ever, and really, to many of the other prongs. Runepaint, charmed objects, etc. Again, it was really only Arc who touched nothing while casting. Nothing physical, e clarified, though thinking this only to emself.

For the mortar, e'd chosen a light, sweet birch sap e'd tapped emself from eir homevillage of Tam. Again, simple. Pure. No mixtures, no paints, no powder of petals. Given the requirements for collection and preservation, e'd conducted the trip as e had the one to To'Arc. Quietly, without being seen, and without speaking to anyone of eir presence. It had felt strange to be there and not stop in, but she reminded emself, once out of the Tower, of the tremendous freedom of time that would be eirs to command.

E would be back. Hopefully, more often.

And so the birch sap sat in a beautiful black glass jar, inside a third case, kept at the right temperature and humidity.

One component eir wand would lack was the essence of an evergreen. E'd thought about this, seriously, and more than once. In the end, e had trusted eir feelings and decided against it. It would be easy, of course: a fine powder of needles stirred into the sap, or a light rub of seed butter on the sap jar. A kiss of holly berry juice. A few threads of pine bark, even from eir daygarden, the hint of essence. But e had not.

In all the ways that Xelle was, emself, evergreen, in all the ways the greens of winter stirred and calmed eir soul, e did not think eir wand needed such an element. Truly, e craved the nakedness of it, the vulnerability. An element different than emself. Ungrounded.

With the materials in place, the second need was the choice and consent of three wanded casters, to birth the wand, as they phrased it.

Of course, in To'Grand that meant there were all sorts of legends about the first wands, from three founding Mages to mythical intervention, to whispers that Mages of other prongs had made the first wand, or even—what if there weren't always seven prongs, but Xelle figured it was like most things. Using a hammer to forge a hammer didn't mean there wasn't a first hammer. Pers loved their drama.

And not unrelated, Xelle had worried quite a bit about the choice of eir Mages. Asking for fewer than three felt disrespectful, as did asking Mage Dram. It's not that he wouldn't have done it, or with incredible skill (stop), but it simply didn't feel right.

Ollia was her first choice. She had been a good mentor, certainly not a friend but with many parallel feelings of warmth. Xelle didn't know if there was protocol against asking the wand lab lead, but Ollia's response was easy and Xelle had the impression she'd probably been in quite a few of these ceremonies, especially with the exchange Studies.

Next, e chose San. E spun over this! Not whether he would say yes or no based on his comfort, but what level of audacity e might be displaying asking a Grand Spire Mage to participate in the birth of eir externally-gifted wand. But, they had taken a water vow, and so, voice shaking, e asked him, and he, warmly, said yes.

Asking another Mage from the wand lab didn't feel balanced, and so e fretted quite a lot over the third choice. Especially as many of the Mages e'd met over the last months could not be assured to not be the turned Mage, and despite em not *thinking* any of them were turned (or of course e would not have grown friendly), e could not fathom the potential consequences of such a risk.

But then, who was e more connected to here than Mage Frealonn, who had stood by eir side, made great unfamiliar efforts for em over untrodden ground. Frealonn could not be the turned Grand Mage, there was just no sense of the pettiness and anger Thunder had seen, and Frealonn spent most of her time here. Mage Frealonn had stared at em a long moment, then unreadably agreed.

Xelle decided to take it. There was no 'rescind the offer over lack of enthusiasm' and the Mage was a diplomat. (And apparently not viewing Xelle as a source of diplomatic influence, ha.)

And then, for Xelle the most complicated component of the three components, were the words. Three words or short phrases: one thought, one whispered, and one spoken. The longer the phrase, the more skill would be needed in its cast, and the harder it might be to give it more potency. But then, one could argue shorter words might carry less. This felt like a lot to consider.

And then, the rules. No one else could touch a Grand Mage's wand. And no one else would hear the words spoken, outside of the three present. The witnesses.

The ceremony started without the formality e would have expected. The witnesses seemed nearly giddy, as though it really were a family event, the caring for another. Ollia went over the ceremony for Xelle one last time, and reminded em the phrase that would signify the start of silence, the actual birth of the wand, ending when Xelle took it into eir hand.

Even the distinction between these leaders of research, management, and diplomacy did not feel significant here. San joked with Frealonn and Ollia like old colleagues at a tavern, and Xelle wondered for a moment how long they might go on. Surely they were busy.

Ollia seemed to be reading eir thoughts. "It is a special moment, no matter how many times one witnesses it. Perhaps there is no equivalent at Arc?"

There was, e suddenly realized. The first moment of traveling the pathways. Of connecting with the inkbloom. But Xelle did not know how that was handled at Arc, because e'd not pledged. E'd not known how it was taught, nor how it was witnessed. They were so used to thinking of Xelle as a Mage, e realized they'd forgotten how much e had not experienced. From preparation, to pledging, to initiation.

San was watching em, and e did see some of that dawn in his eyes. "Mage Xeleanor Du'Tam, we would be honored for you to begin." He nodded toward the table, a fine, old cloth of velvet and beads upon it. Set in a triangle, the cases for the base, the fabric, and the mortar, and in the center, what they called the cradle, a specially-made custom shape of smooth, polished metal, fitted exactly for this wand, and melted back into the supply of such metal after the conclusion of the ceremony.

First, e put on the custom gloves. Some sewed their own, then kept them like one might keep a baby's first cap. Xelle's sewing was not nearly fine enough for such a task (Xelle's sewing was not fine enough for any task requiring a look other than determination and chaos) and so Mage Flav had made them for em. Simple. Black. No adornment other than a small embroidered X at the wrist of each.

After smoothing the gloves against each other, against eir hands, e opened the first case and lifted the twining vines. Realizing e, too, was lifting it like the smallest hu baby, e smiled. Glad to feel some part of what the others felt. Honored. E smiled at San, hoping he saw this too.

He did. And he then looked down at the base. (E had been told over and over, it could not be called a wand until it was complete and the words spoken, and held by the hand or equivalent and touched to the skin of the Mage.)

"As beautiful as it is unique," he said.

Eir chest felt wobbly. A friend. A Spire Mage. Eir find of woods, from a garden that e loved. "They fused," e said. "As they grew."

"I see," he said, not unkindly but acknowledging he had sensed that in them.

Then, e reached into the sap, and layered the sap over the base, turning slowly and gently, ensuring that it fell and dropped over every piece, including the little curves and turns of the shape.

When it felt right, and at this point feeling very nervous and overwhelmed, e reached toward the fabric. Eir hand was shaking, and Ollia asked, "May I?" Knowing Ollia would not suggest anything that might cause an issue, Xelle nodded, and watched as she gently lifted the fabric, not casting, but manually, and guided it onto the metal cradle. She spoke soothingly to Xelle as Xelle lowered the base onto it, and then pulled the fabric around, making sure it adhered to the mortar. The swatch that Ollia had made was perfect, meaning that while the whole thing looked like a mess of fiber and goo, the fabric met exactly at its seam. Xelle lifted eir hand away and removed the gloves, setting them onto a smooth table waiting to the side. This, then, was it.

Ollia looked to see if e was ready. Then, she looked to San and Frealonn, who both nodded.

"Speak thrice. And may a new life begin."

Xelle had been taught those words, the new life, did not actually refer to the birth of the wand, but the part not spoken of so casually, the birth of the Mage. The idea that no matter where one has been, in the pathways of life, many things are possible. Many more things once connected to them, than observing them from the outside.

The birth was Xelle's.

First, the words e would think. A silent cast. Never revealed to anyone else, but the passion of one's true self, concentrated. Remembered.

E gazed at the object on the cradle, and made eir cast: *My heart speaks truth.*

Nothing appeared to happen. E hoped e had done it right. But e could not ask now, not in any fashion. E had to continue.

Second, the words e would whisper. A quiet cast. Heard only here, and only if those e trusted chose to listen. The quiet of one's spirit, open. Breathed.

Whispering into the utter silence, e stared down at the small bundle. "I love you," e whispered.

Feeling an energy rising in em, e needed to complete this now. E needed to say eir last phrase, the one e had chosen, a word only.

Third, this word e would say. A loud, open cast. Released. Shown. Proud. "Together," e stated, looking at each of eir witnesses in turn as they raised their wands and cast together, and then e looked to where their wands pointed, seeing not a bundle below them, but the vines as they had been, but now magically protected, held in this state of beauty and calm as long as e wished them so. E lifted it into eir hand.

The three burst into cheers. Even the normally straight-faced

Frealonn beamed, tears in her eyes. San reached forward for a hug, which e gladly returned. And Ollia looked every part the professor, urging em onward. "Try it!" she said. "Something simple, now!"

Xelle had thought about this from the moment e'd learned you actually were supposed to try it out in front of everyone. Not even for show, but to confirm to the wand the connection that each—the wand and the caster—had offered to each other.

For this first use, e wanted to cast only with Grand, which was quite difficult as Xelle now had much of eir mind connected to the pathways. The Arc pathways, e meant. And so for this, e sought only the Grand pathways. The pathways of life.

And remembered the moment when e'd found the vines, twirled playfully in the wind, jutting out over the path, where they would surely be trimmed, for safety, without their elegant dance noticed by a harried gardener.

And breathing in like the freshest air had filled the old, embedded space, e closed eir eyes, and swayed, around, conducting with eir beating heart, feeling life, feeling its permanence and delicacy, the reach and depth of its pain and the gorgeousness of its passions.

E did not look. E did not worry. E felt the pathways, felt the wand, glad to assist in this natural, wonderful, whimsy, and when e opened eir eyes, the entire lab had been transformed. Tumbling yellow roses, climbing star jasmine, and a mix of springing grasses and ivy filled the spaces, wound on every column, every shelf, around every sacred case, because they were not really here. They were in eir heart, in eir wand, and in every bit of love and openness e wanted to live by now, in this birth, in this new life. Trust, Love, and Connection. The essence of Xeleanor Du'Tam.

Suddenly exhausted, e tripped, and fell back, caught by San's arms, yes, his soft bosom, and a loud "whoa" as the Mage guided em into a seat. Looking overwhelmed, he said, "Thank you. We'll talk soon?"

Xelle nodded, and he turned from the lab. Ollia was silent and went to sit at her desk, watching the blossoms sway and turn.

And Mage Frealonn waited, as if hoping to say something to Xelle. Putting one hand on the edge of Xelle's chair, she leaned forward. "I have never been asked before. To witness. Thank you for these, and thank you for that." It was about as poetic as Frealonn got, and she took a sharp breath and whisked herself out of the room.

"You should go rest," Ollia said. "Use the washroom first, you'll sleep much longer than you expect. I'll make sure no one disturbs you."

Feeling that exhaustion setting in, Xelle rose.

"I'll take care of all this," Ollia said. "And may I keep them?" She pointed at the flowers. "A bit longer, before I call the others back. Not too long." She smiled. "There is work to be done."

"You may. This feeling." E pointed around, realizing e was using eir wand to point. "I used Grand Magic. As simply and purely as I could. But this feeling, a garden in spring. The scents and colors and order in disorder. This is . . . outside of Arc Tower."

Ollia nodded, smiling.

And oh, Xelle had one more thing to say, just to be clear about what that meant.

"This is me."

~

The Independent: Issue Two

The focus of this summer issue will be to communicate the status of the area under operation of Alyssian dragons.

Alyssian is emphasized not to suggest any other type of dragons, but to remind and reiterate that all per should have equal standing in our shared home.

[The illustration above shows a rough map of Alyssia surrounded by symbolical hearts.]

Mage Xeleanor, as dragonfriend, has some ability to communicate with these dragons. The dragons have conveyed to her that they would like to be referred to as a home. The place in what we call Highponds where they now live is best referred to as, per best interpretations, Drophome. As the association of group and place is clearly less distinguished than in hu parlance, we will, instead of vaguely calling them 'the dragons', refer instead to the pers or residents of Drophome.

These residents have offered permission to discuss their building efforts on this land. On their own, they had requested lumber, stones, and various mortars to create a series of structures for shade, rest, and privacy.

Bouncing off of a session of ideas, Bon Rod Du'Highponds has added a series of formal firepits, including one with various bowls, grates, and baskets for ease of marination, roasting, and especially soups, which are the biggest new trend in Drophome. He has also added a raised platform for smoking without disturbing non-smokers, a series of large wood diamondboard pieces to which the per are inventing their own rules, and to one far side of the land, a series of large chimes.

[The illustration above: The set of chimes, with notes bearing symbolic smiley faces on their round parts.]

Once it was all done, a need for group privacy was discussed, and so a tall, latticed structure on the farthest end of the property was added, with a shelf of chairs that could be brought down to accommodate hu.

Most popular of all, though, is the tiered slide. Really an expert-piece of design, the layered set allows pers to land atop various platforms, curl their wings in, and then slide down. The lower slides reach the soft ground below, but the two highest lead into either a pond or a hugely stretched canvas that bounces the per up upon impact where they may again engage their wings, or give it a couple more bounces.

[The illustration above depicts a per happily bouncing down a long slide, surrounded by sparkles.]

Not all is fun. The pers of Drophome have relationships. They have quarrels. They argue over roles. Things around them break, or fail. They feel sad, sometimes. They must comfort each other, when the feelings are too much.

All of this seems wise to remember when considering this new space.

23 – Love in Nature

Xelle wondered if there would be a time Helia would communicate more frequently by calling and other Arc Magic, but her handwritten notes on exquisite paper and with exquisite tapes and marks of colorful ink made her rather hope that she would not.

This one had been a bit brief.

Mage Xeleanor,

I will have several days in a row without obligation, and with wedding plans in work, not much flexibility to change them. With that, I have somewhere I would like to go with you. Please let me know soonest whether you'll be able to meet me, a week from the sending of this note at lunch hour. We'll start with a pair of cocktails? I'll see you there.

With fond anticipation—

Helia

The note having been sent a week ago today, Xelle sat now, in the Enchanted Forest hoping that she hadn't misinterpreted the reference. But surely, if she'd meant Grand Village or Arc Tower, or anywhere else, she would have been more specific. And she knew about Xelle's ability to travel.

"If it's your friend from before that you're waiting for, she'll be here." Klein walked over, and set down two beautiful golden drinks, each with a topping of marigold flower petals that looked like they'd fallen onto a lake reflecting the golden tones of the sun.

If anyone other than Klein had suggested somehow knowing whether a specific per was arriving from across the land based on no information, Xelle would have at least been annoyed. But Klein always seemed to know. Also knowing he'd not let such a lovely set of drinks lose their chill, she swiveled her stool around, waiting.

A minute later, she walked in. Xelle did not think she'd ever seen Helia not wearing robes. She blushed. As clothing, she meant. Out in public.

Not that she looked any less glorious.

"You ever see her in pants before?"

Xelle appreciated Klein's improved wording. "Nope," she answered. "Still as stunning."

And this was true. The pants were a deep, jeweled blue, shaped to her form with a hearty-looking fabric. Over it, she wore a loose-fitting off-white top and a pair of thin gloves clipped to a shoulder-slung plum-colored bag. Her cap was plain and comfortable, lightly covered with a light scarf in the color of the blouse. And, why did she do this to Xelle, her chest was wrapped in the same color as the pants, wrapped and secured in a comfortable and firm x-shape, under the thin blouse. Only Helia could invite her to meet at her favorite tavern then show up in the expensive version of a 'sexy gardener' costume.

Xelle at least had one of her lacier tops on. And not totally black. She, in fact, was wearing a red-colored cap, and had pinned a little red scrap flower she'd made at a craft party with a Charm Mage onto her shirt. Practically fashión.

"My love," Helia said, taking the occasion of her working dress to hop up onto the neighboring stool. "How did you survive at Frond? With only dark clothing?"

"I didn't," Xelle retorted. "Didn't even make it through a summer. What an insensitive question!"

"Pffft." Helia 'accidentally' bumped into Xelle on the seat and turned toward Klein. "It is lovely to see you in the place where we are."

"Indeed," he said, reaching to kiss her hand. Pers didn't kiss hands without asking but Helia didn't even looked surprised, let alone concerned. Xelle had the weirdest friends, and that really was the best thing she could say about any of it.

"What brings you here, if you don't mind sharing with a simple bartender?"

Helia giggled. "I am taking Xelle here to Heartgrove."

"An overdue meeting of just the right moment," he said. "I was considering making you the special a bit early, but how about, instead, while you enjoy these marigolds—a new drink I've just invented for you—I will pack you a lunch."

"Perfect," Helia said. And she counted out a large sum of coins, waving away Xelle's attempts to pay.

The drink, it tasted like sunshine. And they left, a while later, both carrying bagged lunches, and both feeling the actual sun on their faces, and both with a bounce in their steps.

She wondered, with Helia soon to be married, whether a day like this could ever happen again.

"So by Heartgrove, do you mean the sanctuary? For the anima?" Xelle had heard there was a place where non-hu anima could be sheltered and tended, south of Mytil, which was the direction they were walking, but there were anima everywhere, and it didn't seem a place she'd need to go.

"I do! And—" she flung a quick cast around them "—I think the per who runs it will be of interest to you and your efforts with dragonkind."

Xelle's eyes widened. "There are no dragons here, right? Tell me now if there are dragons."

Helia giggled, again. Oh, her giggle was sweet. "Not of the literal kind, no, but the per who has run this for many decades now is Kin Sheli Du'Heartgrove. She and her spouse are deeply familiar with the cultures and needs of anima, especially when relatively confined."

That didn't quite make sense. "Why are they confined, then?"

"That will be a good first question for Kin Sheli, and I would rather she answer it than I. Her answer will be better, and for now, I am enjoying the views of the Lake."

Indeed, Heart Lake wandered in and out of their sight as they walked along the road, sometimes trading sling casts (Helia picked this up quickly) to speed their way.

"Whatever you are doing here," Xelle finally said, "thank you for doing it."

"Mm hmm," Helia only said, her gaze fixed out upon the Lake.

"Confinement is an action, not a state." Sheli had one boot up on a rock, and took the opportunity to lean forward, stretching her leg. This hu was perfectly amazing. Thin, but strong. Tall, but grounded. Gloves that stretched well past her elbows, a snug-fitted tank, and pants whose pockets looked to have pockets.

"Some anima were injured by hu, in their carelessness. Some need extra care for reasons their own. And so we feed them, build them ways to live comfortably. Some lost their original habitats to housing, so we house them here. Some just flock here."

"For your charm?" Helia asked.

Sheli snorted. "No, for hers."

Previously introduced as Sheli's spouse Val, a hu was wheeling her way toward them, down the smooth-paven path, a carafe attached to one of two long poles welded onto either side. "Is she confined? Or is she bringing us coffee?"

"Lectures on language?" Val asked, bringing her chair next to the other hu, who was now stretching her other leg on the rock. "She loves that. If you don't mind serving it," she nodded toward Helia, "there's a tray on the back."

Helia was the one here least used to folding trays or setting out her own service, but being sure the Mage could handle it, Xelle watched as Helia managed, chatting the whole time to cover that she had no idea what she was doing.

Xelle grinned, knowing Helia would ignore it, and nodded courteously when she handed Xelle a small cup of coffee, turning it awkwardly so Xelle could grasp it by the handle.

She took a sip.

"There's something else in this?" Xelle asked. Normally, she wouldn't question an offered drink, but the taste was unfamiliar to coffee, and she was curious.

"Yes, it's a mix of the roasted beans and also windblooms."

Windblooms. The common flower was one of the few constants across Alyssia, blooming the loveliest yellow petals and then seeding into a poofball that flew in the wind. Xelle had sometimes seen the greens in a fresh-made salad, but not as a beverage.

"It's delicious," Xelle said. "Just not a flavor I'm used to."

"Metaphor for life," Sheli said, lowering her leg. "Now, last thing on the previous."

"She wasn't done," Val confirmed, both amusedly and lovingly.

"The closest you might find to confinement are the ones who were trained from birth by hu, as companions or even to work. They didn't learn their own natural survival, and may not understand the care of others. Some do have to be put behind barriers, but we do not see it as confining them, but caring for them as best that we can, given the confinement handed to them by life."

That sounded a lot like a Frond Mage discussing monitored or even restricted hu. Not a topic she had any energy to get into here.

"So, if I might ask?" Sheli finally put her other leg down and sat comfortably on the rock as if her boots had not just been there. "What are two unadorned Mages doing at Heartgrove on a zesty summer afternoon?"

Helia's introduction as Helia Du'Arc would clearly identify her as a Mage, but as Xelle had called herself only Xeleanor Du'Tam, and didn't see Sheli as the sort reading *Protectors of our Populace*, she was a little surprised by the reference. Also, she still wasn't completely sure. She glanced toward Helia.

Helia was smiling sweetly. "Xelle here is the dragonfriend who brokered the transfer of a small patch of lands in the Highponds into dragon control."

Sheli's eyebrows went right up, and Val, who had been about to turn back toward the house, set the brake on her chair.

Well, fine. They would have heard about *that*.

"And so," Helia continued, "knowing your work here, your insights, I thought, first, you should be acquainted, and second, you might have some insight to offer. I greatly appreciate your insights on confinement and apologize, as I introduced the concept to Xelle. However, per that definition, these dragons are certainly confined, as there are more of them in a smaller space than they would prefer, and only one specific place."

"Acquaintances and insights. Always more with a Mage." It was Val, speaking. She nodded toward Sheli. "She knows most anima, but I know hu. Might help to know what the rest is, to better answer the first."

Actually, Helia had only mentioned them meeting, she didn't know what else there—

There was absolutely more. Xelle would have wandered there eventually, with what she could already see of these two and their oddly unsocialized affects, but with Val holding the metaphorical door, she might as well go in.

"How do you feel about independently speaking of that which causes harm, without the permission of the populace or magesphere governments?"

Sheli snorted. "It is the soul of this place, around you. To acknowledge each per, each life, for what it holds, the comfort it deserves, holding none above others. Not everyone loves Heartgrove, young Xelle. Those who wear kindness as an accessory find its embodiment garish." That was quite a line, but she clearly wasn't done. "And speaking? Oh. That is the core of it. Everyone values speech unless they are asked to speak about someone harming another. Then, suddenly, it's not their place. Too complicated. Hu make their choices. And yes, they certainly do."

She was starting to get, as Xelle would put it, 'worked up', so Xelle was a little glad when she turned around suddenly with lowered tone. "Intriguing. Let's walk around and discuss?"

"Sure," Xelle said (that's what she had after all that) and took Helia's offered arm and with a wave to Val, who was turning back toward the house, followed after the quite fast-walking Sheli.

"I try to let per live as naturally as they want, but if I can provide for comfort, I certainly will. So you'll see little crafts I've made around." She pointed to a series of perches here, a feeder there.

Xelle noticed a long, thin set of stairs. About to ask what they were for, she saw a huge bird sitting on a platform at its top. Ae was missing a wing.

"Yes, there ae is."

Sheli made a series of, well, bird noises, and the bird turned their way. "Won't let anyone pet aem but me, but ae sees sharply, and knows the spirit of a per. Likes you both. Especially her."

Xelle was starting to see that this hu spent a lot of time out here with the anima. But also glad she passed the bird test, and not in the least upset ae preferred Helia. Good taste, that one. Helia had moved closer, and was speaking softly to the bird.

"So, it's no secret that the Lunests filed a false transgression against me," Xelle went in while they were waiting for Helia to meet her new admi.

Sheli made some sounds rather like barking. Xelle went on.

"We are working to gain more evidence of what they are doing, with their company, with other pers. Seems per are scared of them, for all their power, but all the while they are using that power to grow bolder in their lack of care for others."

"Yes, so *The Independent*." She squinted at Xelle. "No need to act surprised, the city's right up there." She pointed off in the distance of Mytil. "You don't move a whole home of dragons into popular hu territory without attracting my notice!" She chuckled. "I don't think you're here to ask my advice on doing it, if you're doing it."

Xelle's mouth curled up on one side. "Correct. My question, after meeting you and seeing all this, is whether you'd like to be connected to it. Or if you have enough of your own dealings here."

"Certainly both," she said a bit seriously.

Actually, Xelle had just thought of something. "This land, it's beautiful. When did it start? How do you keep it?" Not just the land, but the entire section of cliffs over Heart Lake. She couldn't imagine what pers would pay to build houses there.

"Keeping it hasn't been easy," Sheli said, looking off to the distance. "It's old. The history of how and when it was designated is fuzzy enough that I wouldn't rely on it. I do think the truth was recorded somewhere, but the same pers who don't really care whether it exists are the same pers who tell stories linking it to their own histories. So who knows. I suspect early on it was harder to build here, with all the rocky ground and unpredictable water pools. But now, we know how to handle that, and every time a caretaker dies, the feasters rush in."

Xelle didn't want to ask about that. The first part.

"No, I don't have anyone," Sheli answered anyway. "At some point . . . Anyway, I like what you're doing with the paper. I'll stand by you as I can. And you'll need to tell me who I can trust to talk to about it. Please, not Bon Tenne. I've met Bon Tenne."

She peered at the hu a moment. "Kwillen Du'Satta," she answered.

"Mmm," she grunted. "Good." She looked over. "Here, sit. Your friend's in love with the bird, and I never interfere in love." She beckoned Xelle over to a rock, which didn't look super comfortable. Xelle started to ask her cloak for a subtle butt cushion, but then remembered, it being quite warm out, she didn't have it on.

She found a place on the rock that wasn't too pokey, while Sheli sat on it with ease. At least it was in the shade. She should have brought a brim.

"I don't have advice for you on dragons, never met one. But I can tell you why she might have brought you here."

Helia was now scratching the head of, fira, what looked like a fox, so Xelle had other thoughts on that, but she said nothing.

"Many hu love anima. Many hu care of anima. Many even ensure their space. But there is something most hu won't give up, when confronted with the issue. Hu-centric choice is not choice."

She paused, and Xelle wasn't sure if it was meant to sink in, or because she was sticking her hand into a dirty-looking puddle on the side of the rock. Which she was doing.

"Think of it like anything," she continued, something small and slimy now crawling across her hand. "If I choose what to make for dinner, and I choose foods I enjoy, without any regard to Val, but then she's sick all evening because of an allergy to one of the ingredients. Then, I say, oh that's terrible. I'll make her this plain side dish, but won't take my own seasoning from the house because I enjoy it. Sure, she can leave, but then I can't say I respected her choice. Can't say I really love her. Sounds obvious. Because she's a hu. But when it's not a hu, we twist basic logic in all sorts of ways."

Sheli twisted, and her back popped loudly. "The only answer I'm giving you today is yes, I'm happy to help with your paper, am beyond worrying about what hu think about me, and then just some ramblings of an old caretaker, in case they're helpful."

Xelle had a hard time believing she was beyond caring what hu thought, but believed she understood the intent of the statement: that she was following her conscience anyway.

"I'd also say"—her pitch lowered—"don't spend half your life trying to put things a way pers will understand. Leave that to the hu with clear brains. You just be truthful, work to be you, and always, always, love yourself too. Ha! It rhymed!"

Helia walked over, beaming. For a moment, Xelle had the

impression she was younger than she was. And then the Magey face returned.

Sheli groaned for the ages while standing, then took off at another pace that made her think it was good Helia was wearing pants.

"Oh, there ae is. Didn't want to bother aem if ae was asleep or resting."

Xelle didn't see anything. Small birds and furry anima, but nothing that would seem to be specifically identifiable.

"Here, here," Sheli suddenly bellowed out, then resumed a speaking tone. "Don't worry, ae knows it's aer choice. With me anyway."

Xelle had metaphorically jumped four feet at the noise, and Helia reached out and squeezed her arm.

A huge dog came running over. Xelle, not really a dog per, was glad that ae seemed content to slobber onto Sheli's hand and glad, she supposed, that Sheli did not seem to care. "This is Bud. Trained to monitor hu for signs of distress in high-risk environments. Ae started to get a bad hip, so ae was retired, as they say it. But not around the hu who'd trained aem anymore, ae was constantly on edge. Always on alert. Now, ae's only got to look after these two old folk, and only when ae wants to."

While Xelle recognized the hu was likely twice her own age, she wasn't *quite* so elderly as to keep referring to herself that way.

Bud kept along with them for a while, as they pulled into a clearing. Then, barking, ae ran off. "Thinks it's going to rain." Sheli scanned the sky. "Maybe over there, but here, I've got a nice bench by the meadow, we should have enough time to finish up."

They walked over, and Xelle was surprised to see that the bench was long enough for at least six hu. Which was good. She was definitely a wide-sitter herself, and on the highly protected outdoor bench, she didn't need to worry about shoetiquette. She sat down against the side rail, stretching both legs before throwing one up to one side. It was really a very beautiful field; she could just imagine what it would look like in spring.

Sheli plopped down on the ground and started chewing a stalk she'd just picked from next to her. She sat for a while, and then spoke.

"Changing minds is hard," she said. "You can't push it. No matter what your 'debate skills' or ability to 'make a case'. And that's not even what makes it hard."

She said those last phrases as if quoting pers but with a great deal of sarcasm.

"Because once minds need changing, you're always late to the match."

Xelle noted Helia was listening intently. Well, she was a diplomatic Mage now. Definitely a subject of interest. Xelle realized she needed to be listening too. And not watching Helia. Who was always distracting. She turned toward Sheli.

"When you see a thing that's needed, when it feels hard, especially to the point where someone is causing harm, that's because they are an old voice. A voice that's been building, creeping, letting pers acclimate for a long time. A voice you would have been seen as rude to point at in the graying green. Then every new step they take isn't a step from zero, they've pulled a thousand advantages to their side for every one new harm you see. It's a little like this place. It gets to stay here mostly because it's always been here. Oop!"

What was oop? Turning up, she did see a fast moving cloud.

"Should have listened to Bud. That's moving in faster than I would have imagined. Well, let's get out from under this tree."

Xelle was thinking the tree would be good protection from the rainshower, if it was quick. The thought must have appeared on her face. Or maybe that she was looking up at all the branches.

"Oh, she's a forestper, isn't she? A forest of trees protects everyone inside it, best it can. But one tree alone tends to get struck by lightning. Unless you want to get struck by the lightning. Seems this one does, huh?" She was now talking to Helia? Pointing at Xelle.

What all hells was Sheli saying?

"You got it," Xelle said, her social capacity running low as it were.

"Zap," she added, but still heeding the warning to stretch her way off of the bench and back to the path.

And as quickly as Sheli had tromped on in the sun, she seemed to take her time in the rain, wandering their way back to the house while both she and Helia (and her light colored tank with the bright blue under) got thoroughly soaked.

Nor did the rain deter Sheli's chatter. "Societies are not anima," she said. "With one individual, you can find change in a moment. Not even a big moment. An act of kindness. A smile. A scare. One per can change, can set their whole life anew, in an instant. With a society," she said, "you are one per trying to talk to multitudes. Pers think they can hold up a sign and reach society, but each of those pers are speaking their own form of the language, when it comes to it. And you can't always read a sign from a distance. You don't always read a sign from a distance."

Xelle thought Sheli was dragging this on a bit far.

"When you're talking to a society?" She stopped now, causing Xelle and Helia to bump into each other, Helia swaying out of the way delicately like she'd intended it. A huge drop of rain dripped off of Sheli's nose, unswatted. "It takes time, dedication, and a commitment to sorrow."

Xelle was not a diplomatic Mage, and she found herself tiredly blurting. "Sorrow? I'm tired of sorrow. Why is it always sorrow for me and not sorrow for the hurt being caused. Sympathy for sorrow, rather than standing in the way of it?"

Sheli turned and walked off. Exchanging a glance in which Helia seemed to find all of this more amusing than Xelle, they both hurried after her.

"Silence, you see," she then said. "Hurts, doesn't it? Remember that when you feel down." After whatever case she believed to have just made, they seemed to be going more slowly down the path.

Silence hurts and comforts? Xelle wasn't going to deal with this while walking in this pelting rain. And that didn't seem to be an issue with the populace, or the Lunests. The Mages were the experts at silence. Even her own Na, who'd never brought her own studies up. Even about things that might protect Xelle, or the dragons, or—

Wait, what the ash? Are they honoring a broken treaty? Do they not realize it? Thunder had confirmed, Xelle had broken the treaty. So zheir home knew, they knew. But Xelle . . . she'd asked the home to wait. They'd said they would wait. For now.

Were they still waiting on this also? Did they think it impolite to nudge Xelle on the issue?

What was it with per and silence when just talking could solve almost all things?

Just as the house came into view, Sheli turned and smiled, her loose cap soaked with rainwater. "May those who travel with peace in their hearts always find their way home again, safely." She barely nodded, a brusque sort of chin flip, turned, and just walked back into her house. The door shut behind her.

"Was that it?" Xelle whispered. Overhead, thunder cracked.

Helia was giggling. Some diplomacy. "We should probably go."

Xelle was overwhelmed, and actually didn't feel like walking back. She had her return pod, but Helia didn't—

She remembered going with Kern. To the Lunest Estate. How he must have pulled her through the pathways. Connected to him, the way one didn't lose their clothes when traveling. Now she laughed.

"What are you thinking?" Helia sputtered, her makeup now officially running. Still pretty. Offensive. She sighed.

"Three things. One, you are beautiful and wearing a virtually transparent shirt, and I am finding it distracting. Two, wouldn't it be funny if when Arc Mages fast traveled, they arrived naked, because the phyta didn't take their clothes?"

Helia looked some level of alarmed now, so Xelle kept going. "Third, I think two pers can fast travel together. Don't know if they both have to be Arc Mages, but we are, so? Would you . . . Would you feel safe if I try?"

"Not just Arc Mages," she said. "Not our travel, I told you, they haven't taught me yet. And I don't know how about two hu . . . But all Mages fast travel. Every prong. They all have ways to do it."

Fast traveling, but not fast fast, right? Well, Frond did have runes, she considered. And Ever enchanted gateways . . . "The Grand ones fly in little footless vrooms."

"Yes," Helia nodded, now shivering at the abrupt change in temperature, but not seeming to want to cast. "And Arc Mages take ground vrooms. It takes a lot to fast travel, and some find it jarring. Anyway, yes, if I trust any caster, ever, it is you. Let's go."

She reached out both hands and took them, and Xelle knew something. Helia was afraid. She did not look afraid. She held her hands as steadily as she could with her own increasing cold shivers. But she was afraid. She felt afraid. And so, Xelle, suddenly with an urge to protect, to shelter, held her hands, so sweetly but so firmly, and reached for the inkbloom. Could they both go? Was this allowed? *She's scared. I can't hurt her. She's my friend.*

The inkbloom, they urged her forward, and feeling into the pod, she went to where felt safest. Not Arc Tower. But her daygarden.

Let's go, she thought. And traveled.

"Xelle," Helia whispered. "I am in awe."

Impressing Helia was not the worst of her accomplishments, but what she had just done was extraordinary, exhausting, and the terror was only starting to hit her of what could have gone wrong, so she kept any half-formed jokes to herself.

"Do they know me? How does it work?" She spun around. "Xelle, they're not even going to tell me where they are for years. I mean, where the others are. Or—"

She glanced around in concern, suddenly realizing she didn't recognize Xelle's room.

"We're wrapped," Xelle said, "inkbloom away." She made her way to the couch and sat down, not worried about her wet pants for the moment, she just needed to sit. This place really needed a cleaning, but, as she'd likely be living here soon and for a long while, she'd have time to do that soon. "I don't think they can just tell you and you go," she said. "The inkbloom, it's a very personal relationship. Even what we just did, the travel here, was . . . They helped. A lot. I don't know how it works in the Tower. Are there hidden gardens, hidden pots, can they ever be shared? I have no idea."

Turning quickly, Helia sat next to Xelle and ran a hand over the side of her face. "I'm sorry. So soon for questions. Are you well? I've never seen you like this."

"Hellie, give me a minute." Her limbs to the point of shaking, Xelle leaned back on the couch, and closed her eyes.

She awoke in her underwear, surely cast dry, wrapped in a sheet from one of her cabinets, and with Helia, on a chair she'd pulled up close, stroking her face. Her cap was still on, over her undercap, and she didn't know how to feel about any of this. Yet, it all felt respectful.

"I fell asleep?"

Helia looked drowsy herself. "You could say that. I could use a rest myself, but I wanted to make sure you were well." Helia's clothes were dry. More notably, it was dark outside.

"Here," Xelle said, rising slowly, "The couch pulls to a bed. Let me do it." She got up, pulled out the bed on its hinges, and put the sheets Helia had found back over it, tucking in the sides, and arranging it best she could. No need for blankets; even here, it was warm.

Moving into the chair Helia had been sitting in, she sat, still a bit groggy, as Helia worked her way into the sheets, and pulled the pillows around her head.

"It's pretty outside. This is the place by Ever Tower?"

"Yes," she answered. "Again, a secret, except Kwill and Rayn know too."

"Good," Helia murmured, wiggling her way further into the sheets and pillow like a cat. Soon, she was asleep. Xelle still sat in the chair, not wanting to wake her, and saw a piece of hair had fallen out of her cap during the wriggling. It was pink, a shade Xelle had never seen, even on her walks through Vattam, where pers had had their crown-hair exposed. Bold colors there, or tired neutrals. This, a beautiful, floral pink.

She wasn't sure Helia would want it exposed, and so she ran her finger against it, tucking the strand back into the cloth. Of course it was soft, too.

Xelle wasn't sure she was totally rested and couldn't really go anywhere while Helia was here, so she laid down, herself, on top of the sheets on the other side, using a pillow from the couch, as the sleeping pillows were framing Helia like a crown of clouds.

Her back hurt. She was sore. She stretched a little, and thought about getting up again, but she still felt heavy, and without realizing she had, gave into it.

The next she awoke, Helia was again up. Fully dressed, and eating a handful of trail mix. "A bit starving, and this smelled good enough." She crunched into another bite.

"I'm going to be living here soon," Xelle murmured. "I'll make a grocery run."

The Mage stopped mid-crunch. Xelle thought she'd told her.

Helia drank from a glass of water. "You mentioned leaving Grand and having places to hide. It didn't really dawn on me you wouldn't have a Tower role at all. Fira, that's . . . big. A conversation for another day. Anyway, get dressed. Now you're distracting me."

Xelle grinned as she pulled on her clothes, noticing that Helia had cleaned them, rather than just dry them. And yeah, it was big.

"And then, you'll need to tell me how to get out of here? I assume we can't travel again, not that I'd even ask you to right now."

"Yeah, to do that again, I'd have to make my way to the inkbloom. I have a way to do that from here, but I couldn't take you with me."

Helia nodded. "I'll find my way quietly to Vi'Ever, take a covert ride to Mytil, then travel back openly from there. I . . . happened to see you have my cloak here, when I was looking for the sheets. Mind if I borrow it back?"

Xelle grinned. She'd forgotten it was here, that's right, she's stored it here when leaving To'Ever, rather than take up suitcase space to Grand. "Well, given that I have to leave directly to get back to the inkbloom, and given the food here is limited—"

"The crackers are moldy; don't eat them," Helia interrupted. "Yes, go ahead."

"Given the food here is limited, I think we should be on our way? Here, I'll show you how to work the door and ladder. In case you need to return."

"Yes, but there's one more thing." Helia shifted with unusual nerves. "I'd like to ask you something, but I feel like . . . we should just make sure we're absolutely clear before I do."

Having just started lacing her boots, Xelle felt glad she was sitting down. Helia, nervous? What was going on? Was she ending things? Changing them? Many pers would. "What is it? Just, say it."

Realizing now that Xelle was joining in whatever nerves she was portraying, Helia seemed to relax. "Between us. I know that we'll be friends. I . . . would have married you, Xelle, but now I don't think that's in your interest or mine." Helia didn't sound convinced. "I don't know how I'll feel about some things. About intimacy. Then. But I'd like to know if it's on the table, off the table, how you feel?"

So, ok, this wasn't bad. Just . . . asking. Asking was good. "Helia, something I've always enjoyed between us is how you've encouraged me to be more open. Be more honest, with myself even." Her cheek rather twitched, and then worrying about it, her shoulder twitched. "So I'm grateful for you. We can see how it goes." She paused, wondering whether this was a good thing to say. Then, realized, she'd just been talking about openness. So here goes.

"I don't remember much from that day. When Thunder . . . brought me back. When you helped me in. The main thing I remember is you telling me to be me, and the rest would work out. Something like that. I want to offer you the same thing. If we're friends, let's be friends forever. Tell me what you need, what you want. Plus or minus. Be you. Just . . . be there. And I will be too."

Xelle was not prepared for the kiss that Helia leaned forward and gave her. Not sweet. Not hot. The kiss was . . . art. Helia stepped back, and Xelle sort of . . . gasped.

Helia looked as smug with herself as Xelle had felt impressing her earlier. "I'd like to ask if you'd be willing to stand for me in my wedding."

"Yes," Xelle said. "Hellie . . ."

"I know," Helia whispered back. "Now show me your foresty ladder, my friend. And hand me the cloak." She winked.

24 – Meeting

Xelle chose the Arc Spire. She valued her relationships within the magesphere, but she was an Arc Mage, whether they saw her as one or not.

Yet she was not the same hu who stood before them a quarter-decade ago. She understood their processes, their structure. She respected their intent, and often their impact. And if she could go back to that day? And just agree to pledge? Would she?

No.

It was simply an unfair question. A cruel question, if meant for any other reason than affirming the answer she had found: Her life was not a game. It was not trade this for that, or erase that which you know for that which you imagine.

She had also thought about Avail's suggestion, that any need unfulfilled here, in this life, was perhaps filled elsewhere, another version of one's self, and she'd come to understand its place in truth. Not the melancholy of a life one would never know, but the understanding that the pathways are more complicated than we grasp. The acknowledgment of a comfort we can imagine, and the peace of letting it rest elsewhere. The reminder that while our wounds and tears are real, and a true bond can be untied but never undone, there are still, in any moment we are fortunate enough to take breath, many things that are possible.

New things, of a nature we cannot even imagine now, the way we can imagine some.

Xelle had enough to do in the weaving of her very real life than to try and reweave another.

Her regret, her only regret, was not being open with Ay'tea when she had the choice. And even that, if it made her the open-hearted per she was today, determined never to let a friend slip past without at least knowing not just her appreciation—but her care—her desire to stay in color and song, when others faded, then even that, she would accept.

"Xeleanor Du'Tam. You petition before us."

"Arc Mage Xeleanor Du'Tam," she corrected. "And I do."

It was odd to see the Arc Spire without the presence of Mage Jehanne. Crown Mage Pelir looked every bit the part, but was not Jehanne. Same height, different tree, she supposed.

And Kern. Sitting, silently. Nothing, nothing about his demeanor to suggest he even knew her. She was not that good of an actor, but as her nerves for this were genuine, she tried to keep her gaze on Pelir.

"I'm here to ask the Arc Spire for a reestablishment of treaty between hukind and dragonkind. I am willing to negotiate this between both parties. I can also confirm that dragonkind considers any existing agreements void, due to my actions in asking the home that I met to move again. They are tenuously honoring the spirit of what was, but would be more comfortable with a redefinition. The brief glimpses I have seen of their power suggest this would be in our interest also."

Silence. Complete silence. She kept her gaze on Pelir, who seemed to be watching her as plainly. The difference was, Xelle had made her offer. It was now on Pelir to respond.

"I am not comfortable speaking on this issue," Pelir finally said. Fortunately with that Magey tone of voice that preceded its own 'but'. "However, I will meet with one representative, you as our communicator."

Ok, ok. This was progress. Almost. Almost there. She wished she could invite Thunder; this was part of the key to getting zhem released. Then, she had considered having two dragons, to match the two hu, but that would definitely give Pelir more of an imbalance than Xelle's presence would give any dragon. "I believe I can arrange this meeting, but I would like to tell you about the communication."

"Proceed," Pelir said.

So warm. So kind. Anyway. "The representative will be able to read your thoughts, as well as mine. Unless you have a way to signal which thoughts they should respect as private, I would not count on that. I will not know what you are thinking, unless this per decides to tell me, or responds in a way that makes that obvious. Zhey will be able to communicate directly with you, and with your expertise in Arc Magic I suspect you'll immediately understand it better than I do now. I will not intervene, if you and the representative do not request it or barring any type of emergency or unforeseen situation. But if there is confusion, I may be able to assist."

Sure, Pelir could have a hidden sigil with someone, but Xelle had a whole handful of consistent cues that Pelir did not. "Thank you," Pelir said, without letting on whether these were things already known to the Mage or not. "Let me know a time and place of the representative's preference and I will be there."

"Yes, Crown Mage Pelir."

"Mage Xeleanor, you are dismissed."

Thunder had balked a little about only sending one per.

I can go back and ask again, if it's that important.

Thunder's response was a wave of frustration. Weirdly, Xelle understood it was not *at* Xelle but rather that frustration you feel when you know the other per is right, or at least as stuck as you are, but are intimidated by the next step.

The main thing is, whoever it is needs to be able to make some level of decision, or even temporary decision, on behalf of everyone, and I don't know if you have that kind of structure.

Thunder imagined lots of cartoon hu bumping into each other (did zhey think this was how hu talked?) and then one leaving with a glowing mind.

Sure, I'll ask them. I guess I should go ask at Drophome this time? And we'll need a time and place. I suppose the place has to be Drophome or the mountains, but I don't want to presume.

Suddenly the idea of light caught her. Truth illuminated. *The sun at its highest?* But then, well, they could count days. The number 'seven' came to mind. *Seven days, the sun at its highest. Would that offend, in any way? Then maybe . . . I pick that time, and they pick which place?*

Thunder thought that was fine.

You'll be out of there soon, friend. And I love you.

Thunder sent back an image of zheir ball.

It was not Drophome that had been selected, but the broken obsidian cliff itself, with Lightning, still there, as their representative. Xelle had traveled there and passed the message along, glad Lightning simply took it as fact that this was the wishes of the home.

Pelir not knowing (or not wanting to acknowledge) that Xelle had access to fast travel, or perhaps still unwilling to cast in the mountains, stated they would walk there together. A long, silent walk, in which nothing was discussed.

Until they were nearly there and Pelir stopped. "What would you give? For others."

A little dramatic. But Pelir was always straightforward, and surely meant the question. So, what, meaning hu, or dragons? Friends? Anyone? Considering it . . . her answer was essentially the same. "I would give much."

Seeing some form of slight uncertainty on the Mage's face . . . Unsurety? Didn't Pelir know? Xelle had already given much. She would continue to give much. Xelle decided it was time to show the per, here in private, just how serious she was.

Xelle looked right in Pelir's eyes, a gesture Pelir likely found disconcerting but yet gave no reaction, none at all, to.

"I would give as much as any true Arc Mage would give, knowing, in fact, that a true Arc Mage would give up public life."

Pelir stared back at Xelle. Stared. Xelle assumed the Mage was trying to figure out if Xelle was implying what she absolutely was implying: that Crown Mage Jehanne had not died, but had somehow gone into hiding to prevent Kern from taking the Ascension. To prevent him having to wrestle with that choice. To provide stability. To work behind the scenes, as Xelle felt sure she was doing, or would be doing. And Pelir, then, knowing a mark of uncertainty on Pelir's own Ascension. A small, silent, weight to bear. Xelle did not break eye contact, until Pelir looked away.

"Very well, then. I ask you to remember that when the day arrives."

Mages did love to be ominous.

And, yeah, this time, it worked. Xelle did not feel comfortable at all. She felt scared. *The day?* What was Pelir really asking her? Was Xelle the proudly stubborn baby of hidden meaning, while all the while Pelir was asking her something more?

Pelir stared, offering a chance for Xelle to change her answer.

Xelle did not.

They walked ahead. The timing, perhaps, was meant to ask the question, but not to give Xelle too much time to unsettle over it, because soon they stood at the clearing, in front of Lightning, who waited there alone.

Xelle did not introduce the two pers by name. Lightning knew that was how Xelle thought of zhem, and had not objected. And she also knew dragons didn't have the same sense of naming. Their identifications were deeper than hu language.

No, that wasn't fair. Hu communication was deeper than language, including issues of identity. But she knew it was different. Yet, it felt some level of formality was appropriate?

Xelle moved from Pelir's side to form, not a triangle, but (in her mind, yes it was still three pers) a U. Standing equidistant from both, while clearly off to the side.

"This is a representative of this divided home." She pointed to Lightning, though it was pretty obvious they knew who was who. "And this is the Crown Mage of Arc Spire, representative to the Crown of Hallinia." She pointed, again. Then lowered her arms. She felt like she was supposed to do something here. Like this was on her. But it wasn't. Not now. She'd arranged this, and she had to let them discuss.

Lightning did not look her way but grunted slightly, in a way Xelle very much thought was meant to remind that her thoughts were being loud. So, she tried to listen.

Zhey began with slowly articulated thoughts. *All upset. Those of meet and age. Displeased. Time. Time.*

The first time felt elongated, the second brief.

"Then why do you meet now?" Pelir asked.

Food is here.

Xelle didn't think it was about food, but more like opportunity? A door being opened? But it felt like a half answer. Lightning cut her a look.

"I understand why you would be upset. I understand why they would be upset. Yet maybe there is fruit in this opportunity. All of this was done before the existence of any hu alive today."

Running. Running away. Cause to run, could sense.

"I am here now. I am here to listen."

Lightning snorted and shifted on the soil. Pelir did not so much as twitch.

Living freely. Living freely. Scattered berries. Eat.

"I don't have a broader solution to offer. The lands where dragons lived are not controlled by Mages, and frankly, I am concerned already about what Ever Tower has done. By forcing an intrusion into this process, it has set a precedent that can be used to scare hu. As you suggested, running before they can listen."

Not. Running over listening. Running with time!

Pelir stood taller. "We are trying to communicate after only just meeting, and what I said was meant in the spirit of your intent. Please do not correct me when the result is unaffected, and I will extend the same courtesy to you."

Lightning's nostrils flared, and Xelle wondered what Pelir would do if Lightning rolled the Mage down a cliff. Or maybe that was just a thing Lightning did to Xelle. Lightning turned toward Xelle and stomped.

"Sorry," she whispered.

Child! Both children!

Pelir waited a moment for Lightning to settle back down before again speaking. "I will not speak regarding eir friend and what you may think of zhem granting Xeleanor a sigil, but Xeleanor is an adult of our kind, and has made more progress on this than any other hu in memory. Perhaps eir age is not of relevance."

Same. Same. Lightning relaxed a bit. *Children touched fire. Touching grows flames.*

"It does. And I must warn you, we hu are younger. All of us. In a sense, you would find us all children. But we are not, as time moves differently through us all. Understanding the parameters of our kind is essential to avoiding an escalation of violence."

Which?

"To us both, in a situation neither of us created. Do you wish for more violence, on top of what is created?"

Burn the world.

Well, that was pretty clear.

Rude. Wrong. Here. Time. Time. Time. Time.

Pelir was . . . not used to being talked to that way. Pelir bowed slightly at the neck before straightening. "You are right. I am sorry."

Heavy rock. Try.

Pelir nodded. "There are other places, not the area hu call Highponds, that I could more easily access. For now. And then I would need time. Not just to find options, but to . . . find others to push the heavy rock."

Forests are crowded. Flat is awake. Trees are home. Green plants. Never dust. Terror over water.

That was an inadequate translation for actually the clearest point Lightning was able to convey. Problem was, hilly green land with some trees but not a forest was the same land most popular to hu. And a clear note that the mostly uninhabited plateaus of Dust Region were not a solution. And the last part, that was something Xelle hadn't known. Dragons were, apparently terrified by the idea of flying over water.

Xelle had never been on a ship and sympathized.

Relate. Stop barking.

Forgetting the need for diplomacy, Xelle stuck out her tongue.

"In hu years also, I am new as Crown Mage. My position is tenuous. This will take time and coordination."

Try.

Pelir bowed, again, a slight bow, but a bow. "I realize that earlier when I spoke of options, you would have seen what I saw. And so let me offer this now. The lands around To'Arc would allow you move freely between here and the Tower, and also protect all that lies here. And allow me to maintain as much help to you as I could."

Hu control.

"I must retain jurisdiction at this point. But I can ensure hu leave you alone, if you agree to stay off the Tower Grounds, out of the village, and not trouble the structures that exist now."

Take.

Then Lightning paused.

Again.

Xelle wasn't sure what Lightning meant by that, and more oddly Pelir stood, quietly. For quite a while. Xelle did not know if the Mage was able to think without the dragons hearing or if the agreement was being repeated and confirmed via thought, but Lightning was clearly agitated, until suddenly silence. Meaning, Lightning was blocking Xelle somehow from hearing zheir thoughts. Or perhaps more likely, the intent was the reverse. Well, Xelle had been chatty. Her mind was a storm! It was who she was.

Enough. Enough time. Enough pushing.

Zheir thoughts flooded back in. The idea of pushing didn't feel violent or rude, but more like what Xelle might call trading? Apparently they had settled up?

"I understand. What we have decided will work for myself and for Arc Tower, and I will ensure coordination with the other parties. Do you need to coordinate this, or are you ready to reinstate this treaty?"

Never! Sealed on spirit and home.

Xelle was confused. Pelir noticed, and turned toward her. "I believe zhey are saying that they no longer wish for a treaty. If we agree, it must be on our honor, on the dragon home, and on Arc Tower."

Same.

And that meant it would last as long as trust lasted, Xelle thought, though surely they both understood that. Lightning turned toward her, maybe to tell her to can it again, but the thought was not that. It was clear and direct. About a per, a specific per. Said to Xelle, not Pelir. "Crown Mage Pelir," she offered. "I believe zhey are saying that it cannot be considered part of this arrangement, but my friend, who is . . . staying at the Lunest Estate," (she did not look at Pelir not wanting to see this reaction) "must leave there, and return to Drophome."

Zhey'd also clearly conveyed something like 'zhey've been there long enough' but that didn't seem necessary to convey.

Same.

When Xelle finally allowed herself to look at Pelir, the Mage had no change in expression. Probably never did. Mages, seriously.

"I trust you, and thank you for your trust. Please allow me some days to make arrangements. I am sure you understand."

Lightning rose to zheir back legs and breathed a huge plume of fire into the air.

Pelir, again, did not flinch, but raised a hand, and cast, with a huge impact, a crackling in the air, and what looked like a streak of lightning that burst into flame.

There was no goodbye. Lightning flew away, over the face of stone, leaving them alone. And Pelir turned, and began to walk away. Xelle, a bit dizzy over all of this, attempted to follow.

The word got out that there was a dragon living at the Lunest Estate. Though at first thought implausible, the story was backed up by an unnamed employee who identified the precise location, and even described the new enclosure. The story was so detailed that it would have seemed absurd to have invented it.

Since the bulletins distributed across Alyssia, at least the ones admis of the Lunests were inclined to read, had enforced the idea of dangerous dragons who must be kept at bay, an outcry emerged of concern and fear.

Had the Mages threatened the Lunests to force a dragon onto their grounds? Were the Lunests under duress from the Amberborn? Surely they were busy and their land vast; had Xeleanor somehow hidden this dragon, waiting for a surprise attack? Or, if these really were lies, they urged the Lunests to let pers onto the grounds, at that location, to show nothing was or had been there. So they could reassure their families, those who believed the tale, or who couldn't sleep, now, at night.

Thunder's 'expulsion' was nearly immediate.

Getting a happy message from her friend, Xelle fast traveled to Drophome, right to the location where her sigil nearly throbbed with excitement, honestly a feeling she was ready to be rid of but not going to tell Thunder to please settle down until she got there.

Thunder rushed over, and urged her toward a shelter and sleeping area that she learned had been built by some of the others, just for Thunder's return. It was lovingly constructed, with bent wood, mortars, and patterns of char, sealing in all sorts of colorful bits not exactly found in nature, but clearly requested from or dropped off by Rod. No, she thought. Not Rod. These were gifts from Mik.

Xelle walked into the space, half shaded and half open, and saw a small pile of items that Thunder hopped around proudly.

"How did you hide and carry all this?" Xelle asked, until seeing that whatever sort of blanket they'd given zhem to sleep on was underneath, used as a huge bag. "Did they allow you to take all this?"

Thunder crouched in a proud and clear 'no'.

Xelle responded to Thunder's query, and allowed thoughts to enter her mind directly, seeing a clear image of Thunder going to leave, surrounded by three hu, and changing course suddenly and swinging up the hidden bundle of goods before anyone had even noticed. Irla was there. Irla was yelling something. To the other hu, not to Thunder.

That was a question to ask, but as Thunder released her mind, zhey pointed again, to the pile of items.

"Ok, ok! This is cool! Let me see."

On top, definitely positioned to be, was the ball that Xelle had made and Thunder enhanced. She picked it up. Good weight, good texture. She knew Thunder was listening to her thoughts anyway, so she let that stand. Then there were a couple of the items that Thunder had shown her during their messaging, toys meant to find what sort of items dragons enjoyed and didn't, and Thunder had tried not to be too accurate about that, but these two, a string of metal flowers that turned in the wind, and a plush baby dragon, zhey had really liked. Oh, she was glad zhey had them, then.

Beyond that, an expensive looking hu shoe. Sure, that one was just for statement, she could respect that. And a few other trinkets and handy items that had not been authorized of varying utility. And, on the bottom, oh, ok, Thunder you win this one, the per had ripped off a wrought metal L, perhaps done when they'd begun to remove the magic barrier? It didn't matter; this was excellent.

"There's some wire out there, want me to help get this hung on the wall?"

Zhey nodded excitedly.

"Oh, look, a piece of the backing came off with it. I could get this hammered over, and it would make a T. Sure, a wonky T, but without doubt of its origin."

Thunder . . . loved that idea.

She thought the next part a bit quietly, even though the dragon rest areas were spaced far enough to allow privacy of thought (including during sleep!) and she thought Thunder would sense anyone listening in.

Ok, so Irla was there? Could you hear her? Xelle was already tapping consent to communicate through the sigil.

The Breath Mage watches Thunder leave; Thunder is a bad choice but Thunder thinks the Breath Mage is a bad choice. Thunder is proud. The Grand Mage wants to try controlling Thunder, with the stick (the wand), the way she makes the walls. She believes she can take Thunder away, that it is time for Xelle's Mage (ugh, Kern) to help. Irla chooses the Breath Mage, chooses to let Thunder go. Irla sees Thunder flying away. Thunder comes back later. Maybe with a stick.

The Charm Mage would be here. The Charm Mage would be here first, and then Thunder would be here. And then emotions. Her. The Charm Mage. Selfish little hu. She would be here. She would be here.

Thunder showed Xelle two versions of the same scene. In one, the Charm Mage, a vagueish cartoon that Thunder had decided to affix to her, was there, and several dragons were there in cages. Silent and sad. In the other, the Charm Mage was not there, and a huge rock fell on the Lunest Estate and crushed it in a gratuitous cloud of stone and wood, and flashes of color, and some curling rainbows.

The rainbows were of course an embellishment to the metaphor, but when Thunder disconnected, Xelle made her way to the floor, sitting, rocking, catching her breath. There was no doubt what worried Irla, even if Xelle didn't know why.

This Charm Mage? Could ruin everything.

25 – Speaking Plainly

Owi'neil Du'Hubo was supposed to win the E'lle Prize. Normally such a scandal would be concentrated in Mytil, especially once the Gallery looked up the tightly guarded records and found evidence of this claim. But this story also burned through Arc Region due to Spire Mage Kern's role there. And to Breath Region, because Bon Tenne himself was now there, and to Grand Region, where Xeleanor Du'Tam was staying, then to the other two cities, each overlapping Grand and Breath Regions, and the publications flowing between them.

And once something was important enough for half of Alyssia's interest, it was sure to spread to the rest.

Xeleanor Du'Tam was behind all of it, as assigned by (or even in some position of leadership of?) the Amberborn. She'd wanted to plant a per in a position of fast power, and what better way than through the most prestigious art prize in Alyssia? At least what better way to a per reported to idolize Mytil since her childhood, to consider it a center of her world.

And what better revenge on Arc Tower, who would not allow her to pledge, than to set up a cura of the presumed (at the time) next Crown Mage, Spire Mage Kern.

But surely, surely, no one would believe such a story. Even the Mages would not stay silent on someone they continued to protect? Whom the Lunests had known and said all along was a serial transgressor, a manipulator of per and truth?

They were not silent. Crown Mage Pelir issued a statement on behalf of Arc Tower. An apology to Spire Mage Kern Du'Arc, who had suspected Xeleanor of manipulation all along, who had met with the failing Study in his office after she'd nearly been transgressed harassing his cura, just before she was removed from Arc Tower.

Ever Tower said they had no comment on the matter. Nor did Charm Tower, or Dust Tower. Grand Tower said they were investigating these claims, and would make their decision soon. Frond Tower never commented on unfiled transgressions; nothing unexpected there.

And Breath Tower said, whether or not this was true and reminding that any remedy would be under the discretion of the Gallery, they believed that Bon Tenne did not know, himself, about the plot, when he accepted the prize, and as Breath Tower had ways to verify the truth of statements that Tenne had agreed to, they would let him continue his work at the Tower, under their protection against his influence by any outside sources. They added, he was an employee of the Tower, not a caster, and so Breath Tower had no basis to control his outside publications, even if he chose to continue to associate with Xeleanor Du'Tam. In fact, if he were so naïve, even better reason to keep him under view at Breath.

Things would change, of course, if he were determined to have conducted transgressions, but of note, Breath Tower did not mention that part. Besides, the Hurts—they did not need transgressions any longer. They did not need Frond Tower, or Grand Tower, or anyone. They had the populace now.

And, then, at the end of Pelir's response, a statement: Xeleanor Du'Tam was no longer welcome in Arc Tower, and their Front Desk had been issued strict guidelines to refuse her entry.

At least, Xelle thought, there was that.

The Independent: Issue Three

Arc Tower has joined Ever Tower, in its own way, in facilitating

additional land for use by dragonkind. We have only prelimi-
nary information, but wanted to release this publication now, so
that truth could have some chance of running alongside rumor
and falsehood alike.

The lands around Arc Tower, all that are within the boundaries
of its jurisdiction, and excepting Arc Village and the Tower
grounds, are now open to use, playing upon, or building upon
by dragonkind.

[Illustration shows Arc Tower, where Bon Tenne grew up.]

These dragons have agreed not to disturb current hu structures
such as benches or gardens, and Arc Tower now restricts any
interference with or occupation of a dragon-built structure
to those who have been invited by a dragon. If a hu does not
know whether they have been invited, they are required to act as
though they have not.

Arc Tower emphasizes that these lands remain under surveil-
lance and control of Arc Tower, and previous restrictions on hu
travel into the adjacent mountain areas remain in effect.

[Illustration shows a hu sitting on a bench reading while a dragon
lounges nearby.]

Arc Tower has issued a statement that the magesphere seeks
additional lands for dragon use. The statement describes the
size and nature of land needed. The only condition is the land
cannot be loaned. It must be transferred permanently for this
use, and put under protection of a Tower. Breath Tower has
not offered any lands at this point, but has agreed to document
and preserve records on all accepted donations of land in the
historical volumes.

[Illustration shows a big glowing book that says 'do good' on its
pages.]

Because of the unplanned earliness of this fall issue, we have decided to issue one further this calendar year, so look for a winter issue this year, sometime before Night's Bell, rather than after the new year.

26 - *Stand*

Helia's family of origin looked like they were wearing the entire stock of the Mytil column shops. It wasn't that Helia didn't wear expensive clothes herself, but she didn't wear them to look expensive, she wore them for comfort and confidence and also she did like nice things.

They had approached Xelle, not because Xelle felt they had interest in meeting her, but rather for an obligation to greet the unknown (to them) hu who had been asked to stand for Helia. And, Xelle couldn't help but think they were also thinking 'instead of any of them.'

Not all hu would think that way; Xelle certainly didn't, nor would she assume it in others. But after a round of 'so nice to meet you' the following barrage of ten ways to ask 'so who are you' and 'so what do you do' ("Oh, I studied at To'Arc") while they certainly must know who she was did set the impression that way.

Xelle was not going to let it get to her. Not today, not any of it. Yes, it weighed on her, well stabbed her right through, that she was now banned from the Tower reaching above them, but Helia had assured Xelle that her inclusion in Helia's wedding, and her departure afterward, would cause no stir, at least with anyone here. And everyone here had been invited directly by either Helia or Drae, so hopefully she'd be allowed this respite.

Reminding herself again and again this was for Helia, she tried to put those issues, well, they couldn't be out of her mind, but she gave them permission to go take a nap, and at least let her enjoy a beautiful few hours.

"Yes, I'm here by myself. Just here for the day." She tried to smile.

Again, she was focused on positivity. "It's an incredible honor to stand at Mage Helia's side."

"It is," one of the sarents replied. Xelle nodded his way. He was absolutely right.

She took a breath, and turned to gaze around her.

Xelle had long gone on about the beauty of Arc Tower in autumn, and she would gladly do so again. Yet on this day—*this day*—Alyssia had surely put all its energy into this spot, this ambiance, this feeling. Oranges and blushy reds in the trees, the colors Helia often favored in winter, marbled in to the preceding fall. Gauzy streamers tinted in all shades of rose swayed in the lightly warmed breeze, draped over the trellises of Helia's favorite garden, a garden of boldly blooming fall roses, coy dance partners to the coordinating streamers. And a natural perfume, a waft on the air, of autumn and rose, sitting only in the presence of the day, as if autumn would last forever.

Xelle resolved to enjoy a moment like this as long as she could, and so excusing herself from Helia's family, she took her seat, one of two off to the side of the front area, and just breathed and absorbed.

The other witness, Grae Du'Estia, saw her and walked his way over to join her. The hu, Drae's sibling, was wearing classic, unabashed forest finery, and so Xelle already knew that she liked him. Soft fabric in stripes of dark dyes, with a loose ruffle at the sleeves, and the pair of pants any forestper knew as 'the good pants'. If Xelle would have known he was going to dress like this, she would have gone to a village tailor, and dressed to match him.

Not that she was at all upset by her own choice. For once, thinking Helia deserved a bit of color from her friend, Xelle was wearing a soft green blouse, and a darker green skirt and matching cap she'd picked up just for this, and had all that atop (shh) her most comfortable pair of black pants.

"I really like her," Grae said.

Xelle grinned. "Me too. I've never met anyone like her, she's just—always like this." She hoped that didn't minimize her. She knew Helia put on a strong face a lot of the time, but her exuberance and elegance were genuine, and stayed through even her tougher moments.

"If she trusts you, then I know all that mud they write about you is lies." He looked at her, as though it were a straightforward remark.

Xelle appreciated that, actually. All the averting or heralding or whatever else really got to her at times. She honestly just wanted to be Xelle. But being Xelle meant doing things that made other pers uncomfortable, and so she wondered if there could ever be a just Xelle again. No, no spiraling on wedding day. "You've seen *The Independent*? Everything in there is true."

"And not everything true is in there." He nodded, as though this was neither a question nor an accusation but perfectly sensible. And so, Xelle didn't answer it.

That seemed to be the extent of their chatter, and so the two, quietly and happily (Xelle didn't mind the hu sitting so close to her for once, and really, it wasn't that close) sat and absorbed the perfect day, the pers walking in, the fluttering over seating arrangements.

"This is us," Grae whispered. Xelle was glad for the prompt; she'd really gone into the zone.

Helia had chosen a flautist from Arc Tower, who stood and played a beautiful, swaying piece. Very unlike the music at a Mage ceremony. Helia loved music and loved poetry, so Xelle wondered where it was from. There was certainly a reference.

She had not seen Helia today, or Drae, as was custom, and so when the two appeared (not magically, but they had rather snuck in) at the back of the center aisle, Xelle found herself gasping. Literally. "Wow," she said.

Grae chuckled. "They make a pair," he agreed.

Xelle's first time seeing Drae was one to impress. He wore a fully tailored suit with shiny collars and cuffs, in a gorgeously perfect arcblack, which reminded Xelle, he was Tower staff. Arc Tower was his Tower too.

And Helia. Xelle had never seen her in black, and now, standing together with Xeleanor Du'Tam in the shadow of Arc Tower was quite a day to do it. A full, layered, lace upon lace upon fabric upon tulle yet looking like every layer was as essential as it was luscious, arcblack gown, and a huge, crown-like cap with a long, trailing, lightly laced, nearly transparent, arcblack train.

Damn.

Grae nodded at Xelle, and together they walked back, past the guests, and joined the two. Grae taking Drae's arm, and Xelle nervously grasping Helia's.

To a more rousing song of the flautist, they walked together, slowly, until reaching the front pavilion. The two witnesses stepped back a step, and honestly, Xelle was just going to stare at her friend. It would probably look like respecting the ceremony, anyway.

Xelle, however, was shocked when the presiding Mage appeared, and she saw that it was Spire Mage Nar. What was this about?

Presumably seeing Xelle's wide eyes, Nar winked, as though to the gathered. She spoke with joy. "Mage Helia and I have made some brief acquaintance over the past months, and though you might not suspect this of a Spire Mage and a career Diplomat, we very much both prefer a brief ceremony and a long party."

The audience chuckled at this.

"And so, I have little to say except to offer my blessings. And also to say that personal ceremony is as sacred to Arc Tower as that of our prong and its supporting institution, and so, if there are concerns about anyone present today, they are certainly noted, and we ask them to be put aside. Every per here was invited through the heart, trial, and path of Mage Helia and Nos Drae. Who wishes to speak first?"

Wait, did they have to decide that now? No, surely they'd planned it. This was ceremony talk.

"I will speak first," Drae said, "because between a handyhu and a diplomat, I'm sure whose words we'd like to let ring."

Actually, that was pretty nice.

"I, Hu Drae Du'Estia, pledge my care, companionship, and trust to Mage Helia Du'Arc. I will love her, support her, offer her grace for rocks, and share with her my life."

That seemed to be it. She suspected Helia would be a bit more verbose. Helia did enjoy a turn of phrase.

"I, Mage Helia Du'Arc, pledge my care, companionship, grace, and trust to Hu Drae Du'Estia. Fear." She paused. "Fear is here, among us today, among us always. Yet there must be some fear in life, for without it, our instincts dull. There are those in life who cause fear and those who do not. Then for each per, there are other pers: special, precious pers, who ease our fear. Who provide safety, comfort, understanding, from all the contexts where fear may manifest. And from our first moment to our last, there is no comfort, none, like a place of safety. A place lacking at least, fear from each other. A place of comfort in this world. As partners in marriage, we offer this to each other. I, offer it to you. Then, with that peace, with that safety, we find our moments. Moments to offer each other a song, a touch, a smile. To find, build, and nourish these connections, and someday, rest what we have made into the true pathways. I love you, and from today, I share with you my life."

Each of the two took a step closer to the other, and engaged in a soft kiss. Xelle found there were tears flowing down her face, happy tears, and she made no attempt to stop them. Yet, feeling awkward standing there crying and not knowing what the protocol was at all for this, she walked over and murmured, "Must be raining up the trees," to Grae. He grinned. "Hugs offered," she added.

She could have put that a bit less awkwardly, or not to add pressure, but they were standing in front of a whole audience and a Spire Mage from her Tower she was now banned from and this all seemed very much. He raised his arms and she gladly added hers. Awkward at first, they pulled each other in. Both seeming glad for the distraction, they lingered in it, a nice and friendly hug, even in all this finery. She hoped she would see Grae again.

Surely, she would.

Helia and Drae turned to face the crowd, and then waved toward an arrangement of tables, chairs, and food brought from the Tower kitchens. "Let's celebrate together," Helia said, her voice radiant.

Nar excused herself, but first glanced fleetingly at Xelle. A tiny ringing, a tiny, tiny cast across the short space. Xelle thought her consent.

"Stay strong," the message said. "We are all with you."

All. Nar had already left, as if she'd barely given Xelle a disdainful glance, and was walking toward the Tower. Xelle looked at Helia. She'd not heard. She was glowing. Just, glowing.

Helia looked so happy.

Xelle felt the warmth in her soul.

Grand Tower had chosen not to make a statement regarding Xelle's status. With a date already arranged for her leaving, they decided to let the unannounced departure speak for itself.

The date had been chosen to complete a year in the wand lab, as at the time, ensuring her stay did not extend past a year kept the Grand paperwork cleaner. A temporary assignment that could be filed away and not entered into the archives.

With that plan already in place, no one involved (at least here) wanted Xelle to leave early. Xelle could complete her work as planned, and yet not so much time would pass that it would seem unreasonable when she left, presumably as a result of Grand Tower rescinding her stay.

She'd come here for protection. For herself, and for her friends, bearing the consequences of Xelle's actions. A small hu with big worries, curling under the security of the large Tower, constructed in the spirit of a tree. Safe in the shelter of the forest, cradled by the pathways of life.

But Xelle was right about one thing. She was an Arc Mage. Arc

Magic was described by many concepts: travel, connection, pathway, reach . . . But what it was? Was change.

She had needed the time here. Needed the time to see herself. To understand the need for others, the need to not always stand alone. To accept that those who chose to stand with her knew the consequences of doing so. And offered it anyway. Or sometimes, because.

They all deserved security, deserved privacy, and Xelle would do her best to find these, but the fact was, as long as she spoke for a change in which pers could not gather wealth in order to take what should never have been theirs, they and all those they used that wealth to control would try to silence her. And Xeleanor Du'Tam would not be silenced. Xelle was not a hero, she was a per who would not be controlled, who had some means to do something about it. Which meant, then, they would paint her as one anyway. Whether a hero, an antihero, or simply in pursuit of either, she was disruptive, disagreeable, discordant.

So be it.

If a voice of discord could not be heard though the harmony of the forest, then, sometimes, she would stand alone.

She remembered what Sheli said, about moving from the lone tree, preferring the fall of chilling rain to the risk of being struck. And now, she could only laugh.

Xelle was the storm tree.

Pers could leave her or stand by her, but there was no shelter from a storm in one's own mind except the friends who offered it rest.

Those friends were busy. Welcome in places she now was not. And Xelle, for now, was here. And again, she had to go.

Then, where? Where was rest for the storm tree?

Thunder. Lightning. She had the power of dragons at eir side, and whether pers saw them or not, e felt them with em, always.

Xelle smiled, remembering, as she'd now learned, what her sigil was called to the dragons. Her own sibling had casually called her 'dragonfriend' and, loving the name, she'd pushed it a bit to stick. But

Hall had actually been so close. The dragons? Called a hu who shared a mark a *firefriend.*

Firefriend.

The first image that came to mind was a per to share the fire with—on ordinary nights, and especially those which were too cold to bear alone. A per of safety, of comfort, the ability to ease fear that Helia had described, the ability to know that in a world of fear, more fear would not be found with each other.

Then, she considered, the fire of the sun. The essence of the world itself. A per to shine light on the other, to say that I see you, and you are beautiful and warm and I'd like for you to see yourself in some facets of the way that I do.

The mark Thunder had given her had not been permanent at first. She'd thought it was, but it wasn't until she'd added her own expression. Her own 'always' and realized what that meant, that the sigil had been sealed.

A pledge not made of institutions, but of heart. Of spirit. Of home.

A mark she would never conceal. She would wear it, publicly, with pride. No matter what other connections she'd make, this mark would remain.

There was one more thing. Something Xelle held close.

Her firefriends?

For them, she would burn down the world.

Storm Tree: The End

About the Author

E.D.E. Bell (she or e) was born in the year of the fire dragon during a Cleveland blizzard. After a youth in the Mitten, an MSE in Electrical Engineering from the University of Michigan, three wonderful children, and nearly two decades in Northern Virginia and Southwest Ohio developing technical intelligence strategy, she started the indie press Atthis Arts. Working through mental disorders and an ever-complicated world, she now tries to bring light and love as she can through storytelling, as a proud part of the Detroit arts community.

A passionate vegan, radiant bi, and earnest progressive, Bell feels strongly about issues related to equality and compassion and loves fantasy as a way to perceive them while offering our minds lovingly crafted worlds in which to settle. Her works are quiet and queer, and often explore conceptions of identity and community, including themes of friendship, family, and connection. She lives in Ferndale, Michigan, where she writes stories and revels in garlic.

E hopes to write many more stories with Xeleanor Du'Tam and perhaps you will join em in them. You can follow eir adventures at edebell.com.

www.ingramcontent.com/pod-product-compliance
Lightning Source LLC
Chambersburg PA
CBHW032342310726

48973CB00007B/1821